DEMON KING

THE BLOODLETTER CHRONICLES

I

ERIK HENRY VICK

RATATOSKR PUBLISHING

NEW YORK

RATATOSKR PUBLISHING
769 BROADWAY #1060
MANHATTAN, NY 10003

DEMON KING/ ERIK HENRY VICK. -- 1ST ED.
ISBN 978- 0-9990795-2-2

For my nephews, Drew and Reid.

My son, why do you hide your face in fear?
Father, do you not see the Erl-king?
The Erl-king with crown and cape?

—Erlkönig,
Johann Wolfgang von Goethe

I hope you enjoy *Demon King*. If so, please consider joining my Readers Group—details can be found at the end of the last chapter.

__Table of Contents__

BOOK ONE:
NIGHTMARE

Chapter 1

1979

I

At the bottom of the hill stood a white clapboard house, dressed with peeling paint and creeping ivy. Dark windows gaped like missing teeth. Over twenty bikes teetered in an unstable heap amidst the mini-tornadoes of whirling fall leaves in the backyard. The pile held all kinds of different bikes: BMX, ten-speeds, bombers, everything. Beyond the house, the gravel road faded into a two-rut track and wound away through the Thousand Acre Wood.

Toby Burton stood at the top of the hill looking down at the house, unsure and anxious. The classifieds had said *one* ten-speed bike was available, not twenty, but maybe the guy fixed them up and sold them? That didn't make much sense, though, because the ad listed twenty bucks as the price. Who would put time and effort into fixing up a bike and sell it so cheap? Unless he got them even cheaper. Maybe he bought them from a junkyard for twenty bucks a truckload.

The twenty-dollar bill in his front pocket was heavy on his mind. He'd stolen the money out of his mom's purse that morning. If he left that second, he could slip it back into her purse without her knowing.

But he wanted a bike. *Needed* a bike.

Toby dithered at the top of the hill, and the temperature dropped with the sun. Anxiety scribbled across his face, he checked the time again. He wasn't allowed to be out past dark, though it would be a rare thing for his mom to notice when he came home.

Everyone else had a bike. He was the only one in his grade left taking it on the arches. His mom had the money, but she didn't want to spend it on him. Not that she thought of Toby much anymore—he was old news. The only thing she had time for now was her new boyfriend. Randy.

Randy the hitter. He needed a bike to get away from Randy.

The house at the bottom of the hill *looked* okay. It was just a house, like any of the others on the street. Maybe in worse repair, but nothing too far out of the norm for the shitburg town he lived in.

"Just do it, Toby," he whispered, but still he dithered. He had to decide. If he didn't leave immediately, there would be no way to make it home before dark. Not without the bike.

"Do it, do it, do it," he said to himself.

He set off down the hill with a confidence he didn't feel, his stride long and lanky, hands flopping loose at his sides. It wouldn't hurt to check out the bike. See if it was as advertised. No charge for looking, right?

The house looked bigger at the bottom of the hill. More imposing. Empty windows stared at him from the second story. The gate of the little white picket fence shrieked as he opened it, sending chills shivering down his spine. He mounted the rotting wooden steps to the porch, watching the windows. The house had an old-fashioned door bell—the kind you had to pull. With a glance over his shoulder, Toby reached out and pulled the lever.

The door banged open. A tall, thin man stood in the shadowy interior beyond the door, looking at Toby with rheumy eyes. His white hair stood up around him in a gossamer halo. Food had stained the front of his shirt in multiple places. He wore an old pair of chinos and black work boots. "Ayuh," the old man said, in a creaky, scratchy voice.

"Huh-hello, mister. I'm here about the bike."

The old man grinned with half of his mouth, but his eyes were hard and cold. "Ad says to come after suppah."

Toby shrugged. "I'm not allowed out after dark."

The old man made a clicking noise in the back of his mouth and jerked his chin to the side, like a weird bird. "Mayhap I'm not allowed out before dark, whaddaya think about that?"

Toby shrugged and looked at his feet. There was a weird scent coming from the open doorway. He'd smelled nothing like it before, and whatever it was, it was foul. "S-sorry, mister."

He turned to leave, and a hand fell on his shoulder. He glanced at it sideways. The old man's hand was inky-black and shriveled like the pictures of that mummy they'd seen in school. The bones of the man's hand pressed against his skin and his skin was loose, drooping. His fingers ended in sharp claws. Toby's mind yelled *Run!* as loud as it could, and he lurched in the man's grasp and tried to bolt for the street.

"Now, now, sonny-boy," crooned the old man. "Nothing here to be scared of. Nothing too far out of the norm for this little town, eh?"

Toby looked at the man's hand. It was back to normal, and he breathed a sigh of relief.

"Now, that's better, son," said the old man with a pat on the shoulder. "You wanted to know about that bike, right? Might as well take a look-see since you came all the way over here from Mill Lane. Can't hurt to check it out, can it? See if the bike is as advertised. No charge for looking, right, boyo?"

Toby stood staring out at the empty street, the old man standing behind him in the way Toby imagined a father would. The longer he stood, the man's warm hand resting on his shoulder, the less afraid he became. He grew more and more confident as the minutes ticked by.

"C'mon, son, let's do it," whispered the old man. "It's right back here in the yard. Through the house is fastest."

Toby glanced back at the growing shadows on the street. Going inside seemed to be a questionable idea.

"Just do it, Toby," said the old man. "Do it, do it, do it."

With a rueful grin, Toby turned and walked into the house.

2

After Toby missed the third straight day of school, Benny Cartwright knew something was wrong. Toby cut a lot, but never so many days in a row—that only got the truant officer on your case. When the three o'clock bell rang, Benny was first through the door.

He ducked the ubiquitous pick-up game of football after school, waved at his friends, and pedaled over to Mill Lane. Benny didn't go in for the BMX bikes like some of the sixth graders. No, he liked racing bikes, and on his last birthday, his dad had given him a sweet Raleigh Record Ace. It was bright yellow with black accents and white handle-bar tape. It was still a little too big for him, but he made do. It must have been expensive, his dad had special ordered it from the Raleigh dealer over in Genosgwa.

He'd never been invited to Toby's house, but he knew where it was. In a town that small, everyone knew where everything was. Benny stood his bike at the curb on the kickstand and ran to the front door. The house was in horrible shape—a bit of the siding next to the front door had gone missing during the last windstorm, and the Tyvek had been left exposed. One of the windows was broken and covered with plywood. Even from where Benny stood, the reek of garbage and rotten food was overpowering. Gritting his teeth, he pressed the doorbell. Nothing happened, no chime, no bell. Benny scoffed and knocked on the door hard.

Toby's mom opened the door, cigarette clenched between her teeth, skin sallow and dirty. She was wearing a housecoat and had her hair up in a do-rag. "I'm not buying anything for that school," she said.

"No, ma'am. I'm not selling anything."

"No?" She raised an eyebrow at him and squinted through a gust of noxious smoke. "What do you want then?"

"Is Toby home?" asked Benny.

The woman turned her head a little to the side and yelled Toby's name, never taking her eyes off Benny. After a long moment, she shrugged. "He ain't home from school yet, I guess."

"Okay, thanks," said Benny, but the door was already closing in his face. He retrieved his bike without a second glance at the house and pedaled to the end of the street. He was worried about Toby, but at the same time, he didn't want to get him in jake with his mother if he really was just playing hooky. She looked like she could raise a welt if she had a mind to. Toby came to school with enough bruises as it was.

He sat down at the end of the road until the sun was threatening to set and then left without seeing Toby.

The next day, Toby was missing from Home Room again, and Benny had a sinking feeling in his guts. At the first period bell, Benny ditched school and rode his bike home. Both his parents worked so if he could get inside unseen, everything would be cool. The only problem was Mrs. Jenkins, who lived next door. She had eyes like a hawk and would say something to Benny's mom if she saw him.

He snuck his yellow Raleigh into the backyard by cutting through from the street behind theirs. He leaned the bike against the back wall of the garage, and with a glance at Mrs. Jenkins' house, sprinted to the kitchen door. He was inside in a flash.

It took a matter of minutes for Benny to find the ad about the bike in the classifieds. It took him five more minutes to sneak away from the house without being seen by Mrs. Jenkins, and another fifteen to pedal to Thousand Acre Drive.

He stopped at the top of the hill, unsure and anxious. Without knowing it, he was tracing Toby's path and miming his actions. He looked down at the run-down white house and its overgrown backyard. He eyed the pile of bikes, and something cold and oily turned over in his guts. He shouldn't go down there. He knew better. If something had happened to Toby in that house, it could happen just as easily to Benny. But it didn't hurt to sit up at the top of the hill and look, right?

There was a flicker of motion in one of the black windows in the sea of white clapboard. He stared at it, but if something had moved, it wasn't moving anymore. *Wait a minute! Why are those windows so dark?* he asked himself. *It's broad freakin' daylight.* The more he looked, the surer he became that the windows were covered with black cloth on the inside. That was weird. Nobody on the up-and-up would cover their windows with black cloth, would they?

Part of him wanted to ride down the hill and get a better look. Part of him wanted to turn tail and pedal away from there at top speed. But what if Toby was down there… inside that house…being tortured?

Toby had wanted a bike bad. He'd been jealous for a week after Benny's birthday and hadn't had much to do with him. *But where would Toby get twenty bucks?* Benny couldn't imagine that hag with a cigarette clamped in her mouth giving up a Jackson for anything Toby wanted. Maybe something else had happened to Toby. Maybe he was cutting school because his mom gave him another black eye. That might explain his mother covering for him. Maybe. But Toby had told him all about the bike ad. He'd said it in a hushed tone like he didn't want anyone over-hearing him—like he was going to go buy it.

Just do it, Benny, he thought. *Just ride down there, quick-like, and stay on the bike. That way if someone comes out, you can ride away fast.*

It was as good a plan as any. He had to find out if Toby had been there. But he didn't want to go to the door alone, and before he brought Mike and Paul here, he wanted to do a little recce, like his dad always said. Benny wasn't sure what that word really meant—his dad was the town manager, and he had to keep track of what all the city employees did during work hours. That meant going on recces. In the summer, he sometimes let Benny tag along.

Do it, he thought, but still, his feet stayed on the ground. *Toby would go down there.* He put one foot on a pedal. *What's the worst that can happen?* Still, he dithered. Something about the house, about the blacked-out windows, maybe, scared him. He glanced down, past the house, at the start of the Thousand Acre Wood. It was silent and dark. Menacing. Benny didn't like it. The house, the windows, the woods, all of them screamed for him to get the h-e-double-hockey-sticks out of there. Even so, he put his other foot on the pedal and scooted his bum up onto the seat. He couldn't bring himself to pedal, though, so he raced down the hill by the power of gravity. The wind of his passing was frigid on his cheeks. *Almost winter,* he thought.

At the bottom of the hill, he squeezed his rear brake and jumped a little as it squealed, heart racing. He slowed to a stop in front of the house, one foot on the pedal, one foot on the ground. The eerie silence was oppressive. Where were the birds? They hadn't flown south yet, at least not on Rabbit Run, where he lived. Where was the sound of the woods—the creaking of tree limbs, the rustle of small animals in the underbrush? Why did the woods look so dark? Had he been grown, he may not—probably *would* not—have noticed these things, but he wasn't a grown man, he was a scrawny eleven-year-old with glasses that always, always slid down his nose.

He glanced up at the windows on the second story. They were blacked-out with heavy cloth, no question. Benny shuddered. The front door was dark green, and the paint was peeling like his skin had after the sunburn he'd earned on the family trip to the beaches of Florida last summer.

Something drew his eyes to the window next to the door, and the cloth moved—like someone had dropped it after lifting it to peek at him. The door creaked open. The entry hall was swathed in shadows, and the sunlight cut a leaning rectangle across the floor. "Come on in, son," said a raspy voice, and Benny jumped.

Inside his mind, Benny was pedaling with abandon, racing back up the hill as fast as he could manage, but in reality, he was rooted to the spot, staring into that space defined by the gloom. Even though he wanted to be riding away from there at the speed of light, even though this whole situation freaked him out, a part of him was shouting to go inside and let that cool darkness wrap its arms around him.

"That's a nice one," creaked the voice. "The bike, I mean. Like buttered corn, it is."

Benny nodded, unsure of his voice. His mind was screaming at his legs to get on the pedals, but still, he stood and stared like a kid waiting for a magician's finale.

"You wouldn't want to sell it, would ya? I'd give you a fair price and your pick of bikes from out back."

Benny shook his head. He didn't want to hear anymore, but at the same time, he did.

"Well, think on it, sport. I'd give you upwards of forty dollars plus a bike. That's a good deal for a young man like yourself."

"No, it isn't," Benny heard himself say. It was like listening to his voice on his best friend Mike's tape recorder. It sounded wrong, too high, too squeaky.

"Shrewd one, are ya?" The man laughed from the shadows. "Well, listen here, Rockefella, my daughter and I have got to eat. You wouldn't begrudge us that, right?"

"I'm not giving you my bike."

"Okay, son, don't get yer britches twisted. I'm just trying to make a deal that benefits us both."

Benny tried to rip his gaze away from the door, but couldn't make his head move. He couldn't even turn his eyes away. "No thanks."

"No, listen here, boyo. Hear me out. I've got a slick bike down to the basement. You'd love her, I'm sure. She's a Raleigh, too."

Benny shrugged, wanting to turn away, and, at the same time, wanting to see the man who was talking to him, wanting to see his face, his eyes.

"Ayuh, she's a Raleigh. I know a bit about Raleighs, see? I know your pops paid out a hundred or more for that bumblebee you're riding. But you didn't pay a cent, didja? The one I got down there is worth three, maybe four times that. It's a Professional Mark 2, you heard of them?"

Benny pursed his lips and nodded. That bike was worth five or six hundred dollars. It had a special paint job, a color you could only get by shelling out the Benjamins, and Italian light-weight racing mechanicals. It was a sweet bike, and the greedy part of Benny wanted to say yes.

"Now, I got it on the cheap, see, but I can't move it. I'd have to sell it to one of them rich kids on Rabbit Run."

"I live on—" Benny slammed his teeth together, avoiding the tip of his tongue by a hair's breadth. He hadn't meant to say anything, just nod, but his mouth and throat had betrayed him.

The man laughed, but it wasn't a pleasant sound. It sounded like a bird caught in a trap. "Don't you worry, son. I already knew that with a bike like that bumblebee there you either lived on Rabbit Run or Deer Vale. But listen, sport. I can't move this Professional. No kid has the kind of money it's worth, and very few people from those two rich streets buy out of the classifieds. No. They want new. Your bike, now, I can sell for fifty or sixty buckeroos. I get a small profit if I pay you forty, and you get a better bike *and* two crisp twenty-dollar bills."

Benny looked down. He wanted out of this conversation but didn't know how to do it without being rude. *Hear the man out,* said an unfamiliar voice in his head.

"Think of what you could do with that money. Think of the toys, the comics. Maybe take your sweetie for an ice-cream. And remember that you'd have a top of the line racing bike instead of the one you're riding." It *was* a good deal. A great deal, but his dad had given him the "bumblebee," and that meant something more than money. "Okay, son, I can see you know how to bargain. I'll tell you what. You get forty bucks, the Pro, and your choice of another bike from the pile out back. You can give that bike to a friend or sell it, I don't care which. Now, technically, I'm out money here, since I can sell the other bike for twenty, but those bikes out back I got for free or close enough. We gotta eat, son."

Benny stared into the black maw defined by the open door. *Is that a man standing back there?* The inky blackness swirled and parted, and the shape *did* look like a man was standing at the back of the foyer, watching him. He blinked hard, and the outline of a man disappeared into the black, sinking into it like an anchor sinking into the sea.

"Why not come in and at least look at the Pro, son? Lookin's always for free. Come see if I'm lying, why don'tcha?"

Benny took his foot off the pedal and shook it a little. It was going numb. He eyed the entry hall of the white house with distrust. Nothing was moving in there. Nothing moved at the windows. How did the man know he was shaking his head? Was that outline really the man?

"Just do it, Benny. You know Toby would."

Something snapped inside Benny, and his strange reluctance to leave evaporated. He wheeled the bike in a tight circle and pedaled as if his life depended on it.

Maybe it did. Behind him, the man made a sound like a rabbit being killed by a cat, and Benny thought it was how the man laughed. "Well, you know where we are, son," he called and then made that awful laughing sound. The door closed with a slam.

Benny didn't slow down until he hit Main Street. Without thinking, without planning, he'd ridden to the safest place he knew—Town Hall, and his dad's office. He'd be in dutch for cutting school, but right then he didn't care. He was scared, and he was scared for Toby.

He wheeled his bike right inside, amidst the chuckles of the town employees, but heck, if the son of the town manager couldn't bring a bike inside, who could?

His dad was in his office, sitting behind his modest desk. As Benny wheeled his bike inside the office, he looked up, met Benny's gaze for a moment, and then his eyes drifted to the clock on the wall. When his gaze settled on Benny, his eyes had that look that said Benny was in it with both feet.

"No school today?" his father asked as if there was nothing amiss.

"I know, Dad, I know, but please listen first."

His dad tilted his head back and pursed his lips, looking down his nose at Benny with squinty eyes. "Go on, then."

Benny leaned his bike against the wall.

"Start with why you have a bike inside the building." His father's voice had that you're-in-trouble-but-I'm-amused ring to it.

Benny sank into one of the chairs across the desk from his father. "Dad, you know I do good in school, right? You know I don't cut."

"Much," said his father.

Benny suppressed a grin and nodded. "Much. I *had* to cut today, Dad. You might not agree right now, but if you bear with me, I think you just might."

His father quirked his eyebrows, and his lips twitched like he wanted to grin, but thought he shouldn't.

"You know my friend, Toby, right?"

"Toby Burton?" his dad said with a sour expression clouding his face.

"Yeah. Look, I know his mom is a real—"

"Yes, she is, son. Go on."

"Yeah, so anyway, Toby doesn't have a bike, right?"

His dad's eyes drifted to his Record Ace leaning against the wall.

"He still has to walk everywhere, and it rankles him. He's the only one of us, and when we're all going somewhere, he gets this look on his face. Like he wants to disappear."

His dad nodded.

"Well, he told me about this ad in the paper. A classified ad selling a bike for twenty bucks, right? He didn't come out and say it, but the hushed-up way he told me about it—Toby wanted that bike and somehow had twenty dollars."

"Son, what's all this have—"

"Just listen, Dad. Please."

His dad made a twirling motion with his index finger and leaned back in his leather chair.

"So, the ad, right? And Toby's been out of school for three days. Well, today made the fourth, okay? He's never cut like that. Not once, and I've known him all my life."

"Maybe he's sick."

"No, Dad. I rode over to his house after school yesterday. I talked to his mom—"

"You went over to Mill Lane? You know I don't want you down there."

"I do, Dad, but you always say we have to look out for our friends, right? I thought maybe his mom…"

"You thought his mom beat him up?"

Benny nodded. "Yeah, it's happened before."

"How many times?"

"I don't know, Dad. A lot. He comes to school with bruises on his face or a black eye or all scraped up."

"Son," his father said gently, "why didn't you tell me?"

Benny looked nonplused. "I... I don't know, Dad. I didn't think..."

"You didn't think it was your business to tell. Well, we need more people who speak up, Benny. Child abuse is not okay. Not in any sense. Discipline should never—*never*—leave bruises, especially on the face." His dad pulled a pad toward him and wrote something down.

"Dad, listen. This isn't about—"

"Well, maybe it is, and maybe it isn't, Benny. Maybe it should be about those bruises."

"Dad, *listen to me*! Please!"

His dad put his gold Cross pen down on his desk blotter and leaned back in the chair, an expression of worry on his face. "There's more?"

"Yes, Dad. There's more."

His dad twirled his fingers.

"When Toby didn't show up again today, I knew something bad had happened. Then I remembered that bike ad, an ad for a twenty-dollar bike. It just didn't sound right to me."

"Too good to be true," murmured his dad.

"Yeah, exactly. I decided I should go over to that house and do a little recce."

His dad sat up straight and put both hands flat on the desk in front of him, but instead of the grin Benny had expected from the use of the word "recce," his dad was frowning. "Tell me you didn't go over there."

"I did, Dad. I *had* to. I had to do a recce, at least. But, I thought if I stayed on my bike, nothing could happen. I figured I'd just ride by the house and take a look."

"And where is this house, Benjamin?"

Benny's stomach soured a bit at being called by his full first name. That was never good. "It's the last house on Thousand Acre Drive."

"You rode over there by those woods? By those *secluded* woods, to see if your friend met with foul ends there, all alone?"

Benny nodded and looked at his lap.

"I raised you to be smarter than that, Benjamin."

"There's more, Daddy. I was stupid, but done is done and can't be undone, right?"

His dad made the twirling motion with his finger.

"The house is…well, it's kind of run-down. Kind of…scary. The windows are all blacked-out with cloth. The paint is peeling like mad, and some of the siding is gone. Out back, there's this pile of like twenty or thirty bikes."

"Is that all of it?"

Benny shook his head, looking at his lap again. "I…I decided to ride by and get a closer look. When I got in front of the house, I stopped without really meaning to. I stayed on my bike though."

"Benjamin…"

"Trust me, Dad, I know it was stupid. The front door opened, but no one came out. It was all dark inside the house. No one moved in there, but a man spoke to me. He saw me somehow even though the windows were blacked-out. He offered me a trade. My Record Ace for a Raleigh Professional Mark 2. *And* forty dollars. He said you'd paid like a hundred for my bike, but that I hadn't paid a dime and that if I traded him, I'd have a better bike and forty dollars to spend how I liked. I said no way, but he kept at me. He said I should come inside and look at the Pro, that looking was free—"

"Benjamin James Cartwright, if you went in that house, I'm going to tan your backside but good!" His dad was half out of his chair and looking at him with hard, worried eyes.

Benny held up his hands. "I'm stupid, Dad, but I'm not *that* stupid. When I said no again, he upped his offer. My bike for a Raleigh Pro, forty bucks, and my choice of bikes from the backyard. He said I could sell it or give it to a friend, he didn't care which. He kept at me to come in and look at the bike."

His dad sank back into his chair. "Is that all of it then, Ben?" his dad asked in a hushed voice.

"Oh! He also said 'Do it, Benny. You know Toby would.' But I never said anything about Toby, Dad, so how did he know?"

His father shrugged.

"When he said that, I suddenly felt free, and I got the heck out of there. I rode as fast as I could and came straight here."

His dad steepled his fingers in front of his face and looked at Benny over them. His eyes were calm. "So, this guy freaked you out a little."

"Oh yeah, he knew where we live, too. I forgot that part. He said anyone with a bike like mine lived on Rabbit Run or Deer Vale."

His father nodded. "True enough, probably. I'll tell you, Benny, I'm glad your recce scared you. Can you guess why?"

Benny shook his head, more than a little surprised by what his dad had said, and by his mild tone.

"Because I never, *ever*, want you to do something that stupid again." His voice had gone hard. "Now, this guy doesn't sound all that bad—" He held up his hand when Benny opened his mouth to speak. "No, Son, I listened to you, now you listen to me."

Benny closed his mouth and nodded. Fair was fair.

"This guy is probably retired and probably sells a few bikes he's salvaged from the dump over in Cottonwood Vale. He probably gets them for a buck a piece, cleans them up and sells them for a two-thousand percent profit. Not a bad idea." He steepled his fingers and tapped them against his lips. "Now, he sounds okay to me, just an old coot, but he might have been something else entirely."

"Stranger danger," Benny breathed.

"Yes, Son, exactly. Now, I know you know better. What I don't understand is why you did what you did today."

"But what about the blacked-out windows?" He leaned forward and came up on the edge of the seat.

His dad shrugged. "Maybe he used to work nights and hasn't broken the habit of sleeping in the daytime. Maybe the light hurts his eyes. Maybe he just doesn't want to be spied on from the top of that hill."

Benny hadn't thought about any of those possibilities. "But Toby wanted his bike."

"Son, there are so many things that could explain Toby's absence. We started this conversation with the most likely of them."

"What, his mom knocked him around?"

"Could be, Benny. And she told you he wasn't home because she doesn't want anyone to know how bad she beat him. Child abusers are ashamed of what they do, Benny. They don't want it out there for everyone to see. They don't want to get in trouble."

Benny sank back in his chair. He hadn't even thought of that reason.

"Now, Son, tell me which sounds more likely: a kidnapper is living on Thousand Acre Drive that no one knows about or even suspects or Toby's mother got a little loose with her fists?"

Benny sighed, letting out the tension and fear that had ridden him since that morning at school. "Yeah."

"Right. So, Benny, what do we do about it?"

Benny thought about it. His mind worked hard, coming up with one scheme to get inside Toby's house and rescue him, discarding it, and then coming up with another. He was a smart kid, but he was only eleven. "I don't know, Dad."

"The first step, you did just now. You told an adult about it. The next step is up to the adult you told, and that's me. Understand, Son?"

"Yeah," Benny said.

"Is it up to you?"

"No, Dad."

"Right. It's up to me, and you can rest assured that I will do something about it. I would do something even if he weren't your friend. Know why?"

"Because you are awesome."

His dad chuckled. "Thank you, Benny, but that's not why. The reason is that I believe it's my responsibility. I'm the town manager, sure, but I'm also a man who believes in defending those who are too weak to do it themselves. I'm duty-bound to do that. Understand?"

"I think so, Dad, but I think we said the same thing. You just used more air. And words."

His dad chuckled again. "So, let's review. What are you going to do to help Toby?"

"Trust you."

"Right. You're going to trust me to do the right thing."

"Okay, Dad."

"Okay." He looked at Benny with a somber expression. "Now, let's talk about this cutting school business."

Benny's heart sank. "Okay, Dad."

"I believe you when you said you had to do something, you just picked the wrong thing to do. Right?"

"Yeah, at first, but I got there in the end."

His dad chuckled again. "Yes, you did. Even so, there's going to be a price here. There's got to be a punishment, don't you agree? For being so irresponsible."

"For going to the house alone."

"Yes, for being so foolish, but also for not telling me, or some other adult, and letting them take the appropriate steps."

"Right, Dad."

"What should that punishment be, Benny."

Benny looked at his shoes. *The bike,* he thought but didn't want to say. "Does there have to be one?"

"Come on, Benny. You know how this works."

Benny nodded. "Ground me."

"How long?"

"A week?" he whispered.

"Let me ask you this. How long would I be in trouble with your Mom if that bike got you kidnapped or worse?"

Forever, he thought. "A long time?"

"You bet your britches, sonny boy." His dad steepled his fingers again. "We'll forego a week's restriction. We'll go with a month without the bike. Maybe a month of hoofing it will help you to remember."

I freakin' knew it, Benny thought. "Yes, sir."

"So, we are agreed?"

"Okay, Dad. A month without my bike."

"Okay. Is it fair?"

Benny worked it over in his mind. His dad always wanted to know if it was a fair punishment, and Benny

30   ERIK HENRY VICK

thought that was one of the reasons he could trust him to look into Toby's bruises. "Yes, Dad. If anything, it's a little…"

"Lenient?"

Benny nodded.

"Should we make it a little harsher?" his dad asked and then laughed as Benny's face scrunched up. "Like I said, Benny. I believe you when you said you had to do something, and it's good that you felt that way. My only quibble is what you chose to do—putting yourself in potential danger. Your welfare is my responsibility, too."

"Yes, sir."

"We'll leave it at a month without the bike, Benny."

"Time off for good behavior?"

His dad chuckled. "We'll see."

That's the best Benny had hoped for, so he smiled.

"Now, let's get you to school." He rested his hand lightly on his son's shoulder and led him out to his brown Oldsmobile Toronado. They joked and laughed all the way to the school.

After the excitement of the morning, the rest of the day was boring. Benny got back to school in time for his least favorite subject: math. When the school bell rang, and Mike and Paul raced to the bike rack, Benny felt the loss of his bike like a physical pain.

Mike glanced back and saw him standing there. "Gonna ride home with us, Benny?"

"No bike."

"Oh." Mike looked at Paul and Paul shrugged.

Benny had imagined he knew how Toby felt, but now he had firsthand knowledge. It was much worse than he thought.

"Let's walk our bikes, Paul."

"Sure," said Paul. "Where's your bike, Benny? At home?"

"At my dad's office. I lost it for a month for cutting this morning."

"Oh," said Paul in a small voice. "Sorry, man."

"Nah," said Benny. "It's a fair punishment."

"Hey, we'd be walking anyway if Toby was here." Mike looked at Benny with surprise on his face. "Where is Toby, anyway? It's been a couple of days."

"Four," said Benny.

"*Four?*"

Benny nodded. "That's why I cut. I…" All of a sudden, the idea of racing across town to find out if Toby had been kidnapped or killed was embarrassing, and he didn't want to say it.

"You went and looked for him, right?" said Mike with a small smile. "That's the real reason you lost the bike, right?"

Benny shrugged.

"Did you find him?"

"No," said Benny. "But I found a scary old asshole."

"Like Paul's?" laughed Mike.

"Worse."

"Nothing's worse than Paul's asshole."

Benny smiled, happy to be with his friends. "I told my dad about Toby, though, and he says he'll take care of it."

"His mom?" asked Paul.

"Dad thinks so. So do I. Now."

"Your dad's okay, Benny," said Mike.

"Yeah, he is," said Benny, meaning every word.

"Let's go to the park. You can tell us all about it on the way."

Benny nodded, and the boys walked toward Neibolt Street. He recounted the visit to the dingy white house and the conversation with the old man.

"Creepy," said Paul. "Do you think—"

"Dad says he's probably just retired."

"Yeah, maybe," said Mike in a voice that said otherwise. "Even so, maybe we should go over there and—"

"Didn't you hear what he said?" snapped Paul. "His dad's *got it*, man, and going there already cost Benny his bike for a month. Leave it."

"Yeah, you're right. Sorry, Benny."

Benny nodded, trying to ignore the little voice inside his head that was shouting Toby needed their help.

3

Jim Cartwright pulled his Toronado onto the cracked concrete that served as the Burton's driveway. The house was a mess, and Jim shook his head in disgust.

He got out of the car and pushed the heavy car door closed with a bang. Walking up to the door, his eyes roamed over the neglected house. Weeds grew in the flower beds, but no plants. Hairy chinch bugs did whatever they wanted in the ignored, browning lawn. Next to the front door, Tyvek was the house's only protection from the elements, and one corner sagged away from the boards it covered. The wood was discolored and rotting.

He pressed the bell, but like Benny's visit, that produced nothing. He shook his head and knocked on the door. The rank smell of the house threatened to overpower his will to wait for someone to come to the door.

Candy Burton opened the door after a long wait. She wore a stained house coat, and her lank, greasy hair fell like an oil spill over her forehead, but it didn't cover the dark purple bruise above her left eye. She held a smoldering cigarette between her middle and ring finger. She squinted up at him with a strange expression on her face. "Who're you? You kinda look familiar."

Jim thrust out his hand. "Jim Cartwright."

There was no corresponding look of recognition on Candy's face. She shook her head, greasy bangs bouncing. "And?"

"I'm the town manager."

"Oh. Yeah." She glanced past him at the Olds. "Big car, big man."

"I don't know about that, Ms. Burton. I need to speak to you about your son. Can we go inside?"

"No," she snapped. "I'm not in the habit of letting strange men in when I ain't dressed proper." Her voice held a liberal dose of hard Yankee accent. "You can say what you've come to say and then get the hell out of here."

"Do you...Ms. Burton, do you have a...is there a man living here?"

She let her eyes wander down to his shoes and then back up to his face, slow, lascivious, and irreverent. "What business is that of yours?"

"I noticed the bruise on your forehead, is all."

She shook her head, making her hair flop to the left. "I'm gonna ask you again, and if I don't get a good answer, I'll be closing the door in your face, Mr. Town Manager. *What business is that of yours?*"

Anger stirred in the back of Jim's mind. "Tell you what, Ms. Burton. I'll answer your question after you answer just one of mine. *Where is your son?*"

Candy pulled her head back, looking like a clucking hen. "My son? Toby?"

"Do you have another?"

"What do you care about my son?"

"He hasn't been to school in four days. Have you seen him in the last *four days?*"

She glanced over her shoulder like the idea that someone might overhear her petrified her. "No, but he knows when to keep his head down and stay the hell outta the way."

"Have you even fed him?"

Candy looked at him and took a drag on her cigarette. She blew the smoke out, almost in his face, and peered at him through the haze of smoke. "He eats when he's hungry."

"And the guy who did that to your forehead...has he seen Toby?"

She stared at him like he was the stupidest man she knew and took another drag.

"Want me to ask him?"

Candy scoffed. "He hasn't seen him. Before you ask me how I know, it's because Toby ain't layin' on the kitchen floor bleeding."

"Nice," said Jim. "Your son has been missing for four days, lady, and you stand here making jokes."

She stepped back inside and slammed the door.

"Yeah, nice talking to you, too," muttered Jim. He turned and walked to his car, but before he could get in, the front door banged open behind him.

"Hey!" A scrappy-looking man came striding across the yard barefoot and bare-chested.

"Yeah?" asked Jim.

"Who the hell are you?"

"I told Candy. I'm Jim Cartwright, the town manager."

"Yeah? Well, Mr. Town-fucking-Manager, I'll tell you something here. You quit coming around here and asking questions."

"Or?" asked Jim, one eyebrow twitched up.

"Or I'll answer you," growled the man. "You want I should start now?"

Jim was at least a foot taller than the guy, but the guy had that crazy, dangerous gleam in his eye. "No. I'm just trying to help Toby."

"Yeah? Great. Help him learn to keep his goddamn mouth shut around me and the world will be a better place. Now, get the fuck outta here, Mr. Town Manager, before I give you something to manage."

Jim slid behind the wheel, shaking his head. One of the perks of being town manager was that he had six guys he could rely on to sort this situation out. The scrawny man stood there staring daggers at him as Jim threw the car into reverse and backed out on to Mill Lane. Jim gave him a jaunty little wave, and the guy flipped him the bird.

Five minutes later, he was sitting with the Chief of Oneka Falls' Police Department. "I tell you what, Matt, that guy is trouble. Trouble for Toby and Candy, both."

Matt Greshin grunted and put one foot up on the corner of his desk. "Seen guys like that before. I don't know who's shacked up with Candy Burton, but we'll get him sorted out, quick-like."

"Yeah, it would be best if we at least know who he is."

"Nine times out of ten, a guy like that is a lot of bluster. Sure, he can beat up on a kid and his girlfriend, but chances are he would have backed down if you'd decided to call him out."

"Maybe," said Jim. "I'm not worried about me, though. I'm worried about the kid. No one's seen him in four days."

Greshin took a deep breath and held it for a moment before letting it out in a long, loud sigh. "Yeah. That's priority one. You know what? I talked to Tom Walton over to Genosgwa just the other day. He called to give me a heads up about a couple of runaways."

"Kids?"

"Aren't they all?" asked Matt.

"I mean *kids*, as in under thirteen."

Matt nodded, eyes grave and mouth set in a grimace. "Course. Yeah, one was ten, the other was eleven. Both boys."

Jim grimaced.

"Not a peep from anyone else. I'll put in a few calls— one to John Morton over to Cottonwood Vale, and another to Bobby Jefferson."

"Okay. Keep me up to date on whatever you hear."

"Sure thing, boss."

"What do you think about the house on Thousand Acre Drive?"

The Chief shrugged. "No idea, but it's easy enough to check out. Feel like riding along?"

Jim smiled and stood. "Yeah. Yeah, I do."

"Good enough, then." Greshin stood up and hitched his duty belt around to a more comfortable position. "I'll have Craig Witherson come with." The three men piled into the Chief's Plymouth Fury, and Greshin drove them to Thousand Acre Drive. They stopped at the top of the hill, just like the boys had, and looked down at the house. It looked forlorn, unkempt. Wild roses had taken over the backyard, including the pile of bikes.

Matt grunted and dropped the cruiser into gear. He rolled down the hill without using the accelerator, and let the car coast to a stop in front of the house. Paint hung from the house like loose skin. The windows were all blacked out, just as Benny had said they were. The three of them got out of the car and strode up to the porch. Greshin mounted the two steps and knocked on the door. The door swung inwards with a shriek of rusty hinges.

"Anyone home?" called Chief Greshin. "It's the police." The house remained silent, not even creaking timbers answered him. "Hello? If you are in there, sing out." Still nothing. "Okay then, we're coming in. If you are home, don't shoot us." Greshin winked at Jim and motioned for Witherson to go in first.

With rolling eyes and a smile, Witherson drew his nickel-plated .357 magnum and crossed the threshold. "Police! Don't be alarmed," he called. He pulled his brand-new Maglite out of his belt and switched it on, piercing the darkness with a beam of brilliant white light.

Greshin followed him inside, also switching on his Maglite, with Jim bringing up the rear. The first thing Jim noticed was the heavy black tar-paper tacked to the inside trim of all the windows. The interior of the house was pitch black in the middle of the afternoon. The house smelled like a cross between a library and a dirty butcher shop: dry, dusty paper, and spoiling meat. "Disgusting," muttered Greshin.

The entry hall was empty, but there was a room to the left, a parlor, and to the right, a dining room. The furniture in both rooms wore a layer of dust an eighth of an inch thick. "Yeah. This looks like an abandoned house," said Jim.

"Maybe they don't like the view from the front."

Jim shrugged and followed the two police officers deeper into the house.

The short entry hall ended in a family room, where the dust wasn't as thick, but still coated everything. There was a bookshelf, the weight of tall stacks of old newspapers warping the shelves. There was a single swinging door to the right and a staircase to the left.

Chief Greshin pointed at the stairs with his Maglite. "Witherson, clear the top floor." He turned his light on the door and pushed through it. Jim followed him into the kitchen. It was the source of the decaying meat smell. Inside the room, the smell was so thick it was almost impossible to breathe without gagging. The cellar door shared the same wall as the one from the family room and across from it was the door leading to the backyard. There was a teal Philco refrigerator standing against the wall, and its door was chocked open about a quarter of an inch. With a grimace, Greshin levered the door open with his Maglite. The smell intensified. Greshin gagged and let the door fall back and then pressed it all the way closed. "You don't want to look in there."

"What is it? Is it…"

"Toby? No." Greshin grinned. "It's the remains of a turkey dinner, and it ain't pretty."

With the door closed, the air quality was better, but still not something Jim wanted to keep breathing. "Let's get out of here then," he choked out.

Greshin nodded, but instead of going to the family room, he opened the door to the backyard. "Place could use an airing out." They stepped outside and stood on the back stoop. An immense wild rose bush had conquered the backyard and was now working on taking the siding off the back of the house. It overran the pile of bikes, which on closer inspection, were nothing but rust and rotting tires.

"No one's been out here in a long, long time," said Jim.

"Too right, boss. I was hoping to get to the cellar from out here, but I guess not."

"No outside door."

"There's nothing for it, then, but to go back through the kitchen." With matching grimaces of disgust, the two men re-entered the kitchen. Chief Greshin opened the cellar door and flipped the switch at the top of the stairs. Nothing happened. He grinned at Jim. "Another flashlight safari, boss." He turned and went down the creaking steps.

Jim nodded and followed him into the cellar. Greshin adjusted the beam to its widest setting as he descended the stairs and then shone it in a slow circle. The cellar was a mess, and not just the detritus of living. It was as if a tornado had been trapped in the cellar. The remains of ripped cardboard boxes drifted up in piles near the corners, rusty nuts and bolts littered the floor like shells on a beach. The furniture was up-turned or broken. Broken picture frames and shredded books lay spread across the floor. There wasn't one thing that was untouched. "Someone had a party down here," muttered Jim.

Greshin grunted a laugh. "Let's get out of here."

Jim nodded.

Witherson stood on the bottom step in the family room. "Upstairs is clear," he said.

The Chief grunted. "Any signs anyone has been here?"

Witherson shook his head.

"How can you be sure?" asked Jim.

With a wry smile, Witherson pointed at the floor of the entry hall, which was hardwood dressed in dust. There were only three sets of footprints. "We'd see their footsteps."

4

The park on Neibolt Street was small, and not all that popular because of it. That's why the boys liked it. Most of the time, they had the park to themselves and had free use of the playground equipment. At most, they might have to contend with a few kids from the elementary school, but even if they did, they were the "big kids" and they got their way most of the time. That afternoon, the park was theirs.

"What should we play?" asked Paul.

Mike shrugged. "Paratroopers?"

"Might as well," said Benny, unable to drum up much enthusiasm for anything.

The trick to playing paratroopers was to go as high as possible on the swing set, and, just before the swing fell on its backward arc, fling yourself into the air and try to stick the landing. There were no winners or losers in the game, but bragging rights were at stake.

Mike and Paul were pumping their legs like mad, building altitude with vigor. Benny tried to get into the spirit of the thing, but the memory of his visit to the house on Thousand Acre Drive kept interfering. Lost in thought, he didn't see the other two leap into space, and he didn't see them land.

"Ah gee, Benny, you missed it."

"Oh. Sorry," said Benny. On his next forward swing, he waited until the zenith of his arc and let go, arching his back. He flew into the crisp fall air, spinning his arms as he went. After he landed, they started over again, but this time, he put the creepy house out of his mind.

"On the count of three," yelled Mike. "All together this time, Benny!"

They pumped their legs harder, trying to go higher and higher.

"One!"

The cool fall air was turning cold as the sky started its plunge toward dusk.

"Two!"

Benny scanned the ground in front of the swing set, looking for stray rocks, sure, but mostly looking to see who had jumped the farthest on the last set. When he looked up at the copse of trees opposite them, a shadowy form ducked behind a tree. *Don't be a sissy*, he thought. *That's just your mind playing tricks on you.*

"Three!" yelled Paul.

As a unit, the three boys jumped, yelling "Geronimo," like all good paratroopers.

Just before he landed, Benny's eyes drifted to the woods and to the place where his mind had painted in the shadowy figure. There was something there. It had dark skin and long fingers that drew to a point instead of the stubby curve of a man's fingers. And, it had *wings*—huge wings, like a demon.

He blinked his eyes hard, trying to clear the image from his sight, and then his feet slammed into the ground. His ankle shrieked, turning as his foot slipped forward. He pinwheeled his arms, but that didn't stop his momentum. His foot shot out in front of him, heel skidding across the hard ground and then flying upwards like he was a placekicker warming up for the big field goal attempt. His other knee buckled, and he fell over backward. He hit the hard-packed earth with a *thud*, and then the back of his head slammed into the ground.

His vision went black, and then color exploded behind his eyes and with it, came the pain. He rolled onto his side, clutching his head and trying not to cry. He had his eyes squeezed shut, so he didn't see what the others saw.

"What is that, Mike?"

"A shadow?"

"What do you want?" yelled Paul. "Are you some kind of prevert?"

"Pervert, you idiot," hissed Mike.

Benny cracked open an eye and peered into the woods where he'd seen the shadow, but there was nothing there. Mike and Paul were looking off to the left, and Benny rolled to that side.

At the end of the playground, where the underbrush and taller trees started, stood a dark, man-like shape—a shape without wings.

"Get the hell out of here, prevert," yelled Paul.

"It's *pervert*," whispered Mike.

"Whatever," said Paul. "Let's get out of here."

They helped Benny to his feet. He limped between Mike and Paul, leaning on them for support. His ankle was already swelling up to the size of a navel orange, and it wouldn't take his weight.

Benny couldn't take his eyes off the dark shape. It didn't seem to have hard edges—like it was composed of black smoke. As his two friends led him toward the bike rack, two points of pale yellowish-green light appeared high in the shadow, and then one of the lights flickered—like a man winking at him.

"Come on, Benny. Get on my bike, and I'll push you."

Benny climbed aboard Mike's bike, and Paul mounted his own. Mike grabbed the bike at the handle bars and on the back of the seat and ran.

As they reached Oak Lane, Benny looked back. The black shape had disappeared. By the time Mike got him home, Benny's ankle felt better—tender and achy, but he could walk on it with almost no sign of a limp. He was dirty and sweaty, though, so he went in through the garage after waving to Mike.

His mother was waiting for him in the laundry room. One look at her face and Benny knew she'd talked to his dad already.

"Stewed spinach and boiled asparagus," she snapped.

"What, Mom?"

"That's what you're having for dinner: stewed spinach and asparagus, and you will eat every last bit. The rest of us are having tacos."

She spun on her heel and walked away.

Benny couldn't stop the sigh from escaping. His two most hated vegetables were spinach and asparagus, and his favorite meal was tacos.

"Sigh all you want, Benjamin. I'm mad at you and for good reason. Don't even think I'm kidding about dinner."

Benny shook his head and left the laundry room.

"And take a shower before dinner. You stink!"

He shook his head ruefully and started up the stairs.

"We'll talk about that limp when you are clean."

Her voice was as cold as arctic ice, and he knew he was in for another tongue-lashing when he came down.

Dinner was…ugly. He had to sit there and watch his brothers eating yummy tacos while he choked down spinach and asparagus — and a huge plate of it to boot. His dad looked at him with sympathy.

"Karen, I think you've made your point. Let's let Benny have some real food."

"Keep talking, James Cartwright, and Benny won't be the only one with nothing to ride for a month," Karen snapped.

Jim looked back at Benny and shrugged. "Sorry, champ. Vegetables it is."

After dinner, Benny stood and took his plate to the sink. When he turned to leave the kitchen, his mom cleared her throat.

"Dishes, Benny."

"It's not my turn," he said.

"Well, maybe it *wasn't* your turn before you went on your little trip, but it *is* your turn now, and it *will be* your turn until I tell you something different." Her eyebrows arched toward the ceiling. "Do you have an issue with that, Benjamin?"

He considered her expression. The corners of her eyes twitched, and her eyes appeared wet, watery. Her lips pressed into a thin line, and still, they shook. He glanced at his dad, but his father had found something interesting to look at in the taco he was holding. Benny sighed. "No, Mom, no problem."

"I said it before, Benjamin. Sigh all you want." With that, she turned her back on him.

"I'm sorry," Benny murmured, but his mother didn't hear, or pretended not to.

He tried to fight it, but another sigh escaped him as he filled the sink with hot, soapy water. After he finished the dishes, Benny went to his dad's study, where Jim had retreated after dinner.

"Hey, Benny," he said.

"Hi." He couldn't keep his lip from quivering.

"It's not forever, Benny."

"I know. But Mom… Mom huh-hates me now."

His dad wrapped his arms around him. "No, she doesn't, Son. She's mad at you is all. You'll understand her anger when you grow up and have kids of your own. Most of it comes from a fear deep in her heart that something will happen to you. Something bad."

"But nothing did, Daddy. And I'm not going back to that house. Not ever."

His dad shook his head. "Doesn't matter, Son. Something terrible *might* have happened, and that fear of what might have happened turns into anger when the danger has passed. It's a scary thing to think your kids might be hurt, or worse. That's the biggest fear I have, Benny, that something might happen to you or your brothers, and I won't be able to do anything about it. I'd rather die than have something like that happen to you guys."

Benny nodded. "Still…"

"Still, you've never heard her talk like that to you."

Benny nodded again, trying not to cry.

His dad sighed. "In a way, the depth of her anger tells you how much she loves you. Can you see that?"

Benny thought about it for a minute, and it made him feel a little better. "Yeah. But how do I fix it, Dad?"

His dad's grin was wry. "Pray." He tousled Benny's hair. "I've known your mom for almost fifteen years, now, Benny. In that time, I've learned that your mom is a very understanding woman up to a point, but once you cross that line, you just have to give her time to get over the hurt, the anger. But this I'll give you for free: cutting out all the sighing will help."

Benny nodded. "I'll try."

"And don't worry, Benny. She loves you until it hurts, even now."

Benny nodded again.

"I'll keep track of the extra chores. When your mom's gotten over it a little more, she'll be more open to time off for good behavior."

"Okay, Dad. Thanks."

"You got it, champ."

"Did you find out anything?"

Jim's face turned serious. "Yes. I think I know who's been hurting Toby. I don't know where he is, yet, so don't get excited. Still working on it, though, and I asked Chief Greshin for help."

"Is it... It's Toby's mom, isn't it."

His dad shook his head. "I don't think so, Benny. I think the person hurting Toby is hurting his mom, too.

But don't worry about all that. You told me, and I told Chief Greshin, and you'd better believe that steps will be taken to doctor that problem."

"Okay. Thanks for everything, Dad. You're awesome."

Jim Cartwright smiled, but inside, he feared that one day soon, he'd have to tell Benny about the police finding Toby's body somewhere.

Chapter 2

2007

I

Drew needed the campus quiet—deserted—and, at four in the morning, it was. He had everything set up back in the lab. He had stopped by the pathology lab and brought the industrial digester up to temperature and had prepped it with lye and water. The only thing missing was the demon.

Swathed in black cotton, Drew stood in the shadows, breathing controlled, no stray sounds to alert a demon to his presence, no shiny bits of metal to catch the moonlight. He wore military grade night-vision goggles that turned the darkest night into day—even if the day glowed with garish green light. He knew the demon was there—somewhere. Drew felt it, even if *seeing* it wasn't possible.

He hated the demons with an intense passion that bordered on psychotic. That most people would consider him a serial killer didn't bother him. Drew knew what he was doing was right. No, more than right, *necessary*.

His prey moved, and his gaze zeroed in on the motion. Across the quad, the demon squatted in a humongous hydrangea. It scratched its arm like mad, making the whole bush shiver and shudder.

Drew increased the magnification on his goggles. A slow smile crept across his face. The thing wasn't even looking in his direction. It stared at a first-floor window of Irene Glass Hall, the freshman dorms. The *female* freshman dorms.

As an experiment, Drew moved his own arm. The demons could be hypervigilant, but he'd never seen one this focused care about anything but its victim. Driven by lust and hunger, the stalk became something like foreplay to them after a while.

This one didn't notice him moving. The thing should be able to hear his movements, and if it looked in his direction, it could pick him out with its unaided eyes—much more easily than Drew could see it. But it didn't turn when he moved his arm, and not when he took a short step. The hunt had it engaged and engrossed.

That was good, but bad at the same time. Good, in that Drew could sneak up on it. Bad in that it meant the thing was old, and that meant powerful and wily. He would have to be careful.

He'd been hunting the demons for ten years—ever since he'd realized the psychiatrists were wrong. The demons *weren't* a product of grandiose delusions. They were *real,* and the demons controlled human senses so that no one saw them for what they were. Instead, humans saw regular people.

He wasn't sure they were really demons—not in the biblical sense anyway—but whatever they were; they were evil, and they needed killing. Some of them looked like biblical demons—leathery wings, horns, fangs, whatever—and those he'd dubbed "traditional" demons. Others had black, rotting skin that hung from them like clothing three sizes too big. Those he called "undead" demons. The rest of them looked…alien. They might have scales or three arms or no skin and those he called "weird" demons. No single weird looked anything like any other weird.

Whatever they looked like, they all fed on human emotions. *Negative* human emotions mostly—fear, anger, hatred—but some fed on things like orgasms or abuses of power.

Drew had been seeing the things since the age of fourteen—all his memories started at that age. It was strange not to have any memories of his childhood, but the doctors called it a response to some trauma he didn't remember. And that was fine with him. Who wanted to remember horrible things that happened in childhood?

The demon in front of him was a weird. It had thick skin like a rhinoceros or an elephant. The night vision goggles made it impossible to tell its true color, other than something dark—it looked black in the green-washed night. It had sharp, cat-like teeth and a wide, wide mouth. It had orbs of pure black for eyes, and its tail coiled around its feet.

As he made his way from shadow to shadow, traversing the quad in total silence toward where the demon hid, Drew unslung his modified tranquilizer rifle. In the beginning, he'd used regular firearms to stun the beasts, but that took a lot of ammunition and made such a god-awful mess, not to mention noise. And, he couldn't kill them that way anyway—not and have them stay dead.

Most tranquilizer rifles had a bolt-action and could fire a single shot. He'd spent a lot of time in the darkest corners of the internet before he'd "met" someone willing to do the job. They believed he was a serial killer, and so they charged him an exorbitant rate to build a semi-automatic tranquilizer rifle with three detachable magazines for the darts. People had no faith anymore.

The demon salivated, offering a clue to its preferred food. Its victim would die (as would he) if Drew failed, most likely through exsanguination, after being sadistically raped. The barbaric malignancy in his sights fed on blood and flesh as well as terror or debasement and shame.

His mouth settled into a grim, determined line. *I will not fail,* he told himself. Drew made one last check of the rifle: loaded and ready, carbon dioxide bottle at capacity. He had two spare magazines that held five more darts each, and an additional supply of darts in the sling-backpack he wore.

He was close, inside the demon's range of lethality. Drew's senses kicked into overdrive as the adrenaline flooded his bloodstream. The demon breathed and scratched its arm—both harsh, ragged sounds that grated against Drew's nerves. Worse, the foul thing reeked like burnt kale overlaid with the thick scent of sex.

Drew brought the rifle up to his shoulder, sighting through the holographic sight that had been customized to fit over the end of his goggles. He centered the weapon on the beast's wide back. He took a deep breath, released it, then squeezed the trigger.

Even as fixated on its prey as this demon had been, the pneumatic hiss of the gun alerted it, and it spun toward the sound, moving faster than the dart traveled. Still, the dart hit the beast in a bulbous shoulder and stuck fast.

The demon's gaze zipped around the quad, peering into shadows, staring at clumps of shrubs. It would perceive him at any second, and the veterinary-grade sedatives he used in his darts didn't work that fast on the demons.

Drew fired the remaining four darts in the magazine in rapid succession, the gun making the *pfft-pfft-pfft-pfft* sound that the movie industry loved so much. He thumbed the magazine release, letting it fall to the ground at his feet, and slammed another magazine in its place.

He looked up and into the hate-filled eyes of the demon and fired five times as fast as he could pull the trigger. His darts hung from the beast's torso, ignored by the demon. It stepped from the hydrangea, its eyes never leaving his. The demon cocked its head to the side, its face settling into that now-familiar expression of confusion.

Yeah, I can still see you, motherfucker, Drew thought and changed magazines. He raised the gun to fire again. *Five more darts. Hope that's enough for this big bastard.* He fired the magazine dry and slung the rifle, getting ready to run for his life. He loaded the darts with a heavy dose of M99, a sedative for large animals—like hippos and elephants. At least he didn't have to worry about killing the demon, so he filled the darts to capacity with the drug. In the TV show Dexter, M99 took instantaneous effect, and he wished for the umpteenth time that it worked that fast in reality.

The demon roared and charged at him. It started more than a hundred yards away, and the beast showed no signs of going out. Drew moved, skipping to the side like a matador in a bull-fight. He hoped that the demon's bulk would mean it lacked agility, but the demon corrected with each zig and each zag, growing ever closer.

Drew turned his back on the beast and sprinted away in a straight line. *Adapt or die*, he thought. As he ran, he pulled the magazine out of the rifle. He reached into the sling-backpack and pulled out five more darts. He leapt a shrub and almost dropped all of them. He fed them into the magazine and tried to push the magazine into the gun.

Instead, Drew dropped the magazine.

The demon kept coming, nostrils flared wide, mouth open like a shark about to bite. Drew's options were disappearing at a rapid pace. He cut to the side like a running-back, eyes frantic, skimming back and forth for the lost magazine. When he saw it, he dove, no time for consideration.

He landed on top of the magazine, grabbed it, and rolled to the side, slotting the magazine. The demon's clawed foot slammed into the ground where he had been a moment before, and Drew wished he'd kept running.

Wouldn't have mattered, he told himself. *It's a faster sprinter.* In fluid, graceful motion, Drew swept the gun up from his side and fired point-blank into the beast's face and neck.

The demon staggered back, holding a massive arm in front of its face. Drew sprinted away, but it was a wasted effort. Behind him, the demon took a step and then fell in a heap.

He approached it, ready to run at a moment's notice, and prodded the demon's shoulder with his booted foot. The demon didn't react, just kept right on tearing harsh, craggy breaths out of the air.

"Three hundred migs of M99. I'll be damned," he murmured. A bull elephant went down in under a minute and a half with just fifteen milligrams of the stuff. *I need more M99*, he thought.

He bent to the task of moving the heavy demon first to his lab, and then to the industrial digester kept for the medical school. He didn't notice the new automated campus security cameras tracking his progress.

2

Like most mornings, Mike Richards had a splitting headache when he rolled out of bed. *Late for my shift. Again. Good thing I'm the boss or I might be in trouble.*

He shuffled into his master bath, kicking aside empty beer cans and an almost-empty bottle of Jack Daniels. The bathroom shined bright, warmed by the mid-morning sun. Too bright—it made him want to throw up, and it made his head pound.

Squinting, he flipped the shower to full-hot and opened the tap. He sank to the toilet and leaned back, resting his head against the wall, and closing his eyes against the barrage of morning light.

He snapped awake sometime later, confused for a moment by the hot steam surrounding him, and the crick in his neck. His head still pounded, and he still wanted to puke, but stepped into the shower, letting the scalding hot water sluice over his head and pour down his back. Mike stayed in the shower for a long time, and when he got out, he felt a modicum less skeezy. He dressed in a hurry and went out to the junk heap the town manager insisted on calling the "Chief's Cruiser," the 1994 Chevrolet Caprice which had seen better days. Mike had no idea how the town mechanic kept it running, but it always started on the first try—even if it smelled like an old can of bear farts. Whatever the town manager wanted to call the car, he called it "Shamu" because it was a whale of a car, and because of how it looked: black fenders, white body. He had no doubt that back in 1994, it ran like a man being chased by demons, but thirteen years later it wheezed like a dying man and rattled like a spray can. It was a run-down whale of a car with a cracked side mirror and peeling dash. He turned the key, the old engine wheezed to life, and then he jammed it into drive.

The car lurched and shuddered out of his cracked asphalt driveway, squealing the belts the whole way. He cranked the air conditioning, despite the cool weather outside the car, and pointed the vents at his forehead. His drive to work took him through the remains of the town of Oneka Falls—empty store fronts, falling down buildings, cracked pavement. Half of the buildings had chain-link barriers in place, or plywood nailed over the doors and windows to keep the kids out.

After that horrific fall in 1979—the crime spree and the mass of child disappearances that followed it, the town had just died. Who wanted to live in a town where the chance that your kid would go missing was more than twenty times the national average? Who wanted to live in a dying town? Mike scoffed. He knew the answer to those questions: drunks, drug addicts, low lifes, and petty criminals. At least he was only a drunk. The town manager was all of the above.

Mike parked the decrepit car in the spot reserved for the Chief of Police and climbed out into the garbage strewn lot. The town manager's 2007 BMW 750i was in its accustomed spot (which was two spots—the only two handicapped spots in the lot). City funds had paid for the damn car, of course. Sport package, Monaco Blue metallic paint, and a beige convertible top. Just the essentials. Mike scoffed again, hawked and spat on the back window.

He trudged inside the run-down town hall, eyes roving over the peeling paint, warped siding, weedy planting beds. The glass door squealed when he opened it, sending an icepick shivering through his head.

Sally McBride sat behind her expansive counter, glaring at him with disdain. "On time again, I see," she snapped.

"Sally, when I answer to you, I hope to Christ someone will have the decency to shoot me and put me out of my misery."

"Such a fine example you set, Mike Richards. Are you even sober today?"

"Fuck you, Sally," he said cheerfully as he walked past the reception desk. "He in yet?"

She glared at him but gave him a terse nod.

Mike turned left into the part of the building reserved for the police department, such as it was. Since the town population had dipped, the police department consisted of a Chief, and three officers, one on days with Mike, and two on evenings. The night shift they had to contract out to a security firm from Rochester. They couldn't even afford to pay a dispatcher anymore. 911 calls were routed to the radio system during days and evenings, and to an on-call cell phone during the night shift.

Mike sat behind his desk in the big room that served as the communal "office" for the police department and slid open his bottom drawer with his foot. He toyed with the idea of taking a quick nip from the pint bottle he kept in the drawer. It would help his head, but it sure as hell wouldn't contribute to getting anything done. With a regretful sigh, he slid the drawer closed.

A mountain of paperwork, file folders, newspapers, dead radio batteries, used Kleenexes, empty Dr. Pepper bottles, and even a pair of dirty socks, covered the top of his desk. He wrinkled his nose at the mess but didn't straighten any of it. Instead, he stood up and walked into the so-called break room—a converted broom closet—and touched the coffee pot. It was lukewarm, and the coffee was guaranteed to taste like piss.

Mike shrugged and picked up a mug, peering into its depths. It had old coffee sludged on the bottom of the cup, but there were no paper-towels or napkins. *Of course not*, he thought. With an apathetic twitch of his shoulders, Mike poured lukewarm coffee into the dirty cup and heaped seven spoons of sugar into it for good measure. Oneka Falls no longer sprang for half-n-half, or even milk, so he sprinkled powdered creamer into the cup and stirred it with his finger.

"Going to make yourself sick, Chief," said Jack King, the other policeman on days.

"That, my friend, would only be an improvement."

"Rough night?"

"Yeah, aren't they all?"

Jack grunted and stood looking at Mike with a critical expression. "Might be better if—"

Mike rounded on him, slopping coffee over his hand. "If what, Jack?" he asked in a cold voice.

King looked away. "If we had a night shift, boss."

"Yeah," said Mike. "That would help, but it's not going to happen."

"No, doesn't seem like it will," Jack murmured.

Mike returned to his desk, still fuming at Jack, but keeping it off his face. *Always has to make a comment. Can't leave it alone, always got to be in my business. Don't see me doing that to him, do you?*

The town manager stuck his head in the door. "Got a second, Chief?" he asked.

Mike shook his head. If the man had any skill, it was perfect timing. "What can I do for you, Chaz?"

"My office?" said Chaz with a look toward King. "We should let Officer King focus on his work."

"Yeah," grunted Mike, pushing himself to his feet. "Your office have fresh coffee?"

"Of course."

Mike tipped his mug into the garbage can next to his desk. "Good. This sludge would kill me this morning." Following the town manager, he couldn't help but sneer at the bounce in his walk. If there was one thing Chaz Welsh had never done, it was work an honest day in his life.

The town manager's office was vast and boasted hardwood-paneled walls. The carpet was plush, the chairs were leather, and the manager's custom-made yew desk was wide. It made Mike sick. All of it.

Chaz held out his hand, and Mike handed him his cup. The town manager glanced inside and made a face. "Shannon, please bring Chief Richards a decent cup of coffee." He held out Mike's dirty cup. "And see to it that the cups in the P.D. office are washed."

Shannon Bertram, the town manager's personal assistant, bustled in with a steaming mug of coffee with the town seal on it. She took Mike's cup with two fingers as if she feared she would get something from it. "Hi, Chief," she murmured.

Mike nodded at her. He could remember being in high school with her though she was a few years behind him. Twenty-one years in the past, high school was already a blur of hazy memories. "What can I do for you, Chaz?"

Welsh closed the door to his office. He turned and walked to lean against the front of his desk. He steepled his fingers and then let his hands fall so that he ended up looking like a kid playing cops and robbers.

All supposed to make him seem accessible, Mike thought trying to keep the scorn from his face, *though all it does is make him seem like an asshole*. Chaz wanted him to ask again, but Mike didn't give a shit. The coffee was good, the chair was comfortable, and the silence didn't hurt his head as much as talking did.

Welsh snapped his tongue against his teeth. "Mike, you know what I want to talk to you about. It's the same thing we've been talking about for months now."

"Refresh my memory," said Mike, hiding a sour frown behind his coffee cup.

"Your...*activities*...are interfering with your job, Mike."

"That's funny," laughed Mike. "I thought my job was interfering with my...*activities*."

"Not funny," snapped Chaz. "You're the goddamn chief of police, Mike. The constant tardiness and missed shifts are one thing, but this...this...insistence on rubbing your drinking in everyone's face is—"

"Did that fat bitch out front complain again? I'll smooth it over. I'll—"

"No, Mike, Sally didn't say a thing."

Mike looked around for a moment, nonplused. "Then I don't see how I'm rubbing anything in anyone's face."

"You don't remember, then?"

Oh shit, thought Mike. "Remember what?"

Chaz sighed. "Maybe it's time we should talk about sending you to a program."

Mike grimaced. "I don't need a program, Chaz. I *like* to drink, but I don't *need* to drink."

Chaz sat in the chair next to him. He held up his hand and ticked off points on his fingers. "Number one, Mike, you're blacking out. Which brings me to number two: you're causing trouble during your black outs. Last night, after downing who knows how many highballs over to Moe's, you decided the jukebox didn't have any good music. Any of this bringing back your memory?"

Mike grimaced and shook his head, avoiding Welsh's gaze.

"Since the jukebox didn't have any good music, you thought you should throw it out. When Brent Spanser tried to stop you, you broke his nose for him. Joe McGilly tried to intervene, you pulled a gun on him. A *gun*, Mike."

Mike put his head in his hands and blew out a long breath. "I don't remember any of this."

Welsh's laugh was sour and humorless. "That's kind of the *point*, Mike."

"What…what happened next?"

"McGilly was two sheets to the wind as well. The two of you ended up leaving together. You bought a case of beer at the Red Apple, and while you were there, McGilly pissed all over the front window. You thought it was funny."

Mike shook his head. "Yeah, last night was…"

"It's not just last night, Mike. You know that."

"I'll rein it in." He gave Chaz an earnest look. "I'll get it under control."

Chaz shook his head and sighed. "Mike, I wish I could—"

"You'll see, Chaz. I'll cut back. I'll quit all together if that's what you want."

Chaz stared at him for a moment, eyes hard, but then his face softened. "Look, Mike, I understand how hard it is for you. Small town and all, what with you being—"

"That has nothing to do with it," Mike snapped.

Chaz shook his head. "If you say so. Mike, no matter what the local idiots might think, I'll back you if you ever decide to—"

Mike stood up, hands shaking. "Whatever you *think* you know about me, Welsh, it has no bearing on this, and I'll thank you for keeping your damn mouth shut about your theories."

Chaz closed his eyes and puffed out a breath. "Okay, Mike. Okay."

"I'll keep it together. I'll cut back on the drinking."

Chaz nodded, the picture of weariness.

"I mean it," said Mike, and he did…at least for a few hours.

3

"Myths, in general, are stories people tell themselves to explain the unexplainable. They exist in every culture, every place human beings band together and form any kind of society. In almost every case, a culture's myths grow out of the mythology of an earlier culture or cultures." Drew tried to keep his eyes off the two men at the back of the room, but try as he might, his eyes kept straying up the amphitheater steps to the shadows at their top.

Cops. They were cops.

Had to be. They weren't dressed like academics— not even those of the administrative bent. Their eyes crawled over him like beetles. He suppressed a shiver. "Someone tell me: what is the most common thing that needs an explanation in any culture?"

Hands shot up around the lecture hall, but Drew wasn't looking at them. The two cops drew his gaze like moths to a flame. One of them—the big one—leaned toward the other and whispered something.

The class fell silent, and the spell broke. He looked around and called on a person at random. "Tell me," he said.

"The weather," said the student.

"That's a good one, but not quite right." More hands shot into the air. "Let's do away with the don't-talk-until-I-call-on-you-thing. Just call out your answers."

"How the earth was created."

"Excellent guess, but not right," Drew said.

"The seasons."

"Doesn't that fall under weather?" Drew asked.

"The cosmos."

"Where we come from, who created us."

"Look, all of these answers are good ones, but we're missing the basic event in every human's life that everyone wonders about, that everyone questions. You are *forensics* students, and I'm a forensic pathologist and profiler. Can you think of something related to what we're here to study?"

"Death," said a baritone voice from the top of the amphitheater.

"Yes! Death. Every culture in history has had death myths."

"What's a death myth?" someone asked.

Drew smiled. "Ever hear of the Grim Reaper? The guy on the pale horse? Heaven. Hell. Nirvana. Valhalla." His eyes tracked up to the top of the stairs yet again. The two cops stepped out of the shadows. One of them put his hand on the badge looped through his belt.

The other one was a demon.

Drew fought to keep his face expressionless. He nodded. "But, that's enough for today, class. For next time, read chapters three through seven. Be prepared to discuss the techniques used in the cases presented in the chapter sidebars." The class groaned. "And…"

Drew held up his hand for quiet. "And write your own myth to explain death."

The lecture hall erupted with the noise of seventy students packing notebooks away. Drew gathered his own notes and shoved them into his shoulder tote. A few female students started to come down the steps for the usual question and flirt session. Drew held up his hand. "I'm afraid I have to take care of something, so let's save your questions for office hours."

He trotted up the stairs, smiling his best "I'm so innocent" smile. At the top of the stairs, the demon cop stared at him with an uncomfortable intensity.

"We appreciate you knocking off early," said the human cop with a smile and outstretched hand. "Name's Scott Lewis. I'm an investigator with the New York State Police. This is my partner, Lee LaBouche."

"Meetcha," said the demon in a baritone voice, never taking his almond-shaped eyes off Drew's.

Ah, Mr. Baritone-voice. "Dr. Andrew Reid. Nice to meet both of you," said Drew, making his "worried" face. "No offense, but I hope you've got the wrong guy."

Lewis chuckled. "Nothing to worry about. We need your help with something is all." He waved his hand in a vague motion. "If you'll pardon the armchair quarterbacking, mythology seems like a strange subject for a criminal justice class."

Drew grinned. "They were all awake, weren't they? And it's a forensics class."

Lewis grinned back. The demon didn't.

"Anyway, I'm a forensic pathologist. Death myths are dead center. I use it as a bridge into the occult."

"That's why we are here, your expertise with the occult," said Lewis. "We are working on a case, and we need a profiler with occult...sensibilities."

"A serial case? I haven't seen anything in the media?"

"Yeah, and we'd like to keep them out of the loop if you take my meaning."

"Oh, sure," said Drew. "Should we go back to my office?"

LaBouche's chartreuse alligator eyes narrowed.

"It's more private." Drew put on his most charming smile.

"Lead the way," said Lewis.

Drew and Lewis walked side-by-side, while LaBouche seemed content to walk behind them. It gave Drew the creeps having a demon so close.

"...nice campus," said Lewis.

"Sorry. I got distracted," murmured Drew.

"It's nothing. I just said it must be good to work at such a nice campus."

"Oh sure. It's beautiful here." The skin between his shoulder blades crawled like it was creeping up his neck. He shrugged his shoulders, but the sensation persisted.

"Something wrong with your back?" rasped LaBouche.

He glanced back at the demon, suppressing the desire to wrinkle his nose at the stench the thing put off in waves. "What? Oh. No, it's nothing. Just a twinge," he said, keeping his voice light.

Drew unlocked the door to his office and motioned the two troopers inside. "Take a seat," he said and walked around desk to his chair after closing and locking the door. "Tell me about your case."

Lewis glanced at his partner, who stared at Drew as if they were the only people in the room. Lewis shook his head with mild annoyance and sighed. "We've got what might be a string of serial crimes."

Drew steepled his fingers in front of his chin. "I note you didn't say 'serial murders.'" The demon was large, almost too large for the chair. Shaped like a large silverback gorilla—wide, wide shoulders, too-long arms, thick torso, massive neck, but bright yellow scales instead of dark fur—he seemed to fill Drew's smallish office.

"No. They may be—"

"There are no bodies," snapped LaBouche.

With arched eyebrows, Drew turned his gaze on the demon. "No bodies?" The thing's mouth was V-shaped, and his shark-like teeth poked through his glistening, rubbery lips.

LaBouche grimaced and looked away.

Doesn't like me looking at him, thought Drew. *Interesting.* He turned his attention back to Lewis. "If *you'll* pardon the armchair quarterbacking, it doesn't seem like your case calls for either a profiler or a forensic pathologist, so I'm at a bit of a loss."

LaBouche scoffed, but Lewis smiled. "Yeah, and LaBouche, here, agrees with you. But there's something…" Lewis shrugged.

"Something seems off?" Drew said. "Gut feeling?"

"There's more than just that, or we wouldn't be here bothering you. This big lug wouldn't go for it if that's all it was."

With a sour glance at his partner, LaBouche leaned back and folded his arms across his wide, scaled chest. He tipped his domed head back and looked down his nose at Drew as if he wanted to get as far away from Drew as possible.

"Okay. Tell me about it," said Drew with a shrug.

"Where to begin?" Lewis mused. "About two years ago, a guy named Walter Flag disappeared. It's no great loss, he was a strange guy by all accounts. Lone-wolf. Gruff, stand-offish. You know the type." Drew inclined his head, watching LaBouche watch him in his peripheral vision. "Few friends and no family, so no one reported him missing. We—"

"Then how did you come across him?"

"Good police work," snapped the demon.

Lewis smiled, embarrassed. "We found links—"

"*Maybe*," interjected LaBouche.

"—between the victims." Lewis spared his partner an irritated glance. "On the surface, there's nothing. No friends in common, no history. But..." He held up his index finger. "But, all twenty-two of them traveled to the same small town in the Southern Tier."

They've only found twenty-two, Drew mused. Drew cocked his head. "Traveled to the same town? That seems a bit thin, Trooper Lewis."

"*Thank* you," growled LaBouche.

Lewis was all smiles and bumbling, aw-shucks charm. "Yeah. It *is* thin. But this town in the Southern Tier?"

Drew nodded.

"Population of eleven hundred and forty-seven."

Drew's eyebrows shot up, and he whistled. "What's the probability that all twenty-two people who don't know each other not only go missing, but are all related to someone in that still lives in town?"

"No idea," said Lewis. "But it's got to be small."

"Town that small, everyone knows everyone else, right?" asked Drew.

LaBouche grunted. "Used to have a bigger population. Late '70s, early '80s."

Drew arched his eyebrow.

"Twenty-two people who all move away from that town to the same town? Tell me they aren't acquainted, at least," said Lewis, shaking his head to negate LaBouche's argument.

Drew was nodding, lips pursed. "Yeah, that seems even more unlikely."

"You bet," said Lewis. "So, if they know each other, if they come from the same town, then why can't we find any link between the twenty-two of them? Why don't they have friends in common? Why don't they have history?"

"Because their histories are counterfeit."

"That's my theory. LaBouche doesn't see it."

Drew looked at the demon, met his hostile gaze, and shrugged. "Still, he could be right."

LaBouche nodded.

"Yeah, and I'm not saying I'm one hundred percent sure he's wrong. He's got a gut for stuff like this that borders on the uncanny." Lewis slapped the demon on the shoulder. LaBouche's gaze never faltered, never left Drew's face.

"But it's weird," said Drew.

LaBouche scoffed.

"I take it one of the other victims was more social? Better liked?"

"Yeah," said Lewis. "A co-worker reported Randall Fiegler missing about three months ago. We were tracking his movements in the month prior to his disappearance and came across a bus ticket to Oneka Falls. It's a little town south—"

"Yeah, I know it," said Drew. He felt hot and cold at the same time, excited and filled with dread, but he didn't know why. Oneka Falls was just a dot on the map to him, a gas stop on a long Saturday drive.

"Well, yeah, so you understand that there's not much there. I was curious why Fiegler would take a bus. The man had money."

"No other way to get to Oneka Falls without driving yourself?"

"That's it," said Lewis.

LaBouche scoffed. He held up a big chartreuse hand and ticked points off on his fingers. "Car service. Train to a nearby town. Plane to a nearby town. Chartered plane. Chartered helicopter."

Drew chuckled. "Points to LaBouche."

Lewis shrugged. "Sure, but I found the link to the others. Even if my initial assumption was wrong." LaBouche glanced at Lewis.

What was that? A flicker of hatred? Why do you hate your partner, LaBouche?

"I traced the movements of the victims we had and then went backward to find the ones no one had reported."

"And you got up to twenty-two?"

Lewis nodded. "From the greater Rochester area, yeah."

"Okay," said Drew. "There seems like there is something to it, Trooper Lewis, but even so, how do you know something untoward befell these people?"

"Yeah," said Lewis, once again all smiles and aw-shucks charm. "Some of them might have just moved on, but *all* of them?"

"Okay. Tell me the rest then."

"Not much left to tell," said Lewis. "They were all male, all middle-aged, all white. All disappeared without a trace."

Drew grinned. "And I supposed you checked with Oneka Falls?"

Lewis laughed. "That we did. Nothing."

Drew hadn't known about any link with Oneka Falls. *Might be worth a visit, see if the whole place is populated with demons.* "Anything on the MO? Trace evidence? Anything?"

LaBouche shook his head. "Nothing."

"Okay. So why do you need a profiler with…what did you call it?"

"Occult sensibilities," laughed Lewis. "Because the only thing we have to go on is Oneka Falls."

Drew looked back and forth between the human cop and the demon. "I don't get it."

"Have you heard of the Temple of the Wolf?"

Drew held up his hands. "Wait a minute. Despite the huge number of claims of ritualistic abuse, there are no substantiated reports of satanic rings or cults who abused children. Zero."

LaBouche nodded with a long-suffering expression plastered on his face.

"Yeah," said Lewis. "But there were findings, in some of the cases, of ritualistic aspects secondary to actual abuse. Most often to intimidate the victim, to keep the victim from telling anyone."

"True," said Drew.

"The Temple of the Wolf sect played a role in a large percentage of those cases of confirmed abuse."

"I still don't get it."

Lewis flashed a half-smile. "I plotted all the cases in the area on a map."

"The cases with ritualistic aspects?"

"Yeah. When I was a kid, all those reports fascinated me. When we looked in to Oneka Falls, something kept tickling the back of my mind."

LaBouche grunted.

"And?"

"And the thing that was bothering me is that Oneka Falls was on that map I used as a kid. It's the geographic center of all the reports."

Interesting, thought Drew. "But no reports were from the town itself?"

"Reports from all around, but not a one from Oneka Falls," said Lewis.

"Now that's interesting," muttered Drew. He pulled on his bottom lip. *Could be the place is a haven for the demons. Like a convention center, a place where they can go and not have to worry about who's watching them. But why would the town be the center of those reports?* "What is it you want from me?"

Lewis looked away. "Look, I get that you can't do a profile on this mess. What I need to know is: whether someone might believe they are an avenging angel or something."

Drew spread his hands. "Like something right out of that book: *Michelle Remembers*? Driving the devil straight back to hell? Sure, anything is possible."

"What other kinds of motivations would there be?"

Drew shook his head. "Anything you can imagine. There's not enough here for more than guesses, and there's nothing here to rule anything out. Yes, it's interesting." He nodded at Lewis. "Enigmatic, even, but I can't begin to build a cogent profile on this. It's all about the victims. About the offender, if there is one, there's nothing."

"That's what I told him," croaked LaBouche.

"Okay, forget the profiling a minute," said Lewis. "Put on your mythology hat. Is there anything about these cases that tugs at you?"

Besides the fact that I killed all twenty-two of the demons you consider victims? "No," he said. "Nothing."

4

"So, what does that huge gut of yours tell you, Lee?" Scott asked as his partner slid into their cruiser.

"Don't like him."

"You hid it well…yeah, no you didn't—not at all."

"There's something…I don't know…something off about him. He's jumpy. He's in his head a lot. I make him nervous."

"You are about as subtle as a rhinoceros in a glass factory. He reacted to your dislike of him, but I got the impression he was nervous, too."

"Didn't want to meet my eye."

Scott laughed. "Neither did the last three boys Becky brought home to meet me."

Lee glanced over at him, mirth crinkling the corners of his eyes. "You don't say. Did you wear your gun all three times?"

Scott laughed. "Jenny wouldn't let me."

"But you would've if she hadn't been there." In the privacy of their car, Lee's gruff, no-nonsense exterior evaporated.

"Well, of course I would've. How else are those little punks supposed to get the message that I'll kill them if they hurt her? I mean, I can't just come out and say it."

Lee chuckled—a harsh, crackling sound in the tight confines of the car. "Next time, I'll just happen to be over when the kid comes to pick up Becky. I'll give him 'the face.' He'll shit his britches."

"Funny you should mention that…I told Jenny we ought to do that."

Lee smiled and cracked his knuckles. He was a big man, three hundred and thirty-five pounds if he was an ounce, but his size was the least intimidating part of him. LaBouche had an air about him, no doubt a cultivated air, that just plain scared people. He could gaze at a suspect with a certain expression without saying a word, and the guy would just start talking, answering any question they put to him. Scott imagined any predator eyeing his dinner would wear a similar expression.

"But, unfortunately, Jenny said no."

"Rats," said Lee. "Might've been fun."

"Yeah," Scott sighed. "What's your opinion—he good for it? Is he the guy in the video?" Lee LaBouche had a sense for criminals, especially for those of the serial variety. He had an uncanny way of getting inside their heads.

Lee rocked his head back and forth—like a lizard. Scott hated it when he did that. "He's the right general size, but…well, that guy doesn't have it in him. What we saw in that video was a cold, calculated professional. No, Andrew Reid is not the guy." Scott looked at him askance. He couldn't put his finger on why, but he had the distinct impression that LaBouche had just lied to him. "Besides, that guy is mayo on white bread, man. The guy in the video has something… Something…"

"Yeah. The guy in the video, he didn't hesitate. Confident, like he—"

"—had done it before. More than once…he has it down pat," finished Lee.

"Exactly. He's done it before, twenty-two times."

"Well…"

"Yeah, but I bet once we know who the decedent in the video is, we'll find he goes to Oneka Falls on a regular schedule."

Lee shrugged. "Maybe."

"Anyway, the murderer in the video wouldn't be so nervous, would he? I mean, you, you can scare the dead, but little old me?"

"Well, you were wearing your gun."

Scott laughed. "That I was." They sat in silence while Scott drove them off the campus and onto 390 south.

"Anyway," said Lee.

"Anyway, can we scratch him off our list?"

"Yeah," Lee grunted.

Why is he lying? wondered Scott.

5

As soon as the two troopers left his office, Drew packed his shoulder bag. Leaving a note on his door canceling office hours, he strode down to the medical school lab building.

He was breaking one of his many rules. He *never* visited the lab during the day. Drew wasn't supposed to have access to it, but the fake university ID card in his palm had master key status. The card had his picture on it, but the name under the picture read: Nathan Hauser, M.D. He wasn't sure why the name gave him a warm fuzzy feeling, but it did.

He peeked through the narrow window in the lab door. The lab looked deserted. He slid his ID through the card reader and pushed his way through the door when he heard the distinctive buzzer.

He dropped his bag near the door and went straight to the industrial digester. The pressure door was still closed and secured. The body of last night's demon had gone into the pressure vessel over twelve hours ago, so it was no doubt already rendered to its chemical components, but he hadn't had a chance yet to drop by and clean out the calcium phosphate that remained. First checking to make sure the digester wasn't running on a new body, he opened the pressure vessel. He scooped out the handful of soft white pellets—the remains of the demon's bones and teeth—and tossed them into the bin set aside for the disposal of legitimate remains from the medical school.

He scooped up his shoulder pack and made his way to the parking lot, surreptitiously looking for the trooper's car. Drew slid behind the wheel of his Honda, the car he called "The Professor-mobile" in his mind. The car drew zero attention from anyone, and he hated the damn thing, but it had the intended effect.

To make sure no one was following him, Drew drove downtown and circled the courthouse three times. When he was sure, he drove to the parking garage where he kept his other wheels. He traded the Honda for his bright red BMW 328i and pulled on a baseball cap and dark glasses.

He had a small one-bedroom apartment near campus—it was a place he stayed, not the place he *lived*. Drew didn't want to be where anyone could find him. He pulled out his cell phone at a light and turned it off. At the next light, he pulled out the battery and put both in the glove box. He headed east out of Rochester and made his way north to Lake Road, following it east to the South Side RV Park. He pulled in behind his 1999 Odin Desperado and got out a remote that looked like a garage door opener. After he pressed the button, the back wall of the toy hauler descended, and he drove the BMW up the ramp and into the claustrophobic "garage" space. He clicked the remote once more and the rear wall began to ascend.

Once the door closed all the way, he breathed a sigh of relief. No one knew about the Desperado—at least no one who knew Dr. Andrew Reid. A traveling salesman named Benjamin Cardrite owned both the BMW and the toy hauler on paper. It didn't matter though. No one looked at the drivers of huge class A motor homes—not ever.

Finally able to relax, Drew dropped his school stuff on the floor, kicked off his shoes, and fell on the couch. He reviewed the conversation with the troopers again and again until he convinced himself that they didn't suspect him—that he'd played them just right. The demon, though, he was a complication Drew didn't need. *He will be a problem.*

With a sigh, he sat up and took out his laptop. Piggy-backing on his neighbor's wifi, he logged in to his VPN and ordered more M99 from a website in Brazil. He found the demons he killed by data-mining the internet data relating to unexplained murders or attacks, possession, alien sightings, and similar items. He configured his data-mining software to add Oneka

Falls and the Temple of the Wolf to its heuristic search parameters.

His head was pounding and pounding by the time he finished. *Too much stress, too much uncertainty.* He hated having the smallest detail up in the air, let alone the life-threatening detail of having a demon in the guise of a police officer on his tail.

For the three hundredth time since leaving campus, he thought about packing up the Desperado and heading west on I-90. The freedom of the open road beckoned him. No more pretense. No more public face to maintain. He could just go from RV park to RV park, finding the local demons and dispatching them. He'd be free, untraceable, invisible.

Until the money ran out.

And besides, something about Western New York called to him, demanded his presence. He'd learned that in medical school. There was a part of him that *needed* to hunt here, *needed* to kill demons here. A voice in the back of his mind kept screaming that he had unfinished business in New York—though for the life of him he couldn't imagine what.

Chapter 3
1979

I

Matt Greshin pulled into the parking lot of the red and chrome monstrosity that was Jenny's Diner. There was a Genosgwa police cruiser in the lot, and one from the Kanowa Sheriff's Department. John Morton, chief of Cottonwood Vale's police department, had the farthest to go, and he was the worst at getting anywhere on time.

Greshin walked into the diner and tossed a smile Jenny's way. The four of them had been having these unofficial meetings at Jenny's place for years, and she knew them all by sight. He slid into the booth next to Bobby Jefferson, the county's sheriff.

Bobby was a working Sheriff, not a politician. He wore a Sam Browne belt and a uniform every day, never a suit. He'd polished over the scuffs in his well-worn shoes, but the heels needed replacing. He tipped Matt a wink.

"Boys, how's the criminal organization coming?" asked Jenny from behind the counter.

"One more still to come," said Bobby in his gravelly voice.

"Morton? He's always late. You three want to order?"

"We can wait," said Bobby.

"You're the Sheriff," said Jenny and turned away.

"I'm glad you called, Matt," said Genosgwa's Chief of Police, Tom Walton. "We got another one reported today. I'm getting worried."

Bobby shook his head. "These things come in threes, Tom. Don't get too worried until you've got a fourth." Bobby was the eldest of the four and had the most experience.

"Well, better get started with the worry. Matt's got one."

Greshin held up his hands. "I don't know it's a runaway. Kid's mom is a piece of work, and her boyfriend is a candidate for a tramp ride out of town if you ask me."

"Abusive?" asked Bobby.

Matt nodded. "Popped off wise to Jim Cartwright."

"Who, being Jim, let it slide," said the sheriff.

"Yep. This guy's a little twerp. You know the kind. Strutting bantam rooster until someone stands up to him, then cries about how he was abused as a kid and he don't know better."

Bobby and Tom both grunted.

The door opened, and John Morton came in.

"Why, if it isn't Chief Morton," said Jenny. "Your partners in crime are over there."

Matt grinned. "She's about to give him the sauce, I'll bet you a dollar."

"Hmph. No bet," said Bobby.

"Say, John," said Jenny. "I've been meaning to ask you… Are you on time for church?"

"I don't—"

"Or maybe to get your kids to school?"

John caught on right about then, so he just stood there with a little smile on his face.

"Nothing to say? Have you been on time to anything? Your own birth, maybe?"

"I think I was late to that too," he said with a chuckle.

"T'wouldn't surprise me," said Jenny with a wave at the booth. "You kept them waiting long enough."

John chuckled again and slid in next to Tom. "Gents. Sorry I'm late, I was delayed." It was the same thing every time. "I was delayed" but he never had anything to say about what had delayed him.

"Huh!" said Jenny with an extra helping of sarcasm.

"You know what we all want, woman," said Bobby. "Get to it."

"Bobby Jefferson, don't you go thinking that your lofty position will protect you from the heel of my shoe."

"Yeah, yeah. Go away."

Jenny made a show of huffing off, and all four of the men grinned.

"So, you think this bantam cock is good for the boy?" asked the sheriff.

"Hell, Bobby, I don't even know the boy's dead. He could've just run off somewhere."

"How long's he been gone?" asked Morton.

"Four days."

Morton whistled. "No one's seen him? Kids?"

"A kid was the one who noticed him gone. Benny Cartwright."

"Jim's boy?" asked Bobby.

Greshin nodded.

"What about you, John? Any runaways or missing kids?" asked Bobby.

"No, nothing. But Cottonwood Vale's forty miles from Oneka Falls. Farther from Genosgwa."

"Hmm." Bobby picked up his spoon and tapped it on the table.

"It's coming!" yelled Jenny from the other end of the counter.

Bobby chuckled. "Still, John, you keep your eyes peeled. Any of you have a new, unsavory type in town?"

Matt shrugged. "No one knows too much about the mom's boyfriend. I'm heading over to see him next."

"I'll ride along if you don't object," said Bobby.

"Things might get...excited."

Bobby turned his steely blue eyes on Greshin. "I think I'm the one who taught you how to handle situations like that."

"Yup, you did, when I was back on the deputies."

"Then it's settled. Now, Tom. What do you know about these two runaways?"

"They all came from the poorer parts of town, o'course. One of 'em is in a situation similar to what Matt's describing. His daddy gets heavy hands when the boy smarts up in school and the like, but he's a good man." Walton shrugged. "The other one is a bit of a mystery. Quiet, that one. No real friends. You know the type."

"This might sound crazy, but just go along," said Greshin. "Did those boys have bikes?"

Walton gave him a strange look. "Um, I'm not sure."

"Why," asked Bobby.

Matt told them about Benny's suspicions about the classified ad. "Might make sense to check the paper over there and see if the same kind of ad has run in the weeks prior to your disappearances."

Bobby pointed his finger at Chief Morton. "There's something for you to watch for, right there."

Morton nodded.

Just then, Jenny bustled out with a tray of food and made a big production out of passing the food out to the wrong person. It was all part of the game the five of them played, and they all played their parts.

After they finished eating, the cabal broke up. Tom Walton and John Morton went their separate ways. Bobby walked to his own cruiser and took his shotgun out of the trunk and then walked to Matt's black and white.

"Just gonna be the two of us, Matt?" he asked.

Matt scratched the stubble on his chin, his finger nails making a harsh scraping noise. "There's one other I could trust with this, but I'm not expecting much trouble out of this guy."

Bobby shrugged. "Better safe than sorry, though, right? And maybe we should get in someone's personal car."

"I'll radio Witherson on the way back to town. He drives a Wagoneer."

Bobby grunted and slid into the passenger seat with an easy grace that belied the white in his hair. "It'll be your show, Matt. I'm just along for the muscle."

"Yup," said Matt as he threw the Fury into gear and drove them back to Oneka Falls. He pulled into Meat World, the town's only grocery store and parked next to a bright red Wagoneer with big tires.

Craig Witherson leaned out the window as they got out of the Fury. "Well, hey there, Sheriff Jefferson. Long time no see."

Bobby Jefferson grunted.

"I don't see the sheriff around here, Craig. I don't see any cops, either. You get me?" asked Chief Greshin.

"Why, sure, Matt. Just three guys helping a buddy move."

"Yup. Get that monstrosity started, will ya?" The Sheriff and the Police Chief climbed into the Wagoneer as it roared to life. "He's on Mill Lane."

"Yep, I know it." Witherson drove to Mill Lane and pulled up at the Burton house, disregarding the drive and parking on the front lawn in front of the door.

"Nice parking, son," said Bobby.

"Easier to load."

"Yup. You want me to knock, Matt?" asked the old sheriff.

"Please."

"Sure thing." Sheriff Jefferson walked up to the front door and slammed the butt of his twelve gauge into the wooden door. The sound of it boomed through the small house.

"*What the fuck?*"

Someone stomped up the entry hall toward the door, and he didn't sound happy. The door flew open, and as it did, Jefferson racked the slide on the shotgun. It was a distinct sound that froze most people right where they were. Jefferson leveled the shotgun at the short guy who had opened the door. "Well, hey there," Jefferson said.

The man was maybe five feet four inches tall and skinny as a rail. His hair was long and unkempt, hippy-style. He wore cutoff jeans shorts and nothing else. His eyes never left the bore of the shotgun, and his Adam's apple bobbed. "Wuh-what is this?" he asked in a small, weak voice.

"Moving day," said Craig.

Candy Burton came up the hall behind the man. She glared at the three men on her stoop. "We aren't moving," she snapped. A cigarette bounced on her lips as she spoke.

"No, Ms. Burton, but *he* is," said Matt.

Candy squinted at him. "Chief Greshin?" she asked. She looked Witherson up and down, and her expression twisted with emotion. Her gaze lingered on the Sheriff's badge pinned to Jefferson's chest. "The police chief, the sheriff, and some loser ain't gonna tell me who can live here."

Matt smiled his best public relations smile. "No, Ma'am. Wouldn't dream of it. But we heard our friend here *is* moving." His eyes cut to the short man, hardening as they did so. "What was your name again, friend?"

Candy opened her mouth, but before she could speak, the short guy elbowed her in the ribs. Hard. "I don't need a bitch to speak for me, Candy. I told you that before."

Quick as a whip, Jefferson reversed the shotgun and jammed it into the short guy's midriff. The air exploded out of the little man, and he sagged to the side, resting against the door jamb, chest heaving. "No way to treat a woman, friend," said Jefferson in an iron-hard voice.

"I'm not your friend, old fuck, and I ain't moving nowhere."

"What's your name, fella?" asked Matt. "I don't believe you're from around here."

"My name is Randy Fergusson, and what business is it of yours where I live or where I'm from?"

Matt laid a big hand on his shoulder and pulled him away from the door jamb. "Two ways this can go, Randy. One, we let you go inside and gather your belongings. We'll be there with you, in case your hands want to go off wandering again. Or two, we'll bag you up, and throw you in the back, your shit be damned. Which option are you keen on?"

"What? You can't come around here and tell me what I will and won't do. You cops don't have no authority—"

"No cops here, old son," said Matt. "Just three buddies to help you move."

Randy's face flushed. "Well, fuck you, *buddy*. I ain't moving."

Jefferson shot a glance at Craig. "Sounds like he picks option number two."

Witherson grabbed Randy's arm and bent it in a hammerlock, lifting the smaller man onto his toes. He jerked him this way and that and then pinned him up against the Wagoneer. "Anyone got a pair of cuffs handy?"

"Wait just a goddamn minute," said Randy. "Just wait a minute!"

Matt slapped his cuffs on the man and bore down hard as he tightened them.

"Ow!"

"Hey!" shouted Candy. "Don't hurt him."

Bobby Jefferson looked at her with disgust and then shook his head. "Woman, he just now bopped you in the ribs, and you want to stand there and defend him? What in the Sam Hill is wrong with you?"

She looked him up and down. "The day you're fit to judge me, I'll be—"

"A dumb woman who *wants* to live with a guy who beats her. Tell me, dumb woman, *where's your son*?""

Candy whirled on her heels and slammed the door.

Bobby shook his head and then slapped Fergusson on the head. "Hey, bozo, she was speaking for you again. Didn't hear you put up a fuss this time though."

Randy went over red and tried to push away from the side of the Jeep, but Craig Witherson was a man of great, wiry strength, and he held him there. "One of you want to get the back?"

Matt opened the tailgate of the Wagoneer, and Craig led Fergusson over, gripping his shoulders so tight that Craig's fingers went white.

"Tell you what we will do, Randy," said Matt. "We are gonna load you in the back of this vehicle, and we will drive on over to Genosgwa and buy you a bus ticket. Anywhere you want, as long as it doesn't cost over twenty, and it ain't here."

"What we're not gonna do, is put up with any shit," said Bobby.

"Yeah, big men you three are," said Randy. "Why don't you come at me one at a time? And without any fucking shotguns."

"Because we don't want you to get hurt, you little pissant," said Craig, punctuating the sentence with a sharp shake.

"Just so you know, things like what you just said, Randy, that all counts as shit in my book." Bobby whacked the butt of his shotgun into Randy's lower back, not hard enough to do lasting damage, but hard enough to make Randy squeal. "Now, you got anything else to say?"

"My stuff," wheezed Randy. "I want option one."

Bobby Jefferson laughed, long and loud. "I bet you do, champ."

2

Benny woke, swimming in sweat and huffing hard. His heart was thumping in his chest like he'd been sprinting. His mouth was so dry his throat hurt. His room was dark, filled with shadows.

He'd been dreaming about something dark, something scary. About something trying to get in through his window.

He flung himself over, eyes searching the shadows between his bed and the window. His mind was still grainy with sleep, and his eyes were bleary, but nothing in his room moved. He kept a sharp watch, anyway.

Outside, the night was lit by the stars and the three-quarters moon. Color had faded from the world. It was like gazing out at a black-and-white picture.

As his heartbeat slowed to normal, his eyelids grew heavy and kept wanting to drift shut. He snapped them open time and time again, sure there would be something creeping up on him, but there never was. The window was closed, locked. He was safe.

Just before sleep claimed him, something rattled against his window, and his eyes snapped open. His room was darker than it had been. He could no longer see his desk, his toy box. He couldn't see the door to the hall or the closet, either. His eyes drifted to the window, thinking maybe he'd slept after all and the moon had set.

He couldn't see anything out the window. It was like the windows of the house on Thousand Acre Drive—pitch black. He gulped and sucked in a breath. Maybe he'd dreamed the bright moon and stars. Maybe it was the new moon, he couldn't remember.

Then the rattle came again. It sounded like someone throwing gravel at his window. The sound didn't scare him, and if his window hadn't gone black, he'd have thought it was Paul or Mike and gone to the window.

"Benny. Benny, help me."

The rattle came again. The voice sounded like...sounded like Toby.

Maybe he *had* run away. Maybe his mom's beau had beat him up, and he'd taken his tent and sleeping bag and went camping.

Benny threw back the covers, shuddering as the cool night air hugged him. He sat up on the side of his bed. "Toby?" he whispered. He threw a glance at his bedroom door. The last thing he needed was his mom hearing him.

"Yeah, it's me. Benny, help me! You have to help me, man."

Benny put his foot on the floor, toes splayed like they were monster sensors. He glanced at the bedroom door again.

"Chop chop, Benny! It's cold out here. Let me in."

"I'm not supposed to, Toby. It's after bedtime."

"Just do it, Benny. Do it, do it, do it."

Something about the voice made the hair on the back of his neck stand on end. It was Toby's voice, he had no doubt of that, but there was something wrong. Something wrong with Toby, something wrong with the situation.

"Toby, I'm already in a heap of trouble. I went to see the bike man, and my mom wants to boil my butt in oil."

"Just do it, Benny," Toby sighed. "You know I would."

Then, like a lightning bolt, the memory of the bicycle man's patter came back to him.

Just do it, Benny, he'd said. *You know Toby would.*

Benny sucked a deep breath, wanting to scream for his dad.

"Don't do that, sonny-boy," said Toby's voice. "No, don't call your pops."

How could he know I was thinking that! He pulled his foot back up into bed and tucked it under the bed clothes.

"Now, son, I don't want to be rude, but what kind of friend leaves a buddy to freeze in the cold night air?" The voice had changed. Now, it was the creaky, scratchy voice of an old man. "What kind of boy won't help a friend in need?"

"Where's Toby? What have you done with him?"

"Come on, now, son. Of what are you accusing me? Just come on out and say it."

"Duh-did you kill him?"

The old man laughed, sounding like a cat stuck in a rusty screen door. "Ah, boy, that's a good one, son! Did I kill him, ha!"

The man laughed for what felt like a long time, but Benny felt no desire to join him. It wasn't that kind of laugh, it was more like the laugh of a bully after he punched you and made you drop your books. The laughter faded into a chuckle with a few guffaws mixed in, and then wound to a stop. Benny thought he could hear the old man breathing, just outside his window.

"How did you get up on the roof?" There was no answer, but Benny could still hear him wheezing. "Did you? Did you kill Toby?" The breathing became faster. "Or are you a pervert?"

"Listen here, boyo. I'm losing patience with you. Are you going to open the damn window or not?" The voice had gone as cold and empty as a baseball diamond in the winter.

"No," said Benny. "Why would I?" He pulled the covers up as if to put an exclamation point on his answer.

"I'll see you again, Benjamin James Cartwright. Oh, you better believe I will."

Chills ran down Benny's back and gooseflesh rippled across his chest despite his fall pajamas. He pulled the covers up to his chin, staring and staring at the black window. The old man breathed, huffing like he was angry.

"What did you do with Toby?"

He didn't think the old man would answer, but after a long time, the man said, "He's with us now, Benny, and with us, he will stay."

Then, with a sharp gust of cold air that stung Benny's eyes, the blackness outside his window shrank to a point that popped as it disappeared. The three-quarter moon flashed like summer sunlight off the water. The stars twinkled, and the fall wind blew.

When Benny woke up the next morning, he laughed. What a dream he'd had. *That wasn't a dream, Benny, and you know it,* said a small voice in the back of his mind. "Yes, it was," murmured Benny. "Yes, it was."

3

"Now, tell me shit-stick," said Bobby Jefferson. "What happened to the boy?"

"The boy?" asked Randy. "What do you mean?"

"To Toby," snapped Greshin. "What did you do with Candy's boy?"

The three of them were in the back seat of Witherson's Wagoneer, squeezed in tight like sardines. They sat parked in a cut out in the middle of the countryside between Oneka Falls and Genosgwa.

Bobby was on Randy's left, and Chief Greshin was on his right. Craig had their guns up in the front seat, but Randy didn't stand a chance, even so, and by the look on his face, he knew it. He scoffed. "That little bastard? The best part of him ran out Candy's cooze right after she banged the kid's dad."

Bobby growled and leaned closer to Randy.

"All right, you grumpy old bastard, all right! I smacked him around a little. So what? He needs a firm hand, or the way he's going, he'll be in trouble before he can get a driver's license."

"And then what," asked Greshin.

"What do you mean, 'and then what?' And then he cried like a little girl."

Bobby reached across and smacked him. "You know what we want to know, skid-mark. Don't play coy, or I'll ask these two to step out a minute."

"Oh, a tough guy," sneered Randy. Even so, he leaned away from the sheriff. "Well, I'll tell you guys, I have *no idea* what you want to know. I hit him. I hit Candy. They both deserved it, and I would do it again."

Bobby looked past him and quirked his eyebrows at Greshin.

"Where did you hide his body, Randy?" asked Matt in a mild tone as if he were asking about the baseball game the previous night.

"His *what*? His body? Whoa, whoa, whoa, whoa. Put on the brakes. There is no *body*. At least, not a dead one. Not that I know of, anyway." Randy's chin quivered.

"Maybe you better tell us about the last time you saw him," growled Bobby.

"Yeah, okay. I can do that, but you're not pinning his murder on me. His or anyone else's. I didn't kill no one."

Bobby leaned in close. "Spill," he whispered, and his whisper was more menacing than his shouting.

"Yeah, fine. It was at dinner Sunday night. Or what you could call dinner, I guess. Candy cooks about as good as she fucks, and I'll save you all the twenty it would cost you to find out. She fucks like an old, dead fish."

Bobby twirled his index finger. *Go on*, his eyes said.

"So, we're sitting there, eating Candy's slop, and boy... You ain't gonna believe this, but the boy looks right at me, bold as brass, and says, he says, 'Why don't you have a job?' Can you believe that? Right there at dinner."

"And then?"

"And then I popped his snotty little puss for him, didn't I? He can take a punch, I'll give him credit for that. Candy goes off like a firecracker. What did I do that for? It's an honest question. Blah blah blah. So…she gets one, too.

"The whole while, Toby's just sitting there, looking at me. A little blood was dribbling down from his split lip, adding color to those watery mashed potatoes Candy makes. He didn't even notice. He's just staring at me, right?

"So, I says to him, I says, 'If you don't get those peepers off of me, bucko, I've got another pop for you just like the first.' He just looks at me, calm as crackers."

"So…" said Greshin.

"So I popped him again. Other side of the face this time. Still, he don't cry like usual. He don't snivel and run to Candy. What's worse is he's still looking at me like I'm a bug.

"Candy, now, she's smarter than the rugrat. She knows one pop to the kisser is better than two any day of the week, so she's keeping her mouth shut, looking at her lap.

"Not Toby, though. No. Toby's eyeballing me like he's got a pair, and the way boys develop these days, maybe his dropped early. I don't know, 'cause I don't go for little boys. Not like Witherson up there."

"You aren't too bright, are you?" whispered Bobby Jefferson in a tone of voice that made the hair on Matt's arms stand up straight. "You're going to sit here bragging about beating up an eleven-year-old, and then crack wise, the whole time sitting not an inch away from me?"

Randy looked at him out of the corner of his eye and gulped. "So, anyway, Toby's staring at me, and I can't have it. You know how it is. I demand respect, and, by God, any kid I'm supporting better give it to me, or he's gonna get popped once or twice.

"Well, the third time I smacked him, I hit him harder, and his head snapped to the side. He turns back to me, slow-like, and stares at me again! Can you believe it? I was thinking, 'My God, this kid's dumb.' Then I said to him, 'School time, Toby,' and pushed back from the table.

"I don't wear a belt, but I keep one handy. You betcha. So, I go and get it and come back. Candy's crying and whispering to Toby. Well, she should know better, so I laid that belt across her back, and she screams, all high and watery.

"Well, does Toby like that? You bet your ass he doesn't. He stands up so fast the dining room chair flips over behind him, and one leg smacks into the wall and punches a hole in the sheetrock. Now, I'm a level-headed guy, most of the time, but right then, right then, everything went red.

"I slung the belt at him side-arm, and it wrapped right around his side and slaps into the small of his back. Now, my daddy taught me that move the hard way, so I know how much it stings. I'm thinking to myself that Toby will cry, he'll snivel, but he doesn't. He looks at me, but I see then that what I took for calm wasn't calm at all. No, it was fury and hate all mixed up like cake batter.

"I shook my head at him, and I says 'You may think you're ready, boy, but trust me. You ain't ready for this.' He cocks his head at me sideways, and then whispers, real quiet, 'I don't know what you're talking about, Randy, but I'm going to tell *you* something. This is it. This is the last time. So enjoy it, you skinny asshole. You hit my mom or me ever again after tonight, and I'll kill you in your sleep. I know how, so you better believe me.'

"Can you believe it? Not even twelve, yet. Well, I'm not much to argue, so I start in with the belt again. Pretty soon, he's crying. He can't help it, see? Candy, well, she thinks it's enough, so she opens her damn mouth and gets a few whacks.

"When I turn back to continue Toby's education, he's not standing there anymore. He's over by the sliding door, and he's got it open already. Fast little fucker.

"Anyway, he looks at me over his shoulder, and goes, 'Was it everything you hoped for? Cause, I meant what I said. Hit us again, and I'll cut your throat when you sleep.' Then he turns and boogies out through the door.

"Since that night, I ain't seen hide nor hair of him. I figured Candy was keeping him away until things calmed down a little, but if I see him again, I'll tell ya for nothing that he ain't gonna sit for a month or more. You betcha. I'll tell you something else—"

"Gonna sit there and brag about that shit, are you?" Bobby's voice was low, almost the growl of an angry dog. His elbow arced up and smashed into Randy's face, and blood splattered all over the back seat. "Sorry, Craig," he grunted.

"No, no, Sheriff. You go on. Do what's right."

Randy sat still, staring down at the blood pooling in his cupped palm. "It's broke," he whispered.

Then the elbow hit him in the forehead, and again on the side of his head, his head snapping this way and that.

When he stopped, Bobby was breathing hard, and Randy was groggy but still conscious. Bobby looked across at the Police chief. "Sorry, Matt. I felt I had to, or I was gonna explode or something."

Matt shook his head. "I didn't see anything. What about you, Craig? You see anything?"

Craig turned to the front of the Jeep and turned the key. "No, siree." He put the Jeep in gear and pulled out on the county highway.

In the ten minutes it took to get to the center of Genosgwa, Randy came around. The blood still oozed from his nose, but it had slowed to a dribble. Still, he was a bloody mess.

"We better stop and clean him up a bit," grunted the sheriff.

"Craig, take us around Tom's," said Matt. "He'll let us use the back door and a cell."

It took about twenty minutes to get Randy sorted out and clean again. His nose had swelled to the size of a peach. He'd done whatever they told him to, but he hadn't said a word or done anything without their prodding.

Tom Walton drifted back into the cells as they were leaving. "That the guy?"

Greshin nodded.

"Is he good for murder?"

"I don't think so," sighed Matt. "He's an asshole, to be sure. He slammed his face into the back of the seat and then started crying about it."

"You bet he did," said Tom. "Right out in my parking lot. Saw it all from my office window."

Bobby winked at him, but his expression was subdued.

Randy looked back and forth from one to the other, face blank, eyes bleary and watering.

They herded him back to the Jeep and drove him over to the bus station. Craig parked at the curb close to the bus depot and flipped down his visor, which had an Oneka Falls P.D. placard on the back.

Randy got out of the car when Matt told him. He stood on the sidewalk, not looking left or right, not talking. Bobby fished his two suitcases out of the back of the Jeep and put them down at Randy's side.

"Now, son," said Matt. "You are going on a one-way trip, ya understand?"

Randy nodded.

"I don't want you coming back."

"Not to Kanowa County, neither," snapped Sheriff Jefferson.

Randy nodded again, not looking at any of them.

"But," said Matt, "if I find out you did something to that boy other than what you told us, I will come for you."

"And I'll be with him," snapped Bobby.

Randy nodded for the third time.

Craig came out of the bus depot and brought over a ticket to Binghamton. "Enjoy your trip, asshole."

Randy's gaze drifted over to Craig, and then he winked.

"I should've got in back," Craig muttered.

The three cops got in Craig's Jeep, and Randy shuffled over to a bench to wait for the bus. Randy muttered and mumbled to himself, glancing over at them, now and again. When the bus pulled up, he stood and came over to the Jeep.

"I'm getting on that bus," he said. "But I want you to know something. I'm leaving because I want to, *not* because you told me to. I was sick of Candy anyhow."

"Whatever you have to tell yourself, asshole, as long as you tell it to yourself on the way out of my county," said Jefferson in a low, menacing tone.

"Yeah, yeah," snapped Randy, eyes blazing. "You three think you are big men, coming at me with guns and all—and the sheriff, here, in uniform. Why not come as men? Why not come one at a time and see how things would be different?"

"You done?" asked Craig in a bored-sounding voice.

"No, I ain't done. I don't know how, and I don't know when, but I promise each one of you this: I will get you for this. I will figure out a way to ruin you. And that goes for that cock of a town manager, too."

"Smart," said Craig. "Threaten three cops. You got a fine mind on you, Randy."

"I'll tell you something else. This one's free of charge."

"Yeah? What's that?" asked Greshin.

"I'm going to get that bratty little boy, too."

"Toby?"

"Nah, I'm done with the motherfucking Burtons. The boy that squealed on us. The town manager's kid. I plan on getting him, too. Just for fun."

"Well," said Bobby in a conversational tone, "I guess that's it." He popped his door open and was out of the Jeep in a flash. He walked right up on Randy and stood nose to nose, maybe a quarter of an inch separating them. "Gonna get me, huh?" he growled. "Gonna get all of us. Gonna get the town manager. Gonna get *another* eleven-year-old, are ya?"

"That's right, you—"

"*Then do it!*" Bobby roared. "Step up. Start with me, boy. Right here, right fucking now."

The people boarding the bus turned to look, but to a one, they turned away tout suite when they saw the guy yelling was Sheriff Bobby Jefferson.

"See?" snapped Bobby. "No one will interfere."

Randy shrank away from him, turned, and picked up his suitcases. Without another glance, he boarded the bus and Bobby got back into the Wagoneer, hands shaking with rage.

"Yep," said Craig in a wistful voice. "I should've taken my turn in the back seat."

4

Randy got off the bus two stops later in Victorsville, still in Kanowa County. It was a place where he knew no one and no one knew him. It was a small town, smaller than Oneka Falls. One traffic light, a police station, fire station, hardware store, and a greasy spoon called Eats defined the downtown area. All by itself about half a block up the road, like it was the kid that stank during lunch, stood a pawnshop and gas station combination named Bud's Bodacious Bargains. No hotel, so Randy bedded down behind Bud's and tried to sleep away the last few hours before dawn, despite his aching nose.

The sound of a V8 muscle car woke him before he was ready. He opened his eyes and jerked away from the front bumper of a 1968 Cutlass.

"Caught you napping, did I?" asked the driver. He was a portly son of a gun with stringy brown hair. "This look like a hotel to you?"

"Well, point me to the town hotel," said Randy with a laugh in his voice. "Why do they let bus routes stop in the middle of the night in towns with no accommodations?"

"Fair point," said the fat man. He hawked and spat out his window. The V8 died, and the man got out of the car. "Name's Bud. This is my place."

"Good enough, Bud. I'm Greg, and I'd like to do business this morning, only I got mugged last night, and they took my wallet." Randy gestured to his swollen face.

"No ID, huh?" Bud scratched his head. "Well, I don't mind if you don't. Less paperwork for me, less hassle for you."

"My man," said Randy with a broad smile.

They went inside, and Randy sold a handful of Candy Burton's jewelry. Bud had a selection of pistols on display in an old jeweler's case, but pistols weren't Randy's style. No, he was a man who liked a little distance between him and the thing he was shooting. "No rifles, Bud?" he asked.

Bud looked him over. "Going hunting, are you?"

"You bet," said Randy, putting on his "honest" face. "Brother-in-law has this cabin—"

"Yeah, I got no rifles. Better get on up to the hardware."

Randy smiled, suppressing his desire to smack Bud across the face for interrupting. "Hardware, you say? They have rifles?"

"Yup." Bud pointed to the east. "Hardware."

Randy waved and left the stinky little shop behind, along with one of his suitcases—the one filled with Candy's clothes. He had three crisp one hundred-dollar bills, two fifties, and three twenties in his pocket. Who knew Candy had such valuable stuff? But it was better he hadn't known, or he'd have no money now and would've had to do day labor to get enough for a rifle.

Victorsville Hardware was a pleasant place. It was one of the older style hardware stores. All the inventory sat out on shelves made of pine, and it smelled like grease, hay, and horse feed. It had a bit of everything, from livestock feed and tack to nails and hammers. And hunting supplies, of course.

Randy parted with his three one hundred-dollar bills and walked out with a brand-new Remington 700 BDL in .270 caliber. He'd have rather had it in .308 caliber, or hell, if he was wishing, 7.62x51mm like the M40A1 Uncle Sam taught him to shoot on, but beggars and choosers, and all that rot. He had a box of rounds for it and a scope. The Hardware hadn't had lawn mower mufflers, but they gave Randy the address of a small engine repair shop where he bought a muffler and talked the owner out of a bit of steel wool.

He knew what he was doing. Those three pigs in Oneka Falls thought he was just some wanker, but that was because he didn't go by his real name anymore. Not since the last time he'd had a rifle, anyway. If they knew his real name, they'd have shown him more respect.

Once he had his supplies, he traipsed out of town and into the woods. He walked a few miles into the forest and then sat down and made a silencer for the rifle using the steel wool and the muffler. He mounted it to the end of the rifle and sighted through the scope. The body of the muffler was a little too big, so there was a big gray smear across the bottom of the scope's field of view, but it was serviceable.

He jacked a round into the chamber and squeezed the trigger. It made noise still, but a lot less than a rifle shot should. Satisfied, he removed the homemade silencer and put everything into the rifle case.

He knew a place where he could crash in Cottonwood Vale, but that was forty miles away. He'd need a car because that fat pig of a sheriff didn't live in Oneka Falls. No, and Randy *needed* to pay that pig a visit.

He walked back out to the road and then trudged away from the little berg's downtown. At the edge of town, a dirt track peeked out of the woods. Randy turned down the track, stepping around the puddles and the mud. He followed the dirt track deep into the woods before he came across what he wanted.

The place was old and more of a shack than a house. It had once been white, but now was more of a dirty gray with green streaks of mold along the edges of the siding boards. Two of the windows had no screens, and another was boarded over with a scrap of plywood. There was no mailbox and no house number.

In the driveway was a 1967 Buick Skylark. The car was black with a white top and rotting white-wall tires.

With a broad grin on his face, Randy high-stepped through the tall grass and weeds of the front lawn. He laughed a little when the driver's side door was unlocked and then slid behind the wheel. A minute and a half later, the Skylark's engine wheezed to life, and Randy broke the lockout on the gear selector. He backed the car out of the drive and looked at the house with a feral grin.

Nothing moved inside the house.

Laughing, Randy drove toward Cottonwood Vale.

5

It was Saturday morning, and Benny had just spent two and a half hours watching Saturday morning cartoons with his brothers. They started on ABC with *The All-New Super Friends Hour* at eight a.m. over bowls of Golden Grahams, even though it meant missing *Hong Kong Phooey*. At nine, they switched channels to CBS to catch *The Bugs Bunny/Road Runner* show, and at ten-thirty, their mother swept in and snapped off the television.

"Outside time, boys. It's Saturday, you shouldn't waste it cooped up inside watching the boob-tube."

"Okay, Mom," said Benny. "Would it be okay if I have Mike and Paul over today? We'll play in the woods or something."

His mom looked at him, and at first, her face was hard and tight, but as she stared at him, something softened in her eyes. She tousled his hair, and said, "Sure, Benny. I'll make you guys a picnic lunch."

He beamed at her. "Thanks, Mommy."

She winked at him. "You still get vegetables for dinner, kiddo."

He nodded. "Yeah. I'm... Mom, I wanted to—"

She put her finger to her lips. "Not yet, Benny. Not yet." Tears glistened in her eyes.

"Okay, Mommy," he said.

"Go call your friends," she said, pressing her index fingers against her lower lids.

Benny went into the kitchen, looking back over his shoulders to see if his mother was still crying. Her tears confused him, and he felt like he would never understand her. He picked up the phone receiver, a clunky, mustard-yellow thing on a long, twisted cord, and dialed Mike's phone number. He felt a vague sense of embarrassment when he thought of the rotary dial phone. Most of his friends had fancy push-button phones now, but his dad said rotary dial was fine.

"Hello?"

"Mike? It's Benny."

"Hiya, Benny. Did you watch *Hong Kong Phooey* this morning?"

Benny shook his head. "Super Friends. Want to come over my house and play? My mom said she'd make us lunch."

"Let me ask," said Mike, and before Benny could reply, set down the phone with a clatter.

Benny waited, listening to the line hum and sing. He smiled as Mike yelled for his mother, sounding exasperated. The phone made a strange noise, but there was always something making noise in the town's old phone system. Unconcerned, Benny fiddled with the yellow cord, unwinding a knot.

"Benny," whispered something in the static.

Benny held the phone away from his face and stared at it like it was a viper.

"Come play with us, Benny. It's nice here."

It didn't sound like a voice — not a human voice, anyway. Benny brought the phone back to his ear. "Funny, Mike," he said. "Really funny."

"Mike's not here, but Toby is. Come on down and let's play."

The sound of the voice was like a rusty file drawn across a cheese grater. "Who's there?" asked Benny.

"What? Benny, you called me. You must be losing it, my man," said Mike.

"Did you hear the other voice? The one in the static?"

"No one here but us chickens, Benny. My mom says it's okay, so should I come now?"

"Yeah," said Benny as he covered his eyes with his free hand.

"See you in three minutes, then."

"Yeah." On the other end of the line, the phone clattered, and then the line went dead. Benny set the receiver in its cradle like it was hot. First the dream, now hearing things in the static? *I gotta get a grip*, he thought. It was just crossed wires. Had to be. He picked up the phone and dialed Paul's phone number.

"If you come of your own free will," said the static voice, "we can have more fun than if we have to come get you. Bring your two friends, there's plenty of room."

"Not funny," whispered Benny as he listened to the last few clicks of the phone number. "You're not funny *at all*, whoever you are."

"Hello? Is that Benny Cartwright?"

"Um, yes, Mrs. Gerber. Can Paul come over to play? My mom says—"

"To whom were you talking? Just then?"

"Oh. No one, Mrs. Gerber, it was just my little brother."

"Well, Benny, your little brother is not 'no one' and one day, you'll enjoy being around him. Trust me on that. Here's Paul."

"Um, okay. Thanks, Mrs. Gerber."

"Hi, Benny."

"Hey, Paul. Want to come over and play with Mike and me? My mom's making us lunch."

"Okay. My mom already said I can come over. When?"

"Now."

"I'll be there in two shakes of the devil's tail."

"You're so weird, Paul."

"I know you are, but what am I?"

"Geek."

"Nerd."

"Hurry up."

"Then shut up and let me leave."

"Always want the last word, don'tcha?"

"You bet."

"Okay, you win. Hurry up."

"Bye."

Not wanting to risk extending the conversation by a few more hours, Benny hung up without saying good bye. He went into his room and changed out of his pajamas and into his army pants and an olive drab T-shirt. When the front door rang, he was lacing up his Nike hitops. He tied them in a rush and took the stairs two at a time to the ground floor.

"Benny, what have we said about running down the stairs?" his mother called from the kitchen.

"Not to do it."

"Then you were just doing what?"

"Running down the stairs to get the door."

"Your friends will wait the extra few seconds. I doubt they will wait for us to take you to the E.D. with a broken neck. Capiche?"

"Sorry, Mom."

"Get the door, Benny. What are you waiting for?"

She's getting over it, he thought. With a wide grin, he turned the knob and let his friends inside. Like him, they wore camouflage pants and T-shirts. It was their mutual Saturday uniform. "Hi, guys."

"Hi fart-face," said Mike.

"Michael, no trash mouth in my living room, please."

"Yes, Mrs. Cartwright. Sorry."

"Let's go out back and play commando in the woods," said Benny.

6

The phone jarred Matt Greshin out of a sound sleep. He rolled over and eyed his alarm clock. 10:41 a.m. Everyone on the police force understood he slept in on Saturdays. They knew better than to call him for something trivial.

He slapped the phone off the cradle and put the receiver to his ear. "Whoever you are, you better have a damn good reason for interrupting my beauty sleep."

"No amount of sleep is going to help you with that, Matt. Tom Walton here."

"Oh, hey, Tom." Matt lay back on the bed with a groan and a sigh. "You calling to ask me to a cookout at your place?"

"Well, I wish it was something like that, Matt, but it isn't."

"So what's shaking this morning?"

"You said we should check the papers last night, right?"

Matt sat up and swung his legs off the bed. "Yeah, for someone selling bikes on the cheap."

"Yup," said Tom. "Guess what I found?"

"A budding entrepreneur."

"You got it in one."

Matt got up and rearranged his boxers. "Gimme a sec, Tom, I want to find what the one over here said."

"Yup," said Tom.

Matt put the phone down and walked into his home office. He shuffled through the stack of loose paper on the top of his desk. "There's the bastard," he muttered when he found the piece of torn newsprint.

"Found it," he said when he picked up the phone.

"Good thing, I was about to call in Search and Rescue to go look for you."

"Har-har. I got a system, see? I call it the one pile system."

"Pile of shit system is more like it," laughed Tom. "Read the thing already."

"One ten speed bike for sale. Twenty dollars is all I ask in return. Come after supper," Matt read. "Then it gives the address."

"Edge of town? Quiet road?"

Matt grunted.

"Mine, too. Ad's almost word for word," said Tom.

"Yeah, but it's all pretty inane."

"Yeah, except for that 'all I ask in return' business, and even that's normal in certain circles around here. It gets a little more suspicious, however."

"How's that?"

"Paper says the ad ran twice. In the weeks before the kids over here lit out. One for each kid."

"Shit," breathed Matt.

"Oh, yeah," said Tom. "I think we better call Bobby Jefferson."

"Let me call John Morton first and see if he has anything new. I'll call Bobby this afternoon, I want to check with the paper here for other runs of the ad."

"Okay, Matt."

Neither of them knew it, but Bobby Jefferson would never hear the news. He'd be dead before mid-afternoon.

7

Randy stalked through the trees. He had his face painted green and brown. His clothes were dark, and he was barefoot, so he wouldn't make any extra noise. He had the Remington slung over his shoulder, silencer attached. He left the Buick parked on the side of the road with the hood open.

The day was perfect—the temperature, the perfect amount of sunlight filtering through the trees overhead, the lack of wind, everything. It reminded Randy of that other day four years before…the day his bitch of an ex-fiancée had tried to marry someone else. On that fateful day, his name had been Owen—Owen Gray. Even now, people remembered his name. But not Stephanie or her imposter-groom. No, they didn't remember a damn thing—not unless your memories went to hell with you. A smile flittered on his lips like a hummingbird's wings.

He had no idea where the bastard of a sheriff lived, but like on Stephanie's wedding day, he knew where he needed to be. And like on that day, a still, small voice was whispering inside his mind, telling him where to go. He knew how to handle the rifle he carried—courtesy of the United States Marine Corps. And he knew how to handle the sheriff. It was like in geometry, follow the two lines until they intersect.

His mind bounced back and forth between Stephanie's Death Day and the present. She had looked so pretty in her white lace, her hair put up in a do, her make-up perfect. He'd added the only thing she was missing—a splash or two of red. The imposter-groom, now, Randy had taken special care with him. His casket had been closed at his funeral. Randy had used a .30-06 that day, and the exit wounds had been immense.

When Randy smelled the barbeque on the wind, he stopped and worked the bolt of the Remington, hands calm and steady, chambering a round. He froze there for a minute, listening hard. After he was sure he was the only one stalking those woods, he started forward again, moving like a cat. As the woods thinned, Randy dropped into a half-crouch.

On Stephanie's Death Day, he'd crept to within one hundred yards of the wedding party. No one had seen him, or even suspected he was there. Stephanie had been all about "getting close to nature" and "communing with Gaia." Randy suppressed a laugh. He'd helped her get close to nature that day, helped her insides get right up and personal with Gaia.

Two or three rows from the edge of the forest, he found a convenient tree. He put the Remington in the crook of a low hanging branch and sighted through the scope. The old man stood staring down at the meat he was grilling. He wore a ridiculous apron over baggy shorts and a white T-shirt.

The little .270 wouldn't leave as much of a mess as that .30-06, but it would do enough damage to drop that son-of-a-bitch *right now*. Randy recalled how Stephanie and the imposter-groom had jerked and jigged as the .30-06 rounds slammed into them, and a small, savage smile spread across his face.

Randy aimed at his eye. "*Pow*," he whispered and aimed at Sheriff Jefferson's Adam's apple. "*Pow*," he breathed. He messed around like that for several minutes, aiming, whispering "*pow*," and aiming somewhere else. He'd done the same thing at Stephanie's wedding, and like that occasion, his little game resulted in an erection.

Jefferson glanced at the woods, eyes lazy, and Randy froze. When the Sheriff looked back down at the grill, Randy aimed at his head. He started to pull the trigger but stopped himself. His first shot at the imposter-groom had been to the head, and it was something he always regretted. The imposter-groom hadn't *suffered*. In hindsight, it would've been better if the bastard had known who shot him; if the bastard had to watch as the bullets slammed into Stephanie. He dropped his aim until all he saw in the scope was the grill, guessing where the Sheriff's gut would be. He took a breath and let half of it out, then squeezed the trigger. The rifle bucked, and he heard the round *twock* into the top of the grill. He took his eye away from the scope, grinning.

Jefferson fell on his side, still facing the tree line. His hands bore down on his gut, above his navel, and blood was seeping through his clenched fingers. His face was screwed up, but his eyes were wide open, mouth working, but no sound coming out.

Randy grinned and lifted the rifle out of his impromptu rest. He stepped through the trees, stopping at the edge of the forest. Jefferson saw him, and it was delicious. Randy gave him a little wave and a ferocious smile. *Hello, shit-stick*, he mouthed.

He raised the rifle to his shoulder, his movements slow and deliberate. Jefferson's mouth was moving, and he was holding out his hand as if he were commanding Randy to stop. Randy put his eye to the scope and aimed. He squeezed the trigger and ejaculated at the same time. The bullet flipped Jefferson down onto his back, and Randy couldn't see his face, but the bullet had flown true—he had a gift with trajectories, so he knew. Jefferson's funeral would be closed casket—like the imposter-groom's. No one would want to look at the mess the .270 caliber round had made of Jefferson's right eye. Randy's grin stretched even wider. He was glad he'd had the opportunity to learn from Stephanie's Death Day. It made this day so much better.

A woman screamed, and Randy crouched, operating on instinct. His eyes snapped toward the house. A woman, Jefferson's wife no doubt, stood inside an open set of sliding glass doors. Her hands mashed her cheeks, and her eyes were the size of silver dollars. A tray, two empty glasses, and a pitcher lay at her feet, ice melting on the carpet. Randy waved at her, and she jerked back as if he'd slapped her. He chuckled and raised the rifle to his shoulder. The woman shrieked and turned. Randy fired, and his bullet hit her in the back of the neck, pitching her face first into the living room of the small house.

Whistling, Randy policed up his brass and turned and walked back into the forest. He felt good again. For the first time since that night in the back of the cop's Jeep, everything felt like it should. *One down, two to go,* he thought. "No, *four* more," he breathed, thinking of the town manager and Toby's asshole friend. He lay the rifle across his shoulder, steadying it with one hand. He whistled *It's a Small World* while he walked.

Something flickered to his left, something he'd seen in the corner of his eye. Something black—a shadow. He spun in that direction, but there was nothing there. He stood still for a moment, staring into the woods. "Are you there?" he muttered.

He would have seen it if he looked up.

8

Mike, Paul, and Benny stalked through the trees. Their faces painted green and brown, they wore camouflage pants and T-shirts, and they carried sticks as if they were rifles. They were careful to make as little noise as possible, or the enemy would suss out their positions and end them with a burst of gun fire.

"Sergeant Benny, do you have eyes on the target?" asked Paul.

Benny scratched his cheek. The face paint Mike brought always gave him a rash. He held out his hand, pointing at an invisible camp of the enemy. "There, Lieutenant."

Paul squinted into the brush. "You sure, Sergeant? Looks like a native village to me."

"I'm sure, sir. That ville needs pacification, sir."

"All right, then. Men, you know the drill. Slow and silent, and not a single commie bastard walks out of that village."

"Yes, sir," snapped Mike.

"Oohrah! Get some," whispered Benny.

The boys crept forward, crouching low—almost bent over—rifles held at the ready. They'd played this game many times before, though Benny doubted they'd get to play it again if their parents found out what playing jungle commando meant. Paul lifted his hand, and they froze.

Paul pointed at his eyes with his index and middle fingers and then pointed ahead and to the left. He pointed at Mike and pumped his fist twice in the air. Mike nodded and skulked away from the other two boys. They waited for him to make his kill, silent and deadly. When Mike rejoined them, he gave a grim nod to Paul.

"Okay, men," whispered Paul. "Let's have us some fun."

The boys charged through the woods, yelling their war cries.

9

Randy watched the three boys running through the woods, screaming like idiots. They had sticks held up like rifles, and as they ran, they made machine gun sounds. Randy couldn't help but grin. He was up in a tree, cradled at the intersection of two thick branches, and he had the Remington locked and loaded. *Just like being in Nam,* he thought. With a lazy grin, he shouldered his weapon and aimed at one of the boys.

Randy didn't know one kid from the other, but he felt sure one of these little brats was Toby's asshole friend. He drew a bead on one boy and whispered "*Pow*" like he had at the Sheriff. Then he aimed at another and whispered "*pow*" again. When he centered the scope on the third boy, something in his chest swelled and burned, and he knew it was the right kid.

He took a deep breath and let half of it out, just like that goddamn drill sergeant had taught him. There was no wind, so all he had to do was lead the little bastard to account for his running and squeeze one off. He tightened his finger on the trigger, slow and steady.

10

They were charging forward, screaming, and firing their machine guns, when Benny heard a buzzing noise and a shower of wood chips and splinters exploded from the tree beside him. Thunder cracked through the woods, and he stood up straight and stared at the crater in the side of the tree. "What the hell?" he asked.

"Sniper!" yelled Paul.

The other two boys dove to the ground, but Benny turned and looked at the crater.

"What are you doing, Sergeant? Take cover for Christ's sake!" yelled Paul.

"That was real," muttered Benny.

"Come on, Benny, don't ruin it," whispered Mike.

Benny cleared his throat. "That was real, guys. There's a bullet hole or something in this tree." He put his back to the crater and followed an imaginary trajectory of the bullet with his eyes.

"What do you mean, real?" snapped Paul.

"There's a bullet hole," repeated Benny. He held up his hand and pointed. The other boys followed his gaze.

Up in a tree sixty yards away, a man stared at them from the branches of a tree. He was talking—more like muttering—and then thrashed as if he were fighting with the invisible man.

"Who's that," asked Mike.

When the hunting rifle came spinning out of the tree, the boys took one short look at it and then turned and ran.

11

As the trigger began to move, something slammed into Randy from behind, and the shot went wild. It felt like a gust of wind, and Randy struggled to stay in the tree. "Mother fuck!" he whispered.

"No," said a voice in his ear.

Randy turned his head, but it only rotated so far—as if he were pressing his face into glass. He could see, but after a certain point, his head stopped fast. "The fuck?" he muttered. "You pick now to come back?"

The little kid just stood there next to the tree, staring. It was a perfect shot—an easy shot. He couldn't miss from this distance. He tried to lift the rifle, to take aim for a second shot, but the rifle was suddenly too heavy to lift.

"I said no!"

Randy shook his head. "What the blue fuck?" he asked. "That bastard owes me."

"He is ours. All the children belong to my father."

The voice came from behind him, and the air in front of him shimmered, but instead of getting brighter, it got darker and darker, blurrier. "No, you don't," he muttered. He tried to lift the rifle again, but lifting the engine block of a semi seemed easier.

"You will not kill him, do you hear?" The voice hissed like a rasp on rough wood. The rifle flew from his hands and went spinning out of the tree. Randy grabbed at the branches he sat on to keep from falling.

"Who the fuck *are* you, anyway?"

"Oh ho, he wants to know us now," said the darkness.

Randy shook his head again. "Who… Whatever you are, get the fuck out of my way!" He climbed down to get his rifle. *Maybe there's still time to catch the brat,* he thought.

"No, Owen, listen!"

Randy stopped and waited, eyes glued to the fleeing boys.

"We can help each other, Owen." The soft voice held a cajoling, begging note. "Like before, in your war."

"Yeah, the invisible woman and Owen Gray, together again."

12

Owen Gray was nineteen and, as the man said, young, dumb, and full of cum. He liked what Uncle Sam wanted him to do. Since the time of the Killer Kane team, Force Recon missions were fun. He liked going into the jungle in a team of four other marines and harrying the enemy, liked setting traps, firing from cover and then watching the enemy run around looking for him. He liked being an agent of death. Owen liked the killing.

When the jungle erupted into chaos, he was up in a tree, star-gazing. He should have been on watch, but it was a beautiful night. Besides, he hadn't thought they were in any danger, so when the VC opened up on his sleeping teammates, Owen almost fell out of the tree into the cross-fire. He held on, but it was a close thing. Once he felt sure he would not fall, he froze in place and tried to calm his ragged breathing, to still his racing heart. No one would hear him over the cacophony of small arms fire, but the firefight would end in minutes if not seconds.

The other two privates died at the start, but Sergeant Bowles, whom he thought of as "Bugeyes," and Corporal Ramirez, or "The Spic," had reacted to the first sound of gunfire. Or maybe they'd been awake already. Both had rolled away and then opened fire. They were moving, trying to find cover, but the enemy's encirclement was complete. They were dead men, they just didn't know it yet.

Owen should've been helping. He should've been firing from the cover of the darkness and the trees, but if he did that, even if some smart slant-eye didn't see him and fire on his position, the VC would know he was there. They wouldn't stop looking for him until they found him.

The Spic was stealing glances up into the trees, no doubt trying to pick Owen out of the shadows. His face wrinkled in an angry rictus that Owen had no trouble reading. If he found Owen's silhouette, the Spic would send his last couple of rounds at it. Leave me alone, he thought at the Spic. Don't give me away! It's better for one of us to live than zero, right?

Bugeyes screamed as the enemy rounds thudded into his torso. He flung his hands up, sending his CAR-15 spinning high into the air. When Owen turned his eyes back to the Spic, Ramirez was staring right at him, face twisted with hatred. Moving as little as possible, Owen shook his head. The Spic's eyes narrowed, and he aimed his own CAR-15 at Owen. Before he fired, something black streaked in from the sky. It wasn't like a shadow, it was like something solid. Opaque and solid. Whatever the thing was, it shoved Owen behind the tree trunk, so hard that he almost fell again.

Ramirez opened up, and bullets slammed into the tree trunk flinging wood and bark away like shrapnel. The distinctive chatter of the ubiquitous AK-47s intensified for a moment, and then silence fell. The VC chattered away in the darkness and Owen held his breath, blind— the blackness surrounded him—but by the noise they made, the VC were coming out of concealment and picking through his teammates' belongings.

"Don't move, Owen," said a strange voice in his ear. The accent was unlike anything he'd heard before—all slithering sibilants and cacophonous consonants. It was

impossible to tell if the voice was male or female, it could've been either.

"Shh!" he whispered, terrified that the VC in the clearing below would hear.

"Don't worry. You are under my protection. They won't hear or see you."

Owen shook his head, wondering if his mind had snapped.

"You are sane," whispered the voice. "Would you like revenge?"

Owen didn't care about vengeance, but he did want to kill more gooks. He nodded.

"I see," said the voice, sounding amused. "I'll make you a bargain, warrior."

Here it comes, *thought Owen.* The catch.

"You don't expect something for free, do you, Owen?"

Owen shook his head, a sly grin on his face.

"Yes," said the voice. "Yes. I'll help you here, now. Later, I'll ask you for a favor."

"A blank check?" laughed Owen. "You must be kidding."

"I assure you I am not. But don't worry, Owen. The favor will be something which suits you. Something you enjoy."

"Sure, sure," said Owen. "It's a bad bargain, but what the hell. Let's do this."

The voice said nothing, but Owen had the distinct impression that the blackness found him both amusing and pleasing. The opaque blackness surrounding him grew translucent. VC were milling around in the clearing, chattering at each other like monkeys.

"Go ahead," said the voice. "Kill them. Kill them all."

"Are you nuts? They'll kill me in seconds."

"No, Owen. They'll never see or hear you. Trust me in this."

"What, are you going to turn me invisible?"

Something tapped his M40A1. "Kill them, Owen. They won't see or hear you."

Owen looked at the men milling around below him. Fuck it, he thought and shouldered the M40. He worked the bolt, jacking a round into the chamber. He sighted on a man at random, zeroing in on the base of his skull, just like Uncle Sam taught in sniper school. He squeezed the trigger and then leaned back behind the tree trunk.

The VC went nuts. They chattered like pissed off monkeys and fired their weapons into the darkness. But none of them fired at Owen, or even in the direction of the tree.

"Oh, hell yeah," he breathed. "I can get to like this."

"Told you so, Owen."

Owen thought the voice sounded just a bit smug, but he didn't care. He was invisible! He leaned out and shot another Vietcong, this time in the face. When the man's brains exploded out the back of his head, Owen laughed aloud.

"Kill them all," whispered the voice.

Owen didn't need to be told twice. He fired the internal box magazine dry and reloaded. The VC were shrieking with terror and either running around without purpose or firing their AK-47s wildly into the surrounding trees. He leveled the rifle at the guy shouting at the rest of them and pointing out lanes of fire. He squeezed the trigger, and the top of the VC's head turned into a red mist.

The rest of the VC broke and ran. Owen stayed calm, picked a target, worked the bolt, took aim, squeezed the trigger. Then he picked a new target and started again. He fired the rifle dry and reloaded as fast as he could.

The VC went insane with terror. A few threw down their rifles and focused on running; others tried to take cover behind trees, but they seemed to think Owen was ahead of them so, they crouched down next to a tree, in Owen's plain sight. Fish in a barrel and Owen let the magic red mist out of them all with a grin plastered on his face. Then, with his new friend, he chased down the rest of the patrol and killed them.

13

A grin stretched across Randy's face at the memory. "That was the shit."

"Yes," said the voice. "And remember the other days. Later. I helped you then, too." The voice was the same, somewhere between male and female, strange accent.

"You here for your favor?" he grunted.

"I hadn't planned it, but you could be useful."

"That boy." Randy took a shaky breath.

"He's ours for now. When we finish with him, I'll give him to you." The voice was calming, placating.

"You said I'd enjoy the favor you asked of me. I don't like being stymied."

"Want to go hunting for us? To reap death and mayhem again?"

Randy discovered he had an erection again. "Like in Nam?"

"Yes. Again, you will stalk the woods, a death god incarnate. Would you enjoy that?"

Randy grinned. "Too fucking right!"

"Then it's settled. One thing, though. You must not harm any children. Not yet. That's the only rule."

Randy made a show of pretending he wasn't sure, but he was. No question. "You'll make me invisible again?"

"Of course."

"The only thing I can't do is kill kids?"

"Yes. It will be best if you stay inside the confines of the forest unless you are with me, but you like it here."

"You know it." He pursed his lips. "There are two kids I want when you finish with them."

"Toby and Benny."

"Yeah," Randy breathed.

"Done and done. But not until we say."

"Why do you always say we? There's only one of you."

"One that speaks to *you*. One you *know*."

Randy chuckled. "One that flirts with me…like in Nam."

"That too."

"Okay, but I want to know what this is all about."

Instead of an answer, the air next to him shimmered, and the darkness enveloping him faded. The shimmer turned into mist in the vague shape of a person. As he watched, two globs of mist thickened and became the greenest pair of eyes he'd ever seen. Then the mist thickened into long blond hair and solidified into the body of a beautiful woman. A beautiful nude woman.

"This time, Owen, let's do more than flirt," she said.

"Your wish, my command," he said and reached for her.

14

Matt Greshin put his leather backed pad into his shirt pocket. The ad had run a few more times than he'd thought, but it hadn't run since Toby had disappeared. Matt grunted and stretched. He flipped the newspapers closed and suppressed a yawn.

"Uh, Chief? There's a phone call for you. They said it was urgent."

Matt sighed. So much for a quiet Saturday. "Where can I take it?"

The short, thin man who had let him into the archives pointed at the editor's office. "Frank's not here, I'm sure he wouldn't mind."

Matt grunted and went inside the office. He picked up the phone and punched the blinking light. "Greshin," he said.

"Matt, it's Gary Robbins."

Gary Robbins was the Chief Deputy of Kanowa County—Bobby Jefferson's second in command. His voice sounded shaky, upset. "Yeah, Gary. What's up?"

"You should... I'm at Bobby's house and... Look, someone shot Bobby. They were all set to have a barbeque, but—"

"Gary! Slow down a minute. Bobby's been shot?"

"Yeah. Him and Meredith."

"When?"

"Today. This afternoon. Bobby was grilling for lunch... Had an invader. Bobby's down out back, and Meredith's inside, shot through the slider."

Matt put his hand to his temple. "Dead? You're sure?"

"Well, let's see, they both have *bullet holes* in important places like the back of the neck and the eyeball, so, yeah, I'm sure they're dead."

"Okay, okay, Gary. It's a shock that's all."

"Yeah. It's a shock."

"Who else have you called? Any of the other chiefs?"

"No. You're first. I want you over here, Matt."

Matt nodded. "Yeah, sure, Gary. Anything you need."

"I-I only took this damn job because Bobby wanted me as his second, Matt. For, you know, administrative stuff. I don't want the big chair."

"We'll help you through it, Gary," said Matt. *Kanowa is so fucked,* he thought. Gary was a good administrator, but a terrible cop. "What can I do right now?"

"I need you over here, Matt."

"Consider me on my way. What else?"

"I... Matt, I don't..." Gary's voice cracked.

"Yeah, Gary. Keep it together, man. Do you want an outside agency involved? The State Police could come down and take over the investigation," said Matt in a steady, detached voice. Cop mode.

"No, no Staties, Matt. Bobby wouldn't want that."

"No, he wouldn't." Matt sighed. "I can't do it, Gary. It's outside my jurisdiction."

"I know, I know," said Gary, sounding miserable. "What am I going to do?"

"Don't worry, Gary. We'll figure something out. Maybe the other chiefs will support someone running things in your name for a bit."

"It's got to be you, Matt. Bobby would want it that way."

"Never mind all that for now; let me get rolling. You call the other chiefs and let them know what's happening, and that I'll call everyone later."

"Okay."

"Okay, I'll see you in twenty minutes or so."

Matt hung up and loosed a string of profanity that would make any sailor flinch. The way to Bobby's house was as familiar as the way to his own. They'd been friends for over twenty years, after all. He stopped off at the Oneka Falls town hall and stuck his head in the dispatcher's office.

"Angie, I'll be out at Sheriff Jefferson's house until further notice."

She flashed a smile. "Barbeque, huh? How come I never get invited?"

Matt grimaced. "Bobby and Meredith were shot earlier today; shot by an intruder."

Angie's mouth made a little O, and she slapped her hand over her mouth. "Are they…"

"The wounds were fatal according to Gary Robbins."

"Oh, Christ," Angie whispered.

"Yeah," muttered Matt. "Tell the OIC, but keep it off the air."

"Yes, sir," she said.

Matt drove out to Bobby's place, his mind flipping back and forth between memories of driving over for a cookout or a beer, and the other night as Bobby got in Randy Fergusson's face and told him to start with Bobby. He had a sick feeling in his stomach.

Four cars from the Kanowa Sheriff's Department fleet lined the road in front of Bobby Jefferson's house.

A big black Cadillac Fleetwood was in the driveway—Gary Robbins car, Matt was willing to bet. He pulled in behind the Fleetwood and killed his engine.

He didn't want to get out, to go inside and see what he had to see. Unbidden, the image of Randy Fergusson's face flashed before his eyes. He pounded on the steering wheel once, then again, before he got out of the car and walked around the side of the house.

Deputies walked a search line across the backyard. The hood of Bobby's fancy gas grill stood straight up, and there was a hole torn out of it. Bobby was on the ground just past the grill, face tilted up at the sky. The yard smelled of steak, blood, and human excrement. Matt shook his head. "Any brass?" he called to the deputies.

"Nothing yet. Found a footprint though."

Matt nodded and turned toward the house. The sliding glass door had shattered, and broken glass glinted in the afternoon sun like so many diamonds. Meredith Jefferson lay face down on the ridiculous pink carpet she'd insisted Bobby buy. There was a small, pristine hole in the back of her neck and a large puddle of blood seeping into the carpet under her. Gary Robbins stood inside the house, well away from the spreading blood.

"Matt, I'm glad you're here. Marty wanted to search the yard, and I thought—"

"I saw them. You thought right." Matt didn't want to talk, not to a prissy putz like Gary Robbins. He rubbed his forehead with his hand and sighed. "You call the coroner yet?"

Gary nodded. "Old Doc Hauser's covering this weekend. He's on his way over from—"

"From Oneka Falls. Yeah. I know him."

"Matt, what should—"

Matt made a savage chopping motion with his hand. "Not yet, Gary," he said, sounding harsher than he intended. He turned away—away from the hurt-little-boy expression Gary was wearing and away from Meredith's blood ruining her prized carpet. Bobby had been gut shot and took a second round to the eye. Matt looked back and forth between the abdomen wound and the hole punched through the top of the grill, imagining Bobby on his feet and tending the grill. He turned and looked at where Meredith lay and estimated how many steps she might have taken after the round hit her. *Not many.*

"Bobby was at the grill, and the first shot took him in the guts," he muttered. "Marty, you said there was a footprint?"

The deputy pointed to a spot near the tree line, and Matt walked over to examine it.

15

Benny, Mike, and Paul sprinted all the way back to Benny's house—they didn't slow as they left the woods; they didn't slow as they ran across the lawn. Benny flung the sliding glass door open, and the boys piled through it. He slammed the door behind them.

"Mom!" he yelled.

"Benny! What in the dickens are you boys *doing*?" called his mom from the living room.

"There's a man in the woods—"

"Is he on fire?"

"Mom! He *shot at me!*"

"He what? Benny, I'm not in the mood for one of these—"

"He's not lying, Mrs. Cartwright," said Mike. "He was up in a tree with a rifle. A hunting rifle."

"What's this about being shot at?" asked Jim Cartwright, sweeping downstairs, the newspaper tucked under his arm.

"We were playing commando in the woods," said Benny.

"We were charging at a pretend gook stronghold," said Mike at the same time.

"Yeah, and then the tree next to me exploded. There was a crater left in the tree. Mike and Paul thought I did it as part of the game, but I didn't. It was a *bullet!*"

Jim took five long strides across the room and pulled the drapes over the sliding glass door. "You boys go in the living room with Mrs. Cartwright."

"Yeah, and that's when we saw the guy up in the tree. He was talking or something, but we couldn't hear him," said Paul.

"Into the other room. Now," said Jim, putting his hand on Benny and Paul's back and giving them a gentle push.

"He acted like a looney-toon and threw the rifle right out of the tree."

"Yeah, but he was still staring at me, so I turned and ran like my ass was on fire!"

"Benjamin James Cartwright!" snapped Karen.

"Sorry, Mom, but that's what I did."

She gave him a glare, but with an expression that meant he would not get into any real trouble for the swear, then she turned her gaze to Jim. "What are you doing just standing there, Jim? *Do something!*"

Jim looked from the boys to Karen and back again. "Now, boys, I don't want you to think I don't believe you, but I need to ask you if you are fibbing. Even a little bit."

The boys shook their heads in unison.

"I'd better go see who this man is and—"

"Have you lost your fool mind?! Get on the phone, Jim, and call Matt Greshin. Stop being an idiot."

A blush crept up Jim's cheeks, but he didn't say anything. He picked up the phone and dialed. After a long moment, he pushed down on the switch hook and punched in another number. With a glance at Karen, he said, "Not at home." He held up a finger. "Yes, this is Jim Cartwright. I need Matt Greshin at my house right now. There's a man in the—"

He turned away, but not before Benny saw him go pale.

"Are they alive?" he murmured into the phone. "Right. I need someone though. There's a man in the woods. He shot at Benny." He said "right" and "okay" a few times and put the phone in its cradle. He looked at his wife's bare feet and snapped his fingers at her. "Shoes."

"Don't snap at me, Jim! I—"

"Now!" he said. "Where are Johnny and Billy?"

"What? They are playing down in the basement."

"Right. Get your shoes on and get the boys. I'm going to start the car."

"Jim, what are—"

"*Karen, just do it!*"

"You don't have to yell."

Jim ushered Benny, Paul, and Mike into the garage and got them loaded into the back seat of the Toronado. "You'll have to scrunch over and make room for Benny's brothers. Now, it will be crowded, boys, but I don't want to hear a peep."

Karen bustled the two younger boys out and glared at Jim. "We have a station wagon, you know."

"I want the Olds. It's more powerful in case we need it."

"Why would we—"

"Get in, Karen," he said in a tight voice. "You can argue with me later."

She made a face, but got the boys into the back seat, then sat in the front and closed the door.

"Now, boys, I'm going to open the garage and back out. I want you all smooshed down in the seat, so no one knows you are there."

"Daddy, what's going on?" asked Johnny.

"Never you mind. Just do like Daddy says," said Karen.

They dropped Paul off first and then Mike. At each stop, Jim went to the door and told the adults what had happened. When only the Cartwrights remained in the car, Jim drove to Cottonwood Vale and checked them into two rooms at the Holiday Inn.

16

Matt Greshin climbed the stairs to the second floor of the Holiday Inn in Cottonwood Vale, moving like a death row inmate on the way to his execution. The stress of the day had left him exhausted—beyond exhausted, in fact—and all he wanted was to sink into a comfortable chair and sleep. He'd also spent the afternoon sinking into the deepest, darkest depression of his life. Randy Fergusson was behind Bobby and Meredith Jefferson's deaths—he knew it in his gut.

With a loud sigh, he knocked on room 295 and stood waiting, shoulders slumped, eyes on the ground. It was 11:15 pm, but Jim had wanted him to come no matter what time it was.

The door opened. "Come on in, Matt."

Matt had never seen Jim Cartwright look so disheveled, so harried. "Thanks. Looks like your day went about as good as mine." He stepped through the threshold and closed the door behind him.

Jim pinched the bridge of his nose with two fingers and let the air gust from his lungs. "I haven't had a great day, no. Even so, I bet yours was worse. Craig told me Bobby was shot. You two were close, and I'm sorry you've got to go through all this."

Matt's eyes swept the room. "Karen and the boys?"

"Next door. Registered under Karen's sister's name."

Matt grunted. "Smart, though maybe not all that legal."

"It is. I told the hotel I was paying, but to only use my name for billing. That makes it all good."

"Huh. I'll remember that next time I'm out chasing fugitives." Jim motioned at one of the bright orange armchairs in the room and Matt sank into it with a sigh. "So tell me about this guy that shot at Benny."

Jim arched his eyebrows. "You don't want to talk to Benny?"

"Maybe later, right now I want to hear it from an adult's perspective."

Jim shrugged. "Benny, Mike Richards, and Paul Gerber were playing in the woods—war or commandos or whatever. They were sneaking up on an imaginary fort, and a bullet smacked into the tree next to Benny. When they looked around, they saw a guy up in a tree, talking to himself. The guy threw the rifle down, and the boys turned tail and ran."

"Think Benny can lead me back to the tree?"

"Benny's not going back into those woods, Matt."

"I need to recover that slug from the tree. Could be important. Very important."

"No way. Tomorrow morning, Benny's on his way to Ohio for a while. Karen and the boys as well."

Matt's lips twitched. "Bobby and Meredith were shot with a hunting rifle, Jim. Two shooting events in or near the woods, both with a rifle? They've got to be related."

"Okay, but I don't want Benny—"

"It's Randy Fergusson. Jim, I know it."

"Fergusson?"

"That prick from the Burton house."

Recognition splashed across Jim's face like paint thrown from a bucket. "That little bastard!"

"Yeah, he is that," said Matt in a weary tone. "Bobby, Craig, and I had a little chat with him the other night. We asked him about Toby, and after that, we encouraged him to seek other living arrangements far away from here. Bobby was…" Matt shook his head. "Bobby got a little hot under the collar, but the guy was a royal prick. At the end of the night, Fergusson made a few comments about coming back and getting us."

Matt rubbed his temples like he had a headache that wouldn't quit. "Bobby called him out on it. Bobby told Fergusson to get started right there, to start with Bobby. Seems he did."

"But why shoot at Benny?"

Matt shifted his position in the chair, looking anywhere but at Jim. "You have to understand, Jim. The guy was just flapping his gums. Or that's what I thought, anyway—I mean, I've heard the same thing from a slew of perps, and it never amounted to anything but hot air. That's why Bobby—"

"Matt," said Jim in a tone he reserved for disciplining his boys.

"Yeah, sorry. This guy, Fergusson, he said he would get us all, and he said he would get you and Benny too."

Jim flushed, eyes blazing. "And you didn't think to warn me? You didn't think it might be—oh, I don't know—*important*?"

Matt looked at the floor. "I thought it was just talk. Bobby... Bobby gave Fergusson a little encouragement, you could say. He was bragging about beating up the kid, and so Bobby—"

"Beat up on Fergusson. That's what you're telling me, right?" Jim's voice shook. "That's why you didn't tell me? To protect Bobby?"

"It's not that…" Matt sighed. "Yeah. Bobby roughed him up a little. But the guy was an asshole."

"You know I've never questioned your methods, Matt." Jim looked away, but not before Matt saw the rage on his face.

"Yeah," said Matt. "I've always appreciated—"

"And anyway, your methods are your business. I don't care if some lowlife gets a bloody nose so you can get a confession. I really don't." The anger was gone from Jim's voice, replaced by an icy calm. "But…"

"We put him on a bus, Jim. Told him not to come back."

"Yeah, but it looks like he didn't care. You should have told me, Matt. You put my life—*Benny's life*—in danger. I can forgive everything else, but that…"

"I should have said something," said Matt. "I fucked that up pretty well, didn't I?"

Jim sat on the bed. "Yeah. So how are you going to fix it? This time, I want to know everything."

"Okay, Jim, you got it. There's not a lot of physical evidence at Bobby's place. Fergusson approached through the woods—we found footprints leading to Bobby's property. He rested the rifle in the crook of a tree and shot Bobby. I assume that was the gut shot because Fergusson came out of the woods and approached the little patio Meredith wanted. Plus, the second shot hit Bobby in the eye, and that would be a hell of a shot to make from any distance. And Meredith was inside when he shot her. She was bringing out a tray of drinks, and it looks like she turned to run, and the guy plugged her in at the base of the neck. No one could make that shot from the woods, the angles are all wrong."

"That's two precision shots," said Jim.

Matt nodded. "I think the gut shot was on purpose. Disable him, but not kill him. Leave time for Bobby to see him—time to gloat a little."

"What are the chances your average hunter could make those two shots?"

Matt shrugged. "Hard to say. We don't know how close he came."

Jim grunted.

Matt cleared his throat. "Gary Robbins is technically the sheriff until the next election."

Jim groaned and shook his head. "Not good news."

"No, it's not—Gary's good at administration, but he's a terrible cop. He's asked me to head up the investigation—unofficially, of course."

"But aren't the State Troopers supposed to investigate the murder of a sitting Sheriff?"

"Yeah, and they will, but it doesn't matter. We'll still be doing our own thing."

"And they'll be okay with that?"

"Are you kidding? They'll bitch, moan, and threaten us, but Bobby was one of us."

"Okay, as long as it doesn't cause too many problems." Jim looked at him. "What's next?"

"Next, I do a bit of police work and find out where Fergusson is staying. I'll start by talking to Candy Burton. After that, I'll be calling hotels in the area."

"What about Benny?"

"I wish I could say that he's out of any danger, but…"

"But you can't." Jim's voice was bleak.

"But I can't," agreed Matt. "Same goes for you, Jim."

Jim shook his head. "Yeah, but I'm not eleven."

"No, you are not, but dead is dead no matter how old your death certificate says you are."

"What are you telling me, Matt? To leave? To tuck my tail between my legs and scamper off somewhere? You want me to teach my boys to run from danger?"

Matt's face tensed and his eyes narrowed. "Yes. You too proud to take precautions? You want your boys to grow up without a dad? Teach them to be smart."

Jim sobered. "How long do you recommend we stay away?"

Matt shrugged and got to his feet. "Not long. Fergusson's not all there anymore if you know what I mean. It's possible our little chat with him broke his brain the rest of the way. Psychotic." Matt shrugged. "He ain't going to give any thought to concealing himself or his actions."

"Okay, then. We'll head to Ohio tomorrow—as a family. I'll call you to give you the phone number when I have it."

"You do that," said Matt. "I've got to get over to the Burton place, and you need to sleep."

Jim shook his head. "Yeah, like that's going to happen."

"Yeah, well." Matt patted him on the shoulder feeling awkward and clumsy.

Chapter 4

2007

I

Tobias shuffled to the dayroom, head spinning. The new medicine they had him on, Seroquel, seemed to be working—as well as anything did, anyway—but living with his head stuffed in a bag of packing peanuts annoyed him.

Tobias wasn't what his mother had named him, but he'd given that name to his best friend. His friend had gotten out of the hell-hole that still housed Tobias, but he had needed a new name, so… *Doesn't bear thinking about,* he told himself. It had been many, many years since all that went down.

The television chattered on, as always. Tobias glanced at it, but he didn't care for television. They *never* showed cartoons anymore, not even on Saturday morning. A Star Trek rerun blathered on, and as usual, drooling or vacant-eyed patients lounged in the three-quarters full dayroom.

Tobias shuffled through the room, into the activities room—a large, square room with narrow windows on the two outside walls. Narrow so none of the wing-nuts could break them and escape. Under each window sat a small wooden table and three wooden chairs—three being the magic number of crackpots who could sit together without inciting a riot. A shelf full of ten-year-old magazines, a few puzzles, and a couple of chess sets accounted for everything the room offered in the way of activities, but to the few patients who eschewed television, it was a refuge. It offered a space to sit and think without being bothered by all that yapping from the other room, alone or in pairs if you could find a patient who didn't have a manic compulsion to talk.

Tobias shuffled to his normal table in the corner between the two outside walls. It had only *two* chairs—no room for three people at that table—and if he put his feet up in the other chair, the chances of solitude increased by at least a factor of ten, unless you accounted for the non-real people in the room; they sat wherever they wanted.

He sank into the chair, facing one of the windows, and pulled the other chair out and put up his feet. Old, torn magazines from the shelves littered the table. Tobias had found that if he had a magazine open in front of him, none of the staff members gave his moving lips a second thought. They all assumed he was reading, though Tobias wasn't sure he remembered *how* to read.

He remembered how to travel, however. Not with his body, with his mind. He visited Oneka Falls, though none of his family lived there anymore. Not since…not since…

He shook his head to break his train of thought. He didn't want to remember that. Not ever.

"Hey, Toby!" called one of the orderlies.

Tobias lifted his hand in what he hoped looked like an absent-minded wave. It didn't pay to talk to those assholes. No, not one bit. He didn't even bother to learn their names anymore.

"You doing okay, Toby?"

Tobias nodded and lifted his hand again.

"Anything you want to talk about?"

Fuck! The guy was heading over. *Must be new.* Tobias shook his head and lifted his hand.

"Hey Toby, can you tell me the day?"

When is he going to catch on? Tobias' chart listed him as non-verbal, but every once in a while, a new guy came to work at Millvale State Hospital who thought Tobias would snap out of it if only the staffer could find the right topic of conversation. The weeks it took for newbies to become disillusioned with the idea caused any number of headaches—for Tobias, if not the orderly. Tobias lifted his hand and turned slightly in the chair, showing the orderly his back.

"How about the President? Can you tell me who the President is?"

Tobias didn't respond, not even his patented go-away wave.

"Okay, okay, that's a hard one. Let's go to something simple. Can you tell me where you are?"

For fuck's sake, asshole! Don't you understand what non-verbal means? Tobias spun in his chair and looked at the guy: tall, blond, lively face—happy face. Tobias hated him already, and he stared at the guy with dead eyes.

"So, my name's Sam. I'm new here."

No shit.

"Don't talk much, do you?"

Which part of non-verbal confuses you?

"Since I've got to be here, and you've got to be here, we might as well shoot the shit. How's that sound?"

It sounds about as fun as hitting myself in the face repeatedly with a brazier of burning coals. Why don't you leave me alone?

"Well, lucky for you, Toby, I like to talk. I can talk enough for two any day of the week."

For fuck's sake…

"Do you like sports? I do. I like them all: football, basketball, baseball, hockey, boxing, MMA, you name it."

How about I don't?

"Listen, I'm working this weekend. If you tell me what sports you like, I'll make sure to turn the TV to a game or whatever. All you have to do is say the word."

Tobias bent his head and pressed his palms over his ears.

"Hey, no pressure," said the idiot. "How about this weather? When was the last time you saw a summer as chilly as this past one?"

Uh, never? I've been locked up since the year I turned eleven, numb nuts. Thanks for bringing that up though. Why don't you fuck off and die?

The idiot grabbed a chair from another table and pulled it over. "Mind if I join you for a while?"

Tobias looked around, desperate for one of the regular staffers to save him. They were never around when you needed them, though, and no one was nearby.

"I see you like to put your feet up in that chair. You know what? I don't think it's about putting your feet up at all. No, sir. It's about keeping people away."

You don't say? What was your first clue?

"Life is better when you're not by yourself, though, Toby. Know that?"

A rumbling sounded deep in Tobias's chest. At first, he didn't realize he was making an actual sound, he thought it was only a vibration. His hands curled into tight fists under the table, and blood pounded in his ears.

"So, even if you don't want to talk, I'll be here. Happy to sit with you. Happy to carry the conversation until you are more comfortable. I'm here to help."

The rumbling in his chest turned into a growl, and when he parted his lips, into a snarl. He lurched to his feet, and the idiot's eyes opened wide. The idiot had his hands up in front of his face, which Tobias thought was strange, melodramatic, overkill.

The orderly opened his mouth to say something, and Tobias brought the heavy wooden chair down with all his strength.

2

Shannon Bertram knew better, but knowing better doesn't help in matters of the heart. She waited in the parking lot after work, waited for Mike Richards—not that he even noticed her—she might as well be a piece of furniture; and not that she would talk to him if he did.

Her little blue car bored even her—as unremarkable as she was. Pale blue, small, and cheap. Not one employee coming out of the Town Hall even looked her way as they came out and jumped in their pretty cars.

When Mike pushed through the door at 5:15, her heart leapt into her throat. His face displayed an expression it often wore these days—an expression that spoke of a headache, frustration, and the want of a drink. Maybe the *need* for a drink.

She wanted to leap from the car and run to him, to soothe his frustration, to put her arm around his shoulders and to tell him it would be okay, to steer him over to her car and drive him to her tiny, unremarkable apartment, and—

She cut off that thought, cheeks blazing with intense heat. *None of it will happen, so why get all worked up?* she thought. No, tonight would be like all the other nights she'd waited outside for Mike: she'd follow him discreetly, parking where he stopped to drink, getting fast food while he went into the watering hole, waiting for him to come out and stumble to his car, then following him to wherever he was going at the end of his evening. She told herself it was to look out for Mike, to keep him from getting in trouble, to keep him safe.

The Chief's cruiser wheezed to life, and Shannon turned the key in her ignition. When Mike squealed out of the parking lot, she waited for thirty seconds by the clock on the lock screen of her phone, and then pulled out of the lot.

Mike's car was heading south from the town's only stoplight, and Shannon rushed to follow. There were seven bars in Oneka Falls, which was remarkable for a town of only eleven hundred people. South of the light, there were three choices, Draughts Men, The Trough, and Lumber Jack's.

A small moue distorted her lips. Draughts Men wasn't too bad, but The Trough and Lumber Jack's were real dives. The only people who drank there were drunks and losers. Her moue deepened into a frown as Mike slowed and turned in under the faded, peeling painting of a smiling lumberjack.

3

Mike bumped Shamu over the curb and piloted the pig of a car around to the back of the buildings. Lumber Jack's was a real shit-hole, but well-drinks were cheap there, and the way he felt, his budget for the night needed cheap.

His headache had never given him a moment's peace. His anger at Frank King and Chaz Welsh had kept the thing alive and roaring. It required a little hair of the dog to get it to shut the fuck up for a while. And he needed to sleep like he needed to breathe.

He turned the ignition off and sat there, head back on the head rest, eyes half closed. That fuckstick Welsh wanted him to cut back on the drinking—and he *had* promised to—but hell, it was Friday night. Work was done until Monday, and he wasn't even on call.

He opened his eyes and looked, then had to suppress a grin when he spotted her. *Poor little Shannon,* he thought. But it was nice *someone* cared enough to see that he got home okay.

He sighed and opened the door. *I should go over there. Just walk up and tap on the window. Tell her thanks, take her to dinner. Tell her she's barking up the wrong tree.* The thing was, Shannon was a beautiful woman, and if she'd just try, she would be a real knock out. She would have her pick of men in a town like Oneka Falls—not that many of them deserved a good woman like Shannon.

Part of him wanted to go over, to skip his nightly worship of the bleary-eyed god of debauchery, or even take the pledge. *I should get the hell out of Oneka Falls, go home, pack a bag or two, and just get the fuck out of here. Go somewhere like New York City. I wouldn't even be missed, not by anyone but Shannon.*

He shook his head while his body moved on autopilot, exiting the vehicle, closing the door, hitching his pants, turning toward the back entrance of Lumber Jack's, and walking inside. He ordered a highball without thinking about anything at all and planted his ass on a stool in front of the bar.

Jack gave him the stink eye as he made Mike's drink. *What did I do to Jack?* Mike wracked his brain, but he couldn't even remember the last time he'd been in Lumber Jack's, let alone the last time he'd gotten pissed there. Jack put the drink in front of him but kept his fat hand on the glass. Mike looked up at him and quirked his eyebrows.

"That'll be $6.50."

"Just put her on my tab, Jack." Mike smiled and reached for the drink, but Jack didn't lift his hand.

"$6.50, Chief," he grunted.

Mike cocked his head, baffled. "Look, Jack, if I did something to you, I don't remember what it was, so how about you just tell me, so I can apologize and we can get the fuck on with the evening? I don't want to drink somewhere I'm not welcome."

Jack scoffed, eyeing Mike through narrowed eyes. "You don't remember? Nothing?"

Mike shook his head. "Can't even remember the last time I was in here, Jack. God's truth."

With his free hand, Jack rubbed his eyes and then squeezed the bridge of his nose. "For God's sake, Chief. Maybe you should look into getting help."

Mike sat there, stiff with anger, and waited, staring at Jack with his best cop stare.

"And you can shitcan that badass stare, Mike. I knew you when you was a snot-nosed little punk, and you don't scare me."

Mike shrugged and shifted his stare to the highball under Jack's fat hand.

"Lookit here, Chief. I like you, always have. I like your trade. Both those things, though, they don't count for fuck-all when you bust up my place, scare off the other customers, break the TV, and then threaten to jerk my liquor license."

Mike leaned back. "I did all that? That was one fuck of a night, eh?" Mike shook his head. "Let me guess. Tequila?"

Jack nodded, trying to keep a solemn expression, but his twitching lips spoiled the effect. Mike always could turn on the charm when he wanted, when his past behavior required it.

"Never serve me Tequila, Jack. I thought we had an understanding?"

"Threatened to arrest me if I didn't pour your damn shots," said Jack, the twitching in his lips growing into a smile.

"Yeah, that sounds like something I'd do," said Mike, pretending to smile along with Jack. "Well, I tell you what, Jack. Give me a pen and one of those napkins."

Jack got him a pen and slid a napkin in front of him. Mike wrote:

I, Michael Richards, Chief of O.F.P.D., do hereby swear that no matter what may occur on the premises of Lumber Jack's Bar and Grill, Jack Laderman is protected by the aegis and auspices of O.F.P.D. and is not to be arrested, threatened, or otherwise bothered by any member of law enforcement working inside the city limits.

"That do her?" he asked, sliding the napkin around so Jack could read it.

"It's a start," said Jack, but he lifted his hand away from the highball.

"First sign of trouble, Jack, you have my permission to throw my ass out."

Jack grunted and walked down to the other end of the bar.

Mike sat, staring at the highball, not touching it, not putting his hand anywhere near it. *Maybe Chaz is right*, he thought. *Fuck, if I can't even remember being here when I raised a stink like that... Am I blacking out that often?* Fear settled into the pit of his stomach like a lump of chilled lead. He tried to count the number of drinks he'd had in the week, but outside of the occasional beer with lunch, and the first couple of drinks each evening, he didn't have much luck. *Maybe I should dry out a little.*

"Something wrong with it?" called Jack.

Mike smiled and winked. "Not a thing, Jack. Just letting the anticipation build."

Jack looked at him like he'd grown a second nose.

Mike grabbed the highball. *I'll leave after this*, he promised himself. *I'll go talk to Shannon, go get a meal with her.*

4

Becky Lewis—seventeen and oh so innocent—LaBouche found her irresistible. He'd crafted his visage based on his light-hearted conversations with the girl. Becky's idea of the perfect guy—athletic, tan skin, wind-tossed (even when no wind blew) sun-bleached hair, like a surfer from Southern California—and it resembled the visage he called his "Lee-look" about as much as an elephant resembled a gazelle, but he didn't mind spending time and energy crafting something special for her. It was the least he could do.

He got out of the silver Subaru WRX he'd purchased for this persona and flipped his shoulder-length hair. The girl's eyes lingered on him from the upstairs window, and he suppressed a lecherous smile. She was like putty in his hands.

He walked to the front door and rang the bell. Scott Lewis opened the door holding an after-dinner beer. "Hello, Mr. Lewis. Is Becky ready?"

Scott grunted and opened the door wider.

LaBouche had to bite the inside of his cheek to keep from grinning at his partner's tough-guy dad act. He kept his eyes down, and the memory of Lewis saying none of Becky's boyfriends would meet his gaze almost made him laugh aloud. He walked in and stood in the foyer, waiting for Lewis to say or do something like LaBouche imagined a teenager would.

Lewis closed the door hard and brushed by him on the way to the family room. He sat without inviting LaBouche to, and un-paused the show he was watching on the DVR, some silly thing—a show about guns and shooting. LaBouche had to avert his eyes to avoid broadcasting his amusement. *So predictable...always has been—he's a human, after all.*

"Daddy! You don't watch that crap, so turn it off," said Becky Lewis from the top of the stairs.

Lewis had the good grace to blush and then he turned off the TV. He didn't look at LaBouche and it was just as well, LaBouche's smile refused to die.

"Hi, Becky. You look great!" LaBouche put as much spunk into the last sentence as he could muster, and almost laughed aloud when Lewis spun around to glare at him.

"Oh, so sweet," Becky said, dripping honey. "Isn't Lane sweet, Daddy?"

Lewis mumbled something no one could make out.

"Daddy?" asked Becky with an edge to her voice.

"I said: I'm sure he is," said Lewis.

LaBouche looked at his shoes. *This is hilarious! After all the stories he's told, after all the interrogations, here he is, brought to heel by his teenaged bitch.* A part of him liked Lewis—well, maybe *liked* was too strong a word, but he sometimes didn't hate every second they had to spend in each other's company. "Ready to go?" he asked, doing his best impersonation of a seventeen-year-old love-struck kid.

"Sure," said Becky, skipping down the stairs.

LaBouche drank her in as she came toward him, staring at her bouncing breasts. She wore a purple halter-top and tight, tight white jeans. He glanced at Lewis out of the corner of his eye. His partner's face glowed red, and he glowered at LaBouche with obvious distaste. *That's okay, Scotty-boy. If you knew what I had planned for your "little girl," you'd shoot me on the spot.*

Becky walked to her father's chair and bent to kiss him on the cheek. He never took his eyes off the apparent teenage boy in front of him while LaBouche stared at her ass. "You have her back by eleven," grumped Lewis.

"Daddy! He'll have me back by one, just like we agreed." Becky was quite cute when she pouted.

Smiling a rapacious smile, LaBouche grabbed Becky's hand and walked her out the door.

It was the last time Scott Lewis ever saw his daughter.

5

Shannon glanced down at her phone. 8:58pm shone from the backlit LCD screen. She nibbled on her lip and thought—for the third time—about going to grab food, but Mike had said he would cut back on his drinking. He'd *promised* Mr. Welsh he would lay off for a while. *What if he makes good on that promise and comes out while you are in the drive-thru line at BurgerWorld? What if he goes somewhere... Silly girl,* she chided herself. If Mike made good on his promise, he wouldn't need looking after. If he packed it in early, she *still* wouldn't have the nerve to go up and talk to him, to invite him home for a late supper. *He's probably already eaten in there.*

She reached for the ignition, but let her hand fall back to her lap. Nibbling on her lip, she glanced up and down the street again. Shannon reached for the ignition again, and this time turned the key, but only to the accessory position. Her radio blared a dollop of pop music, and she snapped the volume down, eyes averted, blush creeping up her neck. She didn't want to be looked at, to be noticed, by anyone.

The thing was, she *did* want to be looked at, to be noticed. She wanted a man to call her "babe" and to be so into her that he wanted to do it with her in public, on the side of the road. She wanted to call him "my love" as he did. It sounded so romantic, so...*hot.*

She glanced around, shoulders up like she was ashamed, but no one out on the street was looking.

Who would give a flip? I could strip naked, and no one would care.

Her stomach growled. It felt like an animal, distinct from herself, that wanted raw meat. Like a wild dog in the woods, hungry, hungry, *hungry*. She reached for the ignition and started the little car. It wouldn't hurt to go get a salad from BurgerWorld. If Mike came out and she missed him, well, that just meant he wasn't drunk, right? That meant he was headed home for the night.

But she knew better, and she hesitated. What if Mike came out, stumbling drunk like he did every night, jumped into his cop car and sped away while she was gone? What would happen if Mike got hurt in a drunken accident? What if he...*died*?

If that happened, she wouldn't be able to live with herself. She reached out and snapped off the ignition. She glanced down at her phone. 9:10pm. *If he doesn't come out in fifteen minutes, I'll go for food,* she promised herself.

6

Tobias smiled as the bolts slammed closed on the seclusion room door. *Blessed silence*, he thought, *for at least twelve hours.* Still, he could have done without the Haldol injection, but everything had its cost.

He relaxed on the bed and tried to pretend he wasn't strapped to it with inch-wide leather belts. The walls were painted a faint shade of pink. *Probably called cotton candy or coral shell pink...idiots.*

To his right, there was one of the narrow windows like those in the activity room. He stared out of it, letting his mind go, letting himself float.

When the pictures flashed before his eyes, he smiled like he was greeting a friend and closed his eyelids.

He was floating near the ceiling, looking down at himself, strapped to the bed. His bed-self was smiling. An insistent tug pulled at him and he didn't fight it. Reality slipped and lurched, and he was looking down at someone else.

An old man—a naked, shit-covered old man. Tobias recognized him, even after almost twenty years. The guy was a monster—hard to forget—but he had *forgotten the man in every important detail. He'd worked hard to forget him.*

"You think you can fuck me and get away with it? You think you can betray me like this," the old man

shouted. He jumped up from his bunk and slammed his shoulder into the reinforced metal door of his cell.

A stranger's voice crackled over the intercom. "Inmate, I've just mobilized the ERT. You know how this always goes, so why not make it easy for everyone today?"

"Fuck you! How's that for easy, you little prick? You fucking Tom. Why don't you come down here yourself? Scared of little old me?" The old man glanced up at the corner where Tobias floated. He grimaced and waved his hand as if in dismissal. "And get that fucker out of here."

"Do you like being strapped to the bed, inmate? Or is it the little chemical vacation you enjoy?"

Information flooded into Tobias's mind. The man on the intercom was Max Tember, the OIC of Sing Sing's SHU. The shit-covered man was a longtime resident.

"Three kinds of convict end up where you're at, inmate. You aware of that? Protection cases, behavior cases, and mental cases. You're starting to fit that last category pretty well, inmate. Is that the rep you want to have? Psychotic shit-slinger?"

"Fuck you, Tom." Despite the tough words, the prisoner sat down on the bed.

"Or is it all an act to keep you out of gen-pop? Are you too much the coward to deal with life in prison?"

The inmate scoffed and spit. At first, Tobias thought the guy was spitting at him, but then he realized it was the camera in the corner behind him that was the target.

"The SHU is hard time, inmate. Locked in that cell for twenty-three out of every twenty-four hours. Showers twice a week. No human contact. Well, unless you classify being held down by the guards as human contact, and knowing you, you just might. You've been in the SHU for over a decade, inmate. Don't you want to go back to gen-pop? Spend a little time outside? Have a few privileges for a change?"

The old man turned his head away from the camera. "My girl likes it better here," he mumbled.

"What? I couldn't make that out."

The guard hadn't heard it, but Tobias had. His girl? *he thought.* Inmates don't have girlfriends, do they?

"So, inmate, what's it to be? The ERT is stacking up outside your door. You can either get down on your knees, back to the door, with your fingers interlaced behind your head, or you can keep on with what you're doing. In the first case, you get a rip and a shower, but you will go back to your cell. In the second case, you get a few bruises, hosed off with the high-pressure hose, and strapped in the chair for twelve hours, give or take. Which is it going to be?"

The old guy looked up at the camera, his face a study in wrath. "You know what, Tom? You know what?"

"What is it, inmate?"

"Send those pussy motherfuckers on in here. You tell 'em to come in swinging, because I'm in here waiting, and I'm a motherfucking killer! *You hear me that time, Tom?"*

Tember sighed into the intercom microphone. It sounded like a series of shotgun blasts. "Calm down, inmate. You remember what happens when you get yourself all wound up, don't you?"

"You're a big fucking man, Tom, safe up there in your little bulletproof tower. When they come back for me, you and I will dance. Why don't you come down here so I can check out your steps?"

"Who is this 'they' you're always jabbering about, inmate?"

The prisoner held up his hands and then pretended to zip his lip.

"Just get down on your knees, inmate. Do it the easy way for once. Last chance."

"You send those faggot fucks on in, Tom. I'll kill every last one of you bastards. Maybe not today, but someday! You know what I did. I can do it again given half a chance."

"Execute," said Tember on the intercom.

The locks on the door rattled, and then the door slid open. Beyond it were six men in body armor. The one in front had a full-length plexiglass riot shield with metal studs protruding through it to the outside face—its built in taser.

"Come on!" The shit-covered man shouted as he danced back away from the door. "Let's get some, you shitbird motherfuckers! Come get some!"

The man with the shield sniggered and stepped into the room. "You need new material, inmate. Get the fuck down on the ground with your nose in the dirt."

"Yeah, you make me, Tom! You make me!"

The guard with the shield walked forward without pause, always keeping all his body parts behind the shield, backing the old guy into the corner.

Contrary to his rhetoric, the man didn't go on the offensive. Instead, he seemed relieved, backed into a corner where he wouldn't have to fight. It all had the patina of an oft-repeated bit of theater.

Once the guard had him pushed back into the corner, the other five guards crowded into the small cell. As Tobias looked down at their Kevlar helmets, he could catch snatches of their thoughts.

Fucking child abuser, *thought one.*

Some hard-ass… Big bad man doesn't want to fight, *thought another.*

Pressed into the corner, the old man looked up, seeming to glare right into Tobias's eyes. "Enjoying this, you little fuck?" he asked. "You little brat! You fucking Tom!"

With a chill, Tobias realized the old man could see him. If he had been in his corporeal form, he would have shuddered.

"Why's he call everyone 'Tom?'" asked one of the guards.

"Short for peeping-tom," said another. "He thinks we're invading his privacy."

The man's eyes bored into Tobias. "I fucking hate your bratty little ass! You're the reason I'm here!"

"What's he talking about?" asked a guard.

"Who knows? Who fucking cares?" said another.

They grabbed the old man and shoved him to the floor, breaking his eye contact with Tobias. They wrenched his arms behind his back and snapped manacles on his wrists, faces portraits of disgust at the feces that dripped off him.

"That's a new one...haven't seen an inmate gas himself before...not such a tough guy, are you, inmate?"

"Fucking Toms," muttered the prisoner.

A cold presence swept through the door, and the temperature of the room dropped ten degrees in thirty seconds.

"Hello, my love," said a female voice.

Tobias turned. The thing standing outside the doorway sickened him. Her skin hung loose on her flesh—as if her skin was several sizes too big. It had blackened like the mummified remains of something long dead. She had long, ivory colored talons where she should have had fingers, and her eyes were like coals of hatred when she looked up at him.

"You!" she screamed and raised her talons.

Fear sang through Tobias. A memory swam into his mind: an eleven-year-old's memory of being trapped in the forest maze, being chased by...by...something horrible. He tried to run, flailing about like a madman until he remembered he had left his body in Millvale. He relaxed and went back to floating in the corner. Nothing that thing can do to me while I'm projecting, he thought.

"Is that so?" she crooned, her voice laden with threat.

But she did nothing. She didn't even try, just stood there staring daggers at him. Without breaking her glare, she floated through the door like a dancer and stood in the center of the room.

"My love," she crooned.

"Yeah, babe," the man whispered.

"The fuck?" asked a guard. "Is he hallucinating for real?"

"The time is coming. Be ready. Father says to tell you that all will be made right. Your revenge on the town will be sweet. On all of them that yet live." She hooked a cruel-looking talon at Tobias. *"Including this one. Father says that when you see this brat in the flesh, you may have him."*

"Excellent, babe. I can't wait. Babe? I love you, babe."

"And I, you, my love."

"What's he jabbering about now?" asked the guard with the shield.

"I don't think even he knows, Sarge."

The blackened, mummified-looking thing reached toward Tobias with a clawed hand. She flicked her talons at him as if she were waving away flies.

Something pulled on Tobias like a long bungee cord at maximum extension. He fought to stay, to see what happened next, but with a loud pop...

...he was back in his body. Strapped to a bed in Millvale.

And he had to pee.

7

"Cut off?" Mike hissed. "What the blue fuck do you mean, I'm cut off, Jack?"

Jack looked at him with hard, cold eyes. "Which part of the concept is confusing you, Chief? I'm not serving you anymore booze. You've been here since, what? 5:30? How many highballs? I've lost count, and you haven't eaten a thing."

"The fuck you saying, you fat fuck? Gimme another highball and do it right the fuck now!" His voice slurred with drink, almost, but not quite, incomprehensible.

"I knew it was a mistake," muttered Jack. He turned and walked toward the other end of the bar.

"*Fine!*" yelled Mike. "Give me something to eat, then! I don't care what…just as long as dinner comes with another highball." Jack stopped but didn't turn back to him. The man's fat shoulders rose and fell with a big sigh. He shook his head…like he *pitied* Mike. "Who the *fuck* do you think you are, you…you…you fat fuck? *Pity*? You pity me? Well, fuck you, chummy! Give me a motherfucking highball, you big tub of lard."

Jack turned then. His face was angry and set, eyes blazing. His hands clenched at his sides, he stomped back to stand over Mike, glaring at him. "Get out, Mike." His voice was soft but cold and distant.

"The fuck I will! Highball!" Mike slapped his hand on the bar. "I want another highball!"

"Get out, Mike," said Jack, tension splashed across his face, voice still soft, cold. "Get out, or I will throw you out."

Mike looked at him, bleary-eyed, red-cheeked. He looked him up and down as if appraising horse-flesh. "You ain't got what it takes to throw me out, Jackie-boy. You'll *try*, sure, but all you're going to throw out is your back."

Lightning-quick, moving with an economy of movement that belied his weight, Jack leapt across the bar and clamped his hands on Mike's upper arms. With a heave, he picked the Chief up and carried him bodily toward the door.

"Hey! Hey!" shouted Mike. "Fuck are you doing, Jack? Put me down! I was just *kidding*!"

Jack didn't speak, didn't slow, didn't lower Mike to his feet.

"Listen to me, you fat motherfucker! If you don't put me down right the fuck now, I'll yank your goddamn liquor license on Monday, and then where the fuck will you be? Out on your ass!"

Jack reached the front door and kicked it open with his big foot. With a grunt and a final heave, he threw Mike outside and slammed the door.

Mike landed on the concrete sidewalk with a bone-jarring *thud*. His teeth snapped together on the tip of his tongue, and he howled in pain. A couple out for a late-night stroll averted their eyes and crossed to the other side of the street.

"Jus' a bartending dispute," he croaked. "Nothin' to see here." He waved in the general direction of the couple without taking his eyes off the door to Lumber Jack's. He climbed to his feet and dusted off his pants, getting angrier and angrier. "Throw me out?" he muttered, voice like molten steel. "Throw me out? Don't know who you fucked with, you fat fuck. I'm…"

He took two steps forward and put his hand on the door, trying to push it open. The door wouldn't budge. He pounded on the door, breathing harder and harder as rage took control of him. "Don't know who you fucked with, Jack! Open this door! Open it!"

When the lock snicked, and the door opened, it surprised him into silence. He stood there, gaping up into Jack's livid face.

The big man had a sawn-off bat in his hand, and he tapped it against the palm of his other hand. "Time to go home, Mike. I don't want to hit you with this, but if you make me, I will, and I'll sleep like a baby tonight. Betcher ass, I will!"

Mike went cold all over, then flashed hot. "Oh, is that so?" The drunken slur had left his voice, each syllable crisp and clean. "And what are you going to do when I arrest you for threatening a police officer? Or when I shoot you in your fat motherfucking face?" His hands shook with rage as he scrabbled around his waist, looking for the Glock 23 that lay locked in the glove box of his Caprice.

"You are unarmed, Mike," said Jack. "Go on! Get!"

"I'm unarmed *now*, yeah," said Mike in a frigid voice. "But that can change, fatso. That can change in a hurry."

Jack sighed, shoulders dropping. Moving with that scary-fast grace he'd shown a few minutes earlier, Jack closed the distance between them, raising the bat as he came. Mike cringed away, arms up to shield his head. "Just go, Mike," sighed Jack, letting the bat drop. "Go and don't you ever come back here."

Mike looked up into Jack's red-rimmed eyes and saw he meant it. Mike's shoulders slumped, and his gaze dropped to the gutter. "Sure, Jack," he murmured.

He turned and walked toward the side lot.

Behind him, Jack hawked and spat.

Mike turned the corner and let the rage come. His eyes teared up with it, his breathing accelerated with it, his hands clenched, unclenched, clenched, and unclenched with it. By the time he got to his car, his thoughts were a jumble of recrimination, shame, rage, and hatred.

Instead of getting in on the driver's side, Mike stomped around to the passenger side and ripped the door open. He bent at the waist and pounded on the glove box until it opened. When he picked up the pistol, his grin was bestial, savage.

8

"Oh, shit!" Shannon squeaked when she saw Mike slam to the sidewalk. She nibbled her lips as Mike picked himself up and dusted himself off. She stuck the tip of her thumb in her mouth and bit it as Mike started to pound on the door and yell.

When the door opened, and the big bartender stepped outside holding a bat, she squeaked again. She fumbled with her phone, meaning to call 911, but dropping it instead.

The bartender seemed to float forward and raised the bat like he was a ballet dancer. Shannon winced, expecting the bat to fall and split Mike's head like an over-ripe melon. Mike flinched and sidled away. Jack said something to Mike she couldn't make out and then pointed up the sidewalk with the bat. Mike nodded and turned to walk away. The bartender spit on the ground and Mike winced.

Her heart raced, and she wanted to run to Mike, to comfort him. "Don't worry, my love," she whispered without being aware of it. Mike turned the corner into the bar's side lot and stomped toward the back of the building. His movements were jerky, angry. She gnawed on the end of her finger, breathing heavily.

Mike straightened by the driver's door of his cruiser. "Just get in, my love," she whispered. "No one saw anything." The Chief glanced around the empty lot, and then almost ran to the passenger side of the car. "Oh, no," she murmured, filled with a terrible fear.

Mike straightened, his face a grotesque mask of frustration, shame, and anger, but he wore a smile on his face—an ugly smile. In his hand was a black lump of something. He turned and almost skipped back toward the front of the bar.

Without deciding to, Shannon popped open the door of her worthless little car. The dome light flashed, and as it did, Mike shot a glance in her direction, but without seeming to recognize her, turned back toward the bar. He rounded the corner and stood on the sidewalk in front of the bar, muttering something.

"No, my love," she said without realizing she was speaking aloud. She shot out of the car and sprinted toward Mike.

His arm lifted the black lump that had to be his gun. His arm came up, seeming to move in slow motion. Shannon poured on the speed but felt like she wasn't getting any closer. Mike's gaze was intent on the door of the bar, and the gun was up, pointing where he was glaring.

"No, my love! No!" she screamed.

Mike spun toward her, gun held at the ready.

She froze, stopping in mid-stride. She put her hands out toward him, mouth working but no sound coming out.

"Oh," he muttered. "It's you."

"Yes, my—" She snapped her mouth shut on the words. "Yes, Chief. It's me, Shannon. Shannon Bertram."

He looked at her like she had a monkey nestled in her hair.

"From Town Hall," she murmured.

"I know who you are, Shannon," Mike said. He looked down at the pistol in his hand and dropped it like it was hot. "Fuck am I *doing*?" he muttered.

"It's okay, Chief," she said, walking toward him.

"Mike. Call me Mike," he said. His head came up, and his eyes found hers. "If you're going to spend your evenings looking out for me, we should be on a first name basis."

Hot blood filled her cheeks, and her eyes smarted. "You...you *knew*?"

He smiled a thin, joyless smile. "Yes. And I let you do it, night after night, because I'm just that kind of guy."

"Oh," she said, not sure what to say. "It...It was..."

"Yes, it was," he said, looking her in the eye. He bent and picked up the pistol. He held it out to her. "You better hold this for a while." His voice shook with emotion.

"Are you...are you sure?" Shannon took the pistol with her thumb and forefinger, holding it away from her body like it was a snake.

"Yes, I'm sure. Shannon..."

"Yes, Mike?" Something inside her belly flipped over and wiggled at the idea of calling him Mike to his face.

"I...I... This is hard to admit."

"There's nothing you can say, Mike, that would make me think any less of you."

One eyebrow quirked, and he flashed a half-smile at her. "Don't be too sure, Shannon."

She made a helpless little gesture with her free hand. "What were you going to say?"

"I need help. I'm a…" Tears glistened in his eyes. "I'm a drunk, and I…"

"Shh, my love," she whispered and wrapped him in a hug.

He let her hug him for a moment and then pulled away. "Since it's a night of confessions, Shannon, I have to tell you something. I'm—"

"I know, Mike."

"But I'm never—"

"Shh," she said, putting a finger to his lips. "Don't say anymore. Come on, Mike. You shouldn't be alone tonight."

"No, I'm fine—"

"Shut up, Mike. I will make you dinner, and you will sleep on my couch. Tomorrow is soon enough to decide what happens next."

"Do you know how beautiful you are, Shannon?" Mike breathed. "You shouldn't waste yourself on me."

Hot blood flooded her cheeks for the millionth time that night, and something in her belly tingled. "I'm not—"

"Yes, you are!" Mike said. "Inside and out."

Shannon wondered if her cheeks were blazing like brake lights. She thought they must be. "I…I…"

Mike looked at her, kind eyes, beautiful smile. "Yes, you are," he whispered.

9

Drew lay awake, unable to sleep, and he didn't know why. His mind kept swirling around in circles, replaying the conversation with the two troopers. "Oneka Falls" kept spinning through his thoughts like a cork bobber in a whirlpool, sometimes dipping under the surface but always popping back up.

It made little sense. Drew had no family there—no family *anywhere*, for that matter—hell, he didn't even *know* anyone from Kanowa County, let alone Oneka Falls. But the town seemed important to him on some level. He couldn't leave it alone, he kept prodding it like a loose tooth.

He never went to bed this early. Sleep and he were not friends, they ignored one another until it was no longer possible. Falling asleep required work rather than the release it seemed to be for others. He didn't dream—never. Sleep was more of an imposition, something he had to do, but hated. A chore. A waste of time.

He twisted and rolled, trying to get comfortable in the RV's bed. Even his eyes refused to cooperate; every time he closed them, they popped right back open after a few moments.

Finally, he gave up on sleep and switched on the little spotlight set into the wall at the head of the bed. He glanced at his book, but he didn't want to read. He considered watching one of the DVDs he bought but never watched, but the thought of sitting still and staring at something flicker on a screen appealed to him even less than reading. *Maybe a game?* He swung his legs over the side of the foam mattress and yawned. "Oh, sure," he muttered. "Now yawn."

Shaking his head, he got up and walked to the entertainment section of the RV. He made it as far as turning on the television and the Xbox before he switched both off again. A game wasn't what he wanted. *Needed.*

He flipped the lid of his laptop open and squinted at the bright screen. "Google Maps," he said while he typed. "Oneka Falls." He waited as the map drew in, and then stared at the dot on the map off 158, but it meant nothing to him. His eyes roved the area around the little dot, skipping over the green clumps that were the state parks in the area. He zoomed in a little, trying to see the roads in the town, and when he saw the words "Thousand Acre Wood," his eyes froze in place.

He couldn't move, couldn't breathe, couldn't even close his eyes. His mind was calm, but his body wanted to be moving, as if in a full-blown panic. The words, the name of the forest, meant nothing to him. *Nothing.* Nothing *at all,* he thought, over and over. He slammed the laptop closed and shoved it off his lap and onto the couch next to him, looking at it as if it were alive.

Drew got up and pulled on a pair of jeans and slipped into his sneakers. Lying there, trying not to, but thinking, thinking, thinking, wouldn't work, he had to be moving, had to be doing something. He went outside and unplugged the power and water tethers and lowered the RV on to its wheels.

"How much is that puppy dog?" he murmured to himself. "Where is the puppy?" He was almost unaware of the phrases he was repeating aloud. It was a cognitive

214   ERIK HENRY VICK

trick a psychiatrist or psychologist had taught him to derail errant thoughts and depressive cycles.

He climbed back into the Odin Desperado, continuing to mutter nonsense sentences, slid into the driver's seat and started the engine. He pulled the RV out of his slip and let it idle up the short lane to the RV park's exit.

He couldn't stay there. He *couldn't*. He had to be moving, had to be on the go. He was going to visit Oneka Falls, anyway, might as well get moving.

It wasn't like he would get to sleep, anyway.

10

It was pleasant not to have a hang-over. By all rights, he *should* have one after all those highballs in Lumber Jack's, but Shannon had forced so much water on him that he'd been up half the night peeing. He smiled at the memory of how sweet she'd been. Then he remembered what had brought her running to his side and blushed crimson.

"It's okay," Shannon whispered.

"But last night—"

"Last night is the past, Mike. Today is the first day of the rest of your life."

Mike scoffed, but not in an unkind way.

"We'll find you a meeting, Mike," she said, as serious as a preacher.

"A meeting," he muttered.

"Yes, Mike, a meeting. Believe me on this, you can't quit drinking without them."

"Who said I was quitting?" he asked.

"Oh… Well, I just…assumed… I mean, after last…" She stumbled to a halt, and her words did the same.

"It was a joke," Mike said, feeling like an utter shit heel. "Not a funny one, I guess. Sorry."

She sighed with relief. "Oh, you had me going. No more of that for a while."

"Too soon?"

"Definitely too soon."

"Sorry," he said.

She led him from the small apartment she rented out to the sidewalk that ran along Main Street. Her apartment was over the garage in a house across from the Town Hall. Mike grinned at the thought of her driving her car across the road and into the rear parking lot every single day. "Did you drive every day just so you could follow me and make sure I didn't get hurt?"

She blushed for about the thirty-thousandth time since last night and hung her head.

"Shannon, I'm the kind of guy who teases to show affection. I don't mean anything by it."

"Affection?" she asked, looking up into his face.

The desperate hope he saw in her eyes almost hurt. "Shannon, there's something I need to tell you."

"Later," she said. "Breakfast, first."

11

Drew had driven through the night, but he wasn't tired at all. When he got stressed, he could go on and on without rest—one of the bonuses from his mysterious past. He'd parked the Desperado outside the town limits—hidden inside an abandoned barn— and switched to the BMW. No one in Oneka Falls would recognize him in either vehicle, but the BMW zipped through tight town streets much better than the lumbering motor home.

Late-season corn fields blurred by on the right and the left, with occasional flashes of greenery at the borders of the fields. He turned down Main Street where it dead ended into 158, trying to look like a tourist from Rochester out on a weekend drive.

At the edge of town, he passed a huge pile of logs and junk wood left to rot on the side of the road. Next to the pile stood a row of old, rusty tractors, each on rotting rubber tires, and each at war with weeds and creeping ivy. Behind the pile of wood, stood an old, crumbling and rotting warehouse. The paint had peeled from the building, and the sign hung crooked from the single post holding it. The sign read: Tri-Blend Meats.

Drew shook his head. *Who would buy meat from a company with a name like that?*

In the next lot, a knot of demons stood and stared at him from the front porch of an ancient Victorian house that had once been white—not to mention that had once had all of its siding attached. The roof was rusting metal.

He smiled at the six demons staring at him and lifted his hand in a friendly wave. Two of the six were the classic demon-type: leathery wings, red scales, horns, tail. The other four were weirds: various colors, shapes, and sizes.

A yellow one with chartreuse, alligator eyes stood in the middle of the others. Its eyes followed Drew. It had a V-shaped mouth and rubbery lips. It didn't wave back. One problem with not seeing the visage the demon projected was that he didn't know if he should pretend to recognize Trooper LaBouche or not.

Heart beating fast, Drew turned his attention back to his driving. Oneka Falls was a typical New York town: creepy, dilapidated houses, with a few fixed up or well-maintained houses interspersed among them. Rusting hulks at the run-down places, fancy German cars at the nicer ones. Roads led to working fields behind the houses on the west side of the road, forest backed the houses to the east. Demons lounged right out in the open everywhere he looked. In yards, on porches, driving tractors, working on cars. He passed various small businesses operating out of old factory buildings or warehouses standing right next door to inhabited houses. He smiled at the garish, red-painted house that had been converted into an antique shop. A huge, hand-painted sign decorated the side of the building. It showed a huge strawberry with arms, legs, eyes, and a big smile pointing to the words: Fine Antiques & Collectibles.

He found downtown a few minutes later. Two whole blocks of two-story commercial buildings from the forties in various states of repair on the west side, and churches, modern bank buildings, and more houses on the east. Between the two blocks, a single stop light swung in the wind where another state road dead ended at 158. On one northwest corner, stood a building that looked familiar. Drew slowed, staring at it. A small brass sign hung on the side of the building over a single glass door. It read: "Town Hall & Police Department." Something nagged at the back of his mind. A fleeting memory or déjà vu.

He continued through the quaint little downtown area, waving at the demons who walked arm in arm with human companions on the sidewalk. After the second block, a small road veered off to the left. Drew glanced at the street sign, and it was like being struck by lightning.

Mill Lane. He slammed on the brakes and the car skidded to a stop. Then Drew faded away for a while.

The loud air horn startled him back to awareness, and, for a moment, he didn't know where or *when* he was. He sat in a car, in the middle of the street, and behind him a grain truck idled. The farmer driving it leaned out the window and shouted something or other.

The driver was a demon with huge, pale wings crammed into the cab behind him.

Drew shook his head to clear it and then smiled in his mirror and waved. A small convenience store (in the shell of an old house, of course) sat on the left. He pulled into the parking lot and put the BMW in park.

It hit him then. *Mill Lane.* He was on Mill Lane. The thought upset him though he did not understand why. A pit yawned in his stomach.

A man and a woman came out of the convenience store, laughing. The woman did not interest Drew, though she was beautiful underneath a plainness that seemed like camouflage. The man, though… Something about the man set bells ringing in Drew's mind. *Something about the eyes, maybe? The mouth?* He couldn't think, couldn't speak, could only stare at the couple as they walked toward him.

The woman noticed him staring and said something to her companion. Drew thought he saw recognition in the man's brief glance, but then the man laughed and said something to the woman, who also laughed. The man had something shiny—a rodeo belt buckle or something—on his belt, but the bag of groceries he held obscured it.

Drew waved and smiled, chin dipped a little toward his chest. Everything about the move was calculated, studied. Over the years he'd developed a whole repertoire of behaviors designed to meet his own needs and wants. This one said: "I'm embarrassed you caught me staring. I'm harmless, though." Like the many other times he'd employed it, it worked like a charm.

The couple smiled at him, and the woman gave him a cutesy wave. They passed his car—less than a body length away, a calculating part of his mind noted—and walked across Mill Lane toward downtown. The man had a Glock 23 stuffed in the back of his jeans, and Drew realized what the shiny thing on his belt must be: a badge. He put the car in gear and turned on to Mill Lane, heading away from the cop and his lady-friend with a feeling of relief.

The houses went from sort-of-nice to decrepit and creepy in less than a block. The farther he drove, the worse he felt.

A house on the left drew his attention. Weeds and rotting garbage choked the overgrown yard. There was something familiar about it… When he saw the house from the front, panic took him by the short hairs, and he mashed the accelerator to the floor. He didn't even see the humor-filled looks flashed at him by demons, nor the angry looks from the humans.

12

The ringing phone interrupted Mike mid-laugh. With a grunt, he flipped the phone open. "Chief Richards."

"Mike?" The voice sounded tinny and far away.

He scratched his cheek. Shannon raised her eyebrows at him, and he held up one finger. "This is Chief Richards. Who is calling?"

"Mike, thank God. It's Tobias."

"Tobias…" The name tickled his memory, but he couldn't pull any sensible thoughts out of his fogged mind.

"Yeah, Mike. Tobias. He's out."

"Wait a minute, wait a minute," he grumbled. "Let a guy think." He put his fork down and turned away from Shannon's tiny "French café" table-for-two. "*Tobias Burton*?"

"Yes, it's me. Listen, he's out and—"

"Wait a second, Toby. Aren't you in Millvale?"

"Yeah, but it's okay. And call me Tobias."

"Well, if you're still in Millvale, then how are you calling me?"

"It's no big deal. I earned privileges back. I'm calling from the phone outside the TV room."

"Okay…"

"What is it, Mike?" Shannon hissed. Mike held up his finger and shook it a little.

"He's out, or he's going to be," whispered Tobias.

"Who's out?"

"*The guy*, Mike. You remember."

Mike shook his head. "Tobias, I don't—"

"Wait a minute, wait a minute. I get confused about the details sometimes. Is that my memory or Benny's?"

"This isn't making a lot of sense, Toby. Is there a nurse available?"

"It's Tobias. Listen to me, Mike, *He* is out. *The guy!* That guy who caused all that ruckus back when we were kids. The one who terrorized us, who kidnapped all those kids."

It hit Mike like a freight train. "No, Toby—Tobias, I mean—you don't have to worry about him. He's locked up and will never get out, not after what he did."

"No, he's out. The invisible woman let him out. Or will let him out. Or something. I get confused with the details sometimes."

"The invisible woman." He tried, but he couldn't keep the derision out of his voice.

"Yeah. You know, they took me and those others. You remember that much, don't you?"

"Of course, I remember, Tobias. How could I forget? But, I'm telling you, he got life with no chance of parole."

"Yeah, okay, Mike, you've got me there, but I'm telling you: the invisible woman got him out—or will get him out—of Sing Sing."

"Toby..."

"Tobias. Listen, Mike—for the love of God, *listen*. He's out. He's on his way there. To kill us. He's out and he's coming to Oneka Falls."

To kill us? Mike ran his hand through his hair and sighed. *"Tobias*, I'm sure you are wrong, but if it will make you feel better, I'll call tomorrow and make sure he's still there. Good enough?"

Static tickled the line for a long breath, then Tobias sighed. "Okay, Mike. Okay."

"Was that really Toby Burton, Mike?" Shannon asked when he dropped the hand holding the phone to his lap. Mike nodded without turning back to the table. "That's so sad," she said. "I wish..."

Mike glanced at her. "Shannon...you were part of that mess back when we were kids, right?"

She forced a laugh. "Was I? I don't remember." She scooped a lump of eggs into her mouth. "Mmm. These eggs are great, aren't they? I love breakfast."

"Shannon," Mike breathed. "You don't remember being kidnapped?"

She flapped her hand at him. "No. Who would *want* to remember that? Besides…I was nine, my love." She clapped her hand over her mouth and looked down, blood burning in her cheeks.

"You have nothing to be embarrassed about, Shan." Mike reached across the table and touched her arm. "Did you ever…did you *see* someone…after?"

"After what?"

"Shannon…"

"And anyway, I've seen lots of people since I was nine."

"That's not what I mean, Shan. I mean a psychologist, a counselor."

She flapped her hand at him again. "Oh, pish-posh. What do you want to do today?"

Mike cleared his throat. "Shan, there are people who specialize in PTSD. They can help you work through it."

"Stop talking about that, Mike. I don't remember, I told you."

For the first time in his memory, Mike heard iron in Shannon's voice. He sighed and patted her arm. *She's helping me with drinking. The least I can do is help her through her past if she will let me.*

Shannon turned to him, eyes bright, a mischievous grin plastered across her face. "Since you didn't say what *you* wanted to do today, I get to pick. Fair's fair!"

Mike smiled. "Sure, Shan. Anything you want."

She cocked one eyebrow and looked at him in a lascivious, challenging way. "*Anything*?" She grinned crookedly.

Mike chuckled. "I should rephrase, Shan."

"Mike?" she asked, the playful, flirty facade gone in an instant.

"Yes?"

"Can you call me 'babe' sometimes?"

13

LaBouche grimaced as the phone rang again. The constant ringing cramped his style. Rolling his eyes toward the ceiling, he flipped the phone over and dug the battery out of it. It wouldn't do to have Scott track him by GPS.

The naked girl in front of him shivered with fear. "Please, Lane, just take me home."

"Don't start that again, Beck. We're beyond that." He liked to preserve the idea he was human until the very end. He liked to spring his true form on them after a day or so. One time, his victim had a heart attack and died when he let the guy see who he was. It had been so good, so sweet...so delicious. "Your old man keeps calling me. Ain't that funny?"

"Please...Lane, please."

"You need to shut up, Becky. Now." He leaned close to her and snapped his teeth, inches away from her face. The girl whimpered, and LaBouche sighed with pleasure. "That's better."

He took the red-hot coat hanger out of the brazier and showed it to her. "I'll give you a choice, Becky. Coat hanger, or I do you again."

Tears streamed down her cheeks. Her eyes flipped back and forth between the glowing coat hanger and his face. "Why are you doing this, Lane?"

"Choose, Becky, or I will."

"Why, Lane? Just tell me why."

"Because, you sniveling little bitch, it's fun!" He whipped the coat hanger down, searing the flesh above her breasts, and, at the same time, rammed himself inside her. Her screams were delightful.

14

His heartbeat slowed and, as it did, so did his flight through the back streets of Oneka Falls. His vision expanded from the tunnel-like view of the street to include the houses, yards, people, and demons he passed. The demons looked amused; the people looked pissed.

He didn't remember turning off of Mill Lane, but the road he drove down didn't look familiar. Not on the street with that *house*. He had no memory of that house. *Why does seeing it bother me? Why does* thinking *about it scare me? What happened there?*

He idled down a pretty street—for the most part. Lined with stately trees and well-kept lawns, most of the homes were maintained with fresh paint, though like anywhere in the western part of New York, there were exceptions.

The old house on his left screamed ugly at the top of its voice. It was a small house with a mish-mash of stylistic starts and stops. The rotting steps in front of the porch sported elaborate wrought-iron rails, but the floor of the porch was plywood. On the ground floor, the front walls of the house boasted ugly fake brick, while the second floor had wood shakes, painted a barbaric shade of red that would make any Italian sports car proud. A metal roof rusted over the porch, but nasty brown asphalt shingles curled up at the sky over the rest of the house. Drew could see two windows upstairs, one covered with roofing tin, and a flowered bedsheet obscured the other from the inside. The windows on the ground floor sported actual curtains, except for the plywood-covered one closest to the front door. A narrow, cracked concrete path led from the sidewalk to the porch, and weeds grew madly from its cracks. The mowed side yard sported nice flowerbeds, but in the overgrown and weedy front, the flowerbeds had been consumed by ivy a long time ago.

As he looked at the house, the flowered sheet in the upstairs window jerked aside, and a demon glared out at him. Drew flashed an uneasy smile. He licked his lips and pulled his gaze away from the bizarre house. His scalp prickled and the hair on the back of his neck stood on end. He excelled at unobtrusive observation. *Haven't blown it this bad since that third demon way back when. Better get it together.* Rousing the suspicions of every demon on this side of town, almost guaranteed he'd be followed. Or worse. With this many demons in one place, he could be attacked with impunity.

How in the hell did a haven like this come to be? The town must be overrun with crimes of all sorts. Either the police here were incompetent, on the take, or demons themselves. The thought made Drew angry, though he couldn't say why.

He passed a quaint little Catholic church on the left with the strange name of St. Genesius' Sanctuary of the Holy Mother. *Strange place*, thought Drew. Besides the saint he'd never heard of, the Spanish sign below the placard bore no English translation.

He drove on; the houses getting bigger and fancier as he went. Then, as if he had crossed an invisible boundary, everything seemed darker: the sky, the houses, the trees. *This must be hell on the property values of those nice houses back there*, he thought with a humorless grin. *As if demons give two shits about property values.*

Ahead, the road twisted to the left, and on the right side of the road, an enormous white church, replete with ugly stained-glass windows and a tall, tall steeple, squatted like an evil frog. A crooked, rusty metal sign hung next to the double front doors. "First Grand Church of the Reformation" read the sign. Two bullet holes stared out from the center of the two Os, and above the door, someone had hand painted "Play Time" with blood-red paint.

Something was very wrong with that church. Drew put his foot on the brake and slowed. The place felt...*evil*. Drew had no doubt that whatever demonic activity anchored in the town of Oneka Falls, most of it happened at the Play Time. It had to be the focal point of the infestation.

As he stared at the church, the double doors banged open. The interior of the place was as black as a moonless night. A weird yellow-scaled gorilla stood in the doorway and stared at Drew with hate-filled eyes.

Drew ducked his head and punched it. *No doubt he saw me that time. LaBouche... What the fuck is he doing here?*

15

LaBouche had learned not to argue with his intuition, so when he felt the need to go have a walk outside, he did it without pause. Leaving Becky moaning and bleeding—dying, most likely—he tossed the coat hanger back into the brazier full of burning coals and then slammed the door of her cell. He walked to the front of the building and shouldered the double doors open with a bang.

A little red BMW idled in front of the door. It was the same car he'd seen earlier. The car he was half-sure

Dr. Reid had driven from Rochester. He looked at the driver. It *was* Dr. Reid.

When the driver of the car saw LaBouche, the man's face turned pallid, and he froze for a moment. Then, in a cacophony of whining turbo-chargers, the car sped off. Half of LaBouche was amused, the other, enraged. He watched the car slide to a stop at the intersection of Main and Union and then speed away to the north.

LaBouche's rubbery lips pinched together, and the corners of his mouth turned down. With a snort, he closed the doors to Play Time and took all three steps between the entry and the sidewalk in one wide step. Easy breaths whistled through the two slits over his mouth that served as his nose.

There was a lightness in his chest and warmth suffused his limbs. But also, his stomach fluttered, and his mouth dried out a touch as he thought of what it would take to get another one like Becky back to his lair. It was always the same when he'd finished one of his projects—when he'd used his pet human up. And, like always, the need to get to work on his next pet screamed in the back of his mind.

He turned toward Main Street without another thought about Becky Lewis. One of his kin would take care of what remained of her, and even if they didn't, no one would look for her at Play Time. No one.

His cell phone buzzed again, and with the start of a tension headache pounding behind his eyes, he took a deep breath and accepted the call. It was Lewis, of course. "Partner," he said, forcing his voice to be pleasant, warm. "How's your Saturday, Scott?"

"Where the hell have you been, Lee?" Lewis demanded.

The substantial muscles of his jaw knotted and his grip tightened on the phone until the plastic and metal case creaked at Lewis' tone. "Well, it's our day off. I've been—"

"Never mind the bullshit, Lee. I need your help. It's Becky—" Lewis snapped his mouth closed on the last syllable. He took several rasping breaths, each one sounding harsh and loud in LaBouche's ear.

"Wait, wait," said LaBouche. "What are you talking about, Scott? What's happened to Becky? Is she hurt?"

"No," sighed Lewis. "It's worse than that."

"She's... My God, Scott, is she dead?" In the background, he heard Jenny Lewis sob. He let the line hiss for several heart beats. LaBouche was a connoisseur of human emotion, and he knew how to play this, how to extend the moment, to get the most out of Lewis' reactions. It was like dessert.

"I… No. I don't… There's nothing to…" Lewis' voice shook, and LaBouche could imagine him standing there, expression slack, eyes wet and dull.

"*Tell* him, Scott!" Jenny shrieked in the background.

"Help me, Lee. I've got to…I've got to find my baby girl, Lee." His voice was flat, torpid.

LaBouche licked his lips, savoring his partner's grief. "We'll find her, Scott," he said. "It's not too late." He smiled at the memory of Becky's cooling body in the old church behind him. "The only problem is…I'm not in Rochester at the moment."

"Well, where the hell are you, Lee?"

LaBouche grinned like a predator and suppressed a chuckle. "Day off, remember? I took a day trip to Hammondsport."

"Hammondsport…"

"Hey, I like the scenery." The line hissed and spit static in his ear.

"How…How fast can you get back here?"

"God, I have no idea, Scott. Couple of hours?"

"How long did it take to get down there?"

"I was enjoying the drive. Paid zero attention to clocks and speed limits both."

"Well, get back here as fast as you can. Okay?"

"Yeah, no problem, Scott. I'm almost to my car."
LaBouche stretched his back and smiled up at the sky.
"Oh, shit…"

"What? What is it, Lee?"

"*What now?*" wailed Jenny.

The blind panic in Lewis' voice was like whipped
cream and a cherry on top of ice cream. "Oh, phew!" he
muttered. "No, it's nothing, Scott. I couldn't find my
keys for a second, but they're right here."

"Christ, Lee. You almost gave me a stroke."

"Yeah, sorry, buddy. Don't worry. I can see the car,
and I'm on my way."

"Is he coming?" Jenny said in a lifeless voice.

"Yeah, honey. Lee's on the way."

"Fuck," LaBouche muttered. He waited, letting the
silence stretch.

"Lee? What is it?"

"Fucking flat tire, man."

"Lee…" Lewis' voice had a distinct edge to it.

"Don't worry, Scotty. It won't take me a minute to
change. I'll be there soon. You and Jenny try to relax."
Lewis didn't answer, and LaBouche tilted his face up to
the sun, reveling in the rejuvenation, the satisfaction
he'd sucked out of Becky.

"What the *fuck*, LaBouche? Are you *humming*?"
yelled Lewis.

LaBouche brought his hand up to his throat. "Uh, sorry… I wasn't…I didn't—"

"My daughter's missing, and you are *motherfucking humming*?" Lewis' voice shook with fury.

"Scott, it's just the stress of the moment, man. It…it doesn't mean anything." LaBouche had to suppress the urge to yawn. The strength of it caught him off guard.

"Are you…are you *playing* with us, Lee?" Lewis' voice had gone from fury-filled to frigid at the speed of light.

"What? No. No, Scott. It's just the stress of Becky being…well, you know."

"Get here, Lee. Get here, *now*."

"On my way, partner. Don't fret." LaBouche couldn't believe his control had slipped to the point that he was now on the defensive. It would take real effort to work Lewis past that little slip. "Look, Scotty, I'm really sorry, I—" The line went dead. "*Fuck!*" he hissed and stomped toward his car.

16

Tobias walked down the middle of the long, institutional-gray corridor, ignoring the other patients, the seclusion rooms lining the left side, and the patient rooms lining the right. As usual, the corridor smelled like old urine and unwashed bodies. The florescent lights buzzed behind the protective mesh screens and the sound of it made him want to shove a pencil in his ears.

The staff pretended not to hear it, of course—said it was just his imagination, but that's what they said about everything. That's what they said about the creep in the woods and the eyeless freaks...the dog-things. And the tree.

The tree full of screaming children.

Tobias shuddered, wrapping his arms around himself and squeezing tight. His friend had learned how to derail such thoughts—such memories—but Tobias had never learned the knack. He needed a distraction, and quick.

He walked down the length of the corridor to the nurses' station. Another corridor stretched off on a ninety-degree tangent, and like the corridor he lived on, ended with a thick metal, electronically-locked security door. The door to the nurses' station was a Dutch door, and except late at night, the top part of the door was always open. A thin counter top had been attached the bottom half of the door, and Tobias rested his forearms on it.

"Hey," he croaked, his voice sounding like a rusty old saw.

An orderly with his arm in a sling and two black eyes glared back at him, some unidentifiable strong emotion burning in his eyes. Tobias cleared his throat. "Hey," he tried again. His voice sounded better, and it didn't hurt as much to speak. Now, if he only had something to say.

"Get off the door," Old-black-eyes snapped.

Tobias stood up straight, taking his arms off the counter and letting them fall to his sides. It hadn't been hard to talk to Mike the other day, but then again, Tobias had known Mike Richards for as long as he could remember. He wracked his brain for something to say.

"You want to talk *now?*" the orderly snapped. "You want my help with something?"

Tobias cocked his head to the side, feeling like he was missing the essential part of the conversation, but not having a clue what it was.

"It was your own fault, Sam," a tanned nurse chided. "We all told you Tobias doesn't like company, but you wouldn't listen."

So that's it! Excitement bubbled through him as the memory of the orderly swam into his conscious mind. He remembered the guy trying to talk to him in the

Activities Room. He remembered the guy introducing himself, but not the guy's name. An image flashed through his mind: the orderly's eyes huge like saucers, his arms up to shield his face. *What does that mean?*

"Tobias doesn't even remember you, do you, Tobias? You can't take it to heart, Sam." The woman was older, nearer to the end of her career than the beginning—sixty years old or more. Her West Virginia twang amused Tobias, and he sometimes sat with her if she wasn't too busy. She never pressed him, never invaded his space.

She was also the one who gave him the shots when he freaked out. He didn't like that part of her, but everyone had their faults.

He refocused on the orderly and cocked his head to the side. "What…happened?"

The man scoffed but seemed less hostile. He gestured at his arm. "You hit me with a chair."

He's lying, sang a voice in the back of his mind. Tobias struggled to make his mouth work, croaking like a frog. "Why?" he asked.

Sam shook his head. "You got me, pal. I was just trying to be nice."

Tobias shook his head, not knowing what to say. He took a step back from the door, fear suffusing his bloodstream.

The orderly stood and walked over to the Dutch door. He beckoned Tobias closer. "I can't leave the station while my arm's in the sling."

Tobias looked at him, scared, not wanting to get within the man's reach. Orderlies sometimes tried to get back at patients who acted out. The tan nurse got on them for it—when she caught them, but nine times out of ten, patients left those encounters with bruises.

"Aww, don't be shy, Toby. I won't hurt you."

TOBIAS! He wanted to scream it in the orderly's face, but he didn't step closer. No way.

Sam glanced around and saw that the tan nurse was busy talking on the phone with a doctor. He turned back to Tobias with a sick grin on his face. "This ain't my first rodeo, pal. Do you have any idea what I do about nut jobs like you?"

Tobias shrugged and took a step back.

"First thing you need to do is get into the Activity Room and look up the word: rhetorical. Once you find out what that means, this conversation might make more sense."

Tobias' gaze bounced from the door knob to the reinforced glass windows to Sam's face and then away in the space of a heartbeat. He scratched his chin and then pulled his ear.

"You've been here a long time, Toby," Sam murmured. "You know what happens when you mess with the staff."

Tobias flinched and turned to walk away.

"Aw, don't go, sport. I've got a message for you…from your old friend in the woods."

Tobias' gaze snapped to Sam's face.

"He says he's bored. He said you'd understand what that meant."

For the briefest of moments, Tobias still saw the orderly, but then his features started to fade, allowing Tobias to see him—*really* see him—for what he was. He was some kind of monster wearing a man-suit.

He walked away as fast as he could, almost breaking into a run. He wanted to be as far away from the monster as he could get, but he didn't want to trap himself in a place where the monster could get him alone. Darting looks over his shoulder every few paces, Tobias hustled to the end of the hallway. Patients were supposed to stay away from the doors, but the tan nurse often let him stand down there by himself.

He had his hands up next to his ears as if shielding his head. Thoughts swirled around like mad dogs chasing insane cats. *He knows him!* No way that was true, though. Herlequin was in the past. He was in Oneka Falls, nowhere near the hospital. There were no forests around the hospital, not a one. *All farm land!* But the orderly had been so cock-sure, and how would he know to say Herlequin was bored?

Tobias shook his head violently, trying to rid himself of the thoughts, the fear, the memories. *Herlequin can't get to me in here. There's no way. No woods, right?* But *Sam* got to him. And once Owen Gray got out of Sing Sing, *Owen* would *surely* get to him.

Tobias scrubbed his hands through his hair hard enough to hurt. *I'm no longer safe here! No longer safe!* He did not understand how Herlequin had found him, but maybe because of his visit to Owen Gray's cell. *Or he's always known, and this idea that I'm safe here is just another errant thought.* The thoughts, the emotions, the memories, they swirled like leaves in a current, banging together, bouncing away. He didn't know how to stop the circular argument or how to stop the panic. The only thing he knew for sure was that he had to get out of Millvale. *I have to hide!* The thought galvanized him, quieted the turmoil in his mind. For the first time in years, a sense of purpose thrummed through him. *Or better yet, I have to kill Herlequin.*

At the other end of the hall, the orderly was leaning out of the top half of the Dutch door, flashing an evil grin at him and…leering. There was something in his gaze…something predatory, something *hungry*.

Tobias slumped against the door, his back resting on the cool metal. The orderly's face filled with fury. "Get away from the door!" he yelled.

Tobias waved and stood up straight.

"Get down here away from that door, Toby!"

Tobias waved again and walked toward the nurses' station. When he was about halfway down the length of the long corridor, he turned and sprinted toward the door, running as fast as his disused muscles would allow. He didn't slow when the orderly screeched at him to stop. Twenty yards separated him and the door. He didn't slow when the tan nurse yelled on the intercom. The door was ten yards away. He didn't slow when someone rang the alarm, the bleating sound that summoned the unit's staff to the nurses' station. Only six more steps! He didn't slow, he lowered his shoulder, pulling his arm tight across his abdomen. The door loomed in front of him, filling his sight, and still, he didn't slow. At the last second, he threw his shoulder into the metal door, and with a crashing boom, the door...popped open.

Shoulder on fire, Tobias hesitated. He hadn't expected to get the door open, he'd just wanted another trip to the seclusion rooms...under the watchful eye of the security cameras. He'd wanted time to think, but now...but now...freedom beckoned, and the man the hospital staff knew as Tobias Burton smiled and sprinted through the door.

His grin stretched when he saw the door for the stairwell across the hall. He ran the three steps to the door and popped it open. When the hospital wide intercom crackled, and the tan nurse's voice rang through the halls calling for security, calling for assistance, his grin stretched even wider.

He raced down the steps, flying from landing to landing. Above him, he heard the booming footsteps of a pursuer, but he didn't know—or care—who it was. *No one can catch me now!*

When the stairs ended on the ground floor, he didn't hesitate—he rammed the emergency door to the outside open with his throbbing shoulder and sprinted away into the gloaming. Behind him, sirens and alarm bells rang. But there were no footsteps—he'd lost his recalcitrant shadow.

He ran on, stretching his stride like he had as an eleven-year-old. When the pain came, when the cramps and stitches in his side came, he pushed through them, just like he had as a kid in the woods. He ran and ran.

Feelings of elation almost overwhelmed him. *There is no fence! I am outside, and no fence stands between me and the world!* He wanted to dance, to giggle like a schoolboy. He wanted to shout his victory from the rooftops of the world.

But he didn't. He couldn't.

Because somewhere, out there, waiting for the coming darkness without a fence to keep him out, was Herlequin. And his fucking mutant dogs.

Chapter 5
1979

I

Toby Burton lurched out of the Thousand Acre Wood a few minutes before dawn. He was missing one shoe, and his skinned knees showed through jagged rips in his jeans. He had blood on the front of his shirt. His face was filthy and streaked with tears.

He staggered up the slight incline to the road and paused on the shoulder, bleary eyes straining to focus. He looked left and right, and then fazed-out for a while, standing like a statue on the shoulder of the road. His head cocked to the side as if he listened to something faint.

When he shuddered and looked around, the sun was peeking over the horizon, and he staggered to the left. Each floundering step looked like it cost him more than he had to give, but somehow, he kept going.

He passed the sign welcoming visitors to Oneka Falls without recognizing it. Cars zoomed past him heading out of town, but he didn't seem to notice. He didn't notice when Craig Witherson pulled in behind him, with the lights of his police cruiser spinning.

When Witherson blipped the horn, Toby didn't acknowledge it. When the siren shrieked once, Toby cringed but didn't stop teetering toward town.

Witherson goosed the cruiser out and passed Toby. He cut in a little in front of the boy and stopped. He got out of the car and sprinted to the rear, but Toby didn't turn toward him.

Toby continued on until the physical bulk of the police car stopped his forward progress. Only then did he stop, but he still didn't look at Witherson, or even turn. He just stood there.

Witherson wrapped him in a blanket and spoke in low, soothing tones. Toby didn't react.

Toby didn't speak with Dawn, old Doctor Hauser's nurse when she gave him a cup of orange juice.

"Has he been this way the whole time?" asked Dawn.

"Yup," said Craig. "A zombie."

Toby didn't react when old Doc Hauser picked him up and sat him on the exam table. He answered none of the doctor's questions. He didn't even wince or cry out when Dawn drew blood.

"I've seen this before," said Doc Hauser.

"Yeah?"

"Hysterical catatonia is what it's called. Comes with a trauma that the mind can't handle—the mind switches over to autopilot, and the consciousness takes a little vacation."

With a glance at Toby, Craig whispered, "You mean *sexual* trauma?"

"Could be," said the doctor. "Where's the boy's mother?"

Craig shook his head. "She'd do more harm than good, if you ask me, Doc." He mimicked drinking from a bottle.

"She's the boy's mother, Witherson. Go get her."

While Witherson was gone, Doc Hauser stayed in the room with Toby. He spoke in low tones of things he thought would interest an eleven-year-old boy. Toby didn't move, didn't respond, didn't even glance at the old man, not even when the doctor pulled out his ultimate kid-icebreaker and waggled his gray caterpillar-eyebrows.

2

Jim woke Karen and the boys as the sun crept over the horizon. He hadn't slept at all, despite his best efforts; every sound had spooked him.

"Come on, sleepy heads," he said. "Let's go on an adventure."

"Where are we going?" mumbled Benny.

"To Ohio."

"All of us?" asked Karen.

"Yes, all of us." Jim treated her to a slight shake of his head so she wouldn't make a big deal over his change of mind.

"What about school?"

"Well, I'm the town manager, and I declare you boys exempt from school until further notice." That got their attention.

After breakfast, everyone loaded into the Toronado, and Jim drove west. He stuck to the back roads, claiming he wanted to see the beauty of nature, but he thought it would be harder for anyone to follow them without his noticing it on the two-lane country roads.

As they passed the Thousand Acre Wood, Billy, the youngest, pointed to the left of the road. "Who's that man, Daddy?" he asked.

Jim snapped his head to the side, sure that Fergusson would be there, pointing a hunting rifle at his family, but it wasn't Fergusson—there was no one there at all. "Must have been a bit of mist that hasn't burned off yet, Kiddo. Nothing to worry about."

"No, it was a man. He had a blanket on like a cape and a shiny hat."

"Okay, Billy," Jim said. "Let me know if you see him again."

"Dad! How could a man in the woods keep up with the car?"

Jim chuckled, even his youngest child was on to his tricks. Karen patted his leg and suppressed a smile. They drove west, feeling safe and content, not realizing the feeling was a lie.

3

Candy Burton reeked of gin in the tight confines of the patrol car, and she looked hung-over as hell. "Don't you judge me, Craig Witherson," she snapped. "Don't you dare. Not after Prom, not after…" She waved her hand and turned toward the window.

Witherson had thought he was doing a good job hiding his contempt for her. "High school was a long time ago, Candy." He glanced at the rearview mirror and met her gaze.

"I bet you still want me. Should come by sometime, Craigy. See if the old sparks still work."

"I don't think so, Candy."

She shrugged, a sly smile flirting with her lips. "S'okay, Craigy. You shouldn't make a snap decision about matters of the heart…keep an open mind."

Craig scoffed. "You should focus on your boy, Candy. Not getting laid."

"Don't tell me what to do, Witherson. You ain't the quarterback no more."

"And you sure ain't no cheerleader, hon," he snapped.

He turned into the lot at Doc Hauser's place and parked. He turned to look at her through the wire mesh that separated the front and the back seats. "Candace, I'm serious here. Your son's in trouble. He's going to need you. See if you can't pull it together."

She'd been staring out the window but turned her head with glacial slowness until their eyes met. Hers were dull, bloodshot, and apathetic. She sneered and spit through the metal mesh that separated the good guys from the bad guys in the police car. "Fuck off, Craigy," she said.

Shaking his head, Craig got out and hauled her out of the backseat. "Don't you care about anyone but yourself?"

She glanced at him, scorn burring in her eyes. "You still here? That's kind of a record for you, ain't it?"

Craig blushed to the roots of his hair. Without another word, he turned, took her elbow, and pulled her toward the doctor's office.

4

The serene calm in the car shattered like candy-glass when Billy slapped his hands over his ears and screamed.

"What's wrong, honey," asked Karen.

"I don't want to hear him anymore," Billy whined. "Make him stop, Mommy."

Karen arched an eyebrow and turned to her two other sons. "Which of you is tormenting your brother?" Johnny looked half asleep, and Benny was staring out the window at the passing trees, a little drool running down his chin—neither looked guilty. "Who is bothering you, Big Bill?" she asked.

"Mommy," he whined.

"I'm here, baby," she crooned.

"Is he dreaming?" asked Jim.

"No, he's awake, staring out the window."

Jim looked out his window, but there was nothing to see but the green blur of the trees they whizzed by. "Then what?"

"Mommy, make him stop. *Please*, Mommy. I don't want to hear it."

"Honey, what can I do?" The mild amusement that had been in her voice a moment before evaporated, replaced by a dollop of fear. "Turn on the radio, Jim."

Jim glanced at her, but reached over and spun the volume knob until the faint sound of country music filled the car.

Billy screamed. "*Mommy! Mommy! Mommy!*"

Karen reacted as if slapped. She sat there a moment, gaze glued to Billy's scrunched up face.

"Shut up, spaz," murmured Benny. Johnny didn't react at all. It was as if he were in a trance.

"Shove over you two," she said and climbed over the seat into the back. She wedged herself between Johnny and Billy and wrapped her arms around her youngest boy. "It's okay, Billy," she crooned. "Mommy's here."

"*He's scary, Mommy! I don't like him no more! Make him leave me alone!*" Billy wailed.

"Who, honey? Who?" Karen asked, shooting a desperate glance at Jim in the rearview mirror.

"*The king! The king!*"

Jim took his foot off the gas and pulled toward the shoulder of the road.

"*No!*" wailed Billy. "*Don't stop, Daddy! Don't let him get me!*"

"Spazoid," muttered Benny.

"That's enough, Benjamin," snapped Jim. With a glance at his wife, he accelerated back onto the road proper. "What do we do?" he asked.

"How would I know? He's never acted like this. Never!"

"*Ah! He's got me! He's got me, Mommy!*"

"No one has you, Billy. It's my arm around you, see?" She rubbed his shoulder.

Billy screamed like he was on fire. "*It hurts! He's hurting me, Mommy! Daddy! Make him stop! Make him stop!*"

"Who?" Jim asked, exasperation and fear warring for dominance of his tone.

"*Drive faster!*" Karen yelled. "Find a doctor or hospital."

Jim floored the accelerator and drove like a madman, the Rocket 455 Oldsmobile engine roaring. The trees flashing by on the side of the road seemed to loom overhead, reaching with crooked branches toward the car. "Get a hold of yourself," he muttered.

5

Candy jerked her arm out of Craig's grasp and tottered into the doctor's office. She walked past the reception area and teetered into the hall outside the examination room, her eyes heavy, a sheen of sweat on her forehead. "Might get sick," she muttered.

Doc Hauser twitched an eyebrow at Craig, who nodded as if to say, "I told you so." Dawn handed Candy a stainless-steel specimen tray.

"Mrs. Burton," said Doc Hauser. "Your son here has—"

"It's Ms. Burton. I never married."

Hauser didn't even blink. "Ms. Burton, your son needs you."

"You're the doctor. What in the hell can I do?"

"You're the mother, dear," said Dawn. "Doc Hauser can only fix the physical injuries. He needs warmth, comfort."

Candy glared at the nurse balefully. "You judging me too?"

"No, dear. You asked, is all." She patted Candy on the arm. "Can I get you a seltzer or something?"

Candy shook her head.

"Fine. Let me take you in to see Toby.

Craig sidled up next to Hauser and grimaced. "She's a wreck."

Hauser nodded, head tilted toward the door.

6

"Drive faster, Jim! Something is *wrong*!"

"Be calm! Everyone stay calm!" Jim yelled over the noise of the engine.

"Mommy," Billy muttered. "The king...the king..."

"What king, honey?" Karen asked and reached to smooth his hair. Billy's eyes rolled up until nothing showed but the sclera. His arms and legs twitched back and forth. Another scream ripped from his lips. "Jim! Jim!"

"What is it? What?"

Billy thrashed violently in the back seat. His head whipped back and forth, flinging spit and white froth through the air. His sclera went pink as blood vessels in his eyes burst. His feet kicked the back of the driver's seat hard enough to cause Jim pain.

"What's he doing, Karen?"

"I...I don't know..."

"Spazoid is having a convulsion," said Benny in a singsong voice.

"Benny, you're not helping," said Jim. "Stop calling him that."

"Tell him to stop being such a spaz and I will."

"Benjamin James Cartwright! You cut that out, or I'll pull this car over and tan your backside!"

"Stop the car, and he dies," said Benny in a flat voice.

"What?" asked Karen. "What are you talking about Benny?"

Benny was still staring out the window, hands twitching in his lap. "The game," he murmured. "I'm talking about the game the king plays."

"What? What game?"

Benny said no more, just stared into the woods speeding by outside his window.

"Benny, answer your mother!"

"Oh, never mind him, Jim! Find a doctor!"

"What the hell do you think I'm doing, Karen?"

7

When Candy started to cry, Hauser nodded. "That's what I was waiting for," he said.

"For her to cry?"

"No, for her to realize her son is in danger. Let's go in." The old man ushered Craig into the exam room. Candy sat on the table next to her son. She had her arm around him and was crying into his hair. "Officer Witherson here brought your boy in, Ms. Burton. You owe him your thanks."

For the second time that morning, Craig blushed to the roots of his hair.

"What the hell happened to my son?" Candy shrieked. "He's so thin!" She stood and stepped a few feet away from Toby, hands limp at her sides, shoulders slumped.

"He's been missing for the best part of a week, Candy," said Craig Witherson. "You'd know that if you ever crawled up out of the bottle." Doc Hauser put his hand on Craig's arm and shook his head.

"He's a little malnourished, Ms. Burton, but it's nothing a few good meals won't fix," said the old doctor. "I've seen much worse in my day, believe you me. You can hug him, he won't break."

As if she'd been waiting for permission, Candy lurched across the space dividing her from her son and wrapped him in her arms. "Oh, my poor baby!" she crooned. "Mommy's here. Mommy's here now."

"Now, now, Ms. Burton. He'll be fine. *Physically*, at least."

She turned her head to glare at Doc Hauser. "What's that supposed to mean?"

"Nothing, dear," said Hauser. "The boy's suffered unimaginable terrors in his time in the hands of his cap…in his time away."

"He was just lost," Candy snapped.

"Maybe that's the truth of it," said the old man. "Maybe you're right. But it doesn't matter. Not really. Just look at him, Ms. Burton."

Candy took a half-step back and looked down at her son. He was staring at her stomach with an expression that might as well have been carved from wood. "Toby," she said. "Look at Momma." The boy didn't move. His eyes twitched to the side like maybe he thought the nurse was his mother. Candy slapped him. "Snap out it, Toby!"

Toby's head twisted to the side with the force of the blow, but other than that, he didn't react.

Candy pulled her hand back for another slap, but before she could loose the blow, Craig stepped forward and grabbed her wrist. "That'll be enough of that, Candy," he snarled.

8

Billy's whole body was jerking, and, despite Karen's best efforts, he was beating himself to a pulp on hard parts of the car. He was making a low groaning noise and frothing at the mouth.

Jim took his eyes off the road long enough to glance at the backseat in the rearview mirror. Karen was crying, and next to her in the backseat, her two other boys were sitting as still as statues. No one spoke. Neither boy looked at either parent or at Billy. Benny stared out the side window, and Johnny had his eyes closed as if he were napping.

Jim brought his eyes back to the road and panicked. A man stood in the middle of his lane, watching the brown car race toward him. Jim kicked the brake pedal hard and jerked the wheel to the left. The big car slewed into the other lane, back end jumping out, threatening to slide off the road.

The man in the road never moved, except to track the car with his eyes.

For a moment, Jim thought he had no face—that bone gleamed where skin should have been—and that his eyes were twin points of red like the light cast off by hot coals. Jim blinked and saw he was mistaken. It was a normal man. The car was still skidding, the rear end sliding closer and closer to the trees.

Jim took his foot off the brake and mashed the gas pedal to the floor. The rear tires spun, leaving smoking rubber skid marks behind as they fought for traction. Jim glanced to his left and gasped, much closer to the trunks of all those trees than he'd thought. Then the rear tires caught, and the car lurched ahead in the wrong lane.

Jim turned and looked at the man in the road, who was now facing the car. His mouth moved as if he were speaking, and Billy uttered a choking scream from the back seat. The man's eyes locked on Jim's and he smiled and winked. The man held out his hand and beckoned, his eyes shifting away from Jim's.

In the backseat, Benny tried to stand up. He hit his head on the roof but never made a sound. His eyes were glued to the man in the road. Benny folded the passenger seat forward and tried to reach the door handle. "Benny! What are you doing!" yelled Jim. "Sit down!" Benny never paused in trying to get the door open. Behind him, Johnny giggled. "Grab him, Karen!"

"I'm holding on to Billy with everything I have!"

"Grab him before he gets the door open! He'll die if he falls out at this speed!"

Karen grabbed Benny by the waistband of his jeans and jerked him sideways. The boy fell over Johnny's legs and ended up in Karen's lap. She clamped her elbow across his chest and went back to trying to hold Billy still.

Jim elbowed the passenger seat back into place—at least they'd have a little warning if Johnny tried to get out.

"Don't stop, Jim," said Karen in a monotone, her eyes tracking the man in the road. "I don't like the looks of him."

"No shit," muttered Jim.

9

"What in the hell is wrong with him?" she asked, half to herself. "Toby, what the hell is the matter with you?"

"Hysterical catatonia," said Doc Hauser. "It results from trauma the mind can't deal with."

"He's not crazy! Don't make him out to be crazy!"

"It's not crazy, Ms. Burton. It's completely normal. You know how when you see something horrific—a traffic accident or something like that—how your mind freezes for a few beats? Well, it's the same thing for Toby. He's suffered a trauma that his mind can't face so to protect itself, it's shut itself off. The thinking part, anyway."

Candy looked from Doc Hauser to Toby and back again. "What kind of trauma?" The muscles around her right eye twitched.

Doc Hauser spread his hands. "I've no idea, Ms. Burton. No one will know until Toby decides to speak to us."

"Give him a pill or something!"

Doc Hauser smiled his benign, I'm-only-human smile he reserved for distraught mothers. "I'm afraid it's not that simple, Ms. Burton. Toby will need specialized care for a while."

"What do you mean specialized care? You're not taking my kid away from me."

"No, no, nothing of the sort, Ms. Burton. I'd like to admit Toby to Strong Memorial Hospital in Rochester. He'd be cared for in a safe setting, by specialists."

"Shrinks."

"Well, yes, amongst others. He'll have constant supervision and constant access to—"

"No," said Candy in a flat voice. "Absolutely not."

"Ms. Burton, if it's a matter of cost, the hospital has a program—"

"I said no. I'm not putting Toby into a nuthatch."

Doc Hauser looked nonplussed. He glanced at Craig.

"Candy," said Craig in a voice just above a whisper. She looked at him and shook her head. "Listen to me, Candy. Toby needs care. If you don't let Doc Hauser admit him, who will give him that care?"

"I will. I'm his mother."

Craig nodded, then shrugged. "And after a few hours have elapsed and you decide it's time for a little drink? After four hours when you're fall-down drunk? Who cares for him then, Candy?"

She sneered at him and rocked her head back and forth like a kid yelling "neener-neener."

"Toby needs you to be an adult, here, Candy."

"Don't you tell me how to raise my kid, Craigy. You had your chance."

Craig blushed to his roots again. "Who are you really worried about, Candy? Toby or yourself? You've spent the last eleven years putting yourself above Toby's needs. You've spent the last eleven years letting monsters like Fergusson into your life, and Toby paid the price for that, too. Hell, Fergusson might be the one who did this to Toby. You ever think of that, Candy? He beat him, maybe he didn't stop there."

"You bastard," Candy seethed.

"Maybe I am," said Craig in a reasonable tone. "Maybe I hurt you back in high school, maybe I'm partially to blame for how your lives have turned out, but—"

"*Maybe?*" sneered Candy.

"—Toby needs this. Don't you want him to recover? Don't you want him to be able to name his attackers? Do you think that *lessens* your responsibility for what happened to him?"

The room was still and silent. Candy was looking at the floor, and a single teardrop fell from her face to the ground. "Fuck you, Craig," she whispered. She turned to look at her son. She cupped her hand under his chin and lifted his face until he was looking her in the eye. Crying silently, she stood there for a moment without speaking. Finally, she let go of his chin and hugged him. When she let him go, she straightened and wiped the tears from her face. Without looking at Craig, she walked to the door. "You'll take care of it, Doctor?"

Doc Hauser said, "Of course. I'll have Dawn call you with his room number."

Candy nodded.

"Can I drive you home, Candy?" Craig asked.

"No. I'd rather walk," she said with frost in her voice. "And about what I said in the car, consider the invitation revoked."

10

Owen followed his companion through the woods, trying to walk as silently as she did. She was as beautiful from behind as she was from the front. Her hair hung to the small of her back and glistened in the sunshine like gold. She seemed to glide along, above the carpet of fallen leaves and twigs.

"Hey," Owen whispered. "What should I call you?"

She tilted her head to the side as if considering the question. "You may call me Brigitta," she said with a bright tinkle of laughter.

"Brigitta? What the hell kind of name is that?"

"A Danish one."

"Are you from Denmark?"

Again, she laughed her bright laugh. "I don't know how to answer that question."

Owen shook his head. "It seems like a simple question to me."

The wind-chime laugh sounded again, and it was his only answer.

"At least tell me where we are going."

"I have a treat for you, Owen. Don't ruin the surprise."

He sighed and shook his head as she laughed at him again.

She led him to the edge of the woods. Beyond the border, a gray ribbon of macadam stretched into the distance, running parallel to the boundary of the forest.

He was about to make a sarcastic comment about Brigitta's navigation skills when he saw Candy Burton walking along the opposite edge of the road. A vicious smile stretched across his face.

"Surprise," whispered Brigitta with a mischievous gleam in her eye. Owen nodded and shouldered his rifle. She lay a cool hand on his arm. "Wait. I'll get her to stop."

"How—" he started, but she was already running through the woods parallel to the road, footsteps making no sound.

As she ran, her form shimmered and jittered, like the image of a decaying old home movie. She was shrinking and fading away. By the time she pushed through the underbrush and onto the shoulder of the road, Owen couldn't see her at all.

"Toby?" Candy yelled. "Toby, is that you?" She lurched out into the road, heading for the other shoulder. "Why aren't you with Doc Hauser?" She paused as if she were listening to something, but Owen couldn't hear what.

Candy came to a halt with one foot on each side of the dashed yellow line in the center of the asphalt. She bent and held out her arms.

Owen didn't need to be prompted. He snapped the rifle up to his shoulder, sighted through the scope, and squeezed the trigger. Blood erupted from Candy's right thigh, a few inches above her knee. The force of the bullet swept her leg out from under her, and she pitched forward into the road. She screamed and grabbed her leg.

His hands jerked the bolt back without having to think about it. The used brass flew through the air, and he slammed the bolt forward. Candy was screaming and rocking side to side in the road when Owen stepped out of the sheltering woods. Her eyes were squeezed shut.

"Candy, you bitch, look at me," he said in a conversational tone. "I promise, baby, I'll never hit you again."

One of her eyes cracked open, and she stopped rocking. When her gaze locked on his, she screamed in fear. Her hands scrabbled on the macadam, looking for purchase as she pulled her good leg under her. Owen let her try to stand, and when she made it up on one leg and tried to hop away, he shouldered the rifle and shot her in the left leg. Candy fell to the side, shrieking in pain. Owen walked toward her, working the bolt on the rifle and enjoying how the sound of it made her flinch away.

"Where are you going, baby?" he crooned. "Don't you want to get back together?"

"No! Stay away!"

Chuckling, he raised the rifle and shot at her without aiming. He was less than ten feet away, and the round took her in the shoulder.

"Hurry, Owen," said Brigitta. "Someone's coming."

Owen turned and looked, but didn't see anything—not Brigitta, not a car. "How do you know?"

"Hurry!" Brigitta hissed.

"I want to savor it, I want to—" Then he heard it. The sound of an engine coming from town. "Damn it! I didn't want this to be rushed!" He turned back to Candy and smiled at the hope he saw on her face. "Don't worry, baby, there's still time." He shouldered the rifle for the final time and aimed through the scope. The bullet hit her above her eye, the force of it smashing her head against the asphalt so hard her head bounced. "Bye-bye, you bitch," he said.

"They are *coming*! Hurry up," said Brigitta.

Owen slung the rifle over his shoulder, eyes twitching around, looking for his spent brass. The sound of the engine was getting louder.

"Come away! Come away now!"

He didn't want to leave the brass, but his desire to get away without being seen won out. Like a wolf, Owen Gray bolted into the forest.

11

Matt Greshin rubbed his aching eyes. After talking to Jim Cartwright, he'd spent fruitless hours trying to track Randy Fergusson's movements. The guy had no arrest record, which, given his proclivity to run his trap, seemed unlikely. What was worse was that there was no record of the guy of any kind. Not anywhere. No social security number, no driver's license, no tax records, no military record—nothing. That could mean only one thing: Randy Fergusson was fictional—an assumed identity—and Matt had no idea who he was really dealing with.

And that was bad. He'd thought he had a read on the guy, and maybe he did, but he'd never gotten even a hint that the guy was more than he was pretending to be. That was worse than bad.

He'd rolled around to Candy Burton's house as soon as the sun came up, but she was gone. Matt wrote himself a note to remember to track her down.

He picked up his office phone and took a slug of cold, bitter coffee. With a grimace, he replaced the receiver and stomped into the break room. Dispatch on the weekends routed emergency calls to the officer on duty, so Matt had the place to himself. He set a fresh pot of coffee brewing and trudged back to his office.

With a sigh, he picked up the phone and dialed Tom Walton's home number. He hated calling people on Sunday morning, but Tom needed to know about Bobby—if he didn't already.

"Walton."

"Hey, Tom, it's Matt. I've got bad news."

"Okay."

Matt could hear the calm veneer of Cop-Mode in Tom's voice. "It's about Bobby Jefferson. Have you heard anything?"

"No, I only just got back from a camping trip. What's up?"

"Someone murdered Bobby and Meredith yesterday. Shot with a rifle."

The line buzzed for a moment. "That's…"

"Horrible, yeah," said Matt. "You remember the dipshit we got cleaned up over to your place the other night?"

"Yeah, squirrelly fellow, right?"

"I think he's the doer."

"Well, fuck." Tom sounded exhausted.

"You can say that again."

"How's Gary handling it?"

"He ain't, he asked me to handle it." Matt sighed and rubbed his hand through his hair.

"No one ever accused him of being stupid. You get any sleep?"

"No, but listen, Tom. I want your help on this."

"Whatever you need me to do, Matt. You know that."

"Yeah, thanks. The guy gave us a fake name."

"Have anything on him?"

"At the moment? Not a thing. I'm going to see his old lady later today, but...well, she's a bit of a drunk. Plus, she's not cooperative. She's the mother of the missing kid."

"Perfect. The little shit good for the kid too?"

"I don't think so. But hell, if he could fool me this bad, maybe he could fool me about that too."

"Don't beat yourself up."

"The guy shot at Jim Cartwright's kid out in the woods."

"Well, fuck. This call's loads of fun, Matt."

"You should be on this end of it."

"Yeah. What do you need? Manpower?"

"No doubt. I've got to go walking in the woods later, looking for a bullet in a tree. And I've got to track down Mr. Not-Fergusson. I'm pretty sure he's not in Oneka Falls."

"But not as sure he's not in Genosgwa or Cottonwood Vale."

"That's right," said Matt.

Craig Witherson walked in, missing his usual grin. "Toby's back."

"What? Hey Tom, Craig's here and says the kid is back. Can you get a few guys going around to your hotels and barns?"

"Yeah, anything you need. I'll call Morton, too. Get him on board and doing the same. Then I'm headed your way."

"Good enough. See you later." Matt set the receiver down in its cradle and looked up at Craig. "He's alive?"

Craig nodded.

"He say who did this to him?"

Craig shook his head. "Old Doc Hauser says it's hysterical catatonia. He's shipping him to Strong in Rochester."

The skin between Matt's eyebrows wrinkled. "We've got to try to get him to talk to us first, Craig. You know that."

Craig shook his head again. "Wasted effort, Matt. He didn't even react to Candy."

"You know where she is?"

"I did, but she wouldn't let me drive her home."

Matt arched his eyebrows.

"I had to…we had words about what's best for Toby. She didn't much like it."

"Let's go track her down," Matt said in a weary tone.

They piled into Matt's cruiser and drove to the Burton residence. Candy wasn't there yet, so they drove toward Doc Hauser's place, using the most likely route, but still didn't find her.

"Well, what now?" Matt asked.

"Why are you asking me?"

"You dated her for a while, right?"

"That was a long time ago, Chief."

"Still."

Craig shook his head. "She was still drunk at Doc Hauser's. Not a lot, but even so. There's no telling what she'd do."

Matt sighed and let the car roll to a halt in front of the doctor's office.

"Maybe…"

"What is it, Craig?"

"She used to hike on the Oneka Trail when she was upset. The one that goes along the edge of the river. Said the sound of the river calmed her."

"Worth a shot," said Matt, throwing the car into gear. The Oneka Trail met the road about three miles outside of town and Matt drove out there.

"What's that in the road?" asked Craig as they crested the large hill on the edge of town. "Someone lying in the road?"

"Is it Candy?"

"I…I think so."

"Oh, for fuck's sake," muttered Matt. "Not another one." He skidded to a halt about twenty yards from the body. It was Candy Burton, no question. "Shot four times," he said.

Craig walked to the side of the road and squatted. When he stood, he had a spent rifle cartridge on the end of his pen. "He got sloppy this time."

"Let's hope there's a print. Better call this in, Craig. Get the ME rolling." Matt turned his cruiser to block the road.

12

Jim brought the Oldsmobile to a skidding halt in front of the Emergency Room doors of Cuba Memorial Hospital. Billy had stopped convulsing, but Karen had been unable to rouse him since then. He got out of the car and slammed the driver's seat forward. He bent down and tried to take Billy off Karen's lap, but she gripped the boy hard. "Hand him to me, Karen. I'll carry him into the ER." She looked up with tear-filled eyes. She let go of Billy, and Jim lifted him out of the car. He sprinted inside, leaving Karen to get the other boys out of the car and bring them into the hospital.

Karen climbed out of the car and told the boys to follow her. Both boys sat where they were, not moving, not even looking up at her. Exasperated, she slapped her hand on the roof of the car. "Boys, get your butts out of the car right now!" Neither boy so much as twitched at the sound of her hand on the roof, but, after a moment, they turned toward her. Benny pushed Johnny's shoulder, and the boys slid out of the car. "Nice to know you can both still move. Now, we're going into this hospital to see about Billy. It will take a long time, and it's going to be boring. Both of you had better sit still, and I don't want to hear a peep." With that, she turned and walked toward the doors, leaving the boys to close the door and follow.

Benny shoved Johnny ahead of him and watched as his brother lurched after their mother. Benny shot a glance toward the woods bordering the hospital campus, and a small smile played on his lips. He looked back in time to watch his mother go through the doors. Johnny stopped at the doors like he didn't know what to do, but when he looked back, Benny made shooing motions, and Johnny went inside with a nod.

Benny turned and sprinted toward the woods. No one noticed him running away from the hospital.

No one, that is, except the king of the woods. As he crossed the border into the forest, the man smiled at him and tossled his hair, and then touched Benny on the cheek. Benny flopped to the ground unconscious. The man's smile stretched wide.

Chapter 6

2007

I

The sun had almost set by the time Drew recovered enough courage to go back to Oneka Falls. Dressed for work as he called it—black cargo pants, black hoodie, skintight black leather gloves, black tactical boots—he parked his BMW a block north of the Town Hall and got out.

He sprinted across the street and stood outside the bank, pretending to look for his debit card while watching the street in the reflection of the big glass panel window. Satisfied that no one on the street gave a shit about him, he turned and walked to the intersection of Union and Main.

The creepy church hunched a block from the intersection on a ninety-degree bend in the road so that the front of the church faced Main Street. The sight of it made Drew a little hinky, a little nauseated.

LaBouche had looked straight at him. *No way he didn't see me,* he thought. *No way he didn't recognize me.* He walked up Union toward the leering edifice of the white clapboard church, tension mounting across his shoulders with each step, nerves jangling. Another run in with LaBouche was the last thing he needed, but he had to know what was going on in that old church.

By the time he reached the ninety-degree bend, night had fallen over the town like a shroud. The night was dead quiet, no shouts of playing children, no traffic noise, no good-hearted banter from backyard barbeques or campfires.

He stood across from Play Time for a moment, just looking at the place. It seemed to loom over that part of Union Street, casting its shadow over everything. Lights flickered inside, making the images in the stained-glass windows dance and leap. The old building creaked in the wind, seeming to breathe in the night air.

With a shiver, Drew darted across the narrow lane, but he didn't climb the steps to the double doors. He sidled around to the north side, trying to mask his nerves—to move like he had every reason to be there.

The side of the old church had been neglected, siding boards warped and bowed, paint peeling, plants dead in the flower beds, garbage drifting across the small side yard in the weak wind. Drew took a deep breath through his nose and almost gagged at the stench the old building gave off. It smelled of old blood, rot, and decay.

He turned the corner to the back of the building and spotted the thing he needed: the bulkhead doors to the cellar. A rusty chain and ancient-looking padlock secured the doors, but that presented no barrier for Drew. With a grin, he fished his lock picks out of his backpack and opened the old lock in a trice. He removed the chain and opened the doors, careful not to make any noise.

The stench that assaulted him from the open cellar put the stench in the side yard to shame. Eyes watering from the reek, Drew descended the narrow steps into the clammy darkness. The odor lashed out at him like a physical attack. He coughed, and the smell coated his tongue, tasting of spoiled meat, mold, and darkness.

The cellar was pitch black, and Drew pulled his night-vision setup out of his pack and slid it on, fighting his gag reflex. He put his hand over his nose and mouth, and that helped to cut the barbarity of the stench but didn't eliminate it.

The cellar flashed to life around him, painted in the fuzzy green light of night vision when he flicked the unit on. He stood at the end of a narrow hall, not wide enough for more than a single man, and even then, the man would have to twist his shoulders to avoid brushing against the grimy walls. Doors lined the hall, spaced about four feet apart. Each door had an iron U-shaped bolt set into its face, and each jamb had an iron hasp bent to attach to the bolt. All the doors were closed, but only some of them had the hasp thrown closed.

Drew took three steps to the closest unlocked door and put his hand on the cold wood. He pushed the door with his fingers, expecting the shriek of old, rusty hinges, but the door swung inward without a sound. Inside, a low table dominated the center of the small four feet by six feet room. The table took up most of the space, and on the edge closest to the door, large, U-shaped clamps hung open on the corners. A single hook sat in the middle of the far edge of the table.

Along one wall hung instruments of savage torture: a meat fork coated in dried blood, a heavy looking cleaver, a set of iron coal-tongs, an icepick, a pruning saw, a one-handed sledge hammer, several lumps of iron whose only function could be branding flesh, and a long-bladed Bowie knife. A narrow counter with a brazier filled with old, cold coals occupied the other side of the room. The table bore the marks of the instruments of torture, in addition to dried blood and other bodily fluids.

Shivering, Drew backed out of the claustrophobic space and went to the next door. The hasp was thrown to the side, so Drew pushed the door open. It swung inward, again without a sound, and revealed the body of a teenaged girl. Her blonde hair was matted to her skull by blood and sweat. The U-shaped clamps at the end of the table secured her thighs, right above her knees, keeping her legs spread. Her arms were wrenched upward and back so that her wrists were behind her head. A mass of burns, cuts, and dark abrasions covered her skin. A rictus of horror and pain twisted her face, her eyes staring blindly at the ceiling. The tools hanging on the wall still glistened with the girl's blood, and some of them still glowed. The brazier glowed with hot coals, and next to it, the girl's clothes and purse lay, contents spilled across the counter and floor.

Drew found her ID card and frowned down at it. "Rebecca Lewis," the card read. He glanced at the picture and then the face of the dead girl on the table. *It's her,* he thought. *Wonder if she's related to Trooper Lewis? If she was, and that's what brought LaBouche here...*

He slipped the ID into his pack and backed out of the room, leaving the door ajar. He knew what Play Time was now—a place of nightmares, a Gehenna, where demons tortured humans to death and fed on their pain.

A restaurant for demons.

He couldn't let it stand. Drew had to do something about it, to call the authorities, but who could he trust?

And what could he say if he found someone trustworthy? He'd never met another soul who could see the demons—not anyone "sane" anyway. He couldn't just call the police and say: "Yeah, I followed a demon to this place and went in the cellar and found a dead body." They'd think he did it. They'd think he was nuts, and he'd end up back in Millvale.

Millvale? What the hell is Millvale? he thought.

You know, answered a small voice in the back of his head. *You remember.*

But he didn't.

He shook his head and checked another room—empty. Then he saw the next door was secured by the iron hasp. He flipped the hasp open, and someone inside the room screamed. "Shhh!" Drew hissed. He opened the door and stepped inside. Above his head, footsteps rumbled across the floor, and a door slammed. The woman secured to the table screamed again. "Shhh! I'm here to help you," breathed Drew. Another door slammed, and footsteps pounded down the stairs. "I'll try to come back for you," he whispered. He backed out of the room and glanced toward the other end of the narrow hall. Vague shadows danced on the wall. Vague, but hulking shadows.

Drew turned and sprinted for the stairs leading up to the backyard. Behind him, the woman screamed a third time. He pounded up the stairs toward the night sky framed by the cellar bulkhead, and over the din he heard a guttural snarl at the other end of the hall. "Who the fuck is down here?" Another loud, guttural snarl followed the question. "Who the *fuck* left the damn cellar doors open?"

Drew burst out into the night air and sprinted for the woods at the back of the lot. If the demon in the cellar saw him, his life would end down there in one of those basement cells. He sprinted through the woods, leaping over fallen logs, dodging old stumps, breath whistling from his throat. Fear had wrapped its icy tendrils around his conscious mind, but it wasn't the normal fear he had of the demons. He was used to that. This was something else...something more. Something old and buried.

The fear threatened to take over, to send him flying through the woods without thought, without plan—a headlong run until he either tripped and fell or broke free of the trees. Something about running through the woods, maybe pursued by a demon, maybe pursued by his own terrors, heightened his dread. Every sound he heard sent a bolt of pure horror screaming along his nerves. Every shadow seemed to loom at him, to threaten him with ungovernable, childlike nightmare images.

His pulse banged through his veins like a trip hammer forming molten metal, thundering in his ears. His jaw ached from clenching his teeth together so hard they creaked. His legs screamed like they would give out at any moment, and his chest hoicked and wheezed like it would burst, and soon. *What is this?* he screamed at himself. *What am I so scared of?*

SHUT UP AND RUN, YOU FOOL! a voice screamed in his head.

An image of an eyeless dog-like creature flashed through his mind, lightning-quick, adrenaline-laden. His vision flashed black for a moment, and he slammed into the trunk of a tree, abrading his cheek, shoving the night-vision set to the side.

He clamped his teeth together against a scream of pure terror, and the darkness fell on him like a pack of marauding wolves. *Something is out there!*

THAT'S WHAT I'VE BEEN TELLING YOU!

Drew ran blind, trying to right the night-vision goggles, but too panicked to stop to do it. He bounced from tree to tree, getting a bruise here, a scrape there. Something tangled between his legs, and he fell. His mind's eye drowned in images of dog-like things pouring out of the darkness, drool glistening from their open jaws, moonlight glinting off their fangs. He rolled, frantic, sweeping his arms to the sides to bat away the creatures.

A horrendous crash sounded next to his head, and the reek of garbage washed over him. He swept his goggles off his head at last. A metal garbage can loomed at him from the side. The hose and sprinkler he'd tripped over lay tangled in his feet. *Someone's backyard...* He sighed with relief.

"A little too much to drink tonight?" asked an amused man.

Drew turned and saw an old man sitting in a deck chair, holding a beer and a cigar. Drew covered his eyes with his hand, knowing, *knowing*, that the man was a trick, a hallucination. He shook his head and jerked his hand away. The man still sat there, still smiling.

"Or something stronger than drink, perhaps?" The man chuckled.

One of his patented "aw-shucks" grins swept across Drew's face without the need for conscious thought. "Damn goggles," he said, pointing at his night vision set, now hanging around his neck. "I wasn't looking and ran into a tree. Knocked them sideways so I couldn't see."

"Oh," said the man, smile widening.

"Yeah," Drew laughed. "Pretty stupid."

"Kind of like running around in the woods at night without a light." The man's droll tone didn't sound unkind.

Drew stood up and brushed off his knees. "That sounds about right. I got all turned around."

"I'd say. Where you headed?"

"I was…looking for deer."

The man cocked his head to the side, a puzzled look in his eye. "Deer?"

"Yeah."

"Out-of-towner, are you?"

"Yeah," Drew repeated. "Rochester."

"No deer in Rochester?"

Drew shrugged and pulled the night vision goggles off over his head. He shoved them into his pack.

"Do I know you?" asked the old man. "You've got a familiar look to you. Grow up around here?"

Drew shook his head. "Nope."

"Rochester?"

Drew shrugged and glanced at the driveway leading to the street.

"Related to anyone in Oneka Falls?"

"Not that I know of. I need to get back to my car."

"Name Witherson mean anything to you?"

Drew looked at the man, expression bland. "Nope."

"Well, I can see you want to be on your way, son. No need to be embarrassed."

Drew chuckled and shoved his hands in the pockets of his cargo pants.

"No, I mean it, son. Stumbling into my yard tonight ain't even on the scale of things around here."

A small grin crinkled the corners of Drew's mouth, but he dropped his eyes.

The man sighed. "Well, I tried."

Drew nodded. "Thanks," he murmured.

"I'll not hold you up, son." Without taking his eyes off Drew, he puffed on his cigar, the coal at the end flaring in the darkness.

"Uh, thanks," Drew murmured again. He started for the drive and then turned back. "Sorry, but—"

"End of the driveway's Pembroke."

Drew lifted his shoulders and let them drop. "Rochester, remember?"

The man laughed and pointed with his cigar. "Head that-a-way. Couple of blocks drops you out on Mill Lane."

"M-mill?"

"Yep. Take it that way," he said, jabbing the air with his cigar. "Half a mile, you come to Main Street."

"Is there another way?"

The man cocked his head to the side and stared at Drew through the fragrant smoke. "Mill Lane mean something to you, son?" he asked.

Drew shook his head. "No. Nothing."

The man narrowed his eyes but then nodded. "Sorry, son. Pembroke's a dead ender. Quarter mile or so, you can take Union Street, but that's the long way 'round."

Drew nodded and waved his thanks. He turned and trudged down the drive. The last thing he wanted to do was retrace his steps through the woods. The next-to-last thing was walking around on Union. He sighed. *Mill Lane it is.*

2

Exhaustion beat down on Scott, not only from the worry, the fear, but from spending the afternoon and half the evening doing nothing—waiting for LaBouche. When LaBouche's car finally turned into the driveway, fury blasted through him with each beat of his heart. He was out the front door before LaBouche even turned off his headlights. "What the *fuck*, Lee!"

LaBouche got out of the car, arms up, palms toward Lewis. "I know, I know, partner, and I'm sorry." He kicked his front tire. "Fucking thing! First the flat tire, and then the fucker broke down! Piece of shit!"

Scott stood staring at him, the sense that LaBouche was laughing at him so strong that if he kept walking, he would be on LaBouche and throwing punches in a flash. "Broke down?" he asked in a flat, wooden voice.

"Yeah. Damn thing popped the radiator hose on one of those long empty stretches of road. I had to walk twenty miles to the next town, buy a hose, then walk twenty miles back." LaBouche slumped onto the hood of the car and lit a cigarette.

"You walked forty miles today?"

"Yeah, I even ran part of it."

Scott looked down at his watch. "In six hours? You walked forty miles and drove, what, eighty, in six hours?"

LaBouche stood up straight. "Now, Scott, I know you're upset, and I'm making allowances, but it sounds like you are calling me a liar. After all the shit I went through to get here..."

Lewis scoffed, arms folded across his chest, eyes blazing.

"Hey, man, if you don't need my help anymore, I can always—"

A pent-up breath exploded out of Scott's chest. "No, Lee. I'm sorry, okay. I can't... I'm just..."

LaBouche smiled from ear to ear. "Letting it all hang out?"

"Yeah," sighed Scott. "What am I supposed to think, to fucking do? It's about twenty-four hours since she left for her date with that little shit-stain. When I find him, I'm going to—"

"Stand back and let your old partner Lee do the talking." LaBouche used his no-arguments voice. "You hear me, Scotty? If he did something, God forbid, if he did something to your daughter, the state will make him pay, not you."

"Yeah," said Scott. "If...*If* we find him. *If* there's enough evidence. *If* the prosecutor is worth a shit."

LaBouche shrugged. "If it doesn't happen, Scotty, you and me will make the fuck pay. Okay?"

Scott nodded. "Let's get going. I need to be doing something, Lee."

"Yep, I get that. Should you leave Jenny alone though?"

Scott nodded. "Neighbor lady's over."

"Okay, let's go. I'll drive."

They piled into LaBouche's Maxima, and as the car settled under Lee's weight, Scott wondered for the millionth time why he would drive such a small car. Like the last sardine wedged into a can, LaBouche hunched behind the wheel. He had to lean to the right to get the driver's side door closed. "Okay, where's the shit-stain live?"

Scott unfolded a now-worn scrap of his wife's note paper. "Jenny, she…Jenny made him leave his address."

LaBouche took the paper and entered the address into his GPS. "I don't know, Scotty. That looks like a bunch of empty land. Did you check this place out?"

Scott hung his head. "Jenny told me not to be paranoid."

"Well," said LaBouche in an upbeat tone that sounded forced. "We'll be paranoid together and go check this shit out."

Scott squinted at the nav system screen. "Must be off that little gravel road, yeah?"

LaBouche shrugged. "We'll find out." He drove, following the navigation systems' instructions. When the car informed them the destination was on the left, Scott's heart fell. The "house" was a big empty space blocked off by a chain link fence.

"You sure this is the address?"

3

Drew drove past the blue Maxima parked in front of the abandoned quarry on Old Penfield Road. LaBouche and Lewis were just sitting there, staring at the empty lot where the quarry used to stage delivery trucks. He continued past and turned onto Sable Oaks Lane. He turned around and tucked his Honda off to the side of the road where the trees made it hard to see him from Old Penfield Road.

Drew had wanted to get Trooper Lewis alone, but by the time he'd gotten the RV tucked in, driven back to Rochester and switched cars, he'd been too late. He'd arrived at the address on Becky Lewis' ID a few minutes behind LaBouche.

He didn't know how he would convince Lewis that he wasn't a serial killer, since he technically was, or how to prove he hadn't killed Lewis' daughter, but if he could get Lewis back to Oneka Falls, back to the crime scene, maybe Lewis would believe him enough to look into LaBouche.

Maybe.

4

Scott sat frozen, staring out at the empty lot. His mind roiled with static as if off-channel snow had filled his skull. His limbs felt too heavy to move, and his tongue lay in his mouth like a dead thing.

LaBouche grunted. "You there, Scotty? I asked if you were sure this was the right address?"

Scott moved his eyes far enough that he could see LaBouche staring at him from the driver's seat. Something seemed weird about his demeanor. He was leaning toward Scott, eyes wide open and staring—like he was drinking in the details, memorizing every nuance. He even panted the tiniest bit. If Scott had been asked to describe LaBouche at that moment, he would have named him a starving man about to eat a steak. "It's the address the kid gave Jenny." The words fell from Lewis like lead weights, leaving him exhausted.

"Maybe she had a dyslexic moment and juxtaposed two of the numbers."

Scott shook his head. "Jenny's precise about this stuff, Lee. You know that."

"For fuck's sake, Scotty, speak up. I can't hear you over the fan for the heater."

Scott tried to wave his hand but settled for twitching his fingers. "Jenny's precise. She wouldn't get this wrong."

"Let's call her, Scotty. Double check the address."

"No, Lee. She's been through enough already."

"But Scotty, if this address is wrong, we might find Becky at the *right* one." He rested a heavy, meaty hand on Scott's shoulder. "Then everything Jenny's going through can be over."

"Yeah," Scott murmured. "Okay."

LaBouche dialed the number, one thick finger punching at his phone like he hated the thing. "Yeah, Jenny? It's Lee." He grimaced and looked at Scott. "No, sorry, hon. Not yet. No, Scotty's right here." Scott fought his lethargy to crook his eyebrows. "No, that's fine, Jenny. I want to double check the address. Can you do that for me?"

Scott turned his head, staring into the dark woods next to the empty lot. The cool darkness between the trees seemed to call to him, enticing him to give up consciousness and sleep beneath the waving boughs of the tree. Forever.

"No, that's fine, Jenny. Okay. Yeah, put her on. Mrs. Carmody? Yeah, Lee LaBouche, Scott's partner…yeah, with the State Police. Listen, I need to verify the address Jenny had for this kid Becky went out with. Can you read it to me?" He paused for a moment and then sighed. "Yeah, okay. No, that's what we have." He tapped Scott's arm, and when Scott turned to him, he mouthed: *Do you want to talk to Jenny?* Scott shook his head. "No, Mrs. Carmody, we'll fill her in when we get back there." He hung up without waiting for any response. "Well, fuck, Scotty. You were right. That's the right address all right."

"Yeah," Scott breathed. "What do…Lee, what can I—"

LaBouche put a meaty hand on his shoulder again. "No, Scotty, listen to old Lee. You know how this works. We've worked MP cases. Tons of them."

Scott sighed and turned his head back to the inviting darkness of the woods.

"Scotty, Jenny needs you right now. More than I do. I'm taking you home, and I'll head down to the Troop E HQ and round up some volunteers from traffic. We'll canvas the shit out of this town, and we'll find a lead. You know how I am, Scotty."

Scott managed a slight nod. "Dog with a bone," he murmured.

"That's right, Scotty. I'm like a dog with a bone. I'll find Becky, and I'll find whoever killed her."

Scott's head snapped around so fast the vertebrae in his neck crackled like a string of firecrackers. He glimpsed an expression on LaBouche's face that turned his stomach. At first, he thought it was pity, but after LaBouche blanked his expression, Scott wasn't so sure.

"Sorry, Scotty. I didn't mean to say that. I meant 'whoever has her.'"

Scott faced forward in the seat. "Drive," he said.

5

When LaBouche's Maxima drove by at the end of the lane, Drew was ready. He pulled out onto the road with his lights off and drove to the stop sign, giving the two troopers time to get a little further down Old Penfield Road before he turned the lights on.

He pulled out behind them, wondering what in the hell had them driving around to abandoned quarries. *Is Lewis a part of this? Some kind of...whatchamacallit...some kind of* familiar *to LaBouche?* But that was too hard to believe. No father would let what happened to Becky Lewis happen to his daughter, demonic pet or no.

No, LaBouche was playing with him, Drew felt sure. Although, what reason LaBouche might have for carrying on with the ruse at this point, he didn't know.

Why torment Lewis? Surely the emotions the demon had fed on while torturing Becky Lewis had sated his hunger.

6

"Who's this idiot?" mumbled LaBouche.

Scott looked up and then glanced in the mirror on his side. "Can't see past his lights."

"Yeah." LaBouche shrugged, but his eyes never left the rearview mirror. "Say," he said, drawing the word out.

"Say what?"

"I've just had one of my brain tickles, Scotty."

Lewis lifted a limp hand from his lap and let it drop.

"Do you find it strange that this happens right after we talked to Dr. Reid about all those other disappearances?"

"No, I don't, Lee. I *saw* this kid. His name is Lamont, some surfer dude. He was in my living room last night. A skinny teenager. It's not Reid."

"So Reid *paid—*"

"No, Lee. In hindsight, there was something off about the kid...something, I don't know...something *smug* about him, but I didn't get a read that he wasn't *interested* in Becky." His voice broke on her name.

"Scotty, you are her dad, and…well, maybe your radar was off with the kid. I say we should check Reid's movements. Find out where *he's* been for the last two days."

Scott grunted. "I don't even like him for the other disappearances, Lee."

LaBouche let air hiss between his teeth. "When did you decide this?"

Scott shrugged. "I have no idea. In the past day, I guess. It's my gut. Besides, you're probably right. That connection with Oneka Falls is *thin*."

"Maybe not," said LaBouche. "Might be you were the one that was right."

Scott flapped a hand. "To be honest, Lee, I don't give one rat's ass right now. I don't care about any MP except Becky."

"Of course," said LaBouche, but there was something off about his tone. "Well, consider it when you're ready to get back to it."

"Yeah," murmured Scott.

"I think the guy behind you is following us."

"Nah. Who's being paranoid now?"

"Let's pull him over, check his ID."

"Lee…I just want to get home, man. I want to be with Jenny."

LaBouche sighed, sounding a little weird. Frustrated or angry. "Yeah, I'll have you home in a few minutes, Scotty."

They rode the rest of the way with a frigid silence between them.

7

Drew drove past the Lewis house for the third time in twenty minutes. LaBouche had left fifteen minutes before, but Drew felt…*hinky*…about it. Like LaBouche was just baiting a trap, just waiting for Drew to pull up so he could swoop in at the last second. Demons thought like that, and it didn't pay to get careless. That shit in Oneka Falls meant Drew had a lot of work to do. *A lot.* He couldn't afford an entanglement with the State Police. To be an effective killer, he had to be off everyone's radar. Just a geeky college professor who profiles and does postmortems as a consultant. No one interesting. No one *threatening*.

He drove around the block again, eyes scouring the darkness, searching for a blue Maxima or any other sign of LaBouche. It was the kind of neighborhood you expected a State Trooper to live in: quiet, respectable, friendly. The carriage and porch lights of all the houses were blazing, pushing the darkness out to the street like a bouncer dealing with a drunk.

Of LaBouche, there was no sign. Now, if he could only work up the nerve to go up to Scott Lewis' house, ring the bell, and tell the man that a demon had tortured and raped his daughter to death. *Yeah. Like there's ever enough nerve for that.*

He parked two houses down from the Lewis' and got out. His muscles were cramped and sore from all the driving, but aside from the emotional aftermath of his trip to Oneka Falls, he felt okay. He stretched his muscles as he walked to their house, up their sloping driveway, and across their walk to the front door. There, he stood for a moment, not thinking, not even looking around, just trying to calm his electric nerves. With a shaking finger, he rang the bell.

An old woman opened the door to the extent of the chain. She had a scar around her right eye, and unless Drew missed his guess, her right eye was a prosthetic. "Yes?" she asked.

"Er, is this the Lewis residence?"

"I'm Melinda Carmody. What is it you want, young man?"

"I'm looking for Trooper Lewis. He's…I have…I have something I have to tell him."

"And you are?"

"Tell him it's Andrew Reid."

She closed the door, and Drew stood there fidgeting, trying not to sprint back to his car. Footsteps sounded on the other side of the door, and the chain rattled. The door opened, and Trooper Lewis stood there, pointing a gun at Drew's face. "Talk," he said in a cold, cold voice. "This had better be good."

"It's not, but it's something you should know." Trooper Lewis looked at him hard, his eyes scanning Drew's face. He moved the pistol, letting his hand fall to his side.

"Who is it, Scott?" The woman's voice slurred over her consonants like a drunk's would.

Lewis glanced over his shoulder and stepped through the door, pulling it shut behind him. He looked back at Drew and frowned. "You've got five minutes. After that…"

"Right," said Drew. He pulled the ID card out of his back pocket. "This will not be easy for me to tell you, but I imagine it's going to be much harder for you to hear."

Lewis' eyes opened wide, and he snatched the ID with his free hand. His eyes scanned back forth between the picture and the text. When he looked up again, fury raged in his eyes, and he leveled the pistol at Drew again. "Where did you get this?" he demanded.

"Oneka Falls. There's an old church there with 'Play Time' painted over the front doors. The cellar is—"

Lewis stomped forward and pressed the gun under Drew's chin. "*Where is my daughter, you fuck?*" His shout echoed back and forth across the street.

"Scott?" The slurred voice of the woman wormed its way through the front door. "Scott?"

Drew raised his hands, his movements deliberate and slow, careful not to jostle Lewis. "I'm sorry to say she's dead."

Lewis' knuckles blanched as his hand tightened on the pistol butt. His eyes blazed and blood flooded into his cheeks. "What did you say to me?" he hissed.

"Trooper Lewis, I'm so sorry. I found that ID on the body of a teenage girl in the cellar of a fucked-up old church in Oneka Falls. But that's not all. I saw—"

"What do you mean, that's not all? What the fuck else could matter?" The man seemed to deflate, to shrink or implode, but the anger blazing in his eyes remained constant.

"Your partner came out of that church," Drew said.

Lewis cut his gaze away, looking out at the night sky. "LaBouche was in Oneka Falls?" he asked, voice mild.

"Yes, I saw him around ten this morning, and again this afternoon. That's when he came out of Play Time. But listen a second, Trooper Lewis. There's more you should know."

Lewis shook his head and sank into a deck chair on the front porch—or rather he fell into the chair as if the bones in his legs had dissolved. "What?" he breathed. "What else could matter? My daughter's dead."

"I'm sorry, Trooper Lewis. I would have saved her if I could. But listen, your partner...the thing calling himself Lee LaBouche, he's not who—not even *what*— he pretends to be. This will be hard for you to—"

Lewis surged to his feet and grabbed Drew by the shoulders. The Trooper spun, slamming Drew into the wall, and pressed his pistol into the base of Drew's skull. "Don't fucking move," he whispered.

"I'm not moving, Trooper Lewis—not resisting in any way."

"I will ask you this one time, and one time only. You'd better not lie to me, you understand?"

"Yes, Trooper. I understand."

"Did you kill my daughter?"

"No, Trooper Lewis. I did not kill your daughter. I *found* her body, and I came here of my own free will to tell you about it."

"You didn't call the police?"

"Yes, I did. I called the Oneka Falls Police Department anonymously and told them where to find her." The pressure exerted on the base of his skull by Lewis' pistol lessened but didn't disappear.

"I can confirm whether or not that call happened."

"Yes, I understand that," said Drew. The calm in his voice surprised him. The calm he *felt* astounded him. "I didn't kill her, Trooper. But I know who did."

"Yeah? Who?"

"Your partner." The gun pressed harder into his neck, but Drew didn't so much as wriggle. "LaBouche hung around Oneka Falls all day, Trooper. And the condition of... Your daughter's murderer...spent a lot of time with her."

"Tell me."

"Trooper, I don't want to tell you. You don't want that image in your brain. I don't even want to have it in mine, and I never met your daughter. She was restrained in a tiny room—a cell. There were...tools...hanging from the walls. You don't want to hear the rest."

The pressure on his neck disappeared, and Lewis sobbed a single, gut-wrenching time. The deck chair creaked under the sudden application of Lewis' weight. "It doesn't make sense," he muttered, voice hitching and breaking.

"It only makes sense once you come to terms with the truth about LaBouche."

They were silent for a moment, Drew leaning against the wall where Lewis had pinned him, Lewis in the deck chair, neither man moving. Lewis sighed, and the sound was horrible—hopeless and lost. "So, what? LaBouche is some kind of…some kind of serial killer?"

"Much worse than that, I'm afraid," said Drew.

"Tell me," said Lewis.

"I don't know why or how, so please don't ask me those questions. Ever since I was a kid, I could perceive…*things*…things that pretended to be humans. No one else I've ever met can see past the…well, I don't know what to call it…the illusion. But I've always had the ability. At first, I believed I was crazy like the shrinks all said, but I realized that what I was seeing had to be real."

Lewis sighed again. "Why? Why would you think that?"

"I watched one of them—a real loner, a real anti-social type. Anyway, I watched him whenever I had free time. I figured that if he was just a man—if I *was* delusional and hallucinating—that I'd never witness him do anything out of the ordinary.

"In the third week of watching, I followed him to a bad part of town. I watched him pick up a prostitute and get her in his car. He drove her to an abandoned building, and they went inside. An hour later, he came out, but the prostitute didn't. I waited until he left, and then I went in the building. He'd...He'd killed her and gutted her like a deer. Parts of her were missing, cut away like meat."

"You expect me to accept this guy was a serial killer?"

"No. At least not in the way you mean it. Not a human killing other people for fun."

Lewis drew a deep breath and released it all in one big whoosh. "What then?"

"He was a demon. He was *feeding* on her. Oh, I didn't know it then, but the more I watched him, the more I learned about them."

"You are insane—you're aware of that, right?" Lewis' voice sounded dejected, horrified, and despondent.

"No, I'm not, Trooper Lewis. I'm not."

Lewis scoffed.

"I've spent a long time—years—learning about these demons, Trooper. I've tracked a lot of them. They all share one thing in common: they feed off us humans. Some physically, like the first one I watched, but others seem to feed on emotion—fear, anger, despair. Some of them—the oldest of them—have developed into master manipulators. Like your partner."

"You expect me to swallow that Lee LaBouche, my partner for the last eight years, is what? A psychotic, flesh-eating monster?"

Drew sighed. "May I sit?" Lewis grunted, and Drew moved to sit beside him in the other deck chair. "Listen, I can't make you see them as they are. I've never met another person who can, but I can show you their den in Oneka Falls. I can show you their dungeons, their torture cells. And if OFPD moved fast enough, they can take you to your daughter's body."

Lewis stared up at the night sky, lips pursed, gun cradled in a loose fist in his lap. "Tell me something, Reid."

"Anything."

"Are you the man we've been looking for? Are you behind the disappearances of those people we spoke to you about?"

Drew pursed his lips, unsure of how to answer. If he said yes, he'd be admitting to killing twenty-two of what Lewis considered people. If he said no, he was certain Lewis would know he was lying. "Let me take you to Oneka Falls, let me show you—"

"Tell me, or I'm collaring you, and you can tell it to a judge."

"No matter what I tell you, you're going to arrest me anyway, and if you do, then I can't help you. Not with Becky, not with LaBouche."

"Stand up," Lewis commanded in a tone that brooked no argument. Drew complied. What else was there to do? "Hands behind your back."

As Lewis snapped cold handcuffs around his wrists, Drew tried one last time. "Trooper Lewis, you and your wife are in grave danger. LaBouche has been playing with your family for a long time. There's a reason for that. I don't know what it is, but there's a reason. LaBouche is getting something out of it. He's—"

"Enough!" snapped Lewis. "Just stand there a second with your trap shut." Lewis moved to the door and then glanced back a Drew. "If you make me come out and chase after you, I'll take you to jail instead of Oneka Falls."

"You believe me?"

"Fuck no. You are a lunatic, but if you have any information, anything real, about my daughter's whereabouts, I'll put up with your bullshit for a few hours." He turned back to the door. "But trust this, Reid. If you are wasting my time, I will make you regret it, crazy-ass fuck or not."

"Fair enough, Trooper Lewis."

Lewis put his hand on the door knob. "I'll be a minute."

"That's fine. I'll wait right here."

Lewis opened the door.

"I'm not, though—wasting your time. *Or* a crazy-ass fuck."

"If you are, you are. Whether you are will become clear in the next few hours. We can wait that long to find out." Lewis stepped inside and closed the door.

I'm committed now, thought Drew. *I hope I can make him accept it.*

BOOK TWO:
BLACKENED

Chapter 1

1979

I

Benny regained consciousness slowly—coming to like a drunk waking up after a long night of pounding down cheap beer. He opened his eyes and gasped in fright.

The king carried him in his arms as a loving father would, but the king no longer resembled a man. His skin was blackened and loose, and instead of fingernails, his hands ended in long, sharp-looking talons. His face was grotesque. Loose skin hung from his cheekbones. His mouth was too wide, and two three-inch tusk-like fangs protruded from his lower jaw, keeping his fat, rubbery lips from closing all the way. The king's ears were long and pointed, with tufts of coarse black hair over them. His eyes were the worst though. Where a human would have whites, he had solid orbs that were silver with specks of black throughout. Oblong pupils split his eyes, giving him a cat-like appearance. His nose hung from his face like an afterthought—huge and crooked.

The king glanced down at him, and his mouth stretched wider in an evil grin. "Get a good look, boyo.

I don't mind." Benny's eyes lingered on the long, tusk-like teeth and seeing this, the thing carrying him laughed. "Don't mind my skull-crushers, Benny. Stay on my good side, and you'll never see them up close and personal."

The ecstatic feeling that had filled Benny during the car trip past the woods had disappeared. Fear took its place. "Are you the man with the bikes?"

The king threw back his head and barked laughter at the treetops. "Why, sport? Have you decided to sell after all? But that ship has departed the docks. Do I look like any man you've ever known?"

Benny shook his head and tried to keep his lips from quivering. "Why are you so…"

"Hideous? Heinous? Monstrous? Grotesque?" The thing laughed again. "I could ask you the same, but I already know the answer, monkey-boy."

"What…what do you want? Why did you make me come to you?"

"You are a fine lad, Benjamin. A sport. You delight my senses, and my daughters will love you. Plus, you showed courage when you came to the house looking for your delectable young friend. It will be fun to play games with you."

"My… Is Toby…"

"Don't worry, sport. Everything is prepared for you. Sensed you'd be coming for a visit, we did, and the girls wanted to dote on you."

"The girls."

"My daughters."

"Daughters," Benny echoed, almost overcome by a wave of lightheadedness.

"Yes. Are you unwell, my fine boy?" He didn't wait for an answer, though. He cackled his horrifying laugh and leaped into the air with an acrobatic flourish. At the apex of his leap, leathery wings snapped open from his back, and they were flying. The king swooped between the tree trunks as if he had memorized the location of each and every tree.

"Who are you?" murmured Benny.

"You may call me Herlequin."

"What kind of name is that?"

Herlequin shrugged. "The kind you may use to address me."

"Are you...are you a demon?" asked Benny, watching the leathery wings flap lackadaisically and more than a little out-of-step with each other.

Herlequin cackled. "Well, People through the ages have called me an elf, a fairy, a brownie, a leprechaun, a kobold, a troll, an ogre, a doppelganger, and a gargoyle; I suppose adding demon to the list won't hurt."

Benny sighed. "Do you ever answer straight?"

Herlequin slow rolled and juked to avoid a low hanging branch, laughing the whole time.

"If you're not a demon, why do you look like one?"

"I can appear to be anything I want. Human senses are easy to fool. That's why games with your kind are so much fun."

"Are you saying you can do magic? I don't believe you." Despite his bravado, Benny's voice wavered the tiniest bit.

Herlequin smiled his nasty smile but held his tongue.

Benny shook his head. "So what do you look like?"

"Well, sport, this is how I look when I'm not playing tricks. I'm not a demon, however, so put that fear out of your mind. There's no such thing as demons or devils."

"What are you? What are you really?"

"It doesn't matter, boyo. I'm here, you're here. We're going to play such games together."

It seemed to Benny that the wood was getting darker and darker as if the sun were setting. He looked up, past Herlequin's head. The branches of the trees interlaced, one with another, until the canopy was like a solid, woven thing. Herlequin followed his gaze, glancing up at the canopy. "No tricks there, boy-of-mine. It took patience and hard labor to train the trees to grow thus."

"Why? To hide the forest from planes?"

Herlequin cackled his tiresome laugh. "No, no, sport. As I said before, human senses are easy to trick. If I wanted to hide, no one would see me. It's as simple as that."

Benny couldn't be sure, but a pinch of falsehood rang in Herlequin's voice. "So why?"

Herlequin sighed. "This constant questioning is irritating, kiddo."

"My name is Benny."

"I get that, sport. You'll answer to hopscotch if that's what I call you. Or pretty-pink-paisley for that matter."

Benny held his tongue. He didn't want to argue with Herlequin while he was flying Benny through the air. "Sorry," he muttered.

"Shall we play a game now?" asked Herlequin. "Are you awake enough? In control of your faculties?"

Fear gripped Benny by his guts. "I…I don't know the rules. I don't know what kind of game you mean."

One of Herlequin's eyes rolled down to stare at Benny, while the other stayed trained on the forest ahead. A smile twitched on the thing's rubbery lips. "It's an easy game to learn, sport. Your friend Toby learned it right away." Herlequin's voice grew wistful. "He was a masterful player. Quite satisfying."

"Is he… Did you…"

"I wish to remind you that those aborted sentences are questions, boy."

Benny sighed. "I wanted to know if Toby is…"

"What, sport? Dead?"

Benny nodded, his agreement marred by his miserable expression.

"No, boy. Toby's heart still beats in his chest."

Again, Benny had the strangest feeling the Herlequin was telling a half-truth. "I'm not stupid," he said with all the petulance of a prepubescent boy.

"Watch that tongue, boyo, or I'll have my daughters rip it from your head." Herlequin's tone was light, teasing, but Benny didn't believe for a second he was joking. "But, we were talking about the game. Do you wish to begin?"

"Not until you explain the rules," said Benny, keeping his voice respectful.

"It's simple." Herlequin dropped his legs and landed without making a sound. He set Benny down on the carpet of old, brown leaves. "Here's how it works. You run. Or hide, whichever. I come after you."

"Hide and seek? You want to play hide and seek with me?"

Herlequin's smile did more to frighten Benny than reassure him. "My daughters and I call it 'The Hunt,' but I guess you could call it 'hide and seek' if that suits you better."

"The Hunt?" Benny's voice sounded weak, even to himself. "What…what happens if you catch me?"

Herlequin's lips split apart to reveal three rows of sharp teeth in addition to the big fangs. Predator's teeth, Benny had learned in science. Carnivore's teeth. "We eat you, of course."

Benny trembled. "I don't want to play."

"Want? Who asked what you want? I asked if you are *ready*."

Benny shook his head.

"Oh, I don't know, sport. You look ready." Herlequin looked him in the eye. His black and gray eyes seemed to spin and dance. "You'd better be."

Benny tried to tear his eyes away, tried to shake his head, but his neck muscles ignored his commands.

"Speak up, boyo. Remember: silence means assent." A sly smile spread across Herlequin's face. "All you have to do is say 'no' if you're not ready."

Benny tried to speak, but like his neck muscles, his voice didn't do what he wanted it to.

"Ah! I thought you'd be a sport! Very well. Let us begin!" Herlequin clapped his hands and hopped in place.

Like a four-year-old, thought Benny.

"I'll tell you what, champ, if you can evade me for three days, I'll let you go back to your boring life. Does that sound reasonable?"

Again, Benny tried to force words out, but nothing happened.

"I'm so glad you agree. Go ahead, boyo. Get started."

Benny stood there, looking up at Herlequin, trying to force words out of his mouth.

Herlequin's smile faltered. "Well?" he asked, sounding like a small child. "Why don't you start?"

Benny got his mouth open, but his tongue lay there like a dead snake. "Nnnnnth!" he managed.

Herlequin's face froze, and his friendly expression shattered. His face twisted with rage, and his rubbery lips twitched while spittle raced down his chin. His eyes blazed: twin pits of black fire, and his taloned hands clenched and unclenched. "What are you waiting for?" he screeched. "The game has begun, boy!"

Still, Benny stood trying to refute Herlequin's words with inaction.

The king's eyes grew wide and his mouth stitched up into a rictus of fury. He bent down and put his face inches from Benny's. "This is not how you stay on my good side, boyo," he hissed. "Now, run! Run!"

Fear engulfed Benny's eleven-year-old mind. All he could see were Herlequin's meat-eater teeth.

"RUN!" Herlequin roared, and, in the distance, dogs howled and brayed. Resolve crumbling, Benny ran.

2

Matt Greshin dropped the phone into the cradle with a clatter. "Fuck!" he yelled.

Craig stuck his head into Matt's office. "Bad news, Chief?"

Matt scoffed. "That was Jim. Benny's disappeared."

"What?" Craig came through the doorway, holding two cups of hot coffee. "Where? When?"

"What is this, Schoolhouse Rock?" Matt rubbed his temples. "They're over to Cuba at the hospital. His youngest boy had a seizure after Jim almost hit a guy standing in the road."

"Shit," muttered Craig, sinking into one of the chairs across from Matt's desk. "He okay?"

"Doctors haven't said, yet."

Craig's eyebrows twitched upward.

"He's still unconscious. He's been that way all day. The ER doctor doesn't have a clue." Matt scoffed and waved his hand.

"So, does Cuba PD have anything to go on? Anything on the guy in the road?"

"They've got fuck-all," grumped Matt. "No one saw the kid leave the hospital—not even Karen, who was supposed to bring the two older boys inside."

"That…"

"Yeah," sighed Matt. "It's *not* like Karen Cartwright, but she was even more flustered than Jim, he said. She was in the back seat with the kid when he seized. He was yelling all kinds of nonsense."

"No one saw Benny? At all?" asked Craig.

"No one saw a thing. It's like the kid turned invisible. But woods surround that hospital on three sides so he could've skipped into the trees and gotten lost."

"With his brother in the Emergency Room?"

"Jim said he was acting…strange in the car. Yelling at little Billy and calling him names while the kid was seizing."

"Well, kids can be—"

"I know. Did you get that shell casing delivered?"

Craig nodded. "Yeah, to the Troop E headquarters in Canandaigua. I asked them to put a rush on it, but it's a Sunday evening, after all."

"Yeah," grunted Matt. "Probably take a week."

"What do we do in the meantime, Chief?"

"Keep your head on a swivel and your eyeballs peeled. We have to find this guy Fergusson. *He's* not invisible, and he's here in our backyards. Morton and Walton will do their parts in their towns."

"I guess I should get on over to the Motor Lodge and check if he's staying there."

Matt grunted. "I doubt he'd be that stupid, but yeah, go take a look."

"Ten-four, Chief," said Craig, getting up to leave.

3

Benny didn't have a guess about how long he'd been running. The skin of his face bore scratches from countless low-hanging branches. His sides ached, and his breath ripped in and out so hard he'd almost forgotten how it felt to take a normal breath. Each gasping breath rasped out of his bone dry and aching throat, leaving his tongue as parched as desert sand. His feet had gone numb, like so much leaden weight at the end of his exhausted legs. Still, he stumbled on, running away from the sounds of pursuit. Running away from Herlequin and his dogs. Or wolves. Whatever they were.

The woven canopy of the trees created an almost perfect darkness beneath their branches. So dark that Benny couldn't see farther than ten feet away. Coming up with any kind of plan was out. He wouldn't even be able to find a place to hide. Stumbling from one gnarled tree trunk to the next took all his concentration.

The animals chasing him were closer. He caught glimpses of black-furred wolves running a parallel course to his own, just at the edge of his vision, keeping him running deeper and deeper into the dark forest's heart. The trees got closer and closer together the farther into the forest's heart he ran.

Behind him, Herlequin laughed and screamed with delight. Every time Benny wanted to give up, the picture of Herlequin's skull-crushers flashed through his mind, and, somehow, he found the will to keep running.

His legs ached, his sides burned, his hot breath cracked his dry lips. His chest heaved. He had to find a place to stop, to catch his breath, to rest…but no place safe existed. No caves, no hunter's cabins, no treehouses. He couldn't keep running.

His frenzied pace slowed until he was more stumbling than running. Out to his sides, the wolves growled and snarled. Fear sank its teeth into him, but try as he might, he couldn't run anymore. He was too weak.

When he fell, he didn't even have the strength to bring his arms up to break his fall. He lay there, face in the thick layer of decaying leaves, panting for breath. Not wanting to see the wolves when they came for him, he closed his eyes. He trembled with fear and exhaustion, and he wished his end would be quick.

When he awoke, he was out of the forest, but still enveloped by dark. He looked around bleary-eyed and muzzy-headed. Grass tickled his ears. He rolled to his side and sighed with relief. Somehow, he'd run all the way back to Oneka Falls. He was in his backyard, facing the sliding glass doors. He sat up slowly, fighting dizziness and sore muscles.

The sliding glass door opened with its signature hiss.

Relief coursed through him. His mom and dad were home after all! Their footsteps thudded across the back deck and creaked down the stairs. Benny smiled and forced his head up. But the figure at the bottom of the step stood hunched-over—shorter than Benny, shorter than Johnny. His heart fell, neither his mom nor his dad had come to help him. It was Billy, face and chest covered in blood.

"Billy?" he murmured.

"Benny, what are you doing?" asked Billy in a gruff, tremulous voice.

"I was so exhausted, someone was chasing me through the woods and—"

"Benny!" shouted Billy.

"What, spaz?" asked Benny with a touch of irritation in his voice.

"The dogs."

"What dogs?" Then Benny heard them, the almost inaudible steps of a pack of four-legged creatures coming out of the forest behind him. If he listened hard, their panting breath sounded like a symphony of impending death.

Benny's muscles locked up and his breath stuck fast inside his chest. Billy stared at something behind Benny, and his eyes were so wide they looked like quarters gleaming in the moonlight. Benny wanted to scream at him—to scream for help and to scream for Billy to get out of there—but his voice betrayed him. His pulse pounded in his ears, and the edges of his vision turned black.

Ever so slowly, Billy raised his hand to point at the things behind Benny. "You should get up now, Benny," he whispered.

Terror still had a lock on his muscles, though, and Benny couldn't get up, didn't even think he would ever move again. When the growling started, however, Benny sprang up and ran before he realized he'd broken free of his paralysis. Pushing Billy in front of him, he ran for the sliding glass door that Billy had left open. He knew those big wolves could break through the glass if they wanted to, but he didn't think the *wolves* would know that. *Get inside! Get inside! Get inside get inside get inside!* The thought swirled in his head, repeating like a scratched record.

The wolves ran after them, their footfalls sounding like thunder in his ears. He pushed Billy—hard—through the open door, and Billy skidded face-first across the deep pile shag carpet his mother liked so much. Benny whirled and grabbed the door handle, ready to slam the door closed, but when he saw what chased him, his muscles locked again.

The things running at him through the once safe-feeling backyard scared him like nothing he'd ever seen before. Hideous. They ran on four legs like wolves, they had tails and fur and long snouts, but they were *not* wolves.

They had no eyes.

Their eyes hadn't been gouged out, they had none to begin with. No eyelids. Where their eyes should have been, only smooth, fur-covered skin stretched over hard bone. Their misshapen ears reminded him more of Herlequin's ears, sharp and pointed, rather than dog ears. Their front legs ended in a knotted, deformed hand, complete with an opposable thumb. Thick, viscous fluid fell from their jaws, and when it hit the ground, the grass sizzled and turned black.

Were these the things that had run next to him in the woods? Had he been so close to these mutant killers? Benny shuddered at the thought.

"Benny! Close the door! *Close the door!*" Billy screamed.

With a start, Benny realized the lead wolf-thing was less than three yards from the open door. He heaved the slider closed with a bang. The lead wolf-thing snarled and snapped at the air. Then it started to pace—back and forth, back and forth it went like one of those windup toy soldiers.

If it had had eyes, it would have been glaring at him. Benny had no doubt on that score. Even without eyes, the thing's face tracked him as the creature paced. It panted, slobbering more of its poisonous spit on the wooden deck. Each drop sizzled and smoked when it hit the deck.

"*Fuck!*" Benny gasped.

"You said the F-word!"

Benny gestured at the thing pacing outside the thin sheet of glass. "I think I'm allowed this time." He glanced at Billy. "What are you even doing here, Billy? Where are Mom and Dad? Where's Johnny?"

Billy shrugged and looked away.

"Tell me, Billy."

Billy glanced at him and then looked out the slider at the wolf-things. Some sat, ears perked at the door as if they listened in on what the brothers said. Others stood, panting, behind their pacing leader. "What are those things, Benny?"

"I don't know. But answer my question. Where are Mom and Dad?"

"Benny, I have no idea! Okay? All I know is that they aren't *here*."

Benny blinked. "Didn't they bring you home?"

Billy shook his head. "Last time I saw them was in the car."

"In the car?" Benny repeated dumbly.

"Right. How did you get here? Why aren't you with them?"

Benny shook his head. "The king...that man in the road...he *called* me to him when Dad stopped the car. I...I *went* to him...Mom didn't notice...no one noticed..."

"I told Daddy he had me. *I told him!* Why didn't they believe me?"

"I… Billy, last time I saw you, you had passed out, and Daddy took you from Mommy and ran inside the hospital. How'd you get from the hospital to here?"

"What hospital, Benny? The king took me out of the car when I tried to tell Mommy about him. He grabbed me and dragged me away."

"Billy, nothing like that happened."

"Yes, it did!" Billy yelled.

Benny turned his back to the sliding glass door and looked at his little brother. Tears streaked the boy's face. "Don't cry, Billy. We'll figure this out."

Billy's gaze drifted over Benny's shoulder, and his eyes stretched big and round. "Oh, no!" he screamed, pointing out at the deck.

Benny whirled. Herlequin stood at the edge of the deck, smiling his wicked smile. "Caught you, sport," he said and opened his mouth wide. Row after row of sharp teeth gleamed in the moonlight. "Now, it's time for you to pay." He skipped across the deck like a little kid and put his hand on the sliding glass door's handle.

Benny was shaking his head, pushing with all his might against the door handle. "You said if I got out of the forest, you'd let me go!"

"You didn't make it out of the forest," Billy said, except his voice sounded a lot like Herlequin's, just a different pitch.

"Yes, I did! I'm standing in my own TV room, at my house in Oneka Falls!"

"Are you, sport?" asked Billy.

Benny ripped his eyes away from Herlequin's leering face and glanced over his shoulder at his brother. Billy raised his hand and snapped his fingers.

The house disappeared...the deck disappeared...the lawn disappeared. The wolf-things didn't disappear, and neither did Herlequin. Neither did Billy. They stood in a small clearing, surrounded by terrifying, twisted trees.

Benny screamed, and everything faded to black.

4

While Craig Witherson was driving across town to check out the Motor Lodge, Owen was setting up a surprise at Meat World, the town's only grocery store. He parked the Skylark about an eighth of a mile down the road from the grocery store and slipped into the woods. The store stood with the woods at its back and a small parking lot and the road at its front. Owen was high up in a tree at the edge of the woods. He had a perfect view of the parking lot and the road, and he had plenty of ammo. He'd removed his homemade silencer—he wanted to terrorize these townie fuckers.

"Brigitta, are you here?" he asked. He was using his own skills to make himself invisible, but he liked having her with him. Unlike most women, she never pissed him off.

"Yes, my love."

Owen grinned. "I like the sound of you saying that."

"I like to say it, my love."

A car went by on the road, rusty muffler blatting away. "Why…why did you pick me?"

"Pick you?"

"In Vietnam. Why did you pick me to save that night?"

"Oh, that," she said. Mist appeared out of the air, and Brigitta coalesced out of the mist, sitting on the branch next to him, and he smiled. "I sensed in you a…like-mindedness. Your thoughts attracted me at once."

"Love at first sight, eh?" Owen chuckled.

"Yes, something like that," she said. "But look!" She lifted a semi-transparent arm and pointed at the parking lot. An old woman was struggling toward her car with a bag full of canned food. "She looks ripe, Owen."

Owen shouldered his rifle and looked through the scope. The woman wore her blue-rinsed hair in a short pageboy cut and wore cat-eye glasses. "At least she's not a pretender," he breathed. Moving the bolt with care so as not to jostle his aim, Owen chambered a round.

"Do it, Owen," said Brigitta. "Do *her*."

"Don't rush me," he snapped. "I want to enjoy this." Brigitta didn't respond, but he didn't get the feeling that his snappishness annoyed her as it would have annoyed Candy. He aimed at the old woman's back. "*Pow*," he whispered. He aimed at her ample posterior. "*Pow*." He raised the gun to aim at the back of her head and gasped with pleasure. "*Pow*," he whispered and pulled the trigger.

The shot echoed across the road and back, and the old woman dropped forward on her face like a felled tree. Owen shivered with ecstasy and closed his eyes, replaying how the old bat had fallen when the round smashed into her brainstem.

"Yesss," hissed Brigitta. "Oh yes, my love."

Someone screamed. Owen snapped his eyes open, and his hands moved automatically, working the bolt, ejecting his spent brass, and chambering another round. A woman in her thirties ran toward the old lady's corpse, no doubt to help. *Good Samaritan*, he thought.

Yes, give her what she deserves, Owen. The mental voice didn't sound like his own, but Owen chalked that up to excitement.

He sighted the rifle at the running woman. Her blonde, feathered hair was bouncing to and fro, her ass jiggling in her tight maroon cords. He aimed at her ass first. "*Pow*," he whispered. His erection pounded with the tempo of his heart. He brought the rifle up, pointing at her back where her breasts would be. "*Pow, pow*," he said, moving the rifle from right to left. Then, his crosshairs floated over the center of the back of her head. Chuckling, he made a game of tracking her as she ran, making himself wait.

When the woman was less than ten feet away from the old woman's corpse, he pulled the trigger and ejaculated as her brains splattered on the back of the old lady's dress. Next to him on the branch, Brigitta was breathing hard, moaning a little. "You are so good, my love," she breathed.

The air stilled for a moment in time, and then a cacophony of screams and shouts sounded from the grocery store. Owen waited, biting his lip, but no one ran out into the parking lot.

"Let's go down there, my love," said Brigitta in a dreamy tone. "Let's go around to the front of the store."

That's the craziest thing I've ever heard, he thought. "Would that be…smart?"

Who cares? Think of the fun! The foreign thought echoed in his head—it had come from Brigitta.

"Can you read my mind?" he whispered.

"Your mind, my mind," she breathed. *What difference is there*?

Owen stared at her for a moment, part of him excited, part of him terrified.

"We can talk about this later, my love. *Let's go*! People are trapped inside the store. Imagine the mayhem we can wreak."

The idea of rampaging through the small store was intriguing, but his mind blanched at how it would end. Owen on the ground, bleeding out, some cop-fuck standing over him with a smoking .357 magnum.

I will protect you.

Owen shook his head and snaked down the trunk of the tree, rifle slung over his shoulder.

"Thank you, Owen!" said Brigitta. "You will love it, I promise."

Owen shook his head again. "Not going in there, Brigitta. It's suicide."

"But, my love, I will—"

"Two shots, at the *most*, from any one location," he recited. "Police your brass, relocate." He stood at the base of the tree, imagining the arc his spent brass would have taken. He had a talent for it, and as usual, walked right to it and picked it up.

"My love, think of—"

"Brigitta, I said *no*." He glanced at her, and though her lower lip quivered like a small child's, her eyes were cold, angry. "We'll relocate across town and find other people to play with." He smiled at her—his best, most winning smile—but she sniffed and turned away, arms crossed. "Don't be that way, babe."

She flipped her hair and looked into the depths of the woods. When she walked away, Owen ran to her side. "Car's this way, Brigitta," he said, laying his hand on her arm. He hooked his thumb in the direction of the road.

She glanced down at his hand and disappeared.

He couldn't even feel her arm. "Brigitta, please. We can go right now, maybe the library or a park. Maybe get a kid or two."

I told you, no kids. Kids belong to my father.

Owen laughed and turned back toward the car. "Your father? Let him find his own fun." He slipped the shell casings into his pocket. Behind him, something growled. With a smile on his face, he turned, expecting Brigitta, but what he saw made him take a step back without a conscious decision to do so.

It was a dog. A dog without eyes. The thing took a menacing step toward him, and the growl transformed into a snarl. "What the blue *fuck*?" he gasped.

Owen, meet my father's idea of fun.

Owen turned and ran for the car, and the dog chased him, snarling and barking. He jerked the passenger door open and jumped into the Buick Skylark he had stolen. He slammed the door just in time, and the eyeless dog crashed into the door, claws clattering against the window, barking to beat all. He stared at the mutant thing's smooth, eyeless head, not quite able to trust what he was seeing. But the dog's slobber coating the window looked real enough. "Nice doggy," he muttered. "Go chase a squirrel or two."

The dog cocked his head as if it could almost understand Owen's words and then barked one more time, louder and more ferociously than before. The dog trotted away. It turned its head back toward Owen as if it were glancing at him over its shoulder. It spun and sprinted toward the car, leaping into the air at the last moment. With a bang and a screech, the dog landed on the hood of the car and stood there, facing Owen through the windscreen, head down as if glowering at him.

"What the hell do you want? I'm all out of Alpo," muttered Owen.

The dog took a step forward, claws sliding and skittering across the hood. It crouched and extended its neck until its nose smeared against the windshield. Its lips peeled back, and then it froze there, mid-snarl.

"Okay, okay. No kids. I get it." The dog jerked as if its owner was tugging on its lead. It turned and barked, then jumped off the hood and ran into the forest. Owen sat in the passenger seat, shaking his head and sweating. He slid over to the driver's side and started the car. "You in here, Brigitta?" He waited for a long time, but there was no answer.

With a sigh, Owen climbed back out of the car, leaving the engine running. "Look, we can go somewhere right now, babe. I'll only shoot adults. It'll be fun." He looked around, hoping to see mist coalescing out of thin air, but there was nothing to see and no reply. "If you're not coming, that's cool. We can catch up later." He got back into the car, and put the car into drive, but kept his foot on the brake pedal.

When she didn't answer, he sighed and screeched out onto the macadam, missing the ambulance screaming in the other direction by a few feet.

5

Benny opened his eyes, feeling anything but rested. His legs ached, and hot spots burned on the balls of his feet and where his shoes rubbed against the back of his ankle. His mouth tasted funny—like he'd licked a 9-volt battery. He felt feverish and a touch nauseated.

"Finally awake, boyo?" asked Herlequin.

Benny moaned. *Not a nightmare.* "Where's Billy?" he croaked. He leaned against the trunk of an old beech tree. The tree was huge, and its thick trunk twisted skyward as if someone had wrung it like a towel.

"How would I know, sport? Omniscience is not in my bailiwick."

Benny leapt to his feet, anger thrumming in his veins. "Where's my brother, you *son of a bitch*?"

"Language, Benny," said Herlequin with a wry smile twisting his grotesque face. "Why do you think I know?"

"I *saw* him! Back at my house when you…when you…*cheated me*!"

Herlequin laughed, and it sounded brittle, a mockery of mirth. "Cheated you? I did nothing of the kind."

"You said if I got out, you would let me go free! I was out of the forest! I got to my house! I saw Billy!" Benny fought the hot tears that wanted to cascade down his cheeks. He fought the rising anger and frustration that threatened to choke him.

Herlequin patted him on the head as if he were a cute puppy. "Tell me what else you think happened."

"It *happened*! You are a big, fat liar!"

"Now, now, sport. Let's not start name-calling." Herlequin held up a finger like a pedantic father lecturing a child. "First off, you absolutely, positively did not get out of my forest. You did not find your house. You did not see your brother."

"Nothing but a liar," snapped Benny. In the distance, he heard the howling of a dog or a wolf. Then the air split with overlapping howls and snarls as if ferocious beasts surrounded him.

Herlequin sighed. "Well, now you've done it, my boy. You've woken them up again." He spread his hands wide and danced a little jig. "There's nothing for it, son. You must run again."

"What if I won't?" demanded Benny, hating the pouting, petulant sound of his voice.

Herlequin smiled and leaned toward him. "Then you will die, and my pets will eat you, Benjamin." His smile stretched wider, pulling his skin tight across his cheeks. His fangs glistened. "Maybe I'll eat you up myself, what with your attitude." A bifurcated tongue darted out to rasp across his lips, leaving a foul, viscous fluid in its wake.

The howling drew closer, and Benny's mouth went dry. He got to his feet on shaking legs and spun in a circle. "Which way are they coming from?" he asked in a small voice. "I can't tell."

"Telling you would be cheating. What fun would that be?"

Benny spun in a slow circle, but it was no good. The howling, snarling, and yipping still sounded like it was coming from every direction at once.

"Better get moving, boyo. Better run."

"You'll only cheat me again."

Herlequin winked at him. "I never cheated you, sport. Told you that, already. If I mislead you, that's part of the fun. Of the challenge. How much of a victory would it be if you could just walk out of the forest? No, boyo. This victory, you have to earn."

A lone dog stepped out of the trees across the clearing from Benny. Its fur was black, like a Doberman, and like the things that chased him before, it had no eyes. Saliva dripped from the thing's jaws.

"What is that thing?" asked Benny.

"One of my daughters, boyo. They love to play this game."

Benny's gaze drifted back and forth between Herlequin and the eyeless dog-thing. "How can that thing be your daughter?" he muttered.

The thing took a step forward, growling and wrinkling its nose. Herlequin shrugged. "Better get a move on, kiddo." The dog-thing took another step forward, and suddenly, there were more of them stepping into the clearing behind it.

Benny turned and ran, his screams echoing through the trees. After too short of a delay, the dogs followed him, yipping and barking happy, playful barks. Behind them, Herlequin laughed and clapped his hands.

As Benny ran deeper into the dark forest, the trees got closer and closer together. Branches whipped across his cheeks, drawing blood. He sucked in huge gasps of air, his lungs already burning. His feet skittered and slid across tree roots slick with fungus.

He fell, and one of the dog-things howled. It sounded like a celebration of victory. Benny pushed himself to his feet, panic gripping his mind with blazing fingers. He'd lost all sense of direction in his headlong flight, and every direction looked the same. *Which way?* a scared, childish voice wailed inside his head. The dogs barked and snarled behind him. He ran on, stumbling across roots hidden in the dim light. His side felt like someone had rammed a white-hot steak knife between his ribs. Tears diluted the blood flowing down his cheeks.

Have to get out! Have to get away from these dogs! From Herlequin! But how? He couldn't even think with the dogs snarling at his back, let alone come up with a plan.

He grabbed a tree trunk and spun around it, running in a random direction. His foot slipped off a slick root and into a hole. His ankle twisted beneath him, forcing a shriek of pain out of him. He sobbed out a breath and stumbled on, lurching from trunk to trunk in the darkened woods.

Behind him, the dogs howled, and Herlequin cackled like a hyena.

6

Owen drove across town, obeying all traffic laws and even waving at people like he was a normal person. He had no plan yet, he was just moving, letting whatever it was that guided him to that damn sheriff's house guide him to his new location. He had another eighteen rounds for the rifle—might as well use them before he drove somewhere to buy more.

Too bad Brigitta flaked, he thought. It was nice having her beside him while the pleasure rolled through him. He got the distinct impression that she got off on his little games as much as he did. "Women," he scoffed.

"I'm no ordinary woman, my love," Brigitta breathed in his ear.

"Holy mother of fuckall!" he screeched. He twitched away from the sound, jerking the wheel of the Skylark and almost running up on the curb. "*Don't do that!*"

Mist swirled in the middle of the backseat as Brigitta solidified. Her laugh was light, but it had a nasty edge. "Why not? It's funny."

He glared at her in the rearview, his lips twisted in a frown. "Like that fucked up dog was funny?"

Brigitta favored him with a one-shouldered shrug. "Not my doing, Owen. And, anyway, that was your own fault. I *told* you."

"Told me?" he snapped. "You *told* me?" His cheeks burned with fury, and every sound he heard took on that tinny cast he recognized from the worst of his rages. He grabbed hold of his temper with desperate strength. He had the feeling that if he tried to beat up on Brigitta, things would get out of control.

That's right, my love. Hit me, and I'll hit you back. You wouldn't like that. The voice in his head was crooning, conciliatory, but the words...the words only fed his fire. He stared at her in the mirror, and she looked back at him with a bored expression on her lovely face. He longed to put his fist right in the middle of her boredom.

Her eyes sharpened and narrowed at the same time. "I doubt you would survive that, my love," she said. "If I didn't break you in half, my father would, you can be sure."

He tore his eyes away from hers, staring out the windshield without seeing anything, marshalling his control. *She's in my head somehow. Don't even have privacy in my fantasies.*

In the backseat, Brigitta smirked. "It doesn't have to be like this, my love. Bitter. Angry. It can go back to sweet and..."

"Sexy," he muttered.

"Yes, that's right. Sweet and sexy. Just promise me."

His eyes snapped back to hers in the rearview. "Promise you what? I'm not willing to pull any stupid-shit suicide runs. I don't care how tight you are."

Her expression soured for a moment, but then, with obvious effort, she smiled again. "Yeah, okay. Not that then. Promise me you won't bait my father anymore. No more talk about killing kids."

He waved his hand in a distracted way. "Oh, sure. I promise. No more kids."

Her smile was slow and lazy—like a cat grinning at a mouse. "And promise me you won't get so angry if I tease you."

He snorted. "Easier said than done, babe."

She shrugged, looking at him from under lasciviously lowered lashes. "It'll be so much more fun that way," she crooned. "*I* promise."

A grin spread across his cheeks, and the dark, bitter anger left his heart. "Well, if you put it that way…"

"I do, my love, I do." She snapped her eyes forward. "Owen!" she screamed.

Without thinking, Owen jammed the brake pedal to the floor. The Skylark skidded and drifted toward the curb, tires smoking and shrieking. Hands locked on the wheel, Owen gritted his teeth. The two little girls crossing the road on their pink Huffys shrieked in unison and, to a one, locked their brakes, stopping right in front of him. "For fuck's sake," he muttered, jerking the wheel toward the curb with all his strength.

With a slight pop, Brigitta disappeared, leaving Owen alone, white knuckled. Everything was too bright, too loud. To Owen, time slowed to a crawl. He could see the people inside Sally's Stationery gaping out the window, hands up to cover stupid, gaping goldfish mouths. Brigitta appeared next to the girls and grabbed a set of handle bars with each hand. With a mighty heave, she flung both of the girls toward the center of the road. A moment later, the bumper of the Buick passed through the space they had so recently occupied. The Skylark bumped up over the curb, smacking the mailbox through the plate glass window of the stationery shop.

When the car stopped, Owen just sat there looking through the passenger window at the biddies inside the shop. They stared and pointed, but not a one of them moved to come outside and see if he needed help. He glanced at the street. The two girls were on the macadam next to their bikes, crying and squealing like the bitches they would become in twenty years. Brigitta was gone again, or invisible, or whatever.

Owen turned back to the stationery shop and scoffed. He flipped the women the bird and mashed the accelerator to the floor. With screeching tires, Owen bumped the car off the curb and raced away. At the intersection in the middle of town, he didn't brake, hanging his hand out the window, shooting everyone the bird.

"That was close, my love." She was back. In the back seat, like nothing had happened, like she hadn't just teleported out of a moving car.

"Gotta teach me that trick, babe."

"If only I could, my love," she said.

To Owen, her tone was a bit lacking in the conviction department, but he let it slide. "That shit put me in a mood, babe. I want to—"

"Shoot some motherfuckers?" she asked with a lilt in her voice. Her laugh tinkled like glass.

"You have a way with words, babe. The thing is, I'm not getting an idea of where to go. My radar's busted. We can camp out at the library and shoot mommies coming to pick up their kids, or maybe shoot a few teachers over to the high school."

"What about town hall, my love? Or that newspaper place?"

Owen shook his head. "Town hall's where the police sit and the paper's just down the way. I don't want to get that close until I can shoot Mr. Town-fucking-manager, and I want to know he's there for sure—"

"He's gone, my love."

"What? Gone?"

Brigitta nodded. "Yes, love. He ran like a coward. Took his stupid wife and kids and ran for the border.

Don't worry, though, my father's dealing with the Cartwrights."

Owen nodded once, slow and deliberate. "That's fine then. Where to?"

Brigitta tapped her front teeth with a long, somehow graceful finger. "Teachers."

Owen smacked his palm on the horn. "I hate teachers," he sang, blipping the horn on each syllable.

"Yes, my love."

They grinned at each other in the mirror.

7

Matt brought his cruiser to a halt half a block away from Sally's Stationery, where he could see the skid marks in the road and up on the curb. The two little ones were up on the sidewalk now, being mother-henned by two ladies with blue hair and eating ice cream. Matt recognized the ladies as Mildred Kenny and Margaret Ward. With a sigh, he opened his door and got out. He strode up the sidewalk toward the girls, hitching up his duty belt as he walked. The girls looked at him with wide eyes.

"Didn't expect the chief himself," said Mrs. Ward.

Matt smiled. "Hello, girls," he said. "I hear you had a little accident. Are you hurt?"

"No, we're fine. It wasn't our fault," said the girl on the left.

"And you're not in any trouble, but I need you to tell me what happened."

The two girls looked at each other, and each took a lick of their ice cream before turning back to stare at him. "We were crossing the road," said the girl on the right.

Matt held up a hand. "Before we get into all that, what are your names?"

The one on the left smiled. "I'm Meredith," she said.

"And I'm Mary Beth," said the other girl.

They turned and looked at each other, smiling. "We're not twins," said Mary Beth. "People think we are, but we aren't."

"Not even sisters," said Meredith. "Just good friends."

"Okay, I'll be sure to remember that." Matt ducked his chin to hide the beginnings of a smile. "Now, tell me what happened."

"We were crossing the road like Mary Beth already said. On our bikes—we both have Sweet Thunders."

"They were perfect before today," said Mary Beth in a mournful voice.

"Yeah, now they're all scratched up," said Meredith in a matching tone.

"Did the car knock you down?" Matt asked.

"No, he screeched his tires and hit the mailbox."

"Sent it right through Sally's window," said Mildred.

"And then the mean lady threw us down into the street," said Meredith.

Greshin arched his eyebrows. "The mean lady?"

"Yeah, she came out of nowhere and grabbed our bikes by the handle bars and knocked us down."

Matt glanced up at the two ladies. Mildred Kenny gave a slight shake of her head.

"What can you tell me about the car?"

The two girls looked at each other and shrugged. "It was big," said Mary Beth.

"As big as a Cadillac?"

Again, the two girls shrugged.

"Did you see the driver?"

Meredith nodded.

"Some old guy," said Mary Beth.

"Okay. Grandpa old or more my age?"

"Like you, I guess. We mostly stared at the lady."

"And why was that, Mary Beth?"

She gazed up into Matt's eyes, the picture of solemn innocence. "Because she appeared right out of thin air. She's a witch."

Matt looked at Meredith, who nodded, then glanced at Mildred. "Okay, girls," he said. "That's all I need for now. In the future, I want you to be extra careful when you ride across this street, okay?"

"Don't you want to know what the woman looked like?"

"No, that's okay, Meredith," he said. "I'm sure Mrs. Kenny and Mrs. Ward can tell me all about her. Are your parents on their way down to get you?" The girls nodded and turned their attention back to their now-dripping ice cream cones. Greshin looked at Mildred Kenny and jerked his chin toward the store and walked over to the door.

When they were out of earshot, Mildred put her hand on his arm. "There was no woman, Chief."

"So I gathered," he said. "Did you see the driver of the car?"

Mildred nodded. "Yes, I did. Brown, greasy hair, about shoulder length…skinny…mean looking."

Something in Matt's guts twisted. It sounded a lot like the guy calling himself Randy Fergusson. "Anyone else in the car?"

She shook her head. "He was speeding, though, of that, you can be sure. And he wasn't watching where he was going. He almost ran those two beauties down, barely missed them by jerking his car up onto the curb."

"Big car like the girls said?"

Mildred shrugged. "A Buick. Older one, I believe."

"How old?"

"Ten years, I'd guess—from the sixties, anyway. I'm not much on cars."

"But you're sure it was a Buick?"

She gave him a look. "I can read, Matt Greshin. Said it was right on the hood."

"Yes, ma'am. What color was this Buick?"

"Well, it was a two-tone. White top, black body."

Greshin nodded. "Anything distinctive? Wheels, maybe?"

"Of course it had wheels!"

Matt grinned. "I mean did it have aftermarket wheels? Mags?"

"Well, I'm sure I wouldn't know. I'm not big on cars."

"Fancy wheels? Polished up to shine like mirrors?"

She shrugged. "No idea."

Matt nodded. "Okay, fair enough. Can you tell me what happened in your own words?"

"Sure, I can. I was standing at the counter, speaking with Sally. We heard a hullabaloo out in the street, and then the big plate window in the front of the shop exploded. I whirled around and saw that car up on the sidewalk and the mailbox lying in the front. The girls screamed and fell down. Or dove, I don't know. The driver floored it and squealed away. Someone should take away his license after today."

Matt nodded. "Yes, I agree. If it's who I believe it is, I'll do more than take away his driver's license when I catch up to him." His expression was grim.

"Know this fella, do you?"

"No," said Matt, shaking his head. "But I'm starting to."

Sally Barnes stuck her head out the hole where her window used to be. "Chief Greshin? Angie called, there's a ruckus at Meat World, and Danny Jones says you better come quick."

"She say what the problem is?" he asked.

"No, sir. Just that they wanted you quick."

Matt sighed. "Well, thanks, Sally. Sorry about your window. You have insurance to cover that?"

"Oh yes, don't you worry. George is already on his way to fetch the plywood to cover the hole until the glazier can drag himself over here."

"Good enough. Anything else you think of, Mrs. Kenny, you give me a ring."

"You know I will, Chief."

With a nod, he sketched them a salute and went to his car. He called Angie on the radio. "What's this emergency at Meat World?" he asked.

"Several people have been shot. Danny says he needs help fast."

"I'm on it, you have Fire Rescue on the way?"

"10-4, Chief."

"Good. In the meantime, put out a county-wide BOLO for a Buick Skylark, late 60s vintage, white over black. Mark it both urgent and approach with caution."

"You got it, Chief."

Greshin started the car and pulled away from the curb. He flipped on his lights and siren, spun the car around, and pushed the accelerator all the way to the floor.

8

Owen took his foot off the gas pedal and let the car roll to a stop in the grass on the side of the road. He got out and slipped into the woods, rifle slung over his arm. "You here, babe?" he whispered. Something touched his cheek, light and feathery, and he smiled.

The high school was on route 19 out near the western edge of town. Like everything on the edge of town it backed up to the forest, but ball fields and parking lots ringed the school itself like a moat. Perfect for a skilled sniper.

Owen climbed a pine tree and made a little nest for himself in the crook of two branches. He sighted through the gun at the main doors. *Fuck*, he thought. The parking lots were empty. The school looked deserted. Only then did it dawn on him that it was Sunday afternoon, and no one would be in school. "Fuck!" he yelled.

"What is it, my love?"

"Sunday. No school."

"Oh," whispered Brigitta in his ear. To Owen, she sounded as disappointed as he was. "That's okay, though. We could go to one of those churches."

Owen shook his head. "Services end at noon. Too late to catch 'em coming out of church."

"Oh," she repeated. "The library then?"

"Closed on Sunday."

"Oh."

He slung his rifle and climbed down the tree, pouting the tiniest bit. "Fuck," he muttered.

"There must be somewhere, my love."

"Well, if you can think of something, just speak the fuck up," he snapped. Instantly, he regretted it. He didn't want to be that way with her. "Sorry, babe. I'm disappointed. I wanted to shoot a teacher or five."

"There's always tomorrow, my love."

"Yeah, but I wanted to do it today," he pouted.

"Let's drive by the churches. Maybe one of them is having a nicpic."

"Picnic," he said. "But you're a genius, lover."

He climbed back into the car and mist solidified into Brigitta on the seat next to him. She slid close and put her cheek on his shoulder. "Did you mean it, Owen?"

"Mean what?"

"You called me 'lover.' Did you mean it?"

Owen smiled. Women were all alike, even the ones made of mist. All they wanted was to belong to a strong man. "Yeah, babe, I did."

"Good," she breathed in his ear and reached between his legs.

9

Benny ran, breath and painful sobs hitching his chest. He couldn't put his full weight on his ankle so he couldn't run fast, but every time he slowed to a walk, the dog-things made a ruckus. Black edged his vision, and he longed to lie down, to give up and let Herlequin catch up to him, but he didn't want the dog-things anywhere near him.

He stumbled against a tree trunk, the rough bark scouring his face and warm blood mixed with the sweat and tears already streaming down his cheeks. Every step on his bad ankle was agony, and every breath he took burned like he was breathing fire. Still, the dog-things weren't catching up, and neither was Herlequin. It didn't dawn on him that the dogs should've caught him easily.

His feet shot out from under him as he tried to cut around the thick trunk of a tree. He slammed to the ground, right on top of a knobby root, and the air went out of him. His vision dimmed as he gasped for breath.

Better get up, sport, or you lose again. The voice rang in his head—an intrusion, an invasion.

Benny rolled to the side, still trying to force air into his chest. His lungs felt like they would burst if he didn't get air soon. Purple and blue shapes swam in his vision—dogs, splotches, things that almost looked like faces. He longed to quit, to close his eyes and let the terror end either in sleep or death, he wasn't sure he cared which.

"Psst! Boy!" said a female voice. "Come on, kid, get up! They're almost here!"

Benny cracked open his eyes, but at first, all he could see was the dark gloom of the forest. Something moved at the edge of his vision, a blotch of white against the gloaming. "Who's there?" he croaked.

"Come on, kid! They're coming!"

Benny groaned and rolled onto his hands and knees. "Can you help me? There's a guy chasing me—"

"I know all about that, kid! You've got to hurry! Run!"

"Can you help me?" Benny repeated.

"Kid, you've got to run!"

He sighed and hung his head. *Just another trick*, he thought. *She's not real.*

"Yes, I am, Benny," said the girl. "Real as real gets. Come on, get up and follow me."

She was about his age, blonde-haired and pretty. Her clothes were immaculate, and barrettes held her hair. He tried to smile at her, but his lips just quivered.

He pushed himself up and took a tentative step in her direction. She held out a hand. On second glance, she might be a little older than him. He took another step. The dog-things howled, and they were much closer. Too close. He darted a glance in their direction and then back at the girl.

"We have to go, Benny," she whispered. "*Now*!" She stepped toward him and grabbed his hand. "Run, Benny. You must run."

Her hand felt cool against his sweaty palm. She smelled familiar, like the flowers his mother grew. Her eyes were intent on him. He nodded.

They ran away, her content to lead, and him content to let her. She led him on with confidence, never faltering. He tried to imagine what landmarks she was using to navigate, but he couldn't spot anything that didn't resemble everything else in every detail.

"I have to get out of the forest," he panted.

"No," she said, not sounding the least bit out of breath. "No, you must hide from them. It's the only way." She increased the pace, and the howling behind them took on a frustrated tone.

"I was at my house. I saw my little brother. Herlequin said if I got out he'd let me go. He didn't—he lied."

"Save your breath for running, Benny."

Benny skidded to a halt, dragging her to a stop. "Wait a second. How do you know my name? I never told it to you."

She stomped her foot in exasperation. "*Benny*! We have to run. No time for this now." She turned and pulled him a few steps.

"No! Not until you tell me."

"*He* told me your name, okay? The bad one."

"Herlequin? Why would he do that?"

She shrugged. "If you keep standing here like an idiot, you can ask him yourself. *Run!*" She tugged on his arm, and he let her pull him into a trot.

"There's something wrong with all this," Benny said.

She scoffed. "You think?"

"No, I mean, there's something off. Something that doesn't make sense."

"Yeah, and it's you trying to figure everything out before we reach safety. We have to get away before we have this—"

"It's important! If we don't figure it out, we're just being herded like sheep. We need a destination. We need a way out of this forest."

She scoffed but refused to look at him. "You will make him mad."

"I don't understand any of this. I don't understand why Herlequin wants to chase me around in these old woods. I don't understand why he didn't let me go."

She erupted in bitter laughter. "You never found your house, you dolt."

"Yes, I did. And my brother—"

"No, you little idiot. He made you *think* you were home. He made you *think* your brother was there."

Benny shook his head but let her pull him up to a faster pace. "But why?"

She huffed a breath in exasperation. "What difference does it make?"

Benny slowed again. "Because if we can figure out *why* Herlequin wants us, then maybe we can figure out how to make him *not* want us."

She scoffed. "Come on!" She tugged on his arm, but Benny pulled her to a stop. She whirled to face him. "They're coming!"

"Listen, you gotta help me. I have to get out of here, and since neither one of us knows how to get out of the forest, we have to figure out how to make—"

Her eyes tracked over his shoulder and narrowed. "I can't help you. I can't save you. It's too late, now."

The growling started behind him. *Close* behind him. Benny shook his head, thigh muscles shaking and aching in equal measure. When Herlequin whistled, Benny sobbed. The girls face melted like candle wax, and Benny screamed. Her joints bent and snapped in directions human joints didn't go. Black fur sprouted along her jaw and neck.

When she growled at him, Benny ran shrieking into the forest.

10

Owen smiled the smile of a satisfied man. He stretched lazily and chuckled to himself. Brigitta was the perfect woman. She seemed to know what he wanted as soon as he imagined it. Plus, she was as gorgeous nude as any other way. In Owen's experience, most women had something to hide. Brigitta didn't.

He picked his pants up off the floorboards and slipped into them. *One benefit of being short and skinny.* With a grin, he fished his T-shirt from the backseat and pulled it over his head. Brigitta sat there, naked as a baby, and watched him, a greedy smile playing on her lips. Seeing her like that was almost too much for him, but he had things he wanted to do.

"Baby, want to go to a church picnic with me?" he asked, a sanguine grin on his face.

She clapped her hands like a little girl. "Oh yes, let's!"

"Though it pains me to say it, you might want to put on a thing or two."

She grinned at him and snapped her fingers. Just like that, clothing covered her beautiful body. Owen's fingers fumbled with his shoelaces and he stared at her, mouth agape, and she laughed a deep, full-throated laugh. "So, going invisible is easy for you to deal with, but this is too much?"

Owen chuckled. "You're the perfect woman, babe. You know that?"

Her eyes twinkled. "Am I? Am I, indeed?"

Owen shook his head, a wry expression on his face. He started the Skylark. "You got any idea *which* church we should visit?"

Brigitta cocked her head like she was listening to something far away. A slow smile spread across her cheeks. "First Methodist of Cottonwood Vale. They're having a barbeque."

"In the fall? Those Methodist fuckers are weird." He pulled the Skylark onto the twisting dirt road that led back to the highway. "Won't take us long to get there," he murmured. He hit the pavement, and fish-tailed the muscle car out onto the road, pointed away from Oneka Falls. Brigitta shrieked in delight.

Soon enough, Owen was up in another tree, this one overlooking a park near the edge of Cottonwood Vale. Members of the Methodist church played frisbee in the open, grassy area beneath him. Others stood around charcoal grills and laughed at inane jokes only they could hear.

Brigitta leaned against his left side, her body warm and soft. She was quiet, but he knew she was excited.

"Pick one," he breathed.

Brigitta glanced at him askance, a crooked smiled on her face. "Really?"

He nodded. "Pick one, babe. You pick the first, and if there's time, the last. I pick everyone else."

She laughed like a school girl. She pointed at a fat man sweating over a grill. "That one," she breathed. "That fat one."

Owen grinned and brought up his rifle. He aimed at the guy's left knee. "*Pow*," he said. He aimed at his right bicep. "*Pow*." He aimed at the guy's jiggling gut.

"*Pow*," said Brigitta, putting her hand on his left shoulder.

"If you say so, babe." He pulled the trigger, the shot rang out, and the screaming started.

II

Matt looked at the pool of drying blood and fought the slow, burning fury that blossomed inside him. *An old lady and the only woman with the stones to try to help her*, he thought with disgust. *Only a coward like Fergusson would do something like this.*

The ambulances arrived in minutes, but neither woman had survived, so they'd left empty, replaced by the county ME vans. Danny Jones was a mess. He was young—nothing more than a kid—and had grown up in Oneka Falls. He stood and stared off into space, hands shaking.

"Danny," Matt said. He had to repeat himself twice before the young cop looked at him. "You're in shock, Danny, and this…" Matt's wave encompassed the parking lot. "This is a lot to swallow all at once. But I need you here, Danny. Can you pull it together?"

Danny's eyes were red rimmed and watery, but he nodded and hitched up his duty belt. "Yeah, Chief. You can count on me."

"Good, Danny. Who were the victims?"

Danny fidgeted through his pad, tearing the pages. "I got it here somewhere, Chief. Oh, here it is. Witnesses said Mavis Kendall came out first and got shot. Then Josie Fredericks ran out to help, and the fucker shot her, too."

Matt turned and looked back at the store. "I'm willing to bet the shots came from over thataway. What do you think?"

Danny turned—a little too slow to suit Matt—and stared into the store. "I don't see how, Chief. He'd have to be *inside* the store, right?" He looked to the side and pointed up the road. "Must've come from down there, right?"

Matt shook his head. "No, Danny. The story's in the blood here." He pointed at the fan shaped splatter. "See this part? See how it's farthest from the store?"

"Well...yeah."

"That's the exit splatter. See how it's in a straight line from Meat World's front doors?"

Danny nodded. "But if someone inside the store had made these shots, someone would have seen him, right? Who would let a guy do that? Why would—"

Matt grabbed his chin and lifted it a little. "What do you see?"

"The woods. Trees. What does that have to do..." He snapped his head toward Matt. "A sniper?"

"*The* sniper," said Matt.

"*The* sniper," echoed Danny. "Same guy. Okay, that makes sense...I guess that makes sense." He scratched his chin. "But, Chief?"

"Yeah, Danny?"

"That's a pretty... How far from here to the doors, you think?"

Matt nodded. *He's waking up.* "A hundred and twenty yards."

"Yeah. Now, how deep is Meat World? Store and warehouse?"

Matt shrugged. "Two, three hundred yards."

Danny nodded again. "Yeah. Then, what, another hundred for the loading dock and back lot, then forty or fifty to the edge of the woods." He pulled on his lower lip. "Boss, that's four hundred and fifty yards, best case. Now, if I was good at math, I could tell you how long the shot would be from up in the tree—"

"It's still about four-fifty. Maybe a few yards more," said Matt.

"Yeah, okay, but even so, Chief. A four-hundred-and-fifty-yard shot takes a serious bit of skill, right?"

"Depends a lot on the rifle."

Danny shook his head with vigor. "Well, sure, but a great rifle and a skell shooter is a miss, right?"

Matt shrugged. "Sure. But, an average shooter and a good rifle could make it."

"But these...the victims were moving, right? That makes it harder."

Again, Matt shrugged. "Well, sure, Danny, but they were moving in line with the shot. It doesn't take much knowledge to lead them—"

"Yeah, but these ladies...the victims were shot with *precision*. They were both *headshots*, right? And the paramedic said the first...victim...the first victim got hit in the *brainstem*. I mean, that takes serious skill, right?"

"They could've also been lucky shots."

"One of them in the head, yeah, chalk it up to luck, but *both* of them? And the second victim was *running*, not walking like the old lady was."

Matt grunted and lifted an eyebrow.

"So, this guy has to be ex-military or something, right?"

"It's possible, Danny, but we can't just assume that he's—"

"But, Chief, it has to be. Look at where he was! Up in a tree. Look at how far away he was when he shot the sheriff! Concealment. He's got to be a trained sniper, right? Like a Green Beret or a Marine guy, what are they called? Force Recon."

Matt held up his hands. "Whoa, there, Danny. Slow down. It *might* be a trained sniper, but it also might be an old redneck with his daddy's shootin' iron."

"What? No, Chief, no. Think about it. Think about how this guy operates. What old redneck polices his brass? What old redneck leaves no sign?"

"First, we don't know if he's picked up his brass at this scene. Yes, he did that at Bobby Jefferson's place, but he left it at the Candace Burton scene, and—"

"Oh! I forgot about her! Weren't you on the scene almost right away? Didn't you and Craig pull up before her body even cooled?" His voice was rising with his excitement, and Matt put a hand on the young officer's shoulder.

"Rein it in, Dan. Keep your voice down."

"Yeah, sorry, Chief. I'm just—"

"It's okay to be passionate, Danny, but as a cop, you have to be aware of your surroundings. You have to be—" The rest of what he'd planned to say was drowned out by squealing tires as Craig Witherson slid his cruiser into the parking lot, going too fast for the turn, red and blues spinning. Matt sighed and looked down at the drying blood, waiting.

Craig bounded out of the car and ran over to them. "Chief!" he said. "Is this Fergusson, Chief?"

Greshin shrugged and looked up at the sky. "We have to work it like we don't know anything, right?"

"Right, Chief," said Craig, looking abashed. "What *do* we know?"

"The guy shot from the trees. I think he must be a military sniper, but Matt—"

"Tell you what. You and Danny go check the edge of the woods. Be *careful*. Don't go in the woods, just check the tree line. You're looking for brass, footprints, anything that might be of forensic value."

"Check," said Craig, taking Danny by the elbow.

Matt looked down at the drying blood, fighting his frustration and helplessness.

12

As exhaustion stole Benny's ability to think, his leaden legs and feet ached and burned. But they were still back there—the dog-things, Herlequin, the pretty girl that changed into a dog-thing right in front of him. Back there, and chasing him, driving him ever onward.

He searched for a clue to the right direction for his panicked flight: light, the sound of a car passing on the road, kids screaming and laughing as they played. But the sound of his pursuit shattered the silence of the forest. Every direction he turned looked as dark as a lark.

He thought he was running in circles, but caring about that seemed too exhausting. Too hard. Behind him, Herlequin whistled and laughed like a madman. "*What do you want?*" Benny screamed. The dog-things howled, and Herlequin howled with them. When the howls faded, the only sound outside of Benny's footfalls and panting breath was Herlequin's mocking laughter.

No one would help him; he had nowhere to turn, nowhere to rest. Hot lead churned in his stomach. Helpless and alone, Benny sobbed.

Herlequin mocked him and laughed louder.

To Benny's surprise, anger at the thing behind him elbowed his fear to the side, and he whirled around and sprinted toward Herlequin and his pack of mutant dogs. His pulse beat in his throat like it wanted to explode through his skin. He still couldn't make his thoughts follow a straight line, but his legs no longer felt leaden, his feet no longer hurt.

The dog-things yelped and jumped out of his way as he ran through the pack, tears of anger and frustration streaming down his face. He burst out of the trees into a small glade, and his sprint slowed to a confused shuffle.

A behemoth tree loomed in the center of the circle. It stood thirty or forty feet high, but the diameter of the *huge* trunk was what made it seem so big. Benny had never seen a tree with such a thick trunk in his life—not even on TV. Twelve or thirteen feet in diameter, with ancient looking black bark, the trunk was studded with hundreds of burls. It looked like a mutated, cancerous growth of malignant tumors covered the trunk.

"What in the heck?" whispered Benny. For some inexplicable reason, the tree terrified him.

"Do you like my tree?" asked Herlequin stepping out from behind the huge trunk.

How did he get around in front of me? How did he get behind that tree with me staring right at it?

Herlequin lay a hand on one burl and caressed it as one would a child's head. "I enjoyed her very much," he mused. "Such fun."

Benny looked closer and the panicky terror his anger had replaced swept back in like the tide. The round bumps weren't burls. Screaming faces of children dotted the trunk where he'd thought he'd seen burls. *Hundreds, maybe thousands, of them*! a panicked voice in his head screamed.

Herlequin cackled. "If you could see your expression, Benny!" He lay his hand on another bump and caressed it. "He ran for weeks. *Weeks*, can you imagine? He never faltered, not until the end."

"Mister, you are a sicko." Benny spoke at just above a whisper, but Herlequin had no trouble hearing him.

"You don't know the half of it, Benny." He waved his hand at the ground like a circus emcee directing the audience to gaze into the ring.

The darkness at the base of the tree swam away like a living thing, and Benny gasped. *Bones* littered the ground at the foot of the monstrous tree—small bones from children. And skulls, some broken, some gnawed on. Benny's mind raced back to when he'd come awake in Herlequin's arms, and, unbidden, his eyes tracked up to Herlequin's mouth. *Skull-crushers* he had called them. Benny shivered, and Herlequin leered down at him.

"Do you see them, Benny?" he asked with an edge in his voice.

Benny nodded, throat too dry to speak.

"The ones you see displeased me. The ones not worthy of the chase." Herlequin looked down at the pile of bones, nudging a skull with his foot. "This one was particularly disgusting. Peed and shit everywhere and, if you can believe it, curled up in a ball to move no more." He looked up and pinned Benny with his eyes. "Do you want to end up in this pile?"

Benny's gaze darted from the pile of bones to the children's faces trapped in the tree. They looked terrified. The faces screamed and cried. He shrugged. "Doesn't look like the others fared much better."

"Oh, but they did! The ones the Tree captures, the boys and girls who led me on a merry chase, they live like kings and queens in the bosom of the Tree."

Benny scoffed. "So why are they screaming?"

"Oh, that's nothing, Benny. That's just for my benefit."

"You like to make children scream, don't you?" Benny said with a hint of his earlier anger.

Herlequin chuckled. "It's my favorite thing. Fear is delicious. Terror is…" He shivered all over. "Ecstasy."

"How does anger taste?" asked Benny.

Herlequin cocked an eyebrow at him, a sly smile twisting his ugly face. "It's not as good as fear, Benny. But it will do."

13

"It's time to go, my love," whispered Brigitta.

Owen took his eye away from the scope, looking out at the carnage he'd wrought. Five people lay bleeding in the grass. Others cowered behind benches, trees, anything. It was like the first time, back in Vietnam, when the VC hadn't known where he was, and he could kill at will. *Delicious,* he thought. *Better than sex.*

Beside him, Brigitta pouted. "Better than me?"

"No way, babe. I meant better than sex with any other woman. Nothing compares to you."

She beamed at him. "That's better, my love." She tugged on his shoulder. "But, it's time to get out of Dodge."

"Why?" Owen flung a hand at the park. "These lemmings are no threat."

"*Lómundr,*" she laughed. "That's perfect. That's what they are. Rodents. But the danger is not from them."

He looked back at the remains of the church picnic. "Shame."

"Yes, my love, but it was grand while it lasted."

Owen sighed and patted her forearm. He slung the rifle over his shoulder and skinned down the tree trunk, quiet as a cat.

"Besides," she said, appearing out of thin air beside him. "It's time for you to meet my father."

He cocked an eyebrow at her. "Taking me home to meet your parents already? This must be serious." He grinned his best grin.

She looked back at him, expression solemn. "Yes, my love. This is serious, indeed."

He didn't know what to think of this latest turn, so he kept his mouth shut. "Will he...will he have expectations?" he whispered.

Brigitta nodded her head. "He will, but you will fulfill them all. Don't worry, my love. He will be very interested in you."

"And will he... Does he know about your...proclivities? Will he be freaked out about what we've been doing?"

She laughed her tinkle-bell laugh. "No, my love. My father is never 'freaked out.' He will approve both of you and of my choice in the matter. My sisters, on the other hand…" Owen made a face and Brigitta laughed. "If you could see your face, my love."

Owen couldn't tell if she was making fun of him or not, but the old, familiar anger was creeping up the back of his neck. "Yeah, I'm a regular laugh-riot."

"No, my love. Don't be that way. This is a *good* moment. Don't sour it."

He forced a smile on his face and forced himself to let go of his suspicions. Brigitta was too perfect to drive away.

That's better, my love. Just enjoy this.

He nodded.

"I respect you, Owen Gray," she said. "Your talents are unique and not often duplicated."

His smile felt a little more real, and he reached for her hand. She let him catch it.

They came out of the woods about twenty feet from the Skylark, both smiling and staring at each other. When the station wagon with fake wood on the side roared by them, Owen's gaze snapped up, and he had the rifle half-unslung before Brigitta's hand restrained him.

"No, my love. No time for that now. Let's away."

"But they've seen us, babe. They've seen the *car*."

"It is no matter, my love. Come." She pulled his arm, tugging him toward the car. With one last look at the station wagon speeding away, he let her.

"Do you know the parking lot for the Thousand Acre Wood trailhead, my love?"

"Yeah, right by where we popped Candy's ugly ass."

"Go there, my love." She turned and looked out the windshield as if they were out for a Sunday drive.

"Back to Oneka Falls? No, babe. We've got to go somewhere else. The town will be hopping with cops after the grocery store."

She turned and skewered him with cold eyes. "My love, do as I bid you."

Again, the rage tried to creep up his neck, but he beat it back down. "Sure thing, babe," he said with a smile.

She treated him to one of her sun-eclipsing smiles and the coldness in her eyes dissipated. "Don't worry, my love. I wouldn't lead you into danger."

"Yeah, I know, babe. You want the Thousand Acre Wood trailhead, then that's where we are going." He put words into action and soon enough, they pulled into the parking lot. The deserted lot stood empty, frozen—not even litter blew in the wind. "Looks like you were right once again, babe."

She smiled and kissed his cheek. "Come, my love. My father is waiting for us."

He quirked an eyebrow. "One day, you'll have to tell me how you can talk to him like that."

She smiled again and patted his arm. "It's like how I can talk in your mind, except both my father and I can see each other."

"Okay," Owen said with a shrug. He reached into the back seat and grabbed the rifle by its stock.

"No, my love," Brigitta said. "We won't need that."

He paused, half-in, half-out of the car, hand on the rifle. "Now that we are…active, I don't want to go anywhere without my rifle."

"No, my love." She shook her head, her expression leaving no doubt that he shouldn't argue with her. "Not tonight."

He shrugged and fished the rifle out of the car. He walked around to the back of the Skylark and popped the trunk. "Don't want to just leave it lying out in plain sight."

"That's fine, my love. Now, come." She held out her hand as a mother would to her child. "Father's waiting."

Owen plastered a smile on his face and let her lead him into the woods. They walked for a long time, going ever deeper into the darkened heart of the forest. He'd never noticed it before, but the foliage up in the canopy was thick and dense. Instead of making him uneasy, the darkness felt like a lover's caress.

When Brigitta led him into the glade, the first thing he saw was the brat that had started all this. The little punk who sicced the cops on him in the first place. His breathing accelerated, and his fists clenched.

"My love," breathed Brigitta, a note of warning in her voice.

"Daughter, who is this that stands in my glade and enjoys such vile thoughts about our guest?"

"Father, meet Owen Gray. Owen, meet my father."

Owen forced his eyes away from the brat. Brigitta's father stood shrouded in the shadow of a tree of enormous girth. "Sorry, sir," he said. "This little guy has caused me no end of trouble. But then again, without him, I may never have found Brigitta again."

The thing that stepped out of the shadows was horrible. It was a gargoyle. A life-sized gargoyle.

No, my love.

Owen shook his head but kept the smile plastered to his lips. He knew how to deal with fathers, he'd been schmoozing them since he'd hit his first girlfriend back in high school. Owen looked the thing in the eye and tried to keep his breathing steady.

The thing quirked an eyebrow at Brigitta. "*Again*?" he asked.

Brigitta nodded. "I first met Owen across the seas. I told you of him."

A sly smile crept across the thing's face. "Ah, the one with the rifle."

"Indeed," she said.

"Your daughter has helped me so much, both then and now. I don't know where I'd be without her."

The thing turned its macabre gaze back to Owen. "Dead."

"Most likely," Owen said, going for a wry laugh that sounded more like a chicken being butchered. Having that thing's eyes crawling all over him unnerved him.

"Call me Herlequin," the thing snapped. "Think of me as a 'thing' at your own peril."

Owen dropped his gaze. This wasn't going as well as he'd hoped. This Herlequin could see right through him.

"But of course," said Herlequin. "And there is no question. No 'most likely.' You owe my daughter your life." His expression hardened, and his eyes narrowed to slits. "And if you even consider harming my daughter in one of your 'rages' I will teach you what true rage is. Am I clear?"

Owen snapped his gaze up and met Herlequin's glare with meek acceptance. "Yes, sir. It was a moment of weakness. An old habit. And I would like to point out that at the time, I didn't know my thoughts were not private."

Herlequin harrumphed. "You offer excuses?"

"No, sir. It was wrong. I admit that. It was weak. Brigitta deserves strength, not weakness."

"I told you, Father."

Herlequin stared at Owen for a long time, not moving, not speaking. The little brat sidled toward the edge of the woods. "Oh yes, Benny," hissed Herlequin. "You go ahead and run. I'll be after you soon." The kid froze, and Owen couldn't keep the snide expression off his face.

"You see, my love? My father has such delectable games for one such as this. Had I allowed you to shoot him, his pain and terror would have ended in a flash. This way, his suffering is *eternal.*"

Owen's gaze crawled to Herlequin's face and smiled at the expression he saw there. "I'm beginning to understand, babe."

"I'm so glad you approve," said Herlequin, but his expression softened a miniscule amount. "Come, my daughter." He held out his arms, and Brigitta stepped into the hug with an air of long-lived familiarity.

As they embraced, Owen let his gaze slither over to the kid. Benny, Herlequin had called him. "Help me," the kid mouthed, and Owen laughed. "I'm the last person you should ask for help, brat."

Herlequin chuckled, and just like that the hostility between them evaporated. He put a taloned hand on Owen's shoulder.

Benny turned and bolted into the forest.

Herlequin smiled. "He's a treat," he said. "But you didn't come all this way to yap about the brat. Tell me, Owen, what are your plans?"

Owen paused, glancing at Brigitta. "I assure you that I have nothing but good intentions toward—"

"Oh, don't start all that Daddy-talk again, Owen. Just be yourself. Besides, Brigitta is a grown...*woman*, capable of making her own choices. And if you think I have sway over her, then you don't know her as well as you believed."

Owen smiled and winked at her. "No, she's a strong woman. Good thinker, too. She's like winning the New York Lotto."

"Damn right, my boy. Now, you were telling me about your plans."

Owen scratched his head. "Well, I had been planning on a little revenge. Already got that ball rolling. But, to tell you the God's honest truth, after meeting Brigitta, and now you, that seems...a little bit..."

"Too small?" Herlequin asked with a grin.

Brigitta stepped close to Owen and linked her arm in his. "One should always strive to finish what one starts. Is it not so, Father?"

Herlequin flashed a lopsided grin at her. "Oh, yes, my daughter. But, there are things—bigger things—that your love may do."

Owen smiled. "I'm all ears."

Herlequin laughed. "You were right, Brigitta. He's perfect."

14

Matt was bone tired as dawn broke across the horizon. He hadn't slept since Friday night, and it was grinding him down. His eyes felt like they were using sand for lubricant instead of tears. Everything was too loud, and the sunrise was too bright.

He opened the Fury's door and put one foot out, fighting a sudden wave of dizziness and the urge to barf a gallon of the bitter, acidic coffee that sloshed in his stomach. The smell of the macadam almost pushed him over the edge.

Matt had spent the night wrapping up the Meat World crime scene and had then driven over to help John Morton deal with the shooting at the church picnic in Cottonwood Vale. Two spree shootings in one day. It had to be the same, slimy little prick, but why he started his shit over in Cottonwood Vale was anyone's guess.

He wanted to—no, needed to—declare an emergency, but with Jim gone, there wasn't much he could do through official channels. Matt was a big supporter of the Second Amendment and didn't want to make law-abiding citizens into criminals, but he wanted to do something. Stop sales of .270 ammunition. Get a list of rifle owners. Put a moratorium on gun sales of any kind until Fergusson could he apprehended. All those things sounded like good reactions to the tragedies, but they wouldn't work for the simple reasons that none of those steps would stop Fergusson from killing again, and none of them would retroactively save Fergusson's victims. But, damn it, he wanted to do *something*. He just didn't have any idea what *to* do. He closed his eyes and rested his head against the door jamb of the car.

"Long night?"

He opened his weary eyes. Jim Cartwright stood next to the car, looking wan and tired. Matt pushed himself up and out of the car. "What the hell are you doing here, Jim? You should be back in Cuba with Karen and the boys."

Jim cocked his head. "Have you forgotten that *all* of my boys are not in Cuba?" His tone bordered on churlish.

"No, Jim, I haven't forgotten about Benny. But he disappeared in Cuba, not here. Your best bet is to get back over there." He kept his tone mild, despite the brief flare of irritation at Jim's tone.

Jim shook his head. "He's not over there, and neither is the guy who's got him."

"And who's that, Jim?" asked Matt.

"Don't do that, Matt," Jim snapped.

"Do what?"

"Use your bereavement voice on me. He's not dead. I'd feel it if he were."

"Sorry, didn't mean—"

"Never mind," Jim sighed. "I was up all night."

Matt rubbed his eyes. "Yeah. I've been up since Saturday morning."

Jim leaned forward, eyes pinwheeling with intensity. "You have a line on Fergusson?"

Matt scoffed. "If only I did. He's...been busy."

"What now?" demanded Jim.

Greshin raised his hands and let them drop to his sides. "He shot up the Meat World parking lot yesterday. Killing two ladies wasn't enough, so he bopped over to Cottonwood Vale, avoiding running down two little girls by a gnat's testicle in the process, and shot up the Methodist picnic."

"Oh my Christ. How many?"

"Counting the Jeffersons and Candy Burton, he's up to ten shot. Eight of those are dead."

"Oh my Christ," Jim repeated. "And he's got Benny. It has to be him."

Matt made a moue. "I don't know about that, Jim. If someone had shot Benny, I'd be with you. But why would Fergusson kidnap him? No, he'd just shoot him."

This time, it was Jim who raised and then dropped his hands. "Then *who*?"

"Maybe Toby can tell us in a few days."

"Toby? Toby Burton?"

"Yeah. Did I forget to tell you he came back yesterday?"

Jim just shook his head.

"He's pretty broken up. Old Doc Hauser wants to send him out to the funny farm up in Rochester."

"And his mom is going for that?"

"Well, fuck." Matt rubbed a hand through his hair. "Look, Jim, a lot happened yesterday. Candy's dead. Fergusson shot her out by the trailhead."

"Oh my Christ."

"Yeah. Look, let's get inside and have a damn cup of coffee." Jim nodded, and they walked toward Town Hall. "Craig and I came across Candy's corpse lying in the road. She was still warm."

Jim shook his head.

"Yeah, oh my Christ," said Matt. "Think we interrupted Fergusson, though. Craig found a shell casing, and we got it over to the Troop E headquarters for fingerprint analysis."

"But we already know who he is. Randy Fergusson."

"Nope. We *assume* it's him, but we can't *prove* it, Jim. Anyway, the name Randy Fergusson is fictitious. It's an alias. No records, nothing."

Jim sighed. "What do we do now?"

Matt made them both a cup of coffee and handed one to Jim. "Good police work, Jim, is ninety-nine percent boredom and one percent ball-busting terror. We're in that ninety-nine percent part."

"So wait? We just wait?"

Matt shrugged. "Yeah. We've got irons in the fire, but until they're hot, there's not much to do, except hope Fergusson takes a day off."

"Excuse me, is one of you Chief Greshin?"

"That'd be me, champ," said Matt as he turned.

"You sent over a shell casing?" The speaker was in a New York State Trooper uniform and had lieutenant's bars on his collar.

"I did, yes. They told my officer it won't be ready for a while, though, so I don't have the results yet. Sorry you wasted a drive—"

"I rushed it."

"You rushed the fingerprint analysis?" asked Jim.

"Yes. I read the report about Sheriff Jefferson's shooting, and it rang alarm bells. When your shooter plugged the woman, I suspected I knew who the shooter was. Turns out I was right."

"Right about what, Trooper…" said Matt.

"Sorry. Jonas Gregory," he said, holding out his hand.

Matt shook hands. "What was your suspicion?"

"Your shooter's *real* name is Owen Gray, and this isn't his first rodeo."

"What?"

The trooper nodded. "Not the killing the sheriff part, but the sniper part. Gray's Force Recon. He trained as a sniper and racked up a bunch of confirmed kills in-country. When he rotated home, Camp Pendleton was his duty station. He got a Dear John from his fiancée.

Turns out she didn't want to marry a "killer" as she put it. Gray went AWOL, drove across the country and shot up her wedding. He used a sniper rifle and shot from the woods."

Matt looked at Jim. "Why do you think it was him?"

Gregory grinned. "I said that I rushed the fingerprint analysis on your shell casing. It matched Gray's service record."

"Ain't that something," said Matt. "I can tell you what he's driving. Or at least what he was driving yesterday."

Gregory crooked his eyebrows.

"Late sixties Buick Skylark, white over black. Almost ran down two little girls in his hurry to leave the scene of the shooting here and get over to Cottonwood Vale to shoot up a church picnic."

Gregory's face screwed up in anger. "Let's get this son of a bitch."

15

Shannon Bertram skipped rope at the end of her grandmother's driveway. She was getting over the chickenpox and had to stay with her Granny during the daytime until she was better.

She didn't know what the fuss was all about. Shannon didn't much care for the hundreds of red spots that had sprouted up on her chest, tummy, and back, and she *really* didn't like the ones on her face, but she didn't feel sick. She felt *fine*. Good, even.

Her best friend, Lizzy Markum, hadn't had the chickenpox yet, so she couldn't come play after school, but they had taken to talking on the phone when Lizzy got home. Shannon was counting down the minutes.

The black car with the white top idled up the quiet lane, its engine rumbling, its tires crunching the dried leaves that littered the street.

Shannon noticed, but she didn't pay it much attention. A man and a woman sat in the front seat, and the woman was all scrunched over next to the man. *Gross*, she thought and turned away without breaking her stride, showing off a little.

The car made a squealing noise and stopped moving behind her. "Hey, girl," said a man's voice. Shannon didn't understand why, but his voice creeped her out. She didn't turn.

"Hey there. Girl." The door of the car creaked open, and, this time, Shannon peeked at him. The man was short and greasy looking, but he was smiling at her. "Hey," he said.

Shannon stopped skipping rope and faced him. "I'm not supposed to talk to strange men."

"And you shouldn't, honey," said the woman from inside the car. "But don't worry, Owen's one of the good ones."

Shannon glanced back and forth between the man and the woman. The man kept a smile on his lips, but the woman wasn't smiling. She looked back at Shannon with a solemn expression on her face. "It's okay," the woman said. "We only need directions."

Shannon shrugged. "I'm only nine. I don't know where anything is."

"Not even the high school?" asked the man. "I bet you know where that is."

Shannon grinned. "Oh sure, it's right around the corner, silly."

The man chuckled. "See, babe? I told you we were close."

A tinkling laugh drifted out of the car. "That you did, my love."

"Well, thank you, Miss…" The man looked at her with that certain expression, the one teachers when you were supposed to answer for them.

"Shannon. My name's Shannon."

"Well, Miss Shannon, I've got a crisp dollar bill for you for your trouble."

Shannon smiled. "A whole dollar?"

"Yep." The man beamed at her and pulled a dollar bill out of his front pocket. It didn't look very crisp, but a crumpled dollar bill bought just as much candy as a crisp one. Shannon dropped her jump rope and ran to get her dollar.

No one heard her scream when the man grabbed her and shoved her in the trunk.

16

It took sixty-minutes to drive to Rochester, and it almost bored Jim to sleep. The country was scenic enough, but he wasn't looking at the scenery. The thought of Benny in the hands of a notorious spree killer whirled around in his head. It was like a low voltage electric charge, interrupting his thoughts, keeping him from focusing on anything.

The psychiatric unit at Strong Memorial looked just like Jim thought a psychiatric hospital should. Built from imposing red brick, it looked like something straight out of a horror movie. Jim parked and walked around to the main entrance. Doc Hauser was waiting out front. He was going to get Jim in to talk to Toby.

"Howdy, Jim. Sorry to hear about your boys."

"Thanks."

"Have they made a diagnosis on little Billy yet?"

Jim shook his head.

"They will, don't you fret," said the old doctor.

"To be honest, I'm more worried about Benny. Johnny's receiving care, at least. Who knows where Benny is…"

Doc Hauser patted him on the back. "Well, that's why we're here." He glanced at the main entrance of the psychiatric center. "Listen, Jim. Toby might not be able to help. He's suffering from hysterical catatonia—the result of his ordeal—and may not talk to us. He may not even acknowledge us."

Jim nodded. "Greshin told me."

"I don't want you to get your hopes up."

"Fair enough, Doctor. Let's go see what happens, okay?"

Hauser ushered him inside, and after a minute and a half of arguing with the attendant at the front desk, they sat in an eight by eight visitation room. It was cold, and the metal chairs and table didn't help. "Now, we wait," said Hauser. "One thing, Jim. Don't tell Toby your son is missing. It might be psychologically harmful to him to think about his own abduction so soon."

"Okay," Jim murmured.

Twenty minutes later, a big orderly wheeled Toby Burton into the room. He stared straight forward, uninterested in where he was going, or who wanted to visit him.

"Well, hello again, Toby," said Doc Hauser in moderate tones. "I've brought someone to chat with you." He patted Jim on the shoulder. "Do you remember Mr. Cartwright?"

Toby didn't move, didn't bat an eyelash, didn't even seem to draw breath.

"Mr. Cartwright is Benny's father. Do you remember Benny?" He waited a moment, and when Toby didn't respond, Hauser sighed. "I'm afraid it's not much use, Jim."

Jim leaned forward and put his hand on the table where Toby's gaze rested. "Toby," he said. "What happened to you? Who kidnapped you?"

The boy didn't move or speak.

"Toby, can you help Mr. Cartwright?"

"Benny's your friend, Toby. He rode around looking for you when you disappeared. He asked your mother where you were and went over to the bicycle man's house. Benny tried to help you, asked about you, and he took a big risk to do it."

Toby sat as still as a statue.

"Damn it, Toby! Benny's missing, maybe because he cared enough about you to go looking for you. Billy's sick, unconscious. He had a seizure the day Benny disappeared."

Hauser put his hand on Jim's shoulder. "That's enough, now, Jim."

"Benny cared enough to go looking for you when he thought you needed his help. Now *he* needs your help."

Toby leaned his head to the side, and his gaze drifted into the corner.

"Jim," whispered Doc Hauser, "this isn't helping anyone. The boy's too traumatized and telling him these things won't help. Come on, now. You've asked him your questions. As he gets better, he might give you the answers to your questions."

"No!" snapped Jim. "Benny needs help *now*."

"Buh-buh-benny?" muttered Toby, sounding like the word was the hardest thing he'd ever said.

"That's right, Toby," said Jim. "Benny needs you."

Toby's eyes drifted away from the corner but didn't quite reach Jim's. "Huh-huh."

"What's that Toby?"

A tear rolled down the boy's cheek, and his chest hitched.

"Okay, Jim, that's enough now."

Toby screamed. It was a scream of pure terror, pure agony.

"Toby, who took you? Where were you kept?"

Toby's chest heaved like he was running, and his eyes grew frantic.

"This interview is over, Mr. Cartwright," snapped Dr. Hauser. "I told you—"

"Benny's in the woods!" Toby shouted, his voice sounding like so many rusted hinges. "The king! The king has him in the glade with the Tree! The king!"

"Who is the king," demanded Jim, shrugging off Hauser's hand. "Toby, who is it?"

"Huh-huh. He will make him run! He's going to...skull-smashers! He's got him in the dark heart of the forest... No! Benny, no!"

The orderly came barging through the door and cast a disapproving look at Doc Hauser. "Now, what's all this yelling?"

Jim pushed himself away from the table and tried to rush around to Toby's side, but the orderly put up one meaty hand and sent Jim sprawling into the corner. "You done enough, mister!"

"The woods! The woods!" screeched Toby.

"Thousand Acre Wood?" asked Jim.

"Watch out… Watch out for… Huh-huh. Watch out! Get to him before the dogs do! Get to the clearing! Get Benny away!"

The orderly snapped the brakes off the wheelchair and spun Toby out of the room without looking back. He kicked the door to the small room shut.

"No!" yelled Jim. "No! He's telling me where my kidnapped son is! Bring him back!"

Dr. Hauser cleared his throat and stood. "Next time you need my help, Cartwright, just remember this scene." Hauser turned and walked out the door.

Jim slouched in the corner and cried. He couldn't stop himself.

17

"Hey, Fatty! Where are you going?"

Bob ducked his ample chin to his chest and quickened his pace. His Husky jeans swished with each step, the inevitable result of his thighs rubbing together. He stared at his Earth shoes and pressed his lips together into a tight line.

"What's the matter, Fatty? Cat got your tongue?"

The guy following him, cat-calling him, was none other than Dennis the Menace, the fifth-grade bully. Bob didn't know why Dennis liked to make fun of him, just that he did it every time he saw Bob.

"Home," Bob muttered.

"What was that, Fatty? I couldn't understand you with my dick in your mouth."

Bob didn't know what that meant, but he knew it was bad. Dennis was the typical bully, not very bright—he'd failed second, third and fifth grades—but gifted at culling the weak out of the herd. And he was loose with his fists. Bob still had bruises from last Friday, and he didn't want anymore.

"I'm going home," he repeated, louder this time.

"Aw, is da diddle bay-bee going home to tell his mommy?"

"No! I'm…I'm just going home," he finished. *Lame!* he chastised himself.

"Aw, Fatty, did I touch a nerve?"

Bob shook his head without raising his eyes. He kept walking, speeding up a bit. *Why are there* never *any teachers around after school?*

"Fatty, you're hurting my feelings—ignoring me, walking away when I'm talking to you."

"Suh-sorry. Got to get home."

The fist came out of nowhere, and when it glanced off the back of his head, tears sprang to his eyes. "Ow, Dennis! Just leave me alone why don't you!"

"That's not very nice of you, Fatty."

Bob groaned when he recognized the change in Dennis' voice. He'd been playing around up until then, but no more. He was out for blood.

"Listen, Dennis, I-I'm suh-sorry, okay? I don't want to fight with you."

Dennis laughed, and it was his nastiest, meanest laugh. "My but, you're just a big ole pussy, aren't you? But don't worry, Fatty. You don't have to." Head still down, Bob only saw the older kid's Pumas edge into his vision in front of him.

Bob saw it coming this time, but it didn't make any difference. Dennis' fist sank into Bob's gut, driving the wind out of him. He fell to one knee, dropping his books.

"Aw, did da diddle bay-bee fall down and get a boo-boo? Here, let me help you, Fatty." Dennis held a hand in front of Bob's face.

Bob ignored it, gasping like a beached fish. He didn't want to get up, he wanted to catch his breath and keep himself from puking.

Dennis waved the hand in front of him. "Come on, Fatty. I ain't got all day."

Reluctantly, Bob grasped the older boy's hand. Dennis pulled hard, yanking him off the ground. At the apex of his trajectory, Dennis punched him again, and this time, Bob did puke…all over Dennis' fancy Puma Clydes.

"Oh, you fat fuck!" yelled Dennis. "These are suede! How am I gonna get your puke out of suede?" Bob lay where he'd fallen, curled around his belly, gasping for breath, eyes full of tears, cheek in the dirt. "This is so gross, Fatty!"

Bob waited. Anything he said at this point would extend the beating.

Dennis bent down and grabbed one of his books, scattering the pile. Papers—drawings, mostly—flew in the wind. "Aw, does da diddle bay-bee like to draw? Is da diddle bay-bee an artist?" Dennis grabbed one of the pictures—one of Bob's car drawings—and used it to sling puke off his shoes and across Bob's jeans. "Have your puke back, Fatty," he yelled gleefully. "You're lucky I don't make you eat it, but frankly, Fatty, you make me sick enough as it is." He wadded up the drawing and threw it side-arm.

As Dennis walked away, Bob reached for the closest of the drawings, pulling them close to his chest. Of course, no one came to help him. No one cared about the fat boy.

Sniffling, and furiously wiping tears from his cheeks, Bob grabbed his books and stood. Dennis had taken off, of course. Not that Bob would have done anything if he was still around, but his absence made it easier to tell himself things would have been different if the bully had stuck around.

He walked away from the school, head down, puke drying on his jeans, thighs swishing together. *I hate that fucking sound!* he screamed inside his head.

When he got home, he was going to have a triple-decker baloney and cheese with lots of Miracle Whip and *two* Ring Dings. Or a Ring Ding and a Ho Ho. He turned down Neibolt Street, wanting to get off the main drag. He lived across town on Mill Lane, but Dennis was always hanging out in the center of town. The last thing he wanted was *another* beating.

He paid no attention to the low rumble of the muscle car until it passed him and cut in front of him. A skinny guy sprang out of the driver's door. "Hey, kid," he said.

Bob didn't answer, cutting his eyes away instead.

"What happened to you? You been to the wars and back, or what?"

Bob angled away from the man, heading for the other side of the street.

"No reason to be rude, kid. I didn't beat you up."

Bob shrugged and kept walking. He didn't feel like talking to *anyone*, let alone some weird guy in a Buick.

"Oh, for Chrissake, kid."

Bob flinched and shrugged away when the man's hand fell on his shoulder.

"Look, kid, you remind me of my little brother, okay? He was always getting picked on. I can't help him no more, but maybe I can help you. Let me buy you a milkshake, and then I'll teach you how to deal with bullies. Deal?"

Bob glanced at him sideways. The guy *looked* okay. "A large milkshake?" he murmured.

"What? Oh, sure, kid. Large it is."

When the guy's hand came to rest on his shoulder again, Bob didn't duck away. Instead, he let the man turn him and guide him toward the white and black Skylark. As they got closer, something started thumping rhythmically in the trunk.

The man caught him staring at the trunk and laughed. "Don't worry, Big Bob. It's just a raccoon."

That doesn't even make sense, Bob thought. *And only Mommy calls me Big Bob.* He turned to walk away, but it was already too late. Far too late.

18

Matt sighed through his nose but tried to keep his exasperation from showing. *Nothing like a cross-jurisdictional search party to destroy the serenity of nature.* On top of having the State Troopers involved, he had police officers from Cottonwood Vale, Genosgwa, and Victorville, and deputies from Kanowa County Sheriff's Department. Adding to the hullabaloo were civilian volunteers from all over the county.

A map of Thousand Acre Wood lay across the hood of Matt's Fury, a pair of handcuffs weighting down each corner. He and Lieutenant Gregory were bent over the map, looking for any place where someone might hide a boy, and trying to identify the best spots to have dumped a body.

"Chief Greshin, you should hear this," said Danny.

Matt straightened. Danny stood ten paces away, almost wringing his hands. Three of the civilian volunteers stood behind him. He waved them all over. "What's up, Danny?"

"Thorndike, here, says they found something. Go ahead, Mr. Thorndike." Danny put his hand on the old man's shoulder.

Thorndike cleared his throat. "We took the Hill Pond trail branch, and then when we were walking, this dog-pack began to run parallel to our course. That didn't seem right, so we tried to follow them.

"The others thought we were bound to get lost pretty quick, but I've walked these woods going on seventy years now, and I can get myself out. As we were working our way out, we came across a pile of kid's things. A jacket, a backpack, things like that. When we went over to the pile, a glade became visible off through the trees. That was strange because of how dark the woods get back in there, and then there was this glade all lit up with sunlight. A huge black tree was in the middle of the glade. Full of cancer, the ugly bastard was. Burls."

Lieutenant Gregory and Matt exchanged looks. *That pile of stuff has to belong to Benny,* thought Matt. *We're coming kid, just hold on.* "Can you lead us back to the spot, Mr. Thorndike?"

"Ayup. Follow me." Without waiting for a response, Mr. Thorndike turned and walked away.

"Well, guess we better follow him, Lieutenant Gregory," said Matt with a wry grin.

"Ayup, Chief Greshin." Gregory wore a grin to match Matt's.

"Danny, you stay here in case anyone else reports something. You call me if they do."

"Yes, sir, Chief."

Thorndike led the two cops down the trail a bit, darting glances into the woods. "You said you saw a dog pack?" asked Matt.

"I reckon I did."

"What sort of dog pack?" Matt asked with a mirthful glance at Jonas.

"Well, some of them were straight out of the movies. One of 'em looked like that one in that devil picture that was out a few years back. The Omen, I think it was called."

"Rottweilers?"

Thorndike grunted. "Scary damn breed, if you ask me. Another one of them looked like a shepherd, but all black."

"Strange set of dogs to be running around in these woods," said Jonas.

"I don't recall ever seeing a Rottweiler or an all-black shepherd in this town," said Matt.

Thorndike harrumphed. "I'm not in the practice of lying about things. This other one looked like that skinny breed of Rottweiler."

"Doberman?"

Thorndike hawked and spat. "If I had the names of the breeds, don't you expect I would have said it outright?" He pointed at a bend in the well-worn path ahead. "That's where we got back on the path after we saw the pile of things and that damn glade."

Matt cocked his head to the side. *Doesn't make sense*, he thought. *Why chase after a pack of dogs?*

"There weren't much sense in us going off after a bunch of feral dogs, and I can't much explain why I took us off that way, except that I got this quirky sensation—a gut feeling if you want."

"You had a hunch about the dogs?" asked Jonas.

Thorndike winced. "Doesn't make sense now," he muttered, throwing a sideways glance at Matt. "But no sense holding back if it might help. I got the feeling that the dogs had themselves a secret, and I wanted to know what that secret was."

Matt smiled, trying to make it a reassuring one. "Mr. Thorndike, if you knew how much of police work boils down to gut feelings…"

"Ayup," said the old man, not sounding convinced. "Nice of you to say. Anyway, we stepped into the forest right here."

"And you're sure you remember where the glade is?" asked Jonas.

"Sure as I can be." Thorndike stepped into the woods before either man could say anything more. They walked for another forty or fifty minutes in silence before Thorndike stopped. "Doesn't make sense," he muttered.

"What's that, Mr. Thorndike?"

The old codger shook his head and turned in a slow circle. "Couldn't have missed the bastard," he murmured. "That damn glade was lit up like a hospital. Should've seen it by now."

Matt looked at Jonas and cocked an eyebrow. He cleared his throat. "Are we lost, Mr. Thorndike?"

"Nah," said the old man with a dismissive wave of his hand. "I know where we are, all right. The problem is, the glade ain't here, and neither is that pile of stuff."

Matt looked around. "You mean this is the place?" It was too dark to see much of anything—everything looked the same in the gloom.

"Ayuh. Right here where we are standing, was a pile of kids' stuff, and over yonder, a glade with a big bastard tree in the middle."

Matt glanced at Jonas.

"Oh, what's running through your noggin is plain enough, Matt Greshin, but I ain't gone off around the bend yet. The others saw the glade and the tree, too."

"Maybe you got turned around coming back? Things always look different from the other direction."

Thorndike's only response was to hawk and spit into the gloom. "Should be right here," he grumbled.

"We could circle outwards for a while. See if we come across this glade." Jonas hitched his Sam Browne belt into a more comfortable position.

Thorndike laughed. "Son, do you know why we call this here wood the Thousand Acre Wood?"

"Well, no."

"Look around, then. This time with your eyes open. We call the place that because it all looks the same. If you've seen an acre, the next thousand acres are all the same."

"But that's—"

"Nah. If that glade were around here, we'd have seen it by now."

Matt shook his head. "So what are you saying, Mr. Thorndike?"

Thorndike shrugged and met his gaze. "That pile of things disappeared while we were walking out. Or someone moved it. Someone must have moved that glade somehow while they were at it." He held up his hand. "Now, that makes me sound a little soft between the ears, but you asked me what I think, and that's it." He turned and walked back toward the trail.

"Matt, is this guy on the up and up?"

Matt peered after Thorndike's retreating back. "Yes. He's old, but he's always been a straight arrow."

"Then what is all this?"

Matt shrugged. "Mass hallucination? A what-do-you-call-it."

"A *folie a deux*? Nah, it's either a hoax or he's trying to cover something up."

Matt cleared his throat. "Thorndike's not involved in any kidnappings. He's all right, Jonas."

"Then this has been a lot of time wasted on a hoax."

"I don't think Mr. Thorn—"

"Doesn't matter, though, does it? We've still wasted half the afternoon on nonsense."

"You boys coming?" called Thorndike.

Matt turned to follow the old man back to the parking lot and then froze, hand drifting to the butt of his Colt.

"What?" breathed Jonas.

Matt held up his hand, head cocked, eyes roaming the surrounding woods. After a minute, he sighed and straightened up. "Did you hear that noise?"

"What?" asked Jonas.

"Thought I heard a dog growling."

Jonas looked at him for a long moment and then brushed past him. "Wasted enough time out here," he muttered.

19

Shannon recognized the fat boy from school, but she didn't know his name. He was a grade ahead and a loner to boot. She inched away from him. He smelled like vomit.

"You were right, babe," said the man. The driver's door slammed. "And so was your old man. This is easy."

The tinkling laugh sounded muffled through the back seat of the car.

"You are good at it, my love. A hidden talent."

The man laughed. "What now, babe? More kids?"

"Well, you promised me a teacher or two."

The man roared laughter and started the car.

"Who are you?" the fat boy asked. He was talking loud over the car's exhaust. "Who is that man? What does he want?"

Shannon shifted away another inch. "Don't touch me, I have the chickenpox."

"Why did he grab us? Why are we in the trunk?"

"How would I know? I got picked up same as you."

"Shit!" said the man driving the car. "Cops, babe."

"Don't worry, my love," said the woman in a lilting voice. "Just pull over here."

The note of the car's engine changed, quieted. Shannon bounced and jounced around as the car pulled off the macadam and coasted to a stop on the shoulder of the road. Another car pulled up behind them, and its driver got out of the car and walked toward them.

"Help!" Shannon screamed. "We're in the trunk! He's kidnapping us!"

The footsteps stopped. "Driver, get out of the car. Slowly!"

"What do I do, babe?"

"Do what he says, my love." The Skylark's door opened. "But take your rifle."

"Babe, if I do that, I'll get shot."

"No, my love. It won't be you getting shot."

The man laughed. It was a nasty laugh. "I think I love you, babe."

"And I, you, my love."

The car rocked as the driver got out of the car. "It's you!" he said. His voice was angry, hateful.

"Fergusson! Get your hands up! Now!"

"Why, Officer Witherson, I'm starting to believe you don't trust me."

"I will not tell you again, Fergusson. Get—"

A soft *crack* sounded next to the trunk. "You are right, Craig. You're not going to tell me again. Not anything. Ever."

The only reply was a gurgling moan.

"Yeah. Your days of telling people things are over, Officer," gloated the nasty man. There was a mechanical sound, part click, part clack, and then the soft *crack* came again, and the nasty man laughed. "See that, babe? His head splattered like a melon!"

"Yes, my love. Just like that comedian with his Sledge-O-Matic and the watermelon."

"Yeah," said the man, but he sounded confused.

"Never mind, my love. Let's get going before someone comes bopping along."

"Right you are, babe." The car rocked as the driver got back in and then the car's engine roared, and they bumped back onto the macadam.

"Did he…did he just shoot a policeman?" Shannon whispered.

"What's your name?" the fat boy asked.

What can it hurt? Shannon thought. "My name is Shannon. I'm in fourth."

"I'm Bob," he said. "Fifth. Yeah, he just killed a police officer. That nice one…Officer Witherson."

Shannon didn't know what to say, so she focused on not smelling the fat kid. The car was moving, the man taking corners without a thought for his "guests" in the trunk. They slid around like sacks of cabbages, bumping and grinding together like an unseemly dance. "Don't touch me," she said. "Chickenpox." The car left the pavement, bouncing along over ruts and holes. When it stopped, she breathed a sigh of relief and slid away from the smelly boy.

The door of the car creaked open, but neither the woman nor the man said anything. The car rocked as the two got out. Something clanked on the roof of the car.

"Well, babe, silenced or loud?" the man asked.

"Let's be loud for a change," said the woman.

"Loud it is."

Shannon heard a ripping sound, and something clattered into the backseat.

"You pick the tree, babe."

"Not this time, my love. No tree. We will need to get out of here in a hurry."

"Oh yeah? Something I missed, babe?"

"Don't worry, my love. I won't let you come to harm."

There was the sound of smoochy kissing, and Shannon's cheeks burned. "I have the chickenpox," she breathed.

"You've said," said the fat boy. "Don't worry. I won't touch you."

A school bus rumbled by on the road, and the trunk filled up with the stink of diesel fumes.

"Okay, babe," said the man. "Pick one."

"Teachers, remember?"

"I remember," said the man, sounding a little annoyed. "Pick one."

"Her."

"*Pow. Pow. Pow*," said the man.

"*Pow*," breathed the woman.

There was a deafening boom, and Shannon screamed. She couldn't help it. The woman laughed her tinkling laugh.

"I scared someone, babe."

"It's no matter, my love. They'll be much more scared come this evening." The woman laughed again. "Him, the one with the whistle around his neck."

"Oh, a *coach*," laughed the man. "I hate coaches. *Pow. Pow. Pow*."

"*Pow*," said the woman, and the deafening boom sounded again. Shannon yelped at the sheer volume of the noise, and the man laughed.

"Oh! Her next," purred the woman.

"She's sexy, babe. Should we—"

"Sexier than me, my love?" There was the sound of a zipper opening. "Sexier than this?"

Oh gross! thought Shannon.

"What are they *doing*?" asked the boy.

"That was her zipper, dummy."

"I *know* that. I mean the booming thing."

Shannon's cheeks burned at the rebuke in his voice. "Oh. I think it's a…a gun."

"They're *shooting* people? It's a game to them?"

Shannon shrugged, and the deafening boom sounded again. This time, she only flinched.

"How sexy is she now?" asked the woman, and the man and the woman laughed.

"Definitely not as sexy as that," said the man.

"Do you just want to look? Or maybe…"

The woman's voice was funny, Shannon thought. *Like the women on her Granny's soap operas just before they kissed someone else's husband.* "Gross," she whispered.

"Someone's screaming," said the boy.

Shannon listened intently, and it *did* sound like someone was screaming. "Someone will come to help us," she said with a wistful note in her voice.

"Oh, put her out of my misery, my love. She sounds like a little girl having a hissy-fit."

The deafening boom sounded again, and the screaming stopped. "Shit," said the man. "They're on to us, babe. I thought we'd get more than three." It almost sounded like he was pouting.

"There will be other days, my love. Other schools."

"Yeah," he breathed. "But for now, let's go find somewhere secluded. You can show me what's inside your jeans again."

The woman laughed, almost like a cat purring.

Gross, Shannon thought.

20

Hour piled on top of hour with ruthless efficiency, and still, Benny didn't come home. Still, little Billy lay in a coma sixty miles away. The shooting at the high school had already made the national radio news programs. They called the shootings a "wave of violence perpetrated by a madman, or a group of madmen." The governor made a speech about declaring a state of emergency and sending in the National Guard.

When the phone rang, Jim winced and twitched, dreading picking up the receiver. Either Karen would be on the other end, demanding news, demanding he *do something*, or it would be Matt Greshin calling to say they'd found Benny's body out in the woods somewhere, raped or who knows what. He reached for the ringing phone, to stop the infernal racket if nothing else. He rested his hand on the receiver and let it ring. If the person calling hung up, he wouldn't have to talk to them. But the phone kept ringing. On the fifteenth ring, Jim picked up the handset.

"Cartwright," he said, sounding as gruff as a lifelong smoker.

"Took you long enough." It wasn't Karen, and it wasn't Greshin.

"Who is this?"

"You know who, Mr. Town-fucking-Manager. Come to your window. I'm right outside."

Trying to be so quiet that his movement wouldn't carry over the phone line, Jim slid out of his chair and crawled into the chair-nook. "Fergusson?"

The caller laughed. "That isn't my name, ass-wipe."

Jim nodded to himself. "Gray, then."

"That's right. Owen Gray. Have you found out I'm a Marine Force Recon sniper, yet?"

"I found out you're a murderous bastard."

The line hissed in silence for a moment. "That's kind of rude, buddy. Come to your window."

"Oh, I'll come to my window if you come out of fucking hiding and face me like a man. But you won't do that, will you Gray? You won't do that because you are a fucking coward." Without feeling the emotion coming, Jim was drowning in a black-hearted fury. "Well, Gray? Do we have a deal? You come out, I come out?"

Gray laughed.

"Uh-huh, I was right about you. The Marine Corps flag is scarlet and gold, right? Or is it *yellow*?"

An odd sound came over the line and a window downstairs shattered. "Still around, Mr. Town-fucking-Manager? I hope you didn't die already." Gray's voice writhed with hatred, slithered with duplicity.

"You are a miserable bastard, aren't you, Gray?"

The line crackled and popped. The sound of Gray chambering another round clattered harshly in its wake. "More where that came from, Cartwright. Oh, hey, I'm an asshole. How's your son?"

"Don't you talk about my kids!"

"Poor little Billy. Dead on the inside. Poor little Benny. I bet he wishes he *were* dead."

"Don't you hurt my boys!"

"Ha! I've got nothing to do with them. Little Billy's already done, he'll never wake up. Your boy Benny…well, let's just say his pain has only just begun. Come to your window. I can make all this go away. All this pain, all this dread…all of it can end right now—"

Jim pressed the disconnect and dialed Matt's home phone number. When he got no answer, he called dispatch.

"Oneka Falls Police—"

"Angie, Jim Cartwright. Owen Gray is outside my house. He already shot out a window downstairs."

"I hear you, Jim." The phone rustled as she dispatched all available units. Matt's voice crackled in reply, but Jim couldn't make out what he said. "Jim? Matt says to hide."

"That's what I'm doing, Angie. Gray thinks I'm downstairs, but I'm not. If he shoots up here, I'll get into the tub."

"Ten-four," Angie said, but Jim didn't know if it was in response to his weak plan or to something Matt said on the radio.

"Mr. Town-fucking-Manager," Gray called from outside, his tone lilting, mocking. Downstairs, another window shattered.

Something bothered Jim about that, but he couldn't figure out what. "Angie? Tell them to hurry."

"Don't worry, Jim, they're coming code three."

"How rude," said Gray. He stood in the doorway, pointing a rifle at Jim. He was dirty, hair tossed with leaves, bare feet almost black with grime.

The sound of the rifle shot was deafening.

21

Matt pushed his cruiser hard—the 440 Magnum shrieked and roared, and the tires screamed on the corners. He knew the streets of Oneka Falls like the back of his hand and took streets that would get him to Jim's house the fastest. The red dash-top light spun, and what traffic existed cleared in front of him

He didn't run the siren. If Jim still lived, a bunch of sirens roaring up outside the house might be a death sentence. Gray was a whack-job, no doubt about *that*, and whack-jobs were unpredictable. And Gray was already making them look like fools. While they searched the woods for Benny, he's miles away, shooting up the high school, and killing cops. All that before he moved on to shooting the town manager. Blood thumped in Matt's temples.

He wanted Craig at his back, but the days of that had ended on the side of the road a few hours earlier. Anger sang in his veins. *Why didn't you wait for back up, Craig? What did Gray do to goad you? What did he say to make you rush in like a dumbass?* As with the previous three hundred times he'd asked those questions, no answer came. Craig hadn't been a foolish man, and he *had* been an exceptional law enforcement officer. Something must have happened that made him confront Gray on the side of the road like that. *But what? Did he catch him in the act of taking the two new missing kids?*

When he turned onto Rabbit Run, he took his foot off the gas and let the car coast up the street. No sense risking having Gray hear him roar up to the house He brought the car to a silent stop and got out, leaving the door ajar.

First on the scene, Matt knew he should wait for back up, knew he shouldn't rush in blind. *Fuck that*, he thought, and the image of Craig Witherson splattered all over the shoulder of the road raced through his mind. He pushed the image away and ran hunched over to the front stoop and plastered himself to the wall. The big bay window had shattered inward, glass shards all over the living room carpet. Gray must have shot from one of the houses on the street. Of course.

He tried the door knob, but it was locked. With a shrug, Matt stepped through the shattered bay window, glass crunching under his boots, Colt in his hand. Inside, he froze, straining his ears to catch any sound.

The house was as silent as a graveyard. *Hope I'm not too late,* he thought. *Better not be for Gray's sake.* Moving quietly, he went to the stairs and climbed to the second floor of the house.

Angie had told him that right before she lost the connection, she'd heard someone in the room with Jim. He thumbed the safety off as he inched down the hallway, listening hard, peering into the shadowed rooms as he passed them.

The door to Jim's study was closed. Matt took a deep breath and edged the door open with his boot and it swung on well-oiled hinges. Matt took a quick glance, and ducked his head back out.

The room was empty. He'd been in Jim's study plenty of times, but couldn't remember where the closet was, or if there even was one in the room. Jim's desk was against the far wall, and the phone cord stretched into the nook of the desk. Matt charged into the room, spinning to cover the only part of the room he couldn't see from the door.

Jim lay slumped against the wall, one hand clamped over his gut. Blood ran down his arm and seeped into the carpet around him, Matt's knees squelched in the blood as he knelt next to his friend. "Jim?"

Jim's eyelids fluttered, and he groaned. Blood seeped through his fingers, thick as sludge.

Matt grabbed the telephone receiver from where it lay beneath the desk. There was no dial tone. He traced the spiral telephone cord to the base of the phone, or what remained of it. It looked like someone had filled it with explosives and set them off. "Shit," he muttered.

Jim groaned again and mumbled something incomprehensible.

"Where is another phone, Jim? What room?"

Jim's fingers twitched and then pointed up the hall. His hands were abraded and scratched like he'd put up one hell of a fight. Matt pushed Jim's hand away and ripped the man's shirt open. The wound was about a quarter of an inch in diameter, surrounded by an abrasion ring and stippling in a wider arc around that. Matt spread the wound and peered inside, ignoring Jim's hissing curses. Everything that should be inside still looked intact. "Looks like he gut-shot you, boss, but the good news is that he didn't rupture anything in there."

"That coward, that bastard," grunted Jim, eyes still squeezed shut.

Matt took off his shirt and pressed it over the wound and then pressed Jim's hand on top of that. "Keep pressure on this, Jim." He ran up the hall and through the door into the master bedroom. He called Angie for an ambulance and told her to get a couple of troopers from the high school to come over to the Cartwright house and start processing the scene.

When he got back to the study, Jim looked a little better. "Jim?"

He opened his eyes and looked around bleary-eyed and in obvious pain. "Where's—"

"Gray ran off, though why he left you alive, I can't guess."

"Girl heard you out front," Jim croaked. "A sick expression washed over his face and he turned tail."

Matt laughed. It was an ugly sound. "I thought I was so quiet. Wait a minute... Did you say a *girl* saw me?"

Jim nodded. "Had his new girlfriend with him. They're all lovey-dovey. Babe, this. My love, that. Almost wanted him to shoot me."

"Did you get a piece of him?" Matt asked, nudging Jim's scraped up hand.

"Yeah," said Jim. "He snuck up on me while I was talking to Angie, shot the phone. I rushed him while he was reloading. Was beating the ever-loving piss out of him when the girl knocked me across the room."

"The woman knocked you down?"

Jim nodded. "Strong little thing. She...she backhanded me and I flew—feet off the floor and everything." He shook his head. "Fuzzy, though."

Matt patted his shoulder. "Don't worry about that, Jim. So, he shot you after the girl—"

"Bridget, or Bridgetta maybe. Something like that."

"Can you describe her?"

"Yeah, blonde hair, high cheeks, full lips. Blue or gray eyes maybe.

"You got beat up by Bo Derek? Some people have all the luck."

Jim smiled, a weak smile not much different from a twitch of his lips, but it was a smile nonetheless. "Nah, no tan."

Sirens shrieked in the distance and Matt patted Jim's shoulder again. "Paramedics will be here soon, boss."

"Gray said to tell you something."

"Oh yeah? What's that?"

"He said to tell you you're next."

Matt laughed. "I sure as fuck hope so."

"He also said to say he enjoyed watching you all run around in the woods."

This time, Matt's laugh was bitter and sour. "Figures."

"Did you..."

"No, buddy. We didn't find anything. Which, while it sounds like bad news, is better than at least one of the alternatives."

Jim's eyes drifted closed. "What the hell is happening to our town?"

"Owen Gray," said Matt. "But I will stop him. I *will* get him, Jim. I promise you."

22

It was 5:30 am, and the sun was peeking above the tops of the trees. Reg Thorndike parked his Coupe de Ville in the Thousand Acre Wood trailhead parking lot. Those cops thought he'd slipped a cog, but that bastard tree had been there, and he was going to prove it. He shoved his Polaroid into an old knapsack and slung the thing over his shoulder. He'd be walking alone into the woods, but he had enough experience not to get himself lost. Plus, sometimes it was better to be alone in the woods—no yapping, no whining, no questions.

He walked down the trail to the cutoff point, lost in his thoughts—almost daydreaming. Thorndike had never much cared for Thousand Acre Wood. He didn't understand it, not on the top layers of his mind, anyway, but when given a chance to walk these woods, or go somewhere else, he always chose somewhere else. Anywhere else.

Out of the corner of his eye, he saw a dark blur of movement, low to the ground, but when he turned, there was nothing there. Shaking his head, he kept walking. *Quiet*, he thought. *Too quiet for day time. Should be birds singing, animals rooting around doing animal things.* He cocked his head to the side, listening hard. *Must be going deaf at last.*

He saw the dark blur again, but on the other side of the trail. He stopped in the middle of the trail, arms akimbo, peering into the woods on either side. "What's this?" he said. "You want my attention?" His voice echoed through the woods, but there was no answer, no stray sound. He shook his head and pulled the map he didn't need out of his pack. He pretended to study it, using his peripheral vision to scan the edge of the woods on either side of him.

When the movement came again, he saw a black dog belly-creeping from one bush to another. It looked like that Omen-dog, all right. Same bull chest and knobby head. *Big dog*, he thought. *Don't want to mess with it, do I?*

"Saw you that time, you big bastard. Might as well come out." He kept his tone friendly and light, despite the meaning of his words. Dogs responded to tone, not semantics.

Growls came from three bushes—two on the left, one on the right. *What the hell?* He folded the map and stowed it away. "Well, I know you're there and you know I'm here. Do we go on pretending we don't see each other?"

The big Rottweiler stepped out of the bushes and looked at him, eyes bright. Eyes *intelligent*. It stood there, meeting his gaze as if it were waiting for him to realize something.

"Well, there you are," Thorndike said. The dog dipped its head but kept its eyes on his. "Smart one, are ya? Care to do my checkbook?" The dog cocked its head to the side, ears perked up. "Oh ho! You like that word? Checkbook?" The dog looked off into the woods, and then met his gaze again. "I guess that couldn't be any clearer, eh, puppy?" He reached out to pet the thing, but it snarled, and he jerked his hand out of range. "Okay, not *too* friendly then. Fine. Going to lead me again today?" The dog stood, still as a statue, and looked at him, not making a sound. The dog held his stare for a moment more, then turned and trotted off into the woods. With an uncomfortable shrug, Thorndike followed.

As they walked, other dogs appeared out of the woods, one by one, until they surrounded him. He glanced at each newcomer—they were all different breeds and sizes. The only thing the newcomers had in common was a distinct lack of eyeballs. Thorndike suppressed a shudder. *That big bastard had eyes, right?* He was no longer sure, but he thought he remembered eyes. These new ones didn't even have eye holes in their skulls—just smooth skin and bone.

"Hey up there," he called, hoping the dog would turn around and look at him. The dog stopped but didn't turn. "You have eyes, don't you, pup?" The Rottweiler growled deep in its chest—a deep rumble that promised violence if not heeded. "Well, pardon my curiosity, then."

The dogs set a fast pace, perhaps trying to wear the old man down, but Reg Thorndike prided himself on staying active. He kept the pace with no more trouble than breathing hard. The dogs surrounding him crowded against him, brushing his legs, growling, snarling and snapping, nipping at his heels, but were never underfoot. They walked for twenty minutes, and to Thorndike, it seemed like it was a straight line, but the sun danced in the sky—first on his left, then behind him, then to the right. *Trying to get me lost*, he thought. *Trying to herd me somewhere I don't want to go. Well,*

I'm no fool, dogs. I won't be herded. Thorndike shoved his way out of the knot of dogs surrounding him, ignoring their snarls and bared teeth. Every time they tried to surround him, he shoved them away, and continued on the course *he* wanted.

One by one, the dogs perked their ears and then peeled away into the woods until it was only Thorndike and the Rottweiler again. "Well, pally, just you and me again. Your friends have somewhere else to be? Or just don't like failure?" The Rottweiler glanced at him over its shoulder and made a sound that was part growl, part whine.

The dog stopped and turned to face him, barring the path. Thorndike looked past it once again ignoring its warning growl. Leaning against a tree were two filthy children. "Well, ain't that a peach? So what now, doggie? Do we fight? Or can we agree to be friends?" He held out his hand for a sniff like he would for any dog he didn't know. The Rottweiler looked at his hand and then looked up at his face. It held his gaze for a mere moment, and then, before his eyes, the skin of the dog's face wriggled and squirmed. The dog didn't move, didn't make a sound. Its eyes shrank back into its skull, like grapes withering into raisins. The skin of its eyelids stretched together and merged without leaving a scar or a blemish or a mark. The wriggling stopped, and what remained was a smooth, eyeless expanse of forehead. Thorndike jerked his hand away from the thing, unable to repress his shudder. The dog opened its mouth, looking for all the world like it was smiling, and let its tongue loll out. Its teeth were ebony and jaggedly sharp. When it growled, he couldn't help stepping back. As if that's what it was waiting for, the dog snarled and snapped its teeth. Thorndike jerked his snub-nosed .38 revolver out of his front pocket and pointed it where the Rottweiler should have had eyes. The dog flinched and backed up a step. "That's right, doggie. I've got teeth, too. Now do we fight or part friends?" The dog cocked its head at him, and Thorndike got the distinct impression it understood and was weighing its options. With a parting growl, the dog turned to the side and sprinted off into the woods.

With a shiver, Thorndike hid the pistol away again. The two huddled forms lay on the ground amidst the gnarled roots of a tree, not touching one another, but close. Thorndike sprinted through the underbrush and knelt next to the children. One of them stirred. It was a little girl he recognized from around town, but he didn't recall her name. Her face was tear-streaked and dirty.

"Are…are you real, mister?" she asked.

"Shush, now, child. What kind of question is that? 'Course I'm real."

"Oh," she said. She was listless, lethargic.

"What's the matter with you?" he asked, kneeling beside her. "Are you hurt? Hungry?"

She turned and gazed into his face. Her movements were slow like she was in a daze. "Are you real?"

"Yes, child," he said. He put a tender hand on her cheek. "You must be hungry, yes?"

She nodded, and her eyes lost focus. "Huh-huh-Herlequin has... I forget his name."

Thorndike spun his pack around and dug out a bag of trail mix. "Munch on this. What's your name?"

"Shannon. Bertram."

"Well, Miss Bertram, I'm Reggie Thorndike, and everything is okay now. I'll have you out of here in a jiffy." He eyed the lump next to her. It was a filthy little boy, whose eyes were open, staring at the canopy of the trees overhead. "Who's this with you, Miss Shannon?"

"I don't know. He was here already. When the nasty man brought the other boy and me. This one doesn't talk or nothing."

"Quiet type, is he?" Thorndike reached over and grabbed the boy's ankle, meaning to shake his leg to get his attention, but the boy shrieked and kicked his feet. "Whoa, there, boy. You are safe, now, settle down.

You're safe." At the sound of his voice, the boy quit screaming and kicking, but he never took his eyes off the dark canopy above them. "All right, Miss Shannon. I need to carry this one. Can you walk beside me?"

Shannon groaned. "My legs burn. He…he made us run and run. My feet…" Her voice drifted away to nothing. Moving like a robot, she reached into the bag of trail mix and scooped a handful into her mouth.

"This boy here made you run?"

"No. No, it was Huh-huh-herlequin."

"Herlequin, huh? Just like in the story about the monk who was chased by the—"

"No. Herlequin's real. He…he chases us. With the dog-things."

"Dog-things?" asked Thorndike. "Dogs like in the Omen movie?"

"I'm not allowed to watch scary stuff. I'm only nine."

"Right you are, dear. Stupid of me."

She reached across and patted his hand. "It's okay. We all say silly things sometimes." He grinned at her, but she didn't grin back. "Can we leave now? Before Herlequin comes for me?"

"We can, dear. But is there a glade around here? A glade with a big bast—uh, a big tree in the center?" He stood and brushed at his knees. "You have more of that trail mix. See if you can get the boy to eat a little, too." He took a single step away from the kids.

"No!" grated the boy. His voice sounded like he'd broken it.

"Stay away from it," snapped Shannon. "He will *know*. He will come and bring the dog-things."

"Okay. Yeah, okay." Thorndike lowered himself beside the boy, and moving his hand slowly, put his hand on the boy's shoulder. The kid shuddered but allowed the contact. "Can you walk, boy? I can carry you, but it will be easier if everyone goes under their own steam." The boy didn't answer. His eyes never left the tree tops above them.

Shannon got to her feet and leaned this way and that, unsteady on her feet.

Thorndike scooped the boy into his arms and creaked to his feet. "Here Miss Shannon, you hold on to my elbow here." Moving as if she were in a dream, Shannon raised her hand and rested it on his forearm, just below his elbow. "Good girl," he said. "Civilization is back this way."

23

Bob lurched forward on bleeding, unfeeling feet. They were behind him again, all of them, eyeless faces snarling as they closed in on his heels. His mind was blank, he had no plans, no ideas left. The muscles on the backs of his thighs cramped each time he put down his feet.

"Is this the best you have, Big Bob?" It was the monster's voice—the gargoyle, the architect of his suffering. "I am disappointed, Bob."

Bob whimpered in the back of his throat. He knew what that meant. The bully had grown tired of playing around with him and wanted to hurt him in earnest. "I'll...I'll do better," he gasped, his voice so quiet he doubted anyone heard him.

"No, no," said Herlequin. "It's much too late now, Bob. I warned you, didn't I? I told you what would happen if you didn't satisfy me."

Tears trickled down Bob's cheeks, and not for the first time that day. They cut paths through the grime on his face from so many faceplants after tripping on roots or stepping in holes.

"Didn't I, Big Bob?" called Herlequin.

"I'll try harder. I...I'll do better. Somehow. Run...run faster." Bob was gasping for breath he couldn't catch, staggering more than running.

"No. I think not, Bob. It's almost over for you."

"No!" Bob cried, lurching forward at a faster pace. "I can do better, you watch."

Behind him, Herlequin laughed. "Hear that, my daughters? He can do better." The dog-things howled and pawed at the ground.

24

"See now?" said Thorndike. "We're on our way and don't you feel better? Don't you just?"

Shannon nodded, but with significant weariness.

"And how 'bout you, boy?" Thorndike squeezed the boy in his arms. When Thorndike had first picked him up, the boy's muscles had quivered with stress, but with each step, he'd relaxed a bit more until he lay in Thorndike's arms like a limp rag. He didn't respond to the question or the squeeze.

Thorndike figured they were about half-way back to the trail. "We'll have you home soon enough—both of

you. I'm sure Chief Greshin knows who you are, boy."
The boy stirred but lapsed back into his stupor.

Shannon squeezed Thorndike's elbow. "Do you hear them?"

"Who, dear?"

She looked up at him, wide-eyed. "The dog-things."

"What are they doing?"

"Howling. Snarling."

Thorndike peered into the trees. "Are they close?" A small sound escaped the boy in his arms. It was a pitiful sound.

"They are always close," cried Shannon. "He'll be mad."

"Don't you worry," said Thorndike. "This Herlequin fella comes upon us, I will have words for him, you better trust in that." Thorndike's mind went to the pistol in his pocket, and he grinned a vengeful, angry grin.

25

The dog things snapped and snarled right behind him. Bob could feel their hot breath on the backs of his legs. Their slobber splashed him as they snapped their jaws and barked. He tried to run faster yet.

But he couldn't do it. He had nothing left. Too much junk food, too many stories on the TV after school, not enough activity. Doc Hauser had been right. His habits had killed him.

He stumbled, and the dog-things snarled. Pain exploded across his left calf, and Bob fell, face-first, into a tree trunk. The bark scraped his face, but the pain of it felt distant, unimportant. The pain in his calf was excruciating. He peeled his eyes open and shrieked. One of the dog-things had clamped onto his calf, blood streaming out of the corners of its mouth and steaming in the cool fall air. His blood. The thing worried at his calf, tearing its head from side to side and with each savage tug, the pain doubled. He kicked the dog-thing with his other leg, but it only growled at him.

Another dog-thing lunged forward and grabbed his right foot, biting down hard. More blood dripped on the carpet of decaying leaves. More pain coursed through him.

Bob screamed, long and loud, and bent to punch at the two dog-things. His pudgy fists glanced off their hard skulls, and the growling increased.

The other dog things sat in a semi-circle around him, looking on, tongues lolling out of their smiling faces. They had no eyes, but he was sure they were watching and enjoying the show.

"Now you fight," said Herlequin in droll tones. "When it's too late."

"Shut up!" Bob yelled. He grabbed the dog-thing that had him by the calf and tried to pry its jaws apart.

"That bully was right about you, wasn't he, Big Bob? You're just a pussy. Aren't you, Fatty?"

The tears streamed down Bob's cheeks, and his blood pattered the ground as another dog-thing lunged forward to grab him by the arm. Pain blossomed in his bicep.

"Now, Fatty, you pay the price for boring me." Herlequin snapped his fingers, and the rest of the dog-things lunged, all at once, each sinking their fangs into his plump flesh and bearing down with all their might. Herlequin stepped from the gloom. "Now, it's my turn to bite," he said with an evil laugh.

He opened his wide mouth, his tusk-like fangs gleaming in the low light. His mouth kept opening wider and wider, past the point when Bob thought Herlequin's jaw would have to break to open any more. Tilting his head to the side, Herlequin leaned in like he was about to kiss Bob's forehead.

The large fangs rested against the skin of Bob's temples and at the back of his head. Herlequin's tongue slathered through his hair.

"At least you finally shut up," whispered Bob, and the big jaws snapped. The pain was brief, and then everything was black, and Bob was no more.

26

Thorndike set the boy down long enough to make sure his snub-nose .38 caliber pistol was still accessible in the baggy front pocket of his pants, keeping it out of Shannon's view. As he picked the boy up again, a horrible scream of raw fury split the quiet air of the forest. It made his blood run cold.

"It's him," said the boy in a flat and lifeless voice.

"Huh-huh-herlequin," whispered Shannon.

"We have to run now, Shannon. Can you keep up with me?"

She looked up at him with mournful eyes. A single tear tracked through the dirt on her cheek. She shook her head, moving in slow motion. "I can't run no more, mister."

Reg's nod was curt. "Then I'll just have to carry you, too." He adjusted the boy so he leaned against Thorndike's shoulder and bent to pick up the girl. "I need you to help me, Shannon. It's your job to keep you and your friend here in my arms. I can hold you, but I can't keep you stable like this."

"Okay. I can do it."

Thorndike moved out at a brisk jog. They ran like that, falling into a rhythm, for what seemed like a long time. The forest grew darker like the sun had set, but his watch said it was 8:35 am. "What's this happy crappy dappy?" he muttered. He didn't need the light to navigate, but it creeped him out.

He trotted around a wide tree trunk and stopped cold. There was a pale lump at the base of the next tree. Gore splattered the ground. As soon as he realized it was the body of a kid, he spun around so the kids wouldn't catch a glimpse of it. "I'm going to set you down on the other side of this tree trunk."

Shannon clutched at his neck. "No, don't leave us alone. They'll come for us!"

"It'll just be a few moments. And I'll be right here." He walked around the tree and set Shannon down, leaning her against the tree. "You see anything, you sing out. You hear?" He set the boy down next to her and gave Shannon a stern look. "No peeking—I mean it."

Shannon nodded and shrugged, both movements enervated and spiritless.

"It will be okay, Shannon," Thorndike said and ducked around the tree.

The pale lump was the body of a rotund boy, ten or eleven years old. His flesh was torn, ripped apart by a fanged animal—dogs, maybe. *Dog-things.* The boy's head was mangled, too. Deep puncture wounds pierced his temples, and the top of his head looked chewed. Thorndike slid out of his jacket and used the garment to cover the corpse. "Sorry I didn't get you, too," he whispered.

The enraged cry came again, and Thorndike thought it was closer. Much closer. He dashed back and scooped up the kids. "Both of you squeeze your eyes shut. Keep 'em closed until I tell you different."

They were close to the path, and if he made it there, he could run faster. *Gotta get these kids to the car and get the fuck out of here,* he thought. He ran in earnest, jouncing and jostling the two kids.

When he caught a glimpse of the first of the dogs running parallel to his course, his breath caught. By the time he gained the path, half a dozen dogs ran through the woods on both sides. They were a distance away, just close enough so he would know they were there.

He ran a few steps toward the parking lot, and the big Rottweiler stepped out of the woods and walked to the middle of the path. Thorndike slowed to a stop. "Back for more, puppy?"

The dog stood and snarled, taking an aggressive step toward them. The dog showed its savage, murderous teeth.

"Okay," said Thorndike. "You want us to stop, okay, we're stopping."

"No," whimpered Shannon.

"Shush, girl." He set the boy down at his feet but kept Shannon where she sat on his forearm. Pretending at a calm he did not feel, Thorndike moved his free hand toward his pocket.

The dog sank back on its haunches.

"See, puppy? No need for all those theatrics." Thorndike tried to keep his voice calm, but at the slight warble in his voice, the dog sprang up and focused its sightless head on him. "Now, now," he said. "Everything's okay." He pulled the snub-nose revolver out of his pocket and snapped off a shot. The round took the dog-thing in its wide chest, spinning it around in a half circle. When it fell to the ground, it made a sound like a human scream. In the surrounding woods, the dog-things raised holy hell and turned toward him.

Thorndike grabbed the boy and hitched him over his shoulder. He sprinted down the path toward the parking lot with dread circling in his guts. *No way I can out run a dog*, he lamented.

At that precise moment, the path in front of him disappeared, and the dark forest surrounded them again. "What the…" he breathed.

"Huh-huh," murmured the boy. "*He* makes you believe things. Not real."

Dammit, have to get these kids out! Grimacing, Thorndike lowered his head and ran straight toward the large oak tree in front of him. He held his breath and squeezed his eyes shut right before he should have smashed into its trunk.

Nothing happened. He was still running in his original direction. A sigh gusted out of him, and he poured on the speed, ignoring the tightness spreading across his chest.

His steps fell on the path he could no longer see. The dog-things looped in from the sides, and when they did, he pointed the .38 at them until they veered away. He only had four more rounds. Maybe the dog-things knew that, maybe they didn't. He didn't care as long as they stayed away.

A nude woman stepped out of the woods ahead of them, blonde-haired with high, angular cheekbones. She flashed him a smile that would have stopped his heart on any other day.

Not real. The boy's voice echoed in his thoughts. *Not real.* He raised the gun and pointed it at her, moving as fast as his old muscles could. An expression of pure rage washed across her face, and for a second, just one second, Thorndike thought he perceived the thing behind the illusion. She was hideous, sagging, blackened skin, talons for fingers. Goop dripped from her maw, and pus ran from her eyes. Without further thought, Thorndike pulled the trigger. The blonde threw her arm up in front of her face and screeched. In the woods, the dog-things squealed and snarled their rage.

Thorndike sprinted past the woman or the corpse or whatever it was. She swiped at him as he passed, but she was too far away to hit him. The telltale tightness in his chest blossomed into a dull, aching cancer.

When he broke into the parking lot, the illusion of being deep in the woods faded. Thorndike raced to his car, ignoring the light-headedness that assaulted him. He shoved the pistol into his pocket when he was three steps from the door and ripped the driver's door open. He shoved the kids in without ceremony and slid in behind them. As he reached for the door, the dull ache in his chest exploded down his arm, and he vomited his breakfast on his baggy khaki pants.

"Mister! Quick!" shouted Shannon.

He looked up and slammed the door, just before a dog-thing careened into the sheet metal. Thorndike couldn't catch his breath. He fished for his keys, dropped them onto the floor, and retrieved them. He slid the key home, cranked, and the Cadillac's five hundred cubic inch mill roared to life.

A dog-thing leapt, snarling, to the hood of the car. It crept forward stiff-legged, stopping right in front of Thorndike. It snapped at the air and howled. A ferocious scream answered. Whatever it was, it was just up the path.

"Go, mister! Go!" urged Shannon.

Thorndike slammed the car down into drive and mashed the accelerator to the floor. Gravel flew behind them like grape-shot from a cannon, and the big car swept into a wide, looping turn. The dog-thing on the hood yelped and went flying.

Reg never let up on the gas, even after the dog-things quit shadowing them in the woods alongside the road. His skin had gone cold, clammy, and the pain in his chest intensified. He was driving one-handed, his left arm hurt too much. His breath came in ragged, tearing gasps.

He swept through town, ignoring stop signs and the furious horns of other drivers. *Have to get them to Greshin*, he thought, vision dimming. *Have to keep them safe.*

27

Matt jumped to the side as the big Cadillac slewed across the pavement and up over the sidewalk. He didn't recognize the car, but whoever was driving was due a piece of his mind. And maybe his foot to their backside.

The car's engine stopped screaming, but it didn't stop. It rolled up across the lawn and bumped into the wall of Town Hall. There was a gray-haired man slumped against the driver's door, and what Matt thought were two filthy little boys in the front seat next to him.

The driver's face was gray and splotchy. His chest was heaving as he put the car in park. His eyes drifted closed.

Matt ran to the front door and stuck his head inside. "Angie! Roll the paramedics!" Without waiting for a reply, Matt turned and sprinted to the car. He grasped the handle, but the door was locked. He knocked on the window. The driver's eyelids fluttered but didn't open. "It's Mr. Thorndike," Matt called, but to whom, he had no idea.

The old man's eyes cracked open and, like it was the most grueling physical task he'd ever undertaken, crawled his hand to the electric door locks and pressed the switch. The locks clunked, and Matt ripped the door open, catching Thorndike as he spilled out.

"Mr. Thorndike! You okay?"

Thorndike made a rude noise and opened his eyes. He looked at Matt and whispered something.

Matt leaned forward. "What was that?"

"Got them to safety. Up to you, now," he murmured.

"Don't you worry, Mr. Thorndike. I'll keep these boys safe."

"I'm a girl," said one of the filthy lumps in the front seat. "My name's Shannon Bertram."

One of the two kids who went missing yesterday! Matt thought. "And is this Bob Gerber?"

"No, he's dead." The little girl's voice was flat, lifeless. "Huh-huh… The bad man ate him up."

Thorndike's hand fluttered against Matt's arm. He was staring up at Matt, eyes bright, intense. "What is it, Mr. Thorndike?"

"Woods."

"The Thousand Acre Wood? What about it?"

"Told you. Yesterday."

"Okay. Listen, Thorndike, don't worry about a thing. I've got these kids now, and the paramedics are on the way. You relax. Try to rest yourself, pretty sure you're having a heart attack." Thorndike, who had taught English at the high school, gave Matt such a look of scorn that Matt blushed to the roots of his close-cropped hair. "Guess you figured that out already. Don't worry, we'll get you help."

As if on cue, the ambulance squealed into the parking lot and skidded into the space next to the Cadillac. Two paramedics that Matt knew well jumped out and grabbed a slew of bags and boxes of equipment and ran over to Thorndike.

"How long?" one of them demanded.

"He's been here about five minutes," said Matt. "No idea how long before that the attack started."

They took Thorndike out of Matt's grasp and lay him flat on the sidewalk and did paramedic things. Matt turned back to the car after a few seconds. "Okay, you two. Slide on out of there. Who's your friend, Shannon?"

"I don't know him. He goes to the middle school." She pushed the boy until he slid out of the driver's side of the car. He stood, eyes downcast, hands hanging loosely at his side. "He was there when the other bad man brought me."

"The other bad man? There are two?"

"Oh, yes. And a bad woman. And a bunch of bad dog-things."

"Two men, a woman, and a bunch of dogs? Did one of the men drive a Buick Skylark?"

"I don't know. I'm nine."

"Right you are. White top, black paint?"

Her eyes tracked to his. "Yes. The bad man that took me into the woods."

"Gray," muttered Matt.

"No, it was black."

"Never mind, sweetheart. Did you recognize the other man?"

She shook her head. "He told me his name, though." She cast her eyes around them, looking at shadows. "Herlequin," she whispered.

"That's one strange name, I bet that man gets teased a lot," said Matt, watching the paramedics load Thorndike onto a gurney.

"He's not a man," whispered the boy. "He's a gargoyle."

Matt looked at him sharply. That voice was familiar. "*Benny*? Benny Cartwright? Is that you under all that dirt?" He squatted and looked the boy in the face, wiping at the filth that crusted the boy's cheeks. "Christ, Benny, your parents will just explode when they see you! How did you get all the way back here from Cuba?" The boy just stood there, staring at the ground in front of him, but he was sure it was Benny.

"I'm from here," said Shannon. "But the man— Herlequin—he made us run through the forest. He sicced his dog-things on us, and they chased and chased us. Maybe they chased him all the way here."

"Not real…" murmured Benny.

"What's not real, Benny?" asked Matt.

The boy's gaze drifted up and seemed to dance around the parking lot, lingering on Matt's shoes, his gun, and the ambulance. "Just another trick."

Matt hugged the boy. "No, Benny. You're free now. You're home." *Didn't Craig say Toby was like this when he turned up?* "Taking Mr. Thorndike to Rochester?" he asked the paramedics over his shoulder.

"Yes, best cardiac unit around."

"We better take these two, as well. You have room in the ambulance?"

"Nah, you better follow us up, Chief."

"Ten-four," he said and shepherded the kids over to his Fury. "Tell you what, Benny, if you want, we can run the siren all the way there."

Benny didn't respond.

28

"He survived, my love," Brigitta whispered in his ear.

"Who did, babe?"

"The man in that house." Her eyes glazed a moment. "Mr. Town-fucking-Manager."

"Dammit! I want him dead."

"I know, my love."

"Where is he?" Owen demanded.

"North of here. A big building with sick people in it."

"A hospital?"

Brigitta nodded, expression solemn. "A big one."

"Strong." Owen said it like a curse. "They will save him, most likely. Dammit!"

"Well…"

"Well, what, babe?"

"Not if you go for a visit, my love. He won't survive that."

A smile blossomed on Owen's face, but the look in Brigitta's eye worried him. She seemed...distant, withdrawn. "You okay, babe?"

"Yes, my love," she said, but she wouldn't meet his gaze. "Let's go to the hospital."

Owen cranked the wheel of the Skylark, spinning it around in a cloud of hazy smoke. "Don't need to ask me twice. How do you feel about nurses, babe?"

Brigitta smiled, but the smile didn't reach her eyes.

Chapter 2
2007

I

LaBouche sat slumped down in the silver WRX he'd used to abduct Becky Lewis. He was down the block and around the corner from the Lewis' house, and he watched as his partner cuffed that asshole Drew Reid and went inside the house. He considered running down there and ripping Reid's throat out and leaving him slumped on the porch while Lewis was inside coddling his dumb fuck wife, but the time for giving in to every impulse that came along had long since passed for LaBouche.

Lewis came out a minute or two later and herded Reid to his cheap little Honda. He pushed Reid into the back of the car and cuffed him to the passenger-side headrest. He walked around to the driver's side and got in. LaBouche's mouth stretched in a wide grin as Lewis backed out of the drive and drove away.

He waited a few minutes to see if Lewis had forgotten anything. Then he started the car and idled up the street. He pulled into Lewis' driveway and got out.

When old Mrs. Carmody answered the door, he didn't speak. He put his big hand in the center of her chest and flung her backward into the house. The old biddy didn't even scream, she stared at him with wide, shocked eyes as he stomped up to her. He let his Lee-visage fade from her eyes and smiled wider as she shrieked in terror.

Upstairs, Jenny Lewis asked what was going on, but LaBouche could tell by her voice that she was doped to the gills on Xanax or something. The thought soured his smile a little—sedated, she'd be much harder to terrorize.

He grabbed Carmody by the foot and dragged her up the stairs. Maybe he'd do Jenny first and feed off Carmody's terror.

2

"Shannon," he asked, putting his hand on her shoulder.

"Wassat?" she mumbled.

"You fell asleep in the movie. Want to just head to bed?"

Her eyes widened, and her cheeks turned pink. "Uh…"

"I meant, do you want to go to sleep? I'm good to be alone now."

"No," she said, shaking her head. "I'm okay. I always fall asleep in action movies. Scary stories, too." She smiled and rubbed her eyes. "See? All better."

"Really, Shannon, if you're tired—"

"Nope. You're up, I'm up." Mike's phone rang, and Shannon jumped. "Oh! That startled me. I'm such a goose."

Mike smiled and handed the remote to Shannon. "Chief Richards," he said in his cop voice as he walked into the other room.

"Mike, I got a strange one," said Jack King.

"What is it, Jack? It's my weekend off."

"Yeah, boss. Sorry, but I don't know what to make of this."

Mike sighed and shook his head. Shannon leaned in the door jamb, blinking and obviously trying to keep from yawning. "Sorry. Work," he mouthed at her.

"It's okay," she said.

"You with someone? Didn't mean to interrupt," said Jack.

"Yeah, just tell me what's wrong, Jack." Mike walked across the room, phone to his ear, and peered through the blinds. Out on Main Street, everything was quiet, but lights burned on the police side of Town Hall.

"I got a call. Anonymous."

"Okay. We can trace it if it's necessary."

"Might be, boss. Guy said there's a body over at Play Time."

"Play Time?" Mike asked.

"Yeah, you know that old abandoned church on Union?"

"Sure."

"Someone's renovating it. It has 'Play Time' painted over the door now. Guy said there's a body over at Play Time. A girl. Teenager. Said she'd been tortured to death down in the cellar."

"Tortured?" Mike said, and then with a glance at Shannon, opened her door and stepped out on the landing, pulling the door shut behind him. "Tortured? What do you mean tortured, Jack?"

"That's all he said about her. 'Teenage girl tortured to death.' He said the cellar is made up like a dungeon, a bunch of little cells with torture equipment and restraints."

"And he didn't leave his name?"

"No, boss. What should I do?"

Mike glanced at the time on his phone. "Well, shit. Fifteen minutes past shift change."

"Yeah, I know, boss. Want me to call the contractors?"

"And have them fuck up the crime scene?"

"Chief, there may not *be* a crime scene."

Mike puffed out a breath. "Well, we can't take that chance. Meet me in front of Town Hall."

"Ten-four," said Jack and then closed the connection.

Mike shoved the phone into his pocket and made a face up at the night sky. "Shit *always* happens on my nights off." With a sigh, he turned and opened Shannon's door. She stood just inside, wearing a light jacket and holding out his fleece. "I'm sorry, Shan. Work."

She shrugged and smiled. "I've always wanted to do a ride-along."

"Shannon, I'm not sure that's a good idea."

"I'll stay in the car," she said, stepping outside and closing the door.

Shaking his head, he opened the door again and squeezed past her. "Need my gun," he grunted. He walked back inside, mind awhirl, trying to find a polite way of telling Shannon she needed to stay home, that this wasn't some fucked-up date night. He grabbed his gun off the top shelf of her pantry where he'd hidden it earlier and clipped it to his belt.

When he went back outside, Shannon was sitting on a step halfway down to the driveway. He climbed down the stairs and held out his hand to her. "Okay. Ground rules." He held up his hand and ticked off the points with his fingers. "You stay in the car. You do what I tell you to, when I tell you, and without question. Plus, you stay in the car. No matter what, you…stay…in…the…car."

"I'm confused," she said with a laugh. "Do you want me to stay in the car?"

"This is serious, Shannon. Jack King and I have to go inside that creepy old church around the corner. I don't want you inside there. Not for any reason."

"That old white church? You know the kids say it's haunted."

"I know." She turned to go down to the drive, but he held on to her hand. "Tell me you agree to the rules."

"Sure, Mike. No problem."

"Okay, then." They climbed down the rest of the steps and got into Shamu. "Seems silly to drive across the street, but there you go." He threw the Chevy into reverse and backed down to Main Street. Then he flipped on his lights, bleeped the siren, and backed straight across to Town Hall

"Hmm, an abuse of power so soon during the ride-along," Shannon said with a lilt in her voice. "Interesting."

"Take it up with the police chief."

"Oh, I plan on it." Her face wore a mischievous, flirty expression.

"You should be careful, flirting with a guy. You might get his wants all out of whack with his needs." He laughed.

"You can have anything you want *or* need, Mike," she said, all signs of the carefree flirt gone.

Mike glanced at her, saw the solemn expression, and swallowed hard. "Shannon, it's not the time, but there—"

"Hey, Chief," said Jack, knocking on the trunk.

"He's got the best timing," said Shannon.

"You don't know the half of it, Shan."

She smiled at him, and he smiled back.

Jack opened the rear door and slipped into the back seat. "Hey there, Ms. Bertram."

"Hello, *Mr. King*," she said, imitating his punctilious tone to perfection.

"Come on, now. You know my name's Jack."

"And *you* know my name." She winked at Mike.

"Okay, playtime is done. Jack, wearing your game face?"

"Ten-four, Chief."

Mike threw the car into gear, drove north a block, and turned onto Union Street. He let the car roll up the street at idle, staring at the huge white clapboard church. He couldn't remember the last time he'd heard anyone talk about the place. He wracked his memory, but couldn't remember anything coming through the police department about anything called Play Time, either. Whatever it was, no one in town seemed suspicious of it. Maybe it was one of those fancy, members-only nightclubs like they had in the City.

He brought the car to a gentle stop facing the main entrance, letting his high beams wash the shadows away from the front of the building. He glanced at Jack in the rearview. The man was sitting forward in the seat, staring out at the building. "What do you think, Jack?"

"Looks quiet, boss. Looks…creepy though."

"Definitely," said Shannon. "What mom would leave her kids there?"

"Kids?" asked Mike. "I thought it was a nightclub."

Shannon shrugged. "I have no idea. I've never heard of the place."

"But you live right around the corner," blurted Jack. "Surely, there's been something."

"Not that I remember," she said. "Nightclubs and childcare, neither one is on my priority list."

"Yeah, me neither," said Jack.

"This is a small town; this place should have been a topic of conversation, gossip, at least," said Mike. "I mean, the new nail salon is nowhere on my list of priorities, right, but at least six people brought it up, for one reason or another." Shannon nodded, and Jack shrugged. Mike met Jack's gaze in the rearview, and he offered a terse nod. Jack popped the back door open and got out. Mike turned to Shannon. "Stay in the car, Shannon." She laughed and shot him a salute as Mike got out of the car.

Mike and Jack approached the steps leading up to the doors that opened on the vestibule. "The caller said the body was in the cellar, right?" Mike asked. "I'll take the left, you go around the right, see if we can find a cellar bulkhead." Jack nodded, and, hand on the butt of his gun, strode around the right side of the building.

Mike walked around to the left and wrinkled his nose at the stink. The distinctive scent of rot was heavy in the air. He glanced up at the stained-glass windows and saw shadows moving around inside the nave. It looked like they were dancing, but Mike couldn't hear any music, not even the faint thump of drums and bass.

He turned the corner and saw Jack standing next to the cellar bulkhead, a grimace covering his face. "What's up?"

Jack shook his head. "That funk...got to be cadavers."

"Yeah, I agree. The stench is too strong to be some little animal that crawled in there and died."

Jack shifted his feet and nudged the shiny new chain and combination lock with the toe of his boot. "Not getting in here."

"No, but isn't it strange that a bright, shiny new lock and chain appear on the night we get a call about a body in the cellar?"

"Yeah," Jack grumbled.

They walked back to the front of the building and climbed the steps. Mike tried the door, but it was locked. With a glance back at the car, he pounded on the door with the edge of his fist. Shannon smiled and waved.

Heavy footsteps approached the door from within. The door swung inward, washing the steps with warm yellow light. The lights burning inside the nave silhouetted a male figure. "What?" said a deep, resonant voice.

Mike squinted and held a hand up against the glare. The timbre of the voice set his nerves on edge. "Who's that?" he barked.

"We're busy in here. State your business or get off the steps."

"I'm Mike Richards. *Chief* Mike Richards of the OFPD. We need to look around the place."

"It's a free country. Come back when you have a warrant."

The man stepped back and started to close the door, but Mike stepped forward and put his hand on the door. "No, it's not going to go that way. We've got a report to check out, and I'll tell you, based on the stench coming from your cellar, I believe exigent circumstances exist that *require* me to search the premises."

"Rats," the man grunted. "Dead in the walls."

Mike stood where he was, hand pushing counter to the renewed force to close the door.

"Dammit, that's why it stinks!"

"We're coming in," Mike said in a cool voice. "Keep interfering, and you'll spend the rest of the weekend in lockup."

"At least the rest of the weekend," said Jack. "Your paperwork might get lost."

The man holding the door growled something under his breath and removed his hand. He turned and stomped toward the nave, with Mike close on his heels.

The interior of the vestibule had been gutted to the studs, chunks of plaster and lath lay around the edges of the room, and plaster had been ground into the carpet between the outer doors and the doors to the nave. The carpet reeked of mold and piss. There was a scarred old wooden door hanging askew from its frame to the left and a set of stairs leading up to the balcony on the right.

With his eyes adjusted to the light, Mike recognized the man at the door from his nights of drinking and debauchery. It was Red Bortha, though why he was called Red when he was as bald as a cue ball was anyone's guess. Red had never liked him, and Mike didn't much care for Red, either. "What is this place, Bortha?"

"The fuck does it look like? It's an old church, dumbass."

Mike scoffed. "Wow. Now I can recognize old churches. Thanks for your help."

"What he means, asshole, is what the fuck is Play Time and why are you fucks in here this late on a Saturday night?" demanded Jack. "And show some respect."

Red stopped, shoulders rippling as his muscles tensed. "*Fuck* respect," he said in ragged tones. "I don't give a shit."

"Come on, Red," said a woman from inside the nave. "They're just doing their jobs." Mike would have recognized her voice anywhere. Sally McBride.

"Hey there, Sally," he said.

"Since we're not at work, I get to answer you like you always answer me. Fuck you, Mike."

Mike grinned. "Yeah, I've earned that."

"In spades," she said, but her tone was a touch friendlier.

"So? What is this place, Sally?" He walked into the nave. Like the vestibule, the walls had been stripped to the studs, but the plaster and lath had been cleaned up. The old carpet had been ripped out, exposing the old pine floor that had moldered beneath it for decades. Throw rugs had been spread on the floor without a thought toward interior design—almost as if they were there to cover stains rather than because the place was being refurbished.

"It's okay, Red. Let me handle the Chief, here. You go on with your work."

Without looking at either cop, Red walked past them to the vestibule, grumbling under his breath with every step. He slammed the vestibule doors, and a moment later, the front doors of the church.

"This place, Mike, will be a community center. For the under-privileged kids."

There was something in her voice that rang false, and it wasn't just the preposterous story. Possibilities slipped through his mind like eels: a sex club, an S&M

club, an adult store, a drug den. Most of those weren't illegal, though, so why all the secrecy?

"Sally, we've had a report. We've got to investigate."

"So you said." Sally's hands jerked out to her sides and then dropped to pat the pockets of the loose house dress she wore. "We take no liability if you get hurt. This place is a work in progress. A construction zone if you will."

"I assume you have permits then?" asked Jack.

Sally's face reddened, and sheen spread across her forehead and cheeks. "Well…"

"Doesn't matter," said Mike with a wave of his hand. "We don't care about small shit, right, Jack?"

"Uh, right, boss."

"Have your little party then…investigate away." With that, Sally turned her back and knelt. She took a brush out of a metal pail and scrubbed the floor.

Interesting, Mike thought. He pointed at one of the carpets with his chin. Jack nodded and walked over to it, turning up one edge.

"*What are you doing?*" screeched Sally.

Jack looked up at Mike, eyebrows arched. "Nothing, Sally. Just looking at the floor."

"Well, you can see there are no bodies under there! Leave it alone!"

Jack pursed his lips, but when Mike nodded, he let the corner of the rug fall to the floor. He straightened with a loud sniff. "Something's gone off, Sally."

"Rats," she snapped, turning her head away. "In the walls." She tried to re-wet her scrub brush, but slammed it into the lip of the bucket instead, spilling water all over the floor. "I told them to get someone else," she muttered.

"Told who, Sally?"

She didn't answer—she sat there with her back to them, water spreading across the floor, wetting her house dress.

Mike gestured to the vestibule. "Cellar door the one hanging crooked in there?"

Sally grunted.

"Guess we'll head down there," Mike said. He and Jack tramped back to the vestibule and moved the broken door out of the way. Mike flipped the light switch next to the door several times, but no lights came on in the cellar.

"Great," said Jack.

Mike smiled and pulled out his flashlight. The beam sliced through the darkness in the stairwell, illuminating a set of old, worn steps. The first step creaked under his weight, and he froze for a moment.

"Be careful," Sally called, sounding for all the world like that was the last thing she wanted them to do.

"She's not so good at lying," whispered Jack.

"No." Mike climbed down the stairs, careful where he put his feet, playing the light across the steps. The steps led to a tiny room, perhaps six by six. The room was bare, just the bottom of the staircase and a single door.

Mike walked across to the door, the stench of decay filling his nose and mouth. "There's the vile stench," he said.

"Rats," said Jack. "In the walls."

"My ass," said Mike.

The single door was locked from the inside, but the wood felt spongy, weak. Mike put his shoulder to it, and the screws holding the door to the hinges squealed and popped out of the wood. The door fell inward with a crash.

"Be careful!" Sally cried from above them.

Beyond the door was a long, narrow room. The wall parallel to the back of the building held three doors. As with the first room, all the doors were locked, but this time, each door had a deadbolt that required a key. With a shrug, Jack kicked the first door, sending it flying down the narrow corridor it hid.

The funk that rolled out of the hallway was atrocious, and both men grimaced and coughed. "Cadavers," Jack said.

Mike's face was grim and set. "I believe so." He gestured down the door-lined corridor, each door with an iron hasp holding it closed. "We better get to work."

Jaws clenched, they started opening the doors. The small cells were empty—at least of human remains—but there were signs of torture and perhaps more. They made a quick check of the other two hallways, but there were no bodies, just effluvium, and evil-doings.

"Call the SD," said Mike. "Get backup down here fast. Then call the Staties and ask for forensic support. Tell them I'm the one making the request."

Jack nodded. "What are you going to do?"

"Arrest that fat bitch upstairs. I want this place guarded, Jack, so call the security guys in. No one in or out of this building without my express approval."

"Ten-four, Chief."

Mike stomped back up the stairs, Jack close behind him. When they reached the vestibule, Mike pointed at the front doors and turned into the nave. "Sally, you're fucked well and good." The puddle of water was creeping across the wooden floor, the carpets lay where they had been, the up-turned bucket rested where she'd tipped it, but of Sally, there was no sign. "Dammit!

Now, I have to chase your fat ass!" He pressed the tips of his fingers against his eyelids until all he could see were swaths of purple, blue, green, and pink. He'd never wanted a drink as bad as he did right then.

"Jack!" he called. "BOLO on the fat bitch. Red Botha, too."

3

Mike was still standing in front of Play Time when the silver Honda pulled up and parked outside the crime scene tape. There was a familiar man driving, but Mike couldn't place him. A man in an NYSP windbreaker got out and nodded. Mike sketched a salute and turned back to watch the other Staties—the forensics team—ferrying evidence bags out of the church and over to their van.

"Chief Richards?" someone asked.

The trooper who had just pulled up stood there looking at him. He had one hand on the elbow of the familiar man. The familiar man in handcuffs. "That's me," Mike said.

"Scott Lewis," the trooper said. "Do you recognize this man?"

Mike shook his head. "He looks familiar, but I have no idea who he is."

"His name is Andrew Reid. He says he reported this." Lewis gestured at the church. "Said he called to report a body. Know anything about that?"

"Yeah, one of my officers fielded the call. It was anonymous though."

The trooper nodded. "So he said. Listen, though. My daughter's missing, and this guy had her ID. He says he got it from the cellar of that place."

Mike narrowed his eyes and looked the familiar man up and down. He didn't remember him, no matter how familiar he looked. He turned and looked at the crowd of law enforcement officers milling around in front of the church. "Jack!" he called.

King came on the run, equipment jingling in time to his steps. "Yeah, Chief?"

Mike hooked his thumb at the stranger in cuffs. "This guy says he's the one who called you."

Jack turned on his hard cop face and looked the man up and down. "Tell me what you said."

The stranger cleared his throat. "I told you that there was trouble at Play Time, that I found the body of a teenaged girl in the cellar."

Jack nodded. "That's him." His eyes tracked down to the handcuffs and then over to Trooper Lewis. "Something I should know?"

"This guy claims the body he found is the trooper's missing daughter," said Mike.

"It is," said Reid.

Jack looked him up and down. "That had better not be some bullshit story, fella."

"I'm telling the truth," said Reid. "Though, I understand your reaction, Officer. To be honest, I'd feel the same way."

Trooper Lewis caught Mike's eye. He reached into his back pocket and flipped a newspaper clipping open. "Do you recognize this man?"

Mike squinted at a picture of a large, heavyset man standing next to Lewis, each holding up a commendation. Mike nodded. "Yeah, I've seen him."

Lewis leaned forward. "Yesterday?" The question was sharp, clipped. "He drives a blue Maxima."

Mike shrugged. "He's around a lot. Not sure he's a resident, though. I think he stays with Red Bortha sometimes." He looked into Lewis' blazing eyes. "Why?"

"That's a picture of my partner, Lee LaBouche. This guy says LaBouche killed my daughter."

Mike looked at Reid. "Is that so?"

"It is," Reid said, as calm and composed as a judge. "But I bet he wasn't driving his own car yesterday."

Lewis glanced at him, horror drawing deep lines on his forehead. "A Subaru WRX? Silver one?"

"Yeah, that car came into town last night, but a kid was driving it," said Jack.

"A kid?" asked Lewis. "Tan? Looked like a surfer?"

Jack nodded. "Come to think of it, I saw the car around all day, but the kid disappeared. A big lunk of a man drove the car around this afternoon."

"Was it this man?" Lewis held the newspaper clipping out.

"Yeah, I believe so."

"Do you see, Trooper Lewis? I wasn't lying to you. LaBouche is dangerous and—"

Mike stopped listening. *Either the guy's telling the truth or he's a great liar. Time will tell us which.* He glanced at the crowd of looky-loos standing around gawking at the crime scene. A tall, bearded man caught his eye.

His beard and his hair were long and unkempt, with wisps of dirty blond woven throughout. He wore hospital scrubs and had nothing on his feet. He had piercing blue eyes that seemed to latch on to Mike's gaze. A slow grin spread across the man's face. He lifted his hand and flashed a nonchalant wave.

Mike cocked his head to the side and walked over to the crime scene tape. "Can I help you, sir?" The guy stank like he hadn't showered in a month and had then rolled around in a cow pasture.

"Hi, Mike. Long time no see. Since we were eleven, I'd guess. That day in the woods, remember?"

"What?"

"You'll remember. I did after I left Millvale. I remembered a lot of things."

"Who are you? Toby?"

"Tobias."

"Right, Tobias." Mike tugged on his ear like he wanted it to come off.

"What's Toby doing here, Mike?"

"What?" Mike shook his head like he was trying to clear out the cobwebs.

"He's right over there." Tobias lifted his arm and pointed at the man in handcuffs.

Mike shook his head. *Don't have time for this shit tonight.* "Come with me, Tobias. Let's get you inside out of the cold. Your feet have to be freezing."

Tobias ducked under the tape. "Okay. Let's go say hi to Toby, first."

Mike scowled down at the street and let his breath rattle out between his teeth. "You are Toby Burton."

The man glanced at him sideways, an idiotic grin floating on his lips. "Come on, Mike. Quit teasing."

Mike gritted his teeth. *Humor the poor bastard,* he thought. He put his hand on Tobias' shoulder. "Okay, no more teasing. Come with me." He pointed at Trooper Lewis, Reid, and Jack. "Tobias, do you remember Jack King? He was a year behind us."

Tobias shook his head. "No, no I don't. A year behind, you say?"

Mike nodded. "Anyway, that's him, the Oneka Falls officer."

"Oh."

"Jack, remember Tobias Burton?" Mike called. The three men turned to look at them, and Reid's eyes stretched wide. Jack nodded politely.

"Say, Chief," said Jack. "Did you take Shannon home?"

"No, she's right over..." He trailed off as he looked over at Shamu. The car was empty. "Maybe she walked home. It's not far."

The skin between Jack's eyebrows knotted. "Should I go check on her?"

Mike nodded. "Yeah. Do that."

"Hi, Benny," Reid said. "When did you get out?"

"A week? No, a month?" He shook his head and laughed like a kid. "I don't know, the details are still fuzzy. But don't call me Benny. I gave you that name so you could get out last year. Anyway, someone might hear you, and then the game is up."

Reid frowned. "Benny, I…" He grimaced and lifted both hands to rub his chin. "So I could get out? Get out of *where*?"

"Tobias. Call me Tobias, Toby. And don't joke, I've already had my fill of it from Mike here."

Reid's ears turned red, and he shuffled his feet, looking away into the darkness. "Why is he calling me Toby?" he muttered.

Mike cleared his throat. "Tobias called me from the Millvale State Hospital yesterday." He cast a meaningful look at the other men.

"He's Benny. Benny Cartwright," said Reid. "How do I know that?" he murmured.

Lewis looked back and forth between the three of them. "What the hell is going on around here?"

Mike shook his head. "I have no fucking idea."

4

Shannon cowered in the darkness of the tumbledown wooden shack. The air in the shack tasted like rotten wood and damp earth. She pressed back into the corner farthest from the only door. There were no windows in the shack, so the only light was the moonlight that snuck through the cracks between the old planks that made up the walls.

That pig of a man, Red Bortha, had walked right up to Mike's cruiser, bold as brass. Before Shannon had even considered hitting the power locks, he'd grabbed the door handle and yanked the door open. He hadn't spoken a word to her—he'd just hooked her arm in his paw of a hand and jerked her right out of the car. He hadn't said anything to her when he'd shoved her into his old pickup truck, nor when he'd plucked her out of it and pushed her into the shack.

She thought he was still outside—the pickup hadn't started up—but he either moved like a mouse, or wasn't moving around out there. She couldn't even hear him breathing. It was as if he'd shoved her inside, closed the door, and disappeared into thin air. So far, she hadn't been able to work up the courage to get up and check to see if Bortha had locked the door.

Despite what she'd told Mike, she *could* remember what happened to her when she was nine. At least the part about being left in the woods, and old Mr. Thorndike leading them to safety and then dying of a heart attack. She didn't know why that made her think of Benny Cartwright. *Was he there when Mr. Thorndike dropped me off at the Town Hall? His dad worked for the town, right?*

That mess had been buried in the substrata of her mind for a long time, and she wanted it to stay there. Besides Mike and Jack, she didn't waste time reminiscing about anyone from school. She liked Jack—as a friend—and Mike...well, Mike was Mike. None of the other kids in school had made enough of a dent in the cotton candy world she'd lived in after the kidnapping. She vaguely remembered a girl she used to play with before—

What the hell am I doing? Woolgathering like a drooling idiot! I've got to find a way out of here before Red rapes me. Or kills me.

Or both!

She pushed with her legs and slid up the wall, the rough wood burning across her shoulders. Her knees shook with fear as she pushed herself away from the wall. She took a baby step toward the door and then froze, listening for Red—for anything outside the door. The night seemed frozen. There was no wind sound, no animal sounds, no breathing, no explosions, no sirens wailing in the distance. Nothing. She crept across the small space and pressed her ear against the door. Cars passed on a road somewhere in the distance—too far to be of any use. She pressed her eye to one of the cracks between the planks of the door and peered into the night. She couldn't see anything moving, not even branches or leaves fluttering in the wind—it was too dark.

Being as quiet as the church mouse most people in town assumed she was, she opened the door a crack and then froze. Nothing crashed out of the woods, nothing lunged at her from the side of the shack.

She wiped her clammy palms on the denim stretched tight across her rear. Her stomach ached from the effort of keeping her breathing under control and quiet. She nudged the door open farther with shaking fingertips. Unbidden, the image of Red slapping the door open and grabbing her by the throat flashed through her mind. The vision was so violent, so foreign, that it felt like a violation—an assault in and of itself. All she wanted to do was find a safe place to curl up and hide until Mike came to rescue her. *Where is he? Why hasn't he come?* she asked herself. *It's been hours and hours. Hasn't it?*

Red had broken her phone. Her *new* phone. Her nostrils flared like a bull at the thought. *That damn thing cost me two whole paychecks, and now it's nothing but broken glass and smashed up aluminum lying in the road somewhere.* She wanted to punch Red Bortha right in the mouth for that...or knee him between his fat thighs. Her lips peeled back from her teeth as she imagined slamming her knee into Red's groin and the big man crying out as he fell to the ground. She shoved the door open, hard this time. Her heart was beating an angry tempo in her ears. She stepped outside like she owned the place. She glanced to the right. Nothing moved. She glanced to the left and screamed.

Red Bortha stood inches from her face, his mouth opened wide—so wide it looked like his jaw hinged like a snake's. His filed teeth ended in sharp points and it looked like there were far, far too many of them. His breath washed over her, smelling like a polluted river full of rotting corpses. Lightning quick, his tongue shot out of his mouth and slapped against her cheek like a frog nabbing a fly.

Shannon froze. There was a weird noise filling the clearing where the wretched old shack stood. It shrieked like air sliding out of a balloon with its throat pinched.

Bortha snapped his mouth shut, just missing the tip of her nose. "Shut your *fucking* mouth, you worthless sow!" he hissed.

She closed her mouth so fast her teeth snicked together with a sharp pain. The keening wail stopped. *Was that me making that god-awful noise?*

"Yeah, you idiot," Red breathed in her ear. "Make it again, and I will bite your nipples off." Shannon shuddered at the image the words brought to her mind. Bortha slapped his hand between her breasts, and she had to slap her hand over her mouth to keep from shrieking again. Red laughed, sounding like a vicious schoolyard bully. He pushed her, and she fell reeling back into the shack, arms pinwheeling, feet shuffling to stay underneath her. "Don't you come out here again, piggy. I might forget that your old friend Herlequin ordered me to leave you alone." Threat oozed from the words.

Shannon backed into the corner. Red slammed the door so hard dirt showered down from the ceiling. Her tight muscles quivered with strain and gave way like a tire with a slow leak. She sank to the earthen floor, friction from the rough wooden planks burning across her shoulder blades. Her butt hit the dirt, and she sobbed.

5

"Mike," said Benny.

Reid shifted his hands, rattling the handcuffs, earning himself a hard glance from Lewis. "They're a little tight," he said.

Chief Richards scoffed. "One of you two better start making sense, or, childhood friends or not, I'm locking you *both* up."

"Mike," said Benny.

"We were friends?" asked Drew. "I…I don't remember anything from before I was fourteen."

"Fourteen? If I remember right, that was the year Benny Cartwright got out of Millvale. He never came back to Oneka Falls though."

"Dr. Reid has legitimate ID," said Trooper Lewis. "I checked. Did a deep background check, too, and this man is Dr. Andrew Reid."

"Mike," said Benny.

"This is like this weird nightmare," said Drew. "How do I know—"

"Cut it, Reid," snapped Lewis.

"MIKE!" yelled Benny.

"What? For God's sake, what?"

"Where's Shannon?" Benny stood hunched, half turned away from the other men. His shoulders were up like he was tensing for a blow, and sweat poured from him, despite the chill in the air.

"She went home."

"No, Mike, I don't think so. She's…"

Drew stared at the bearded man. He *knew* him somehow, but he didn't understand how or why he believed it with such vigor, he didn't *remember* the guy at all.

"Relax, Tobias," said Richards. "Everything is okay. I sent Jack over to check on her."

"Jack?" asked Benny, tilting his head to the side.

"Yeah, Jack King. You met him a minute ago, standing right here."

"Is he one of them?"

Richards shook his head and tugged his belt into a more comfortable position. "One of who?"

"Them. The demons."

Chief Richard's eyes flicked toward the heavens as if sending a silent plea for patience. "Demons, Tobias? What are you—"

"No," said Drew, his voice firm. "Jack isn't one of them, Benny." Lewis' gaze crawled over his face, but he didn't turn. He didn't want to watch the man's face when the truth hit him.

Benny turned to Drew and put his finger to his lips. "Tobias," he stage-whispered. Then he smiled. "I sure am glad we're together again, Toby. One of them came to the hospital. Got a job there. Threatened me. That's why I left."

Drew averted his eyes as a furious blush crept up his cheeks. "I'm sorry I don't…I'm not this Toby person. My name is Andrew Reid."

Benny winked and put his finger alongside his nose. "Right. Andy, is it?"

Drew tried to slip his hands into his pockets, forgetting about the hand cuffs for the moment. "Uh, no. Drew."

"Right. Drew." Benny leaned forward and winked, in plain view of everyone. "Your secret's safe with me, Toby. I mean Drew. I won't tell the c-o-p-s. Just *op-stay* with the *Enny-bay* stuff."

"Um, okay."

Chief Richards watched the exchange like a spectator at a tennis match and then shook his head. He turned to Lewis and shrugged.

Lewis cleared his throat. "So, uh, this body—"

"Mike," said Benny. "Mike, Shannon's in trouble."

Richards closed his eyes and scowled. "No, Tobias. Jack will take care of her." He opened his eyes, turning away from Tobias and toward the trooper. "We didn't find one."

Lewis' eyebrows peaked. "No body?"

Richards shook his head. "No, but there was evidence—"

"Mike! One of them has her! We've got to help her!"

"—of recent assaults that ended in death." He jabbed his finger at the old church. "The whole fucking cellar is a warren of tiny cells set up for torture."

Lewis glanced at Drew. "That's what he said. That she was in a tiny room with torture implements on one wall." Lewis shook his head, looking exhausted and grim. "I..." After a moment, he pulled Drew closer by the handcuff chain and unlocked the restraints.

Richards' cell phone rang, and he stepped away to answer it.

"I'm sorry, Trooper Lewis. I wish I—"

"Yeah, save it," said Lewis in a gruff voice. "You're not off the hook. The forensics—"

"Not there? Did she go across the street to work, do you think, or up the street to the store? Zip over and check Town Hall," Mike said.

Benny shook his head. "She's not there, Mike. I'm telling you, she's in trouble."

"Benny..." said Drew. "Benny, just give him a second."

Benny shot him an exasperated look and held his finger to his lips. "Shhh!" he hissed.

Mike Richards turned back to them. "Jack's doing a little recce. In the meantime, Trooper Lewis, we can head—" His cell rang again, and holding up a finger, Richards turned his back again.

Lewis stood there, shoulders slumped, thumbs hooked in his front pockets, staring at the church. "You say LaBouche came out of there this afternoon?"

Drew nodded. "Yeah. I'm sorry. I was sitting right over there in my car." He pointed to where Richards' cruiser stood. "And he came through the double doors. We were almost face-to-face. No way I confused someone else for him."

Lewis grunted.

"*What?* I can't do that, Chaz. The State Police…Yeah, I realize that, but…" Richard's voice was rising, both in volume and pitch. "Well, fuck, Chaz, I can't just…"

Benny stepped closer to Drew. "Uh, Toby? I mean, Drew? Is Mike *really* Mike?"

Drew arched an eyebrow at him. Lewis seemed lost in his own thoughts.

"Well, I mean, he's not one of *them*, right?"

"No. No, Benny. None of these men are demons."

"So you can still see them? I mean, really *see* them?"

Drew wrapped his arms around his chest and squeezed. "How do you… How can you know what I can see and—"

"We are best friends, Toby. You *told* me." His tone sounded off, and he looked a little hurt. "Don't you… The amnesia thing isn't just an act?"

Drew looked him in the eye, reading the hurt there. "I'm sorry. You are Benny Cartwright, but I don't remember how I met you, or when."

"So you don't remember Oneka Falls?"

Drew shrugged. "Before yesterday, I'd never been here."

"I get things wrong—sometimes, but I *know* I'm not wrong about this. You are Toby Burton. You grew up in Oneka Falls."

"I don't remember any of—"

"Well, until we were eleven, anyway. You wanted a bike. Bad. And your mom…well, I don't want to speak ill of the dead, but she was a real piece of work. She wouldn't get you one, and we all had bikes and there was this ad—in the newspaper, not like this internet crap—that was offering bikes for a Jackson, and you wanted it and—"

"Hold on," said Lewis and Benny turned to gaze at him, head tilted like a bird. "Did you say Dr. Reid grew up here? In Oneka Falls?"

Benny shrugged. "Well, of course he did. He grew up on Mill Lane, right around the corner—"

The world faded to a dull gray, and a weight fell on Drew, pressing him toward the ground. Everything was spinning, and his breath whistled out of him like the air was being sucked right out of his lungs. Lewis grabbed his shoulder, saying something that Drew couldn't hear.

Mill Lane—what is it about that road? Why does it feel like someone's dropped a million volts across my spinal column every time I see or hear about Mill Lane?

Suddenly, he wanted—no, needed—to puke. He squeezed his eyes shut, willing away the spinning, shrieking maelstrom that had settled around him like a weight around a drowning man. *It's nothing. Nothing!* Even with his eyes closed, the world spun and spun. His hands flopped outward, grasping for something solid, something to anchor himself to. "How much is that puppy?" he muttered. "Where's my little puppy?"

"What's he saying?" The voice sounded like it was a million miles away.

"Why can't I find my puppy?" he murmured, willing the craziness to subside, willing a sane reality into existence. The spinning slowed, his nausea subsided.

"Why is he talking nonsense?"

"It's a trick he learned in Millvale. It helps him stop thoughts he doesn't want to think—"

Just like that, Drew was off again, spinning and spinning. Nausea rolled back in with a vengeance, hitting him like an out-of-control semi-truck.

Mill Lane. Thousand Acre Drive. The man with the bikes. The man with the claws—

6

"No fucking way, Chaz. I can't just roll out of here and pretend none of this ever happened."

Static hissed in his ear for the span of ten heartbeats. "That's a mistake, Mike."

"Maybe so, Chaz, but there's no way I can go to the Staties and say 'Oh, sorry. False alarm.' I mean, they've already *mobilized*, Chaz."

"Be that as it may, Mike, I need you to find a way to back out of this."

"Look, Chaz, you have a…a liberal bent toward law enforcement. I get that, and I can't always say you are wrong, but how in the blue fuck can you *want* a place like Play Time operating in Oneka Falls? Even if no one *died* in the cellar, even if it's all consensual as you say, even if it's all in good fun. I mean, the stuff down there in the basement…branding irons and hot coals. That's grievous bodily harm, *even with consent*. I can't condone the sort of behavior that leads to…to…to branding and…and—"

"Listen, Mike, let me—"

"—and *crazy* shit like that. Anyway, there *has* to be an investigation. Even if I didn't want one, now the

State Police are involved, and that means there *will* be an investigation. Their forensics people are already—"

"You leave all that to me."

"Chaz, I—"

"Tell you what, Mike, I'm on my way down to the scene right now. I'll talk to the Staties and then meet you for a beer. Say down to Lumber Jack's?"

"Chaz…"

"Let me help, Mike," Chaz crooned. "I'll handle everything. It's your day off unless I've got my wires crossed. It is, right?"

Mike turned back toward Trooper Lewis. Reid was down on his knees, and both Lewis and Tobias crouched next to him. "Yes," he said.

"Well, okay, then. I'll be right there to relieve you. I'm coming up Mill Lane, now. Talk to you in two shakes."

"Chaz, I…listen to me a—" The call ended.

With a grimace, Mike shoved the phone into his pocket. He walked back over to the trooper. "Listen, Trooper Lewis. My boss is on his way here right now. He wants to put the kibosh on this whole investigation."

Lewis snapped his head around and his gaze bored into Mike's eyes. "No."

"Yeah, I know. In so many words, he told me to go get drunk and relieved me of duty. He's a bit of a—"

"I don't care what he is. This investigation will not be—"

"Take it from me," Mike said, leaning toward Lewis and staring him in the eye. "Take jurisdiction. Take the case. He can't sweep it under the rug if it's a state case."

The headlights from Chaz Welsh's fancy blue BMW washed across them. Lewis' eyes strayed to the car and then back to Mike's. He dropped his chin once and pushed Reid toward Tobias. "Give me a minute," he muttered.

He stood and faced Mike, waiting for Chaz to get out of the car. The BMW's door swung open, he said, "No, you listen to me, *Chief.* It's obvious that at least one serious crime occurred inside that building." He crooked his thumb toward Play Time. "That is a *crime scene*, plain and simple. I'm taking over this case. As of right fucking now."

Chaz sprang out of the car, all smiles and twinkling teeth. "Now, Trooper, that's not very friendly, is it?"

"Not here to make friends, sir, and don't you dare take one step inside the crime scene tape. It's there for a reason."

"I'm the town manager of Oneka Falls, and this place is inside my town. I go where I like."

"One step," said Lewis, holding up a finger. "One step past that tape and you can tell it to a judge."

"Mike, tell this guy—"

"It's my night off, remember?"

Chaz glared, first at Lewis, then at Mike. "You two are making a mistake. I have…*friends* who will be quite upset at your behavior. You are—"

"Shove it up your ass, Town Manager," said Lewis. "You want a collar for threatening a law enforcement officer?"

Chaz glowered at him.

"Careful," hissed Reid from behind them. Mike glanced back. Both Tobias and Reid were staring at Chaz Welsh like he was the devil himself.

"I think you've just ended your career, Trooper," snarled Chaz. He turned and slid into his car, slamming the door. He revved the engine and then threw it into reverse, leaving two long, smoky black tracks up the block.

"That went well," said Lewis.

"You should call in the troops," said Mike.

"Yeah. Let me get on the horn." He stepped away and started making phone calls.

Mike squatted next to Tobias and Reid. "What was that all about?"

"He's one of them," said Tobias.

"The town manager?"

"Yeah. He's a demon," said Reid.

"I picked the wrong weekend to quit drinking," muttered Mike.

7

Jack stirred cream into a steaming cup of brown water, grimacing in anticipation of the flavor of the swill. He had no idea where Shannon was, but he knew where she *wasn't*: not at home, not at the store, not here. He'd expected to find her at home, warm and safe. Maybe she'd gone somewhere for a late dinner, but her car still sat in its space below her apartment. He thought it was possible she'd gone out with friends, but the probability was low. Everyone knew she carried a torch for Mike Richards. She followed him around when he went drinking. It didn't sit right that she would have gone off somewhere while Mike stewed over at Play Time. She would want to keep him company. Jack had a bad feeling about the whole thing, but neither he nor the chief believed in all that hocus pocus.

The front door slammed open and heavy footsteps pounded through the lobby. Jack froze without knowing why. He turned the light off in the closet that served as the police department break room. It might be one of the night guys, but he didn't think so. It wasn't Mike—the chief would neither slam through the door nor stomp across the lobby like a spoiled child…at least not while sober, which he had been not long before—miracle of miracles.

"I did what I could. Don't be angry with me." The voice sounded familiar and yet strange, like whoever spoke usually pretended at an accent or different pitch.

"Shut up, you worthless bitch!" bellowed Chaz Welsh.

In the darkness, Jack's eyebrows shot skyward.

The sound of a heavy blow reverberated through the town hall, followed by a whining cry. "One job!" shouted Chaz. "You had one, simple little, motherfucking teeny, goddamn thing to do, and you *fucked…it…up!*" The sound of a heavy blow underscored each of the last three words.

"No, Chaz! I'm *sorry!*"

That voice. Jack had the sense he heard a voice like that every day. *Someone's mother? Someone's daughter?*

"*No, Chaz! I'm sorry, Chaz!*" mocked the town manager. "That's all I get from you, you worthless hen!

I should send you back. I should send you *back* and leave you there to *starve*! This place is for can-doers, not for apologizers!"

"Chaz, I—" The sentence turned into another yowling cry.

"Sally Fuck-it-up McBride! That's what we'll call you from now on."

Of course! But that meant Chaz *sent* Sally to that damn church… *Fuck. Chaz is* behind *whatever is going on at Play Time.*

"Sally, is there someone here with you?" Chaz asked in conversational tones. "I smell something."

"Coffee? It's just the pot for the PD night shift. It's always burning away in that closet of theirs."

"Hmm," said Chaz, sounding anything but convinced. "Well, no matter, Fuck-it-up. Tell me, did Bortha do *his* part of it at least? Did he grab that mouse Bertram?"

"I don't know, Chaz. I came here after Mike—" Again, the sentence stopped, cut off with a whingeing cry. "Please don't hit me anymore, m'lord," she whimpered.

M'lord? What the fuck?

"Herlequin will be most displeased if you allowed the woman to get away. *Most* displeased. If you think

I'm hard on you, Fuck-it-up, well, you are in for one rude awakening."

Sally's only reply was a mewling moan.

Chaz didn't bother to respond, beyond muttering while he punched a number into the phone at reception. "Red? Chaz. Do you… Ah, great news. Yes, I'm sure Herlequin will be pleased. Expect him soon. I don't need mention she'd better remain untouched, do I, Red?" Chaz grunted and hung up the phone with a clatter. Sally yawped like Chaz had yanked her up by the hair.

"Now, then. Where were we, Fuck-it-up?"

Jack's stomach ached like he'd swallowed a hot coal. *They've got her! They have Shannon.* He pulled his cell phone out of his pocket and called Mike.

"Richards."

"Mike, listen and don't interrupt. I'm at the PD. Chaz is out in the lobby, beating the piss out of Sally McBride. He's in on it, behind it. They have Shannon, or Red Bortha does. Said they are holding her for someone named Herlequin."

"Why, Jack," crooned Chaz. He stood so close that his breath tickled Jack's ear. "I'm so disappointed."

"Chaz! Shit, you scared me, boss!"

"You haven't seen anything yet. Look at me, Jack."

Jack turned and screamed. Chaz took his phone out of his numb fingers and crushed it with one huge, scaly hand.

Chapter 3
1979

I

"I'm sorry," said the doctor dressed in scrubs and a lab coat. "Mr. Thorndike succumbed. We did all we could, but our efforts were not enough."

"Well, shit," said Matt.

"Did Mr. Thorndike have a family? Anyone we can contact? Or will you be doing that?" His expression and tone of voice left no question he wanted Matt to do the notification.

"Yeah, I'll handle it," groused Matt. "What about the kids?"

The doctor narrowed his eyes, lips pressed into a tight white slash. "They are not my patients. I'm sure I don't know their status. Ask one of the nurses."

Matt angled his head away from the pedantic little man and cracked his knuckles. "No, wouldn't want to put you out. I mean, you're *important*."

"Now, see—"

Matt spun on his heels and walked away from the man, leaving him grumbling. The nurse's station crackled with the clamor of Emergency Rooms everywhere. Matt caught the eye of a pretty, red-headed young nurse. "Excuse me," he said. "Can you help me?"

She nodded and came toward him. "Yes?"

"I brought two children in several hours ago. Boy by the name of Benny Cartwright and a young girl named Shannon Bertram. Can you give me their status?"

The nurse glanced down at his badge, then his gun, and back to his face. "Sure, Chief." She turned her back and fished the charts out of their slots. "Hmm. The Bertram girl is rehydrating, and her parents are on the way. The Cartwright boy...well, we have two issues."

Matt nodded.

"We can't contact his parents, that's the first thing. Add to that—"

"His mother is away, but his father is right upstairs. He's a patient. Room 409."

The nurse smiled and jotted something in the chart. "Good. That will make things easier. The second problem is the boy. He's suffering from hysterical catatonia, and—"

"Oh, good Christ, not again," Matt mumbled.

The nurse's eyebrows arched, and she tilted her head to the side.

"Nothing," said Matt. "He's the second kid to come from my town with that in the past few days."

She glanced down at his badge again. "Oneka Falls? Oh! Because of the shootings?"

Matt shook his head. "No, because of the shooter. He also kidnapped these children."

"Oh, my lands," she said. "That's terrible!"

"The first kid's already up here—over to the psychiatric center."

The nurse nodded. "That's where little Benny will be headed when he's done with his IV and we get his father's permission."

"Well, shit," Matt muttered. "No chance he can talk to me? I've known him all his life."

"I don't see why not. Tell you what, let's get his IV finished, and then you and I can take him up to visit his father."

"Deal," said Matt. "Is there a payphone I can use? I need to get in touch with my dispatcher."

"Sure," she smiled at Matt. "There's a convenience room for law enforcement off the lobby. I'll take you there."

2

Owen smiled at the women in the lobby, allowing his true self to shine through. That was enough to make them look away. Both he and Brigitta were dirty and bare-foot. He'd left the rifle in the car, so he had to do something to keep people from throwing him out.

He walked up to the information desk. "I need a friend's room number, please."

The portly woman behind the desk raised her eyebrows. "Name?"

"Randy Fergusson."

The woman turned to a rolodex and flipped through it. When she got to the end, she looked up at Owen, loosing an exaggerated sigh.

"Sorry, I thought you wanted my name."

Her face pinched up like an old prune and she looked at him over her cat-eye glasses. "What's your *friend's* name?"

"Sorry." Owen smiled at her, though he wanted to punch her in her fat face. "His name is…Joe, uh… No, it's Jim."

The woman huffed another sigh. "His *last* name?"

"Oh, uh…" Owen looked at Brigitta and raised his eye brows.

"If you don't know, my love, neither do I," she whispered.

"Uh... His last name is... Okay, this is embarrassing." Owen plastered his best sheepish grin on his face. "I've forgotten his last name for the moment. He's the town manager in Oneka Falls, so if you could—"

"This is Rochester, sir, *not* Oneka Falls. You can't expect me to follow your town's leadership."

"Yeah, no. I don't, I mean. I was wondering if you could—"

"Sir, if you don't know your friend's name, I can't help you." She turned in her squeaky chair and looked out the window.

Owen wanted to jump right across the desk and teach the fat bitch a lesson, but Brigitta's cool palm rested on his forearm. "Do we have it in the car, my love?" She winked at him.

"Yeah," Owen seethed. "In the car. Yeah, in the trunk." He turned and stomped away from the information desk.

"Put on a damn pair of shoes while you are out there, hippy," called the woman at the desk.

Owen stood up straight at her tone, but Brigitta pulled him toward the electric doors. "No scene, my love. Not until after."

"Right," Owen snapped. "After." The way he said the word made it sound like a promise.

3

The pretty little nurse led him to the lobby, smiling and chattering away like a humming bird. Matt thought he'd have to ask for her number before he headed back home. He was watching the way her lips quirked when she smiled, and just happened to glance up at the man at the information desk. Their gazes locked for a moment. Matt grabbed the nurse's shoulder and sent her spinning back into the hall that led to the ER. She squawked with surprise, but Matt was already moving, already pulling his 1911 and crouching for cover. "Freeze!" he boomed.

The fat lady behind the information desk looked at him with obvious distaste, but when her eyes tracked up to his gun, a bleat escaped her lips and her eyes went wide behind her cat-eye glasses.

4

Owen saw that chief fuck walk into the lobby, and their gazes locked for a moment. Then the dumb-fuck shouted "Freeze!" and Owen ducked down, the information desk between him and Chief Greshin. He looked around for Brigitta, but she was either invisible or gone. "Wish she'd teach me that teleport shit," he muttered.

"What? What?" squawked the fat lady on the other side of the desk.

"Shut your fucking hole," he said.

"Gray! Get out here where I can see you, hands up and empty. Do it now."

"Aw, fuck you, Matt," yelled Owen. "Not such a badass without your pals, are you? Let me tell you, son, there's only one badass in this lobby, and he's Force Recon."

"Badass? You're hardly that, Gray."

The fucker was moving around, flanking him, Owen could tell by the sound of his voice. Owen slid around to the back side of the desk and yanked old cat-eyes clean out of her chair. She fell to the ground, landing on her side. "Oh, you *fuck*!" she screamed. "You broke my ever-loving hip, you bastard!"

"Good," Owen snapped. "Maybe you'll learn respect from that pain…*if* I let you live long enough to learn anything." *Where's Greshin? What's he doing?* "Hey, Matt," he yelled. "I got a friend down here with me. Her name's… Well, to be honest, I don't give a fuck. I think I broke her hip."

"So she said," said Greshin.

He sounded *close*. Owen swiveled his head back and forth, scanning each end of the desk and skimming across the top edge. "Don't you fuck with me, Greshin. Do that, and this old bag is a dead motherfucker! You know I'll do it."

"Yeah, I do," said the chief, sounding closer than ever.

"Good. Here's what we're going to do. You, drop that cannon and *get the fuck back*, and I might let this old bitch live."""

"No," said Greshin, his voice cold.

"What? What do you mean, no? I told you I'll kill her, Chief." Greshin didn't answer, and now Owen could hear his breathing. "Don't think I won't. You should know by now I don't give a fuck. Not one."

5

Matt squatted behind the folding panel set up behind the information desk. Gray sat on the floor on the other side of the panel.

"I'll do it, Greshin!"

Matt duck-walked to the other end of the panel, and keeping his movements slow and careful, peered around the edge of the screen. Gray sat with his back to Matt, head turning back and forth, trying to keep all the edges of the desk in sight at the same time. Matt allowed himself a grim smile.

He cocked his arm back and threw the empty Coke bottle he'd grabbed out of a garbage can. It arced high over the top of the panel, and, as it soared overhead, Gray's head snapped up to track it. Matt moved, exploding out from behind the panel, knocking the panel away with one hand, leveling the gun on Gray with the other.

Gray shrieked like a little girl on Halloween, and Matt fell on him, hammering Gray with the Colt, and slamming his hand down on the side of Gray's head, pushing his face to the side and into the cold tile floor. He pressed the end of his 1911 into Gray's throat, right under the bend in his jaw. He sat astride Gray, knees pinning Gray's arms. He leaned forward, breath hissing in and out like a locomotive at full throttle. "Move," he hissed. "*Please.*"

"You'd enjoy that, wouldn't you? Well, I'm not going to give you the satis—"

"Then shut up," Matt sneered. With a fast, savage strike, he pistol-whipped Gray across the face. He rolled Gray onto his stomach and cuffed him to the radiator that the folding panel was supposed to hide. He glanced at the big woman who worked the information desk. "You okay?"

"Sure, I enjoy lying on the ground and writhing in the dirt! No, I'm *not* okay. I think I broke my hip!"

"Help's coming. Where's the woman?"

"What woman?"

"The blonde. She was with this guy when I came in."

"How should I know?"

"She ran toward the stairs," said the red-headed nurse. "Are you okay?" Her eyes held Matt's gaze, steady, calm.

Competent woman, Matt thought. *I should get her number. I'm a fool if I don't.*

"No!" said the fat lady. "Why does everyone keep asking me that? Do I *look* okay?"

The nurse smiled at Matt and winked. "You know we have to ask you, Matilda. Where does it hurt, hon?"

"Call 911," he said. "Get the local cops over here, and tell the dispatcher to contact Lieutenant Gregory at the Troop E barracks. He'll want to be here." He flashed her a smile and sprinted for the stairwell.

6

Jim Cartwright lay in his bed, trying not to move. Everything hurt when he moved, but if he kept still, it wasn't so bad.

"Mr. Cartwright?"

Without moving his head, Jim looked toward the door. A sexy blonde nurse stood there. She had one of those funny little nurses' hats on, and when she smiled, the hat waggled back and forth.

"Yes?" Jim said.

"Hello. I'm an ER nurse here, and I've been treating your son, Benjamin."

"Benny," said Jim. "He's…he's *alive*?"

"Well, of course, silly. We don't treat the dead."

"Oh, thank Christ!"

"No, thank an old man named Reginald Thorndike. He found your son in Thousand Acre Wood and led him out."

"Old Reg Thorndike?"

"Yes," the nurse smiled. "It is unfortunate."

Jim snapped his head toward her, groaning at the burning pain in his gut. *What is unfortunate about my son being alive?*

"Oh, sorry!" she said with a self-deprecating laugh. "I mean, it's unfortunate about Mr. Thorndike's demise. Heart attack."

Something's off. This nurse is…wrong.

"I'm sorry you feel that way," said the nurse, and her clothes and skin faded, revealing a rotting corpse.

Jim screamed.

7

A scream rent the air above him, and Matt poured on the speed, taking the steps three at a time. The scream sounded again as Matt passed the fourth-floor landing, and he skidded, mid-stride, to a stop. He hit the push-bar on the door and stepped into the hall. He looked both directions and drew his gun.

To his right, a few patients stuck their heads out into the hall, and to his left nurses did the same from the nurses' station. "Which way?" he demanded. A nurse pointed, and Matt pounded up the hall, head twisting back and forth as he scanned the rooms on both sides.

The door to room 409 was closed—Jim Cartwright's room. He kicked the door as hard as he could and burst into the room, trying to see everywhere, every*thing* at once.

At first, he thought a blonde nurse was screwing Jim, but then the blood splattered everywhere registered. "Get the fuck off him!" he bellowed and leveled the gun on the nurse.

She glanced at him, and she was no longer a blonde nurse. She *changed*, she became a thing out of nightmare. Her black, rotting skin hung from her like clothes on a line, and blood dripped from her maw of a mouth. Instead of fingers, she had talons and they were buried in Jim's throat. Her eyes dripped a viscous green goo—pus—over Jim's face. "Too late," she rasped.

He squeezed the trigger, the gun boomed, but instead of the bullet slamming into the thing on top of Jim, it shattered the window behind him. The thing had vanished.

Matt shuffled forward, thinking she'd dove off the side of the bed, but the space between the bed and the wall was empty. His eyes tracked up Jim's body, noting the exposed organs, the ruptured blood vessels in a clinical, methodical way. "Well, fuck," he muttered.

"Indeed," hissed a voice in his ear, and pain erupted from his throat.

8

Owen came to, his head throbbing like a funny-car engine. He jerked his hands, and the cuffs bit into his wrists. The warm metal almost burned his skin. "Fucker cuffed me to a radiator?" he croaked.

He opened his eyes. Pandemonium ruled the hospital lobby. If he could get free of the goddamn cuffs, he would slip away in the confusion. He glanced down at the cuffs, hoping Greshin had forgotten to lock them. *Pipe dream*, he thought. *Greshin has had a hard-on for me since I shot his pet, Witherson.*

He gazed around the lobby, hoping something would leap out at him, a tool, someone he could manipulate. "Hey, this burns," he yelled, but no one so much as glanced his way. "This is cruel and unusual punishment!" Again, no one batted an eyelash. "Fuckers," he muttered.

He looked around again, and across the width of the lobby, he glimpsed blonde hair. She stood near the door, blood dripping from her fingers—Brigitta, his love. Their eyes locked, his pleading, hers sorrowful. He rattled the handcuffs, and she frowned, shaking her head.

Babe, get these cuffs off me and I can walk right out of here. I can—

No, my love. My father says this is how it must end. For now. There will—

Fuck *that! Come on, babe! We can get away clean. We can—*

Owen, my love, no. Father says things have gotten too far out of control, that strategic retreat is called for. You can understand that, can't you?

Owen kept his mind still. Stopped the thoughts before she picked them up.

My love, the time will come again when we are together. Trust in that. We will be apart for a while, but we are meant to be together, and we will be again. Believe *me.*

Brigitta! Babe, no! Don't leave me! Tears sprang into his eyes, and his throat burned as if he'd been eating live coals. "Please," he sobbed.

Her face crumpled and she shook her head. *I'm sorry, my love. Father requires us to make a sacrifice. But the rewards will be equal to the cost—more than equal. And, Owen, I took care of Jim Cartwright and Matt Greshin for you.*

He stared at her, mind racing.

Yes, my love. I ripped their throats out with my bare hands. They suffered, my love, they suffered as much as I could make them suffer. She turned and walked out the front door. No one noticed her. No one except Owen Gray, tears and snot streaming down his face.

Brigitta!

Chapter 4

2007

I

"Jack? Jack! What's happening?" Mike spun and faced the town hall. "Chaz, you leave him the fuck alone!" He took two steps toward Shamu before Benny caught him.

"No, Mike! That Chaz guy is a demon! You can't do anything."

"Yes, we can," said Reid. "But not how you think."

Mike jerked his arm out of Benny's hand. "I can't just stand here while he does whatever he wants to Jack."

Reid turned his face up to him and rose to his feet. "Bullets don't do enough damage. You might kill the thing after a while, but it won't stay dead."

"*What*?"

"No, the best way is to exsanguinate the beast, and then dissolve the body in a strong base. Back in Rochester, I use an industrial digester to get rid of their bodies. Once the body and blood are gone, they can't come back."

Mike put his hands up to the side of his head. "No, no. This isn't happening."

"If you insisted on using bullets, you'd need hard calibers and a lot more ammunition than those pistols hold. When I first learned how to kill them, I—" Reid snapped his mouth shut like he'd just realized what he was saying to two law enforcement officers.

Mike glanced over at Lewis, and the trooper's expression mirrored what he was feeling. These two men were obviously insane. Psychotic. Delusional. They both belonged in Millvale.

"No, it's not crazy, Mike," said Benny.

When did I start thinking of him as 'Benny?' Mike wondered. But Benny or Toby or Tobias, he was rat-shit crazy.

"I'm not, though, not 'rat-shit crazy,' Mike. I *pretended* to be crazy for a long time because it was safer *inside* than out."

Mike shook his head. *Did I say that aloud? The part about rat-shit crazy?* Benny chuckled and shook his head. Mike glanced at Reid, but the man was staring at Benny in rapt attention. Reid muttered something that sounded like "I can see it."

"Mike, trust me here. Jack just told you that a man named Red Bortha took Shannon. Am I right?"

Mike nodded, face as hard and cold as ice.

"And he said someone named Herlequin is coming for her?"

Reid's face blanched and his eyes went wide. He shook his head from side to side, faster and faster until Mike thought it would fly off.

"It's okay, Toby," Benny whispered. "It's okay."

Reid looked anything but okay.

"Red Bortha, he's from around here, but who's this Herlequin?"

"It's a long story, and one we don't have time for right now. Have I satisfied you as to the contents of your phone conversation with…What's-his-name?"

"Jack. And, yes."

"And could I have tapped into the airwaves? Overheard your call? Had a trained parakeet listen in and tell me those things?"

Mike shook his head.

"Then how did I do it?" Benny put his hand on Reid's shoulder.

"I have no idea," said Mike.

"He read your mind," said Reid. "Or something. I don't know what it is, but it comes from having survived Herlequin." He shuddered and began to shiver.

"There's that name again," said Lewis.

"Yeah. I need to understand who this guy is," said Mike.

"No time," said Reid. "We can't let Huh-herlequin get to her."

Mike slapped his fist into his palm. "Well, how the fuck do you expect me to save her?"

"Just like I could read your thoughts, I can hear Shannon's. I can take you to her, and Toby can see *them,* so he knows who is a good guy and who isn't."

"This isn't cops and robbers," said Lewis. "I'm not shooting anyone based on your say-so."

"No. Don't shoot *anyone,* either of you," said Reid. He walked to the back of his little silver Honda and popped the trunk open. He pulled out a strange looking air rifle and grinned at them. "*I'll* do the shooting."

"No, you won't," said Lewis.

"Don't worry," said Benny. "It's a tranquilizer gun." He smiled at Reid, and Reid grinned back.

Lewis looked at Mike and Mike shrugged. "She's in danger."

"*If* we can believe this happy crappy dappy."

Mike gestured to Play Time, looming in the darkness behind them. "Do you believe your daughter was there?"

Lewis looked into Mike's eyes for what felt like a long time, then he turned to Reid and gave him the same treatment.

"He does," said Benny.

Lewis' gaze snapped to Benny's face. "I can speak for myself."

Benny held up his hands, palms out. "Sorry, sorry. I've suppressed this for so long, it's fun to let it out to play."

2

They all thought they knew him—the crazy sniper fuck who didn't want to fight up close and personal. He'd cultivated that belief for years, waiting...biding his time.

He'd awakened fifteen minutes before, the cool hand of Brigitta caressing his cheek. "The time has come. Be ready, my love," she'd whispered in his ear. Then she'd disappeared.

Owen was dressed and ready. He'd wadded up his sheets and towels, winding them around his arms, shoulders, neck, and head. He'd used his foot-high stack of newspapers to wrap his abdomen, and he looked a bit like the Michelin Man. Newspaper and sheets didn't make the best armor, but it would afford him a modicum of protection from clubs, and a lot of protection from those damn taser darts. He bounced on the balls of his feet, eager to kick some Tom ass.

He heard the shouting and caterwauling first. A weak-minded person would say blood-curdling screams, but to Owen, the screams sounded pleasant, like a concerto of classical music. Mozart, maybe. He wished he could see what was happening. What Brigitta was doing to those motherfucking Toms.

The first gunshots rang into the night, ricochets whining down the hall in front of his cell. Owen cackled like the insane idiot he'd pretended to be. It was time…he didn't want to be standing there anymore, waiting. He sprinted around the edge of his small cell, leaping to his bed, running its length, leaping to the sink, then the commode, then back to the floor. Each time he passed the door, he leapt into the air and kicked at the glass view port. On his third circuit around the room, he realized he was yelling. "Come get me, babe! Come get me, babe! I want to play! I want to come out and play!"

Other inmates shouted and pounded on their cell doors, but they didn't rise to the level of Owen's notice. Somewhere in the building, fans of beautiful crimson splashed on the walls and puddled on the floor, and he didn't want to miss it. He wanted to see the blood of

Toms, to smell their fear, to hear their death rattles. "Let me out! Let me out!"

When his cell door clanked and then slid open on its automatic track, Owen laughed like a maniac and charged out into the hall. He looked both ways. To the left, the hall led to the showers and the laughable "yard" for the SHU—nothing more than a bunch of six by six cages outside, like that was worth a fuck, but they *were* out in the air and sun. To the right was the guards' control room. The place where the fucking Toms sat on their asses and watched him with their fucking little cameras.

"Which way, babe? Which way, babe?" he shouted, laughing like a kid. "Oh, Tom, I'm going to stomp your shit runny!" Without waiting for a sign from Brigitta, Owen turned right and sprinted up the corridor.

As the doors of the other cells on the SHU flashed by him, Owen caught snippets of what his fellow inmates shouted at him.

"—out of here, Gray! I've got *money*—"

"—motherfucking ass-licking carpet-sucking mother—"

"—door! Open the motherfucking door! Open—"

"—trying to sleep here! Shut that goddamn—"

Owen laughed with glee and hopped a few dozen paces. He hugged himself fiercely and punched himself in the chest, psyching himself up. *Those Tom motherfuckers are in for a surprise tonight! No more Mr. Nice-guy. No more weak little Owen. No more no more no more!*

The emergency klaxon blared away into the night. As Owen neared the guard station, radios squalled and screamed in a perfect storm of static. He pounded on the bullet-proof glass of the guard tower with his fists. Blood painted the interior of the station red—the blood of that chief Tom motherfucker—but no body was visible. Owen kept running.

Both doors of the SHU airlock stood open, the door controller a smoking mess and Owen danced through them, pretending he was John Travolta in that disco movie. He looked up at the camera on the other side of the air lock, grabbed his crotch and pretended to skull-fuck someone. *Let those Toms get a load of that!*

"Babe!" he yelled. "Where are you, babe? Leave a bunch of these Toms for me!"

He slid around a corner, and his eyes lit up like roman candles. A *rifle* leaned against the wall. A rifle with a scope. "Oh, I love you, babe! You're the best!"

Laughing like a kid at Christmas, Owen scooped the rifle up and kept running.

3

The nightmare held Shannon fast, and she couldn't find her way out of it. An infinite nightmare, as soon as the damn thing ended, it began again. She wasn't sleeping, not exactly. She was trapped in a shack by Red Bortha, she *knew* that even if she didn't always believe it.

"Lizzy," she called. "Come play with me."

"No way, Shannon, you're sick!"

The blister-like pox covered her face, it was true. It's why she couldn't leave Granny's shack. That's why Granny stood outside, guarding her. Keeping her inside.

"Cut out that racket, Shannon!" called Granny in a low voice that made Shannon think of a growling bear.

Shannon whimpered and backed into the corner. Squeezing as far from the door as she could.

Shannon forced her eyes open, blinking rapidly. She didn't want these…these daydreams. She didn't want to think about when she was nine.

Outside, a car fired up and idled, growling and snarling like a race car.

"Hey girl," said a man's voice. But it wasn't like Mike's voice at all. The voice creeped her out. It was the

man's *voice. Shannon shook her head, trying to deny the man even existed.*

"Hey there. Girl." *The car's engine rumbled and gurgled, but she still heard the car door slamming shut when the man got out.* "Hey," *he said.*

Where is Mike? *She screamed inside her head.* I want Mike!

"Mike?" *asked the man.* "Who's this Mike guy? You been stepping out on me, babe?"

"No!" Shannon screeched, shaking her head back and forth with a violence that made her sinuses hurt.

"Shut up," snarled Bortha. The shack shuddered and boomed as he beat on the wall. "Just shut up."

"I'm not supposed to talk to strange men!" she yelled.

"Shut—"

"And you shouldn't," *said a woman.* "But don't worry, Owen's one of the good ones."

Shannon shook her head, pressing her hands over her ears, squeezing her eyes shut.

"It's okay, Shannon," *said the woman.* "We need directions."

"I'm only nine," yelled Shannon. The ground was cold beneath her buttocks, and the earth smelled of fertilizer and engine oil. "Leave me alone, I'm only nine."

"Woman!" roared the monster outside. "Shut your damn mouth! You're pissing me off, and that's the last thing you want to do. Anyway, if you're nine, then I'm the president of these fucking United States."

"I don't know where anything is!" she wailed.

"Not even Thousand Acre Wood?" asked the man. "I bet you know where Thousand Acre Wood is. Bet you know exactly *where it is."*

"I hate *that place," hissed Shannon. "I'm never going back there again."*

"Wanna bet?" said the man. "But anyway, I told you you'd know the place we wanted to go."

A tinkling laugh drifted in through the cracks in the shack's walls. "Yes, you did, my love," said the woman.

"Stop it! Stop it! Stop calling him 'my love!' That's for Mike!"

The walls of the shack shook, and dust poured down on her from the ceiling. "The fuck? Are you having a goddamn fit?"

"Well, little Miss Shannon, I've got a crisp dollar bill for you for your help. All you have to do is come out here and take it."

"I don't want your fucking money, you...you...you asshole!"

The tinkling laugh floated through the air again. Beneath it, footsteps approached the door of the shack.

"Aw, come on, Miss Shannon," said the man. *"All you have to do is come to the door."*

"No!" she screamed. "I'm not coming out!"

Outside, Red Bortha roared like a lion.

4

Drew pointed at the demon and then held his fist up in the air like he was some sort of special forces guy. The demon was getting agitated about something. Drew raised his tranquilizer rifle and thumbed on the holographic sight.

They were at the edge of Thousand Acre Wood, and the shack was almost in the backyard of the last house on the street. The creepy looking house stood at the bottom of a hill. *That's strange,* he thought. Something about the place tickled the back of his mind.

The demon guarding the shack was a "weird." It was bright red like a traditional might be, but it had three, triangular-shaped mouths and tentacles instead of arms. Its body drooped like melted wax that had dripped into cold water and hardened. The demon wailed on the wall of the shack with his three tentacles, the single horn-shaped claw at the end of each leaving a

544   ERIK HENRY VICK

long gouge in the old wood. Drew wanted to stay clear of those things at all costs.

"That's Red Bortha, all right," breathed Mike. "I'd recognize that big bastard anywhere."

"I doubt I'll forget him either. He's old—I can tell by his size."

"Okay," said Richards.

"I'm going to load him up with M99, but it will take more than one shot...who can say how many to bring him down—ten or more is my guess. Once he's down, you and Lewis should see the truth."

Richards shrugged. "Maybe. Maybe not."

"He will come after me, and that's okay. I know how to deal with these brutes. I'm going to run, to dodge, and keep plugging him full of M99. Once he has enough in his blood, he'll go out, guaranteed."

"What do you want us to do?" asked Trooper Lewis.

"Stay back. No matter what. Don't let the demon see you or hear you. Who knows what he'll do then—kill Shannon, or worse yet—"

"Hey! Fuck-face!"

Drew swept the woods with his night vision goggles, but he knew who it must be: Benny.

The demon stopped beating on the shack and turned, his honeycombed eyes sweeping the woods.

Benny stepped out of the woods on the other side of the clearing.

"*Fuck*," muttered Drew. He'd missed it when Benny crept away from him and the others.

Bortha roared, sounding very much like a pissed off lion, and charged across the clearing. Drew stood, snapped the tranquilizer rifle into firing position and pulled the trigger five times in rapid succession. Across the clearing, Benny took his eyes off the demon and looked at Drew, smiling.

"*Run, you fool!*" screamed Drew. He was ejecting his empty magazine and slamming a new one home. "Reload that one," he said to Richards. "More darts in the bag." Without waiting for a reply, he sprinted out into the clearing, raised the gun again, and fired five more darts into the demon.

The demon roared and, lightning-quick, spun to face him. Bortha's tentacles writhed in the air, snapping out like striking snakes, rolling up like fiddlehead ferns, going straight and rigid, all without pattern. His mouths snapped open and closed. The demon's honeycombed eyes snapped on Drew, and the three tentacles slapped together. When the horn-shaped claws met, they made a sound like hedge-clippers closing. Drew didn't know anything about the demon or where it came from, but that gesture spoke to him anyway. "Come on," it said. "Let's dance."

Drew ejected the empty magazine, flipping it over his shoulder, hoping it would land in the woods where Richards or Lewis could retrieve it. Drew slammed his last magazine home, hoping the demon would fall soon, or at least that the M99 would slow the thing—those weaving tentacles looked *fast*. Benny was still standing on the other side of the clearing, grinning like an idiot. When Drew looked back at the demon, it was less than five feet away, barreling at him like an insane sprinkler.

Drew dove to the right, rolling when he hit the ground. Three loud thwacks sounded just behind him—the sound of the clawed ends of the demon's tentacles plunging into the earth. Drew came out of his roll on his feet and drove forward, away from the demon, pumping his legs with as much speed as he could. Every fourth or fifth step, he juked to the right or left, trying to keep the demon from guessing where he was going and coming in on an intercept course.

Sprinting into the woods, he threw out his arm, encircling the first tree he came across. He whirled in a half-circle around the trunk of the tree, eyes snapping back and forth, seeking the demon. He snapped his gun up into firing position, but the demon was gone.

"*Down!*" screamed Lewis.

Drew dropped to the ground as Lewis' pistol went off—*ka-BLAM, ka-BLAM, ka-BLAM*! He rolled to his side and stared up into the demon's ugly visage, drool from the closest mouth dripping down to spatter on his chest. Bortha's tentacles arched high into the air above Drew, horn-like claws pointed down at him. Lewis fired three more shots, and each shot hit the beast in the torso but seemed to do nothing.

Drew whipped the tranquilizer gun up and fired point-blank into what served as the beast's face. One of the darts hit the demon in the mouth, and the demon howled—but in pain or anger, Drew had no idea.

Tranquilizer gun empty, he tossed it toward Lewis and rolled away from the demon. One of the claws scraped across his back as he rolled, and the shallow cut it left behind burned like salt packed the wound. Drew screamed and forced himself up, running back toward the clearing. His only hope would be to keep the thing at bay long enough for Richards or Lewis to pump more M99 into the thing until it fell.

Drew dodged a tree, and, with a sound like a heavy axe striking wet wood, one of Bortha's tentacles slammed into the tree hard enough to fracture the trunk. He dove into a forward roll. A scream of rage from the demon followed on the heels of the *pfft-pfft-pfft* of his tranquilizer rifle. Without pausing, Drew leapt to the side. He landed badly, his ankle erupting with burning pain.

The demon was close—too close, and Drew was almost out of tricks. He could hear the beast breathing, and it sounded heavy, somnambulant. The tranquilizer gun spat twice more in rapid succession, and the demon shrieked.

Drew rolled at random and slammed into the side of the wooden shack. Inside, a woman screamed. *At least she's still alive.* He pressed his back against the wall of the shack and pushed himself up with his legs. The thin cut across his back burned.

The demon stood swaying in front of him, honeycomb eyes glaring down at him, tentacles hanging loose. Its three mouths worked, snapping open and closed, but without a sound. Drew jerked his arms up to cover his face, knowing one of those horrid claws could come at any instant.

The demon lifted a tentacle, but the spastic, writhing speed he had shown before was missing. The claw wavered and trembled as if the effort of holding it up was almost more than the demon could bear.

"Duck!" screamed Benny.

Drew didn't think about it, he dropped to the ground. Above him, the claw thwacked into the wooden plank where his head had just been. The tranquilizer gun spat again, this time a rapid stream of five shots. The demon grunted, tried to lift its tentacles and fell against the shack.

"Don't put me in the trunk with it!" screamed the woman inside the shack. "Gross!"

Drew scrambled to the side. Across the clearing Mike Richards stood, changing the magazine of the tranquilizer gun. Behind him, Lewis was reloading an empty magazine. "Move!" Lewis hissed.

Drew took two giant steps away from the demon and then stumbled, his back burning and numb at the same time. Jagged fingers of ice stabbed down toward his waist and up toward his shoulders.

The demon was still on its feet, but it was staggering side to side. It glared at Richards and then heaved its bulk against the door of the shack. The door exploded inward in a shower of splinters and kindling. Richards sprinted toward the door, a look of abject terror on his face.

Drew took a step back toward the shack and fell, unable to feel his feet any longer. "Poison," he breathed.

The woman inside the shack was screaming, Richards was bellowing, and the demon was hissing like a tea pot about to boil. The woman stumbled out the door, and her beauty struck Drew dumb.

"Toby?" asked Benny. "Are you all right?"

"Poison," Drew mouthed through tingling lips. He looked up at the bearded man's face, marveling that it seemed so familiar.

"Mike! Mike!" yelled Benny.

The shack shook with violence, dust and dirt flying off the roof in clouds, and it sounded like world war three had stepped off. Lewis sprinted to the door, his firearm drawn and ready. "Get down!" he yelled. "Get down, goddamn it!" He checked his fire—aiming at one spot, then moving the pistol to point at another.

"My love! My love! My love!" shrieked the beautiful woman. "Help him!"

A look of concentration slid over Benny's face, and unconsciousness slid over Drew.

5

Smiling, LaBouche closed Scott Lewis' front door. More than just sated, he felt full for the first time in eons. He imagined Scotty's face when he got home and laughed, the cackling screech echoing down the street like bats. He thought of the bloody presents he'd left inside and grinned.

Whistling tunelessly, he jingled his car keys as he walked toward the Subaru.

6

Red Bortha glared at Mike, then threw his shoulder into the door of the wooden shack and exploded inside. Mike sprinted in after him, holding the tranquilizer gun at the ready. Bortha was either a real demon like the two crazies said, or the darts weren't loaded with M99.

Bortha was across from the door, leaning against the wall, breathing hard. Richards snapped off two quick shots, both darts thudded home and hung loose from Bortha's skin like all the rest.

Bortha screamed and lashed out, too far away to hit him, but even so, the gun jerked from his hands and flew away into the shadows. Red leapt at him, arms held wide. Mike stepped into the leap, swinging hard, throwing punches at Bortha's liver. If he landed the shot just right, and with all his strength, even a heavy lunk like Bortha would fall to his knees.

"Get down!" Lewis yelled from behind him. "Get down, goddamn it!"

His fist smacked into Bortha's abdomen, right under his ribs. Perfect, except instead of grunting and going down, the demon chuckled. It felt like Mike's hand sank into soft wax. Bortha slammed into him, carrying him against the wall.

Mike rocked to the left, lifting his knee as hard as he could, going for another body shot. Bortha was breathing hard but seemed unaffected by anything Mike tried. Red grabbed his shoulder and hooked between his legs, jerking Mike up to shoulder height. "I never liked you, you weak fuck," Bortha grunted. He threw Mike across the length of the shack, and Mike slammed against the far wall, still three feet off the ground. Pain exploded through him on impact, and he sank to the ground.

"Liver shot, eh?" Bortha grunted stomping toward him. He grabbed Mike by the chin and lifted him as if he weighed no more than a toddler. He held him there for a moment, grinning into Mike's face.

"My love! My love! My love!" screamed Shannon. "Help him!"

He hoped Shannon got clear of this, got clear of the entire fucking town. Summoning what saliva he could, he spat into Bortha's face and grabbed his wrist, trying to wrench it away from his own chin. A moment later something whipped across his abdomen. At first, it felt like the demon had slapped Mike's belly, but after a few seconds, the pain sank its teeth into Mike, burning as if someone had injected boiling acid in his side. Breathing seemed impossible, but he *could* breathe fine. His arms fell slack.

"Tha's a liber shop, you numb suck!" Mike sagged against the wall behind him, and Bortha lurched toward him, then away, reeling like a drunk. "Naw fur da cup d'grass. Ima love killin you." He towered over Mike, grinning, and his ugly mug started to fade. Behind it stood something that looked like a melted candle with three tentacles. The tentacles jerked and spasmed up over the thing's head. "Injoy wat you say?" the thing crooned. "Las' tink you eber say." Dagger-shaped claws tipped the tentacles, and those claws plunged downward at him, only to stop before hitting him and return to the air.

Then, the demon slashed the air with its claws, it juked and jived, lurching this way and that, but ever away from where Mike slumped. The beast spun in a circle, tentacles whipping out like one of those creeping sprinklers that drove across the lawn. It was as if it were fighting something Mike couldn't see.

The battle took it to the far corner of the shack, and the beast stayed there, backed into the corner, tentacles weaving in front of it as if in defense. Mike watched with wonder as the monstrous thing fought nothing.

He lurched to his feet, eyes scanning the ground for the tranquilizer rifle. If the thing's slurred speech was any indicator, Bortha was close to going out. He almost tripped over the gun, then scooped it up and fired the remaining darts into the thing's face.

It screamed and shrieked, but the thing didn't come out of the corner. The thing bent at the waist and fell forward, one of his mouths digging a furrow in the damp earth.

Mike stood, staring down at the thing. Lewis stepped inside the shack, gun in one hand, loaded tranquilizer magazine in the other. "Did you see it?" croaked Mike.

Lewis nodded. "He went a little crazy there at the end."

"No! Did you *see* it?"

"See what?" Lewis asked with a shrug.

"Tentacles. Mouths. Red…"

Lewis stared at him without speaking and shook his head. "He was just a man. A big man, granted, but a man."

Mike shook his head. "No, he was much more than that. It's…it's like those two said. A…a demon."

Lewis stared at him, not moving, not speaking. He shrugged. "Either crazy is catching, or there's something going on here I'm not party to."

Mike nodded. "Where's Reid? We need to know what to do next."

Lewis hooked his thumb toward the clearing. "He's out. The bearded guy said Reid thought he was poisoned or something, but that Reid's okay. Unconscious, but okay. Who's the woman?"

"Friend of mine," grunted Mike, staring down at the tentacled monster that shouldn't have existed.

"Seems she sees it another way," said Lewis. "You should go to her."

Mike looked at him in confusion for a moment but nodded. "Yeah. She's been through it tonight."

"What do we do about your friend?" Lewis asked pointing at the tentacled lump.

"Reid said something about having a place in Rochester. We take him there. We'll keep pumping him with M99 until Reid wakes up."

"Dangerous," muttered Lewis. "That might kill him."

"I don't think so," said Mike as he stepped through the door and wrapped Shannon in his arms.

7

In the back of Shamu, Shannon smiled a small, secret smile. Mike had paid her little attention since they'd gotten back to the car, but his attention was on the road. He drove like his ass was on fire, lights flashing, siren screaming, but he'd put his arms around her back at the shack. *That means something, right?*

The other cop sat up front and stared out the front window, not talking, not even grunting when Mike tried to get him to respond. The man Mike called Toby sat nestled between Benny and her, head lolling with each bump in the highway, oblivious to the world.

Lost in her thoughts—at least that's what Shannon told herself—because she didn't want to remember the nightmarish fugue she'd gone into back there in the shack, she was thinking about cleaning. Cleaning her house, her workspace at the town hall, her car, Mike's place, anything, *anything*, but the trunk and that evil man.

Mike said he saw something, so Shannon believed him. Mike also said the smelly guy with the unkempt beard in the back seat with her was Benny Cartwright, so it must be Benny, but my goodness he stank. It was like a mixture of sweat, chemicals, and old, rotten cheese. *Gross.* "How much longer?" she asked.

Mike glanced at her in the rearview mirror. His eyes looked scared, and she'd never seen him like that before, except for that night at Lumber Jack's when he'd almost—*No, I won't think about that either.* She could tell he was fighting the urge to get a drink—she could almost feel his want, his *need* for a drink. "Not long now," he said. "How is he?"

"Still out," Benny said. "He likes to sleep."

Shannon looked over at him, trying to guess if he was making a joke, but he sat pressed up against the car door with his window cracked and his nose pressed into the crack as if *she* was the one that reeked like an elephant. He was mumbling something into the wind, something repetitive. She strained her ears until she caught his words: "...an elephant. *Not* an elephant. *Not...*" She blushed and ducked her head. *Did I say that aloud?* she wondered.

The tires thumped over the expansion cracks in the highway's concrete surface. *Ka-thump. Ka-thump, Ka-thump.* The engine whined like Mike was asking too much of it. Mike rubbed his eyes, and Benny muttered into the wind. The other cop stared out the window—she thought he might be crying. Toby nodded to the beat of the tires against the cracks.

Shannon shivered and turned her mind back to methods of cleaning her car.

8

Scott had a painful, sinking feeling in the pit of his stomach. The muscles across his upper back and shoulders stretched so tight they hurt. He stared out the car window, watching mile markers flit past through the veil of his tears.

Becky was *gone*. He knew that now. LaBouche…*maybe* LaBouche had done it, had *tortured* and *murdered* her. Each thought brought reams of fresh pain shivering across his shoulders and back. He drew a breath, and it burst from him with an evil-sounding hiss.

"You okay?" asked Chief Richards.

Scott ignored the question, licking his lips, scared that if he tried to speak, he would end up screaming. He feared that if he started screaming, he would never stop.

He wanted to be alone, to curl up in a ball somewhere. Jenny would be so angry with him when he told her…when he told her Becky was dead. Jenny would be furious, would blame him for their loss. And she would be *right*.

This fucking car ride is taking too long. Why is he creeping along like an old grandma? He glanced at the speedometer. It was buried. Pegged. *That's strange...I would have sworn he was going forty. Why does it seem like we are going so slow?*

He had to decide what to do. These three men he was with...he wasn't sure what was going on, but the crazy seemed to be spreading. The woman, well, as traumatized as she was, what she said didn't matter, but Richards... *What's his excuse?*

They were going to kill the man who'd kidnapped the woman—if they hadn't already with whatever weak tranquilizer they thought was M99. *That shit will kill an elephant. Kill anything in the amounts they'd shot into this Bortha character. How in the hell can they believe it's M99? That's not rational.*

But images of LaBouche hiding a smirk of a smile as they drove around looking for Becky kept flashing through his mind. He kept hearing LaBouche humming—*humming*—while he told Scott not to worry, that changing the flat would only take ten minutes. His expression when Scott yelled at him so many hours later when he'd showed up. *Something is...*

He didn't want to complete the thought, didn't want to believe LaBouche could do something like that to Becky. He didn't want to believe Becky was...

Jenny's going to kill me!

They were going to kill the man in the trunk, these three from Oneka Falls. There was no doubt in his mind what they intended to do. *Am I going to let them? Am I going to* help *them?*

He imagined Jenny sitting on the couch next to Mrs. Carmody, listing to the left due to the Xanax. He imagined her watching the local twenty-four-hour news channel on cable, searching for signs of their daughter. Their *only* child. Their baby. She would kill him, for sure.

Can these jokers be right? Can Reid be right about these...these...demons? Could LaBouche have been this evil the entire time we worked together? How could I miss it? I'm supposed to be a trained fucking investigator! A profiler!

"Oh Jenny," he murmured. "Forgive me."

"What's that?" asked Richards.

Scott stared out into the darkness and closed everything else out, and his thoughts began their cruel, savage cycle again.

9

Benny sat with his nose pressed against the crack between the window frame and the cold glass. Mike was hauling ass, and Benny liked the sensation. He hadn't ridden in many cars, not since his daddy's Oldsmobile.

He glanced at Toby's reflection in the window glass. *Toby's having a dream. Hope it's a good one.* Shannon was still ruminating about cleaning things. And she thought Benny was insane…

The other cop in the front seat worried Benny. His thoughts had taken on a spiraling quality that Benny recognized from other patients in Millvale. *He's driving himself insane. He needs a way out; he needs someone to guide him.*

Benny could be that person, but he didn't know if he *should* be that person. He still didn't understand what the polite limits of his ability were or should be. When should he let on that he knew what he did and when should he keep quiet?

Life outside Millvale was so hard.

He almost longed for the simplicity of life as a mental patient. *Almost.*

He wondered where Owen Gray was that night. What the man was doing. He wondered if the LaBouche guy was with him. He had the feeling the two were together. What could they be planning?

He sighed and leaned back in the seat. *Let Shannon think I'm gross,* he thought. *What do I care? She's crazy. Fantasizing about cleaning all the time.*

I should be helping someone. He took slow, even breaths, trying to steady his thoughts, to make the surface of his mind as smooth as a mirror. *But should I help Toby? Trooper Lewis? Shannon?* He let his eyes drift closed, letting the *ka-thump, ka-thump* of the tires against the surface of the highway soothe him, carry him away from himself. *Or should I go see what Owen Gray is up to?*

With a deep sigh of relief, Benny floated into the ether.

10

Owen pulled the stolen pickup off the freeway, angling down the off ramp with an ease that belied his long incarceration. Brigitta snuggled next to him in the bench seat, just like he liked. "Why are we getting off here, babe?"

Her laugh tinkled like broken glass. "I *told* you, my love. We're here to meet a friend."

He glanced at her sideways, and a harsh note crept into his voice. "A *guy* friend?"

"Ah, my love, it's so endearing that you are jealous after all this time. He is a male, and he is a friend, but there is only you, Owen Gray."

Mollified, Owen turned his attention back to the road—just in time to slam on the brakes. The back of the truck jittered sideways, but he brought the vehicle to stop before he plunged out into the intersection.

"It's okay, my love," said Brigitta in a quiet voice. "This far out, there's little traffic. Especially at this time of night."

Owen wiped his brow with a shaking hand. "Still, that was a close one. Which way?"

"Go left," she said. "Pull in to the diner on the left about three miles up."

They drove the three miles in silence, each lost in thought. *No one but me? And her still looking like Miss America? Not fucking likely.*

Oh, Owen. LaBouche is no one to be jealous of. You'll see, my love. You'll see.

It still freaked him out when she spoke in his mind. It had been so long since she'd...since his arrest. So long since he'd had any constant contact with her—with anyone other than Toms—that it was surprising all over again.

He put on his left blinker and pulled the car into the narrow lot in front of the Cascade Diner. It was garish—polished chrome and cherry-snow-cone red. *Doesn't anyone have taste anymore?* There was a little silver car in the lot. A Japanese thing, by the look of it. He didn't enjoy driving the modern cars, not one bit. Under-powered lumps of plastic and aluminum. He wanted good old American iron beneath his right foot—something with a big block.

He put the truck in park and got out, Brigitta sliding out behind him. He stretched his back and groaned. "Getting old sucks, babe. You're lucky you don't have to do it."

"Don't I?" she asked, an amused lilt to her voice.

"Freeze! Both of you!" snapped a baritone voice.

Owen reacted instantly, leaping back toward the truck, ripping the door open and grabbing the rifle. Deep booming laughter echoed across the lot. "Did you see him, Brigitta? Did you see him jump?"

Owen straightened and turned, the old, familiar anger tingling in his spine and stinging his eyes. A hulking man stepped out from the side of the diner. Anger thrummed through Owen's torso, contracting his muscles until they were hard nuggets of burning ache.

"LaBouche!" snapped Brigitta. "It *wasn't* funny!"

The big guy laughed harder, even slapping his thigh and wiping away a tear. *Doesn't know who he's fucking with, eh? Well, I can fix that happy horse-shit right the fuck now.* With a smooth, continuous motion, he brought the rifle up one-handed and fired from the hip. The report boomed across the parking lot and flew away into the surrounding country side.

"Owen! No, my love!" yelled Brigitta an instant too late. She stepped between Owen and the big asshole.

The big asshole was still *laughing at him*. Owen worked the bolt on the rifle he'd stolen from a guard at Sing Sing, sending spent brass flying into the big plate-glass window and jacking a new round into the chamber. "Keep laughing. Go ahead," Owen murmured

"It's his way, my love. He doesn't mean anything." Brigitta whirled to face the big man. Something in her demeanor changed, and her voice, when it came, cracked like a whip and sent chills down Owen's spine. "He's *mine*, LaBouche! You invoke *my* anger when you toy with him."

LaBouche sobered and stood straight. He performed a perfunctory half-bow. "My apologies, Brigitta. My sense of humor is…well, you know my proclivities."

"And you know *mine*. Find your own meals."

Meals? Owen thought. *What the fuck?*

"A manner of speech, my love," she said over her shoulder.

He would have to learn the trick of thinking his thoughts quietly again and *tout suite*. "Yeah, well, we better get back on the road, babe. This guy can find his fun with someone else."

"Oh, no," said LaBouche. "I'm going with you."

"No," snapped Owen. "No, you're not."

Brigitta turned to face him and put her hand on his forearm, cooling most of his anger. She looked up into his eyes, her expression imploring. "My love, this is how my father wants it."

"Ah. Your father."

"Yes, my love. He's calling us to him at long last."

Owen looked over at LaBouche, whose expression was hidden by shadows, but Owen was sure he was smirking. "Fine. Let the big asshole drive, and you and I can hang out in the back. You can sit on my lap, and we'll talk about whatever pops up." When LaBouche's head snapped back as if slapped, Owen smiled. He swung the rifle across his shoulders and took Brigitta's hand. "What do you say, babe?"

"That sounds perfect, my love," she said, glancing over her shoulder to look at LaBouche. "LaBouche doesn't mind. Do you LaBouche?"

Without a word, the big man brushed past them and got in the driver's seat of the little silver car. "If you have room back there, knock yourselves out." There was a *thunk*, and the little car's trunk popped open. "Rifle goes in the trunk, though."

Owen put the rifle down and secured it to the floor of the trunk with a fancy little net. He slid into the back seat, loosening his belt as he did so. Brigitta slid onto his lap.

LaBouche started the car, the purr of the little engine sounding like an anathema of everything good to Owen. He got them back on the freeway, headed south.

As they got back up to speed, Mike Richard's cruiser passed them going the opposite direction, but no one in either car noticed the other.

11

Scott stared into the blackness. It seemed to beckon him, to invite him to come on in and stay awhile. It tempted him in a way he'd never been tempted. He'd never have to think about what Jenny would say again. He'd never have to find out whether LaBouche killed Becky. He'd never have to learn Becky's DNA was found in that torture chamber. All he had to do was drift away, stop making decisions… He let his eyes drift closed, relief soaring through him.

Daddy. Daddy, look at me. It was Becky's voice. Talking to him in his head? He cracked his eyes, head still pointed out into the night.

Ten feet from the car was a luminous being—a luminous *girl*. It was hard to see her features with the bright light emanating from her pores. "Becky?" he gasped.

Daddy, it's okay. I'm not suffering anymore. I don't want you to…to…to go to the dark place. It won't help.

"Oh, baby," he breathed. "How can I not? You're…you are…you're—"

Daddy, listen to me. These people you are with, these men…they can do something right. *They can fight the demons that have tortured and murdered hundreds...thousands...I don't know how many people. The whole town is...it's a haven for the...the things that can make everyone see them as humans. For the demons.*

"What are you saying, Becky?"

They need you, Daddy. They need the strong you, the decisive you. The you that stood up to the red thing back there at the shack. The you that knew bullets would do no good, but stood up and shot at it anyway, so Toby could get a little space. The you that is angry, Daddy. The you that is filled with rage that these demons may even exist here. They need *you, Daddy.*

"I don't..." *How does she know Toby's name?* "I don't feel strong anymore. Becky, I am weak, stupid. Your mother is—"

Scott gasped when the images slammed into his mind. Images of blood, of death. Jenny lying across Mrs. Carmody as if she'd tried to shield her from something. Jenny's back flayed to the bone, tears coating Mrs. Carmody's face. LaBouche standing above them, leering down at them with a greedy expression on his face. LaBouche stabbing Mrs. Carmody again and again, never in a vital area, not stabbing her to kill her, but to hurt her more and more until she bled out.

"No!" Scott screamed, bolting up in his seat. "Oh, you *motherfucker!*"

"What is it?" asked Richards. "What?"

LaBouche changing, fading away. What stood there afterward was crazy. A yellow gorilla with a V-shaped mouth. Long, strong arms. Wide mouth, rubbery lips.

That is what LaBouche really is...what he really looks like. He's a demon.

Anger poured like hot lava across the surface of Scott's mind. He wanted to be moving, fighting, *killing*. In his rage, he didn't realize the last voice he'd heard inside his head had been Benny's.

12

Shannon was thinking about washing her little blue car, about getting the exact right mixture of soap and water in her pretty pink bucket (*not about the forest, not about the old man*). Two squirts of soap, then add water from the hose—not too fast! Watch the suds, (*don't think about him—about* them) don't mix it so fast that all the bubbles form on the top of the water. Let the water do the work.

She visualized the natural sponge she kept in water year-round so that it stayed soft (*don't picture the dog-things*) exploring each nook and cranny with her mind's eye. She thought of the chamois she'd bought from the specialty place on the internet and how it had special cleaning instructions that she'd always followed to the letter (*not about the instructions about how she had to run...*).

She didn't think about Mike (*my love*). Or Toby. Or even Benny (*gross*). She thought about cleaning and *only* cleaning. The rest of it was (*the truth about her pitiful life*) noise. No, she was the one in control.

Shannon was in charge.

She imagined washing the car. Starting from the driver's side front and working her way back (*don't remember having chickenpox, don't visualize a crisp dollar bill*). Short, circular strokes, that was key. She imagined turning the corner to the back of the car (*STOP*). She pictured cleaning the bumper, washing it twice, just to be sure (*STOP! STOP!*). She would clean the brake lights with the soapy water, and come back with the Windex and make sure they shined (STOPSTOPSTOPSTOP!). She would move up to the trunk—

The trunk. The trunk slamming shut with her inside. The mustiness of old rubber and rust and the acrid funk of gasoline and old oil invading her sinuses. The trunk.

Her mind rebelled, ran away from those thoughts, as she'd spent years training it to do.

She'd vacuum the cockpit (*haha that's a funny word*) first, paying special attention to where the edges of the floor mats left that cute little dent (*the boy ohmygod the fat boy*). She'd put in her winter mats—yes, it might be too soon, but better too soon than too late (*too late! Too late for the boy! Too late for old Mr. Thornd—*)

No. No, she was focusing on cleaning the car. *Where was I? Oh, yes, the trunk.*

The TRUNK! I'm trapped in the trunk with the boy! The fat boy. I spent his last hours holding him in contempt, refusing him comfort because he was fat and might have smelled a little. We were all alone in the trunk!

It's okay, Shannon. The mental voice was male.

No! It's not okay! My-love and Babe kidnapped us, they kept us in the trunk! They...they... GROSS! I'm not remembering anything *they did! I'm thinking about CLEANING!*

Shannon, I'm here. Hold on to me. Pretend I'm Mike and hold on to me.

We didn't know what the sounds were. We didn't! I was nine! *The boy was only ten! We'd never heard a rifle in our young lives. How could we know? And even if we did, how could we stop Babe and My-love? They locked us in the trunk!*

Shannon, it's okay. You were a kid, you couldn't have done anything, and no one ever expected you to do anything.

I should *have! I should have held the fat boy. I should have screamed and kicked and bit and scratched My-love! I should have—*

SHANNON. The voice roared through her mind like a screeching 747 on take-off. The force of it cut through her thoughts about the trunk, about cleaning, about everything. It shattered the walls she'd built around herself. *It's okay, I promise.*

That voice. It wasn't the boy's voice. It was...it was...

Benny. I'm Benny. I was with you at the end.

At the end?

With Mr. Thorndike. He saved us from Herlequin—

DON'T SAY HIS NAME!

—and the dog-things. He carried us out of the forest and put us in his car. Mr. Thorndike—

He hit the dog-things with his car.

Yes, Shannon. He fought the dog-things to save us. I was so scared I thought I'd die. I couldn't move, couldn't speak. You walked beside him while I lay there in his arms and he ran. I thought I was already dead.

But you didn't die. Mr. Thorndike did. And...and the boy. He died, and he left me alone. You *left me alone.*

I did, and I'm sorry. I had to work through it, to process everything. My mind shut down, like a TV after Saturday morning cartoons. It just went off. Herlequin—

Don't say it. Don't say his name.

—had me for a lot longer than he had you. He played such tricks, such vile tricks on me. He made me run and run and run and run and run. He showed me the kids trapped in the—

IN THE TREE! Oh my God, how could I forget about the tree?

You had to forget, Shannon. Or you'd have been with me in the mental institution.

I guess you're right, my lo—oh my God no! My love, babe—that's what they *called each other! That's what—*

Shannon, open your eyes.

What? Why?

Open them.

And she did. Her walls had been torn away, and she saw the world—the real world—for the first time in years. She looked at the man slumped between her and Benny. He was beautiful. She looked at Benny and felt a pang. *Did I really say he smelled like an elephant?* She looked at the trooper in front of her. He was sitting bolt upright in his seat, hands up by his head, fingers splayed. His fingers were shaking.

She looked at Mike. Beautiful Mike. Perfect Mike. But he wasn't beautiful or perfect. He was an ordinary man. She knew he didn't love her. He wasn't even interested in her.

Shannon didn't believe Mike had *ever* had a girlfriend, serious or otherwise. She didn't even think he'd ever dated anyone. Well, except for Jim Beam, Jack Daniels, Jose Cuervo, and Sam Adams.

Of course, he's never dated a woman. Mike is gay. Duh. He told himself the lie that he'd kept it a secret, but everyone knew. Everyone except poor, dumb Shannon Bertram. But she'd known. That's why she'd set her cap for him.

She groaned. She'd pursued him because he was *safe*. Because he would never take her up on it. Never ask her out. Never want more of her than she was willing to give. Never love her. Never *want* her.

Memories of pretending they were lovers flashed through her mind. Each imagined "my love" and "babe" made her want to vomit. The way she'd preened when he paid her the slightest attention. *Why the hell would I play out scenes between the man and woman— no, fuck that—between Owen Gray and his girlfriend? Why would my mind hold that as an ideal? That's...*

"Gross," she said. She looked at Benny, his eyes remained closed, but he wasn't asleep. He'd saved her from spending the rest of her life as a zombie. She owed him.

She owed him a lot.

Plus, under all that hair, he was kind of cute.

13

Drew dreamed:

He was a boy, running and running from something. He didn't know what was chasing him, but if it caught him, he would be d-e-a-d, dead. His feet felt mired in thick, sucking mud, and each step got harder and harder to take.

Something breathed behind him. It sounded like the bear he'd seen on that show, Grizzly Adams. It huffed and chuffed, hot breath washing across his neck.

Up ahead, a woman solidified out of the mist. He recognized her but who she was evaded him. Friend? Foe? He veered away from her, not seeing her fade back into the mist.

He ran through Thousand Acre Wood, his feet throbbing, his ankles scraped and cut, his cheap K-Mart tennis shoes sloshing with blood. The small of his back felt like Muhammed Ali had used him for a speed bag.

Up ahead, the woman solidified out of the mist again. She held up a hand, palm toward the sky as if inviting him to come to her. "Who are you?" he screamed. She recoiled as if he'd slapped her and disappeared with a pop.

On he ran, ever forward, each step jarring his teeth together with a bone-aching clack. The thing behind him sounded like it was laughing at him, delighting in his suffering. Two tentacles shot past his head, one on either side and slammed together in front of his face, horn-like claws coming together with a sound like a hammer on stone. "Who are you?" he screamed, and the chuffing laughter got louder.

The woman appeared out of the mist, this time off to his left. She beckoned him with one hand and pointed past herself with her other one. She looked so familiar it made his heart ache. "Toby," she called. "Toby, dear, run faster."

The sound of her voice hurt him to hear, but at the same time, it felt like coming in out of a fierce winter wind. "Muh-mom?"

She smiled at him, a perfect study of beatitude. Her eyes seemed to blaze with happiness. "Run," she mouthed without sound.

He veered toward the woman, sprinting with new-found determination, but once again, she dissolved into *the mist.* Why won't she stay with me? *his mind shouted.* I *need* her help!

"No one can help you, sport." The new voice was also familiar, but instead of warm feelings, it invoked frigid terror.

He ran on and on, abrading his skin on the bark of trees, vines with vicious thorns vexed his ankles, both drawing fresh blood. His lungs burned and ached. His eyes filled with tears. What's the use of running? I can't get away.

"No, you run, Toby! You run for me!" It was the woman's voice, he was sure of it, but he didn't associate it with the loving, caring tone with which she now spoke.

Ahead, the forest thinned. A murky gray light filtered through the trunks, washing out the dark shadows. He dug deep, into a reserve he didn't know he had, and increased his pace, the muscles in his legs shrieking in protest, the air whistling in and out of his lungs.

"No!" shouted the awful bear-like voice behind him. "Don't you do it, boyo! Don't you even think *it! Not again! Never again!"*

A heavy tentacle slapped down on his shoulder like a dead fish. It reeked of sewer and decay and burnt meat. He swept it off his shoulder, counting on adrenaline for strength. He jigged to the right, juked back left, and, as he approached the edge of the forest, dove toward the gray light of dawn.

The thing behind him screeched, the sound of it almost drove Toby insane, the volume of it tearing at his eardrums. "Not again!" the thing screamed.

Toby wanted to laugh, to cry for the woman in the mist, to scream in triumph, to sink to the grass and fall asleep, all at once.

Instead, Toby woke up.

14

Beside him, Benny sat up straight and cleared his throat.

"What's happening?" Toby asked in a blurry voice.

"Mike knocked the demon out," said Benny.

"With a lot of help," said Mike.

"He's in the trunk," grunted Trooper Lewis, hooking his thumb over his shoulder.

Toby turned in his seat and looked at Shannon. "Hello," he said. "I'm Toby Burton."

"Shannon Bertram."

"You remember now?" asked Benny, voice cracking like an excited kid's.

"Yeah. Well, I remember Oneka Falls. Not sure what other goodies my mind is hiding from me."

Benny shook his head. "Nothing. Nothing."

Toby glanced at him. "I had a nightmare—or whatever you call a nightmare when you're knocked out by demon poison."

Benny nodded and looked out the window.

"What was it about?" asked Shannon.

"I was running through Thousand Acre Wood. Being chased by a demon. A woman—" His voice cracked. "I think it was my mom. She kept appearing out of the mist, guiding me. Helping me. When I got away, I woke up."

"I, uh...I had a dream, too," said Lewis. "I was...well, I was circling the drain that leads to the nuthatch." He glanced back at Benny, blushing. "Sorry." Benny didn't appear to have heard either comment. "I saw..." His throat worked, and his jaw muscles clenched. "Maybe I dreamed it?"

"No," said Benny. "It wasn't a dream."

"You seem to know an awful lot about what goes on in everyone else's mind," grumbled Lewis. "Anyway, my...my daughter, she...she was...She...she was made of light—warm, golden light. She told me...things, showed me things." He turned in the seat and pinned Toby with a glare. "Tell me what LaBouche looks like."

"What he wants you to see or what I see?"

"What you see."

Toby took a deep breath and leaned forward. "Well, he's what I call a 'weird.' He's yellow like a—"

"A weird?" asked Shannon.

"Yeah. There are three main kinds of demons—at least from what I've seen. There are your 'traditional' demons. They look like what you hear about in the bible or religious paintings. Then you've got your 'undead' demons. That's self-explanatory, black, rotting skin that hangs loose, claws instead of fingers, weeping pustules, dry hair. Ugly as—"

"And the weirds?" asked Lewis with an edge to his voice.

"Yeah. Well, they are…weird. Their appearance is truly alien. Like LaBouche or Red Bortha back there. No two of them look alike."

"And LaBouche?" demanded Lewis.

"LaBouche is a big, yellow gorilla. Chartreuse eyes; wide, V-shaped mouth; gross, rubbery lips, two slits over his mouth for a nose; teeth like a shark's that stick out of his mouth."

"Gross," said Shannon.

"That's what I…what Becky showed me. It must be true, then. All of it." Lewis slumped in his seat, facing forward.

Toby glanced at Benny, but he was still staring out the window. "All of what?" Toby asked.

"The bastard murdered my Jenny after we left," Lewis said in an emotionless monotone. "Mrs. Carmody, too. He killed them all." Shannon leaned forward and put her hand on his shoulder, squeezing gently. "Thanks," he said. "Buh-Becky also said you four needed me. That I had to stick around." He said the last sentence at just above a whisper, but even so, everyone in the car heard him.

"We do," said Shannon with another squeeze of his shoulder. "Each of us," she began, looking at Mike's reflection in the rearview mirror. "We're all broken in our own way. Each of us used our own methods to forget, to keep the horror of 1979 at bay." Mike glanced at her, and she smiled. "I was the worst. I built an entire fantasy world around myself to keep me safe from the memories." She shook her head. "I incorporated parts of my kidnapping into that fantasy, though. It was sick."

"It's okay, Shannon," said Benny. "We're here with you now."

She glanced over at him and smiled. "Yes. Thank you."

Above his matted beard, Benny blushed.

"One of you will have to tell me what happened to you as kids," said Lewis. "But first, what are we going to do with Red Bortha?"

Toby cleared his throat. "It isn't pretty, but I've learned through trial and error how to kill one of these things. Or at least how to make them leave our plane of existence. I'm not sure they ever *really* die."

"Tell us," said Mike.

"We have Bortha unconscious, and we keep him that way. We have to separate his blood from his flesh. That breaks the immortality. Afterward, we have to break the body down into component molecules. The blood, we kill with boiling acid."

"Uh… You're not kidding? You've done this before?" asked Mike.

Toby nodded.

"How did you…learn how to do this?" asked Lewis.

"Trial and error. Old legends. Experimentation. Oh, and I stole the idea for the M99 from the TV show, *Dexter*." Toby cleared his throat. "First, I stalk one, making sure I catch it unaware. Otherwise…otherwise we have something like what happened in the clearing."

"A mess," muttered Benny.

"A mess that almost got people killed," said Toby. Benny blushed again. "But we'll get better at it."

"What do you mean 'we'll get better at it'?" asked Lewis, turning to face the backseat. "You want to do this *again*?"

Toby looked back at him, as calm as the Dalai Lama. "I do. I've done it…I've done it sixty-one times."

"Sixty-one…"

"Yes." Toby looked Lewis in the eye. "They are *demons*, not people. Humans are their prey animals; they commit such acts of atrocity that even Stalin would find them offensive. They are *evil*." Lewis returned his gaze, as silent as a mute. "I killed every demon I could. When I saw one, I set about finding out everything I could about them—their habits, their predilections, their routines. Some, I lost and couldn't find again. Until this weekend, my record was pretty good."

"What does that mean?" asked Mike.

"Well, before going back to Oneka Falls, I never saw more than one or two demons at a time. In Oneka Falls, they are *everywhere*."

"What?" gasped Shannon.

"About one in three people I saw were demons. I've never seen such a concentration of them. Not anywhere." The tires thumped against the pavement beneath the car, and Mike shifted in his seat, but other than that the car was silent.

"But…*why*?" asked Shannon.

"Something…*someone*…has made Oneka Falls a sanctuary for them." Toby looked down at his lap. "Mike, tell me something."

"Anything, Toby."

"What happened after Benny and I got shipped off to Millvale?"

"After Owen Gray's trial and all that?"

"Yeah."

Mike cleared his throat. "Well, life went on. Paul and I…well, we sort of drifted apart. I don't even know where he is."

"What happened to the town?"

"Oh. Everything was quiet during the two years it took to get Gray convicted and sent away, what with the sheriff, and most of the Oneka Falls Police department being dead and gone. But everything picked up after the trial, and things stayed good for, oh, I don't know…three or four years more. After that, kids started disappearing all over Kanowa County. Sometimes, bodies turned up in ditches or old, abandoned buildings, but most often, the kids disappeared into thin air. No one else disappeared and staggered out of Thousand Acre Wood a few days later. No more old men stumbled across brutalized kids in the forest and drove them back to town." Mike shrugged. "As time passed by and more and more kids disappeared, people…*good people*, mind…they drifted away. Property values plunged into the toilet. Lowlifes of all kinds moved in and set up shop. By the time I became a cop, there was already an unofficial policy in the town—live and let live. If you didn't see it for yourself, it didn't happen."

Lewis whistled.

"Yeah," said Mike. He glanced at Shannon in the rearview mirror. "People developed ways of dealing with things… Anyway, the town became a haven for criminals and the like, and property values fell even further. Bars sprung up everywhere it seemed. Churches closed."

"The fall of civilization," said Benny.

"Well, it wasn't as bad as all that. For the most part, if you didn't go looking for it, trouble left you the hell alone. After a while, even the disappearances stopped inside the city limits. It was like Oneka Falls was protected."

"And the rest of the county?" asked Lewis.

"You've seen the stats."

"Yeah. They're horrible. When I was a kid, there was this scare… The whole satanic thing we talked about when Reid—I mean, Toby—and I first met. I think I might have told you that Kanowa County is the geographic center of the reported abuse in the Northeast."

"Yeah," said Toby.

"Anyone want to guess what the geographical center of Kanowa County is?" burbled Benny.

"I think it's clear," said Toby.

"So, what then? Is it only that Play Time place?"

Toby shook his head. "No. I'm sure things like that old church exist in a lot of different places."

"You think it's Herlequin?" asked Shannon, her voice failing her on the last syllable.

Toby nodded. "I do. Him and his damn dogs."

Benny shuddered, but he nodded. "I think he moved on for a bit after we got away. I think he laid low, so to speak, which means he went somewhere that no one suspected his existence and got up to his old tricks under the radar. After people in the town forgot the horror-story part of the whole deal, Herlequin moved back into Thousand Acre Wood."

"Who is this Herlequin?" asked Lewis.

"Have you heard of the character Harlequin from French theater? The mischievous devil?"

"I'll take you at your word."

Toby nodded. "Well, Harlequin was most likely derived from an even older myth from 11th century France. *Mesnlee d'Hellequin* told the story of the Great

Hunt, in which a pack of demons led by a black-faced devil, chased the damned souls of evil people to hell."

"Nice," said Mike.

"But it doesn't end there. There is an even older myth from Scandinavian mythology, the name of which was the *ellekonge*—the elf king. This elf king had a bunch of daughters, and together they haunted forests. The daughters lured men into slavery using desire, jealousy, or lust for revenge, while the elf king himself was a goblin who lured little children to the land of death."

"Whoa," breathed Benny. "A goblin?"

Toby nodded.

"And the dog-things?"

Shannon made a strangling sound in the back of her throat. "Babe."

"What?" asked Mike.

"Owen Gray's girlfriend. He always called her 'babe,' and she always called him 'my love.'" Mike raised an eyebrow at her in the mirror, and Shannon blushed to the roots of her hair. She ducked her head. "She…she used her feminine wiles to goad him into bigger crimes."

"The *ellerkongens datter*," said Toby. "Herlequin's daughter."

"So, what are the dog-things?"

Toby shrugged. "Other daughters? The pack of demons used to chase the damned to hell? Maybe they are just things Herlequin painted in our heads."

Lewis whistled. "You don't need me. You need an army of exorcists."

"No," said Toby. "You are *exactly* what we need. You have the resources to help us find more of them, to find other hotspots like Oneka Falls."

"*And* you can keep the cops off our backs," said Benny in a bright voice.

Lewis looked at Benny without speaking. "No," he said at last. "I want to be more than the research guy."

Toby smiled. "I knew you would."

15

With the body of Bortha tucked into the school's industrial digester, Scott wanted nothing more than to curl into a ball, to disappear into sleep for a while, but he was afraid. Afraid he'd dream of Becky, or worse yet, Jenny. He'd called home, he couldn't resist, but there was no answer. Same for Mrs. Carmody next door.

"What now?" asked Shannon.

They had set up shop in Toby's apartment near the school. Exhaustion showed on everyone's face, but no one was sleepy.

"We have to—"

"I need to go home. To check. To be sure," said Scott.

Benny turned to stare at him. "It's true, I—"

"Yeah," sighed Scott. "But I don't care. I have to see her. I have to call it in, to get her taken care of."

"That's understandable," said Mike. "Do you want company? I could go—"

"No. Thanks, but no."

"You'll need these," said Mike, tossing the keys to his cruiser to Scott.

He caught them and nodded his thanks. "I'll head home, but I'll be back…sometime. I guess I don't know when."

Toby stood and walked with him to the door. "Don't worry, Trooper Lewis—"

"Scott. If we're going to be demon hunters together, you can call me Scott."

"Scott. Don't worry about us. I've got plenty of food, and if we need something, I've got another car."

Scott nodded. "Okay. I'll…"

"Scott, are you sure you don't want one of us, all of us, to come with you?"

"Yes, I'm sure, but thanks."

Scott left them as the sun was threatening to rise in the east. He was used to pulling all-nighters, every homicide investigation had its share of them. All the emotion, though, left him feeling crippled with exhaustion.

He drove to the house he'd shared with Jenny and Becky, and with each passing mile, his heart grew heavier and heavier. He'd spent twenty-three years with Jenny, and seventeen with Becky, and in the space of a single weekend, he'd lost them both. His hands tightened on the steering wheel until he thought his knuckles would burst through his skin.

His cell phone rang, and he yelped in surprise. He fumbled it out of his pocket and answered it. "Lewis," he said.

"Scotty!" said LaBouche. "How the fuck are you, partner."

Heart-piercing fury slammed into his veins. "*You fuck!*" he screamed. "*You miserable fuck!*"

LaBouche chuckled. "I fucked Becky, now that you mention it. She was a virgin, can you believe it? In this day and age…"

As quickly as it had come, the fury vanished, leaving him gutted, empty. "I'm going to kill you." His tone was flat, cold. It was too much effort to add inflection to his words.

LaBouche laughed. "Yeah. I get that. You and Dr. Reid have a good time? Where'd you take him? County lockup?"

"Why do you care?"

"Thought I might pay him a little visit."

"Yeah. He's in jail. I charged him in the campus disappearance. Why don't you go visit him?"

LaBouche laughed, and in the background, someone said, "Jesus. Shut up."

"Where are you, LaBouche?"

"Oh, I don't think you need to worry about that, Scotty."

"Don't you ever call me that again."

"Scotty. Scotty. Scotty."

"Have I mentioned that I'm going to kill you?"

"Yes, you did. But, before you get too far with your planning, you should go talk to Jenny. I talked to her a while ago, and she's a mess, Scotty. All those drugs. Yech."

A sigh burst out of Scott before he could stop it. "What do you want, LaBouche? Why are you calling?"

"Oh, I see. You already know."

"I'm hanging up now." Scott took the phone from his ear and was about to press the disconnect when he heard LaBouche yell.

"I fucked Jenny, too, Scotty. She said she'd never had it so good. She—"

Scott thumbed the disconnect button and fought the urge to throw the cell phone out the window. Instead, he laid it on the seat next to him, glancing at it from time to time as if it were a spider.

He pulled into his driveway, his stomach sinking, dread rising like a behemoth from the depths. Suddenly, he didn't want to be there. He wanted to be far, far away. On the moon, maybe, or the bottom of the ocean. He forced his hand to the door handle and opened the door. The sun broke over the roof of the house across the street, stabbing at his eyes. He wrestled one foot out, and with a significant effort, the other.

He glanced across the yard at Mrs. Carmody's house, hoping against hope that he'd see her puttering around her kitchen as he often did when leaving or coming in at that hour. Her house was dark, quiet. It looked forlorn, abandoned as if it already knew its owner was no longer alive.

He pushed himself up and closed the door. The walk to the front door was the longest walk he'd ever made in his life, but he kept plodding forward until he reached it. He pulled the storm door open, and stopped and listened. He wanted, more than anything, to find Mrs. Carmody puttering around *his* kitchen, chatting with Jenny, and for a moment, he heard them.

Excitement percolated inside him, and his hands shook as he tried to put the key into the lock. He dropped the keys and had to try again, but he got the door open and stepped inside.

Reality crashed back on him like a huge wave, and he knew it had either been a trick of his mind or wishful thinking. There was no mistaking it, no second guessing it.

Mrs. Carmody lay on the hardwood floor, the skirt of her ever-present calf-length dress hiked up. Her eyes were gone, and gore splattered her cheeks as if she'd cried so hard her eyeballs had burst. Jenny lay across her, missing the skin from her back, naked. Her legs were propped open like some gross caricature of a seductive pose—too wide. Her hips looked like a bag of broken glass. Blood had congealed beneath the two bodies and dried there.

Scott fell to the floor, his legs no longer able to support him. He didn't sob, he didn't even cry. He just stared.

16

LaBouche looked at the asshole in the backseat. "You never want to do that again. I don't care whose pet you are."

Next to the asshole, Brigitta sat up and hissed at him, as if she were a fucking snake or cat or something. LaBouche scoffed and rolled his eyes. "You know I'm within my rights. Your...*pet*...disturbed my feeding. I have every right to take retribution, *right now*, but instead, out of respect, I'm issuing a warning. To him, not to you."

Owen laughed. "Fuck you, chum. Who're you that you think you're so badass? I'm Force Recon, motherfucker, and let me tell you, *I'm* the badass."

LaBouche turned his eyes toward the man. The face of his visage was blank, but his face—his *real* face—wore what served him as a sadistic grin. "You sure?"

"Do you want to find out?" asked the man, puffing up his chest and pushing Brigitta's soothing hands away.

LaBouche stared at him and let his visage flicker. The man's eyes opened wide, and LaBouche laughed, long and hard. He let the man see him, to see *all* of him, and laughed all the harder as Owen shrank away as far as he could.

"Stop this, LaBouche!" snapped Brigitta, her voice pulsing with power and promise. "Stop this, or *I will*."

Sobering, LaBouche recast his visage on the man's perceptions. "It was a joke, Brigitta. And he asked."

She sank back into the seat, looking weary and annoyed. "I wish you'd both whip them out, measure, and be done with it."

LaBouche smiled. "I did, and your pet withered up like an old prune." Owen didn't even glance LaBouche's way, he was staring out into the darkness. LaBouche laughed again.

"Wh-what are we waiting for?" Owen asked in a timid voice.

LaBouche scoffed.

Brigitta put her hand on the back of Owen's head. "My love, we're waiting for word from my father. He has a plan, and so far, everything is going according to that plan. Don't worry, sweet Owen."

Owen turned and looked at her, fear still dancing in his eyes. "Do you look like him?"

She shook her head, and LaBouche snickered. She cast a baleful glare at him and turned back to Owen. "No, my love. You see me before you. That is what I look like for you."

"I mean…I mean what you…what you *really*…"

Brigitta sighed and glared at LaBouche. He knew she wanted him to get out of the car, to leave them alone, but this was too much fun. The man's fear was an aperitif.

"Owen, my love," she said. "You are the first to have seen me, to have seen my heart, for eons. You *see* what I look like in every way that matters."

"Oh, how sweet," sneered LaBouche. "And how nauseous."

She turned to glare into LaBouche's face. "Windbag," she snapped. "Blabbermouth. Cackler. Magpie." An evil smile broke across her face. "Yes. *Magpie.*"

"What?" asked LaBouche, a hint of fear in his voice.

"Magpie. That is the punishment I will ask my father to impose on you for your insolence."

"No," said LaBouche, his tone bordering on wheedling. "Please, not a bird."

She continued to stare at him, expression imperious.

"No, please. I apologize. I was kidding. It was a joke. A bad one, but a joke." LaBouche hated the way his voice sounded—like he was *begging*.

"You'll not do it again." Brigitta waved a hand at him as if to dismiss him from her mind. "You will be quiet."

LaBouche faced forward again, staring out into the coming dawn. For solace, he imagined doing to Brigitta what he'd done to Jenny Lewis, and he smiled.

17

Scott came to himself sometime later, back sore, hips and knees stiff. Jenny was still dead on the floor before him, congealed and dried blood spread beneath her like a macabre carpet. He knew what he had to do.

He knew, but he didn't want to do it.

Doing it would make this nightmare real. It would become a fact. The world would spin on without Jenny, without Becky, and Scott would have to move on with it. He didn't want to.

He took his cell phone out of his pocket. He dialed 9-1-1 and waited for the operator to answer. When she picked up, he did it. He made it all official.

Then, the tears came.

18

"Now, doesn't that feel better, Benny?" Shannon asked, letting her hand linger on the side of his face.

"Y-yes. It does, Shannon."

He was so cute, so boyish. She didn't imagine he'd had a lot of experience with women in Millvale, but there was an innocence to him that made her heart lighter.

Benny was smooth shaven, and his hair was trimmed and neat. He'd bathed and put on deodorant at Toby's suggestion. With each day that passed while they all waited for Scott to come back, he'd seemed to become more and more normal. Toby had always seemed normal, but he was changing, too. He was becoming Toby again, integrating his memories, his personality, from his childhood with the memories and personality he'd evolved since then. She supposed she was changing too, doing the same thing both Benny and Toby were doing. Of the four of them, only Mike seemed constant.

"Does it... Do you..." Benny sighed with exasperation.

"Yes, Benny, it pleases me. You're cute, you know that?" He blushed all the way to the crown of his head, and Shannon laughed and kissed him on the cheek. "No reason for embarrassment, Benny. It's okay to be handsome, for a friend to appreciate your looks."

Mike cleared his throat from the doorway. "It's more than okay, Benny. It's a *good* thing, and finding a better friend than Shannon will be tough."

Her face burned hot, and she knew she was a burning shade of crimson to rival Benny's blush.

"No reason to be embarrassed, Shannon," Mike parroted. "It's okay to be appreciated, for a friend to like you for who you are."

Still blushing, Shannon threw a wet washcloth at Mike. He caught it, laughing, but he sobered. "Shan, I owe you a lot, and I'm sorry I couldn't give you what you wanted. I wish it had been different, believe me."

"Mike," she started, but he held up his hand to stop her.

"Thank you, Shannon. For all the looking out for me you did. For being there to stop me from becoming…from becoming someone I—something—that…that would have killed me inside."

She left Benny standing at the counter, watching them in the mirror, and stepped close to Mike. She wrapped her arms around him. "It's okay, Mike. It's what friends do."

His eyes sparkled with momentary wetness before he pulled her close. "I'm glad to have a friend like you."

"Oh, my! Seems like I stumbled into an episode of Oprah," said Toby from the bedroom. "Is there a car under my seat? Did I win a lifetime supply of cheeseburgers?"

"Can it, Burton," Mike said in his cop voice.

The doorbell rang, and Toby left to answer it. Benny looked from Mike to Shannon and back. His expression was hard to read, but he didn't look jealous.

"No, I'm not," Benny said.

"Not what?" asked Mike.

"Jealous."

"Okay…I'm going to need cue cards, here." Mike chuckled. "How come I didn't get a superpower like you and Toby?"

"Because I haven't decided what you need yet," said Benny. His face wore a serene expression as if he'd said nothing more shocking than "I like breathing."

"What? I—"

"Got you," said Benny.

Shannon didn't believe he was kidding, though she didn't know why. "I don't have a superpower, either," she murmured.

Benny gazed at her. "Are you sure about that?"

"Well, I—"

"Hey guys," yelled Toby. "Scott's back. Get out here, we need to talk."

They filed out to the living room in silence, no one sure what to say. Scott stood in the short hall that led to the door. A few days' worth of stubble spread across his cheeks, and his eyes were bloodshot like he'd been drinking or not sleeping. Maybe both.

Shannon's heart went out to him, but what could she—the woman who'd spent her life in a fantasy world because she was too weak to face the truth—what would she say to him? *He* was facing his horrors. She couldn't even imagine how devastating losing his wife and daughter within twenty-four hours would be. How could she offer him comfort?

Stop it, Shannon.

It was Benny's voice in her mind, but was it him or her own mind? She glanced at him, but Benny was looking at Scott with an intensity that bordered on obsession. Scott returned his gaze as if he were a condemned man waiting for judgement.

"Would you two like a little privacy?" asked Toby with a grin.

"What?" asked Benny. "Oh. No, we're fine."

"Are we?" asked Scott. "What was that all about?"

Benny blushed and looked at his feet. "Sorry. I forget how to act sometimes. You know...*out here*." He waved his hands around, looking like a spastic orchestra conductor.

Scott grunted. "Don't beat yourself up, I feel the same way half the time."

"You do?" asked Benny with such incredulity in his voice that everyone laughed, and the spell broke.

Shannon thought there was more to the exchange than Benny was letting on. She tried to catch his eye, but he was either oblivious or ignoring her plaintive glances.

"So, uh, is…" said Mike.

"Yes. I handled…everything," said Scott in a despondent voice. He blinked in rapid succession and took a deep breath. "What's the plan?"

"No calls from Oneka Falls," said Mike. "But I figure I'm fired." He shrugged and grinned. "Troopers have any spots?"

Scott flashed a smile that quivered around the edges. "Always." He cleared his throat. "Toby, there was a riot at Sing Sing, and nineteen inmates escaped. Your… Owen Gray was one of the men who escaped."

"Benny told me."

"Oh…okay. He was—"

"He's in Oneka Falls," said Benny, his expression leaving no room for doubt. "With LaBouche."

"Well, well," Scott said in a tone that would have frozen open flame. "At least I don't have to worry about where I'm going later today."

There was an uncomfortable silence that stretched across the space of ten heartbeats. Mike cleared his throat. "Yeah, well, about that…"

19

"Where's the big monkey, babe?" he asked.

"Father is *speaking* with him. Put him out of your mind, my love." Brigitta slipped her small, perfect hand into the crook of his arm. "Father asked me to convey his thanks, his appreciation, his *respect* for what you've done for us. For everything…for Sing Sing. He regrets the necessity, and hopes you bear him no ill will."

"How could I, babe? The way I was back then, I'd have ended up in prison with no help from him or anyone else. And anyway, he got me out. Or you did, which amounts to the same thing. I'd say everything's jake."

"I knew you would, my love."

"Does Pop have something for me to do? I hate to sit around like a lump in the carpet. I've done enough of that to last a lifetime."

"Oh, my love, no! Never call him that. Either call him Father or Herlequin. He hates to be called 'pop.'"

"Oh. I didn't mean anything."

"It's okay, my love. And to answer your question, he does. You will enjoy the task." She smiled at him sweetly. "And so will I." She stood on tip-toe and kissed his cheek. He couldn't remember for sure, but he imagined she'd been taller. "Oh, I almost forgot," Brigitta said. "Father has a few gifts for you." She pulled a set of keys out of her pocket.

"What is it?" he asked, looking at the keys.

"You'll find out when we get back to the parking lot."

"It's not... I hate to sound this way, but I'd rather not have LaBouche's car."

Brigitta laughed. "I wish you could see your expression, my love. But no, Father knows you better than that. I'm to remind you to look in the trunk."

Owen felt like a kid on Christmas morning, waiting for his parents to come down so he could open presents. No one had ever given him gifts—not since he was small, and he felt a ridiculous amount of gratitude. "I'm sure I'll love them."

"As am I, my love. Now, can you run back to the parking lot or are you too old?"

Owen laughed. "I'll show you too old." He reached for her, and she smiled and tilted her head back. When she closed her eyes, Owen sprinted away toward the path, laughing.

"Oh, my love! You cheater!"

He won the race, and deep down, he knew she'd let him. But that didn't make him mad, like it might have once. Instead, it endeared her to him. "I love you, babe," he gasped between breaths.

"And I, you, my love," said Brigitta. She wasn't even breathing hard.

"Can you... Never mind."

"Ask me, my love."

"Well... No, it's stupid."

"My love," she said, resting her hand on the back of his neck. "Anything that's in my power is yours."

"Can you...can you teach me magic? Can I stay young?"

"Oh, my love," she said in a tone filled with regret. "There are limits that even my Father can't break. I'm sorry."

"Yeah," said Owen, suddenly on the brink of tears. "I just... We never had much time together and I..."

Her small, cool palm caressed his cheek. "Our time has been short, my love. But we lived what we had back in 1979 to the fullest, didn't we? And we will live the time we have left the same way."

"Yeah," he said, dashing tears from his cheek. "I don't know what's the matter with me. I'm not blubbery."

"Shh, my love." She turned and pointed toward a sleek car parked in the lot. "I wonder if your keys fit that beast."

He blinked a few times and turned and looked. "What in the hell is that thing?" The car was mean looking, he had to admit. It was a two-door beauty with a fancy hood and fancy wheels, slinky and low to the ground, but what struck him most about it was that it looked *mean.*

"Father knew you would like something from before, but we didn't have much time to procure this gift, and these days, cars from that era are rare. This, my love, is called a Dodge Viper."

"That beauty's a *Dodge*?" he asked.

"Yes, my love. Do you like it?"

"Oh, babe, I *love* it."

"Go open the trunk. The other gift Father bought you is inside."

"Tell him I said thank you, babe. From the bottom of my heart, thank you."

"He knows, my love."

He glanced in the window as he walked around the car. Red leather interior, fancy seats, manual transmission… "I think I'm in love, babe."

"With me or the car, my love?"

He glanced at her, and his grin matched hers. "Both."

"Open the trunk. Let's see if the last gift can compare."

With a broadening grin, Owen popped the trunk. "*Holy fuck, babe*!" His eyes stretched wide, and his hands shook. "Is that…is it what I think it is?"

Brigitta smiled, eyes glistening. She walked over to him and glanced down at his crotch. "I guess you approve?"

"Oh, babe…I don't even… Is it a…" He gave up on speech and picked up his new rifle. "I saw these on a show in prison—a show about those pansy SEALs, but this weapon is a thing of beauty." The rifle was long-barreled, and *heavy*, even for a rifle. It was a semi-automatic and had a bipod built right into the front of stock. "I wish I'd still been in the Corps when they went into Iraq. The first military branch to use these beauties was the Corps."

Brigitta smiled like an indulgent mother, encouraging her child's excitement. "Tell me all about it, my love."

"It's got an effective range of over a mile—*over a fucking mile, babe*—and can punch right through walls, through armor plates, even!"

"Can it?"

"Oh yes. The show was about Somalia. Snipers would wait for the enemy to pop up and take a shot, and then duck back down. They aimed *below* the window. *Shot them right through the wall*! Bang! Dead enemy."

"It sounds wonderful, my love," she said.

"I can't believe it. I just can't believe it."

"It's all true, my love."

"A motherfucking Barrett M82A1! I never even thought I'd *see* one of these, let alone fire one. Even once!"

"It is our hope you will fire it more than once, my love."

"You and your father, babe… I can't say it in words. I'm not good with words. Can you look inside me and see how this makes me feel?"

She snuggled up to him, pressing her breasts against his side. "I can, my love, and so can Father. He is pleased you like the gifts."

"*Like* them? I *fucking love* them, babe. And you. And him! Tell him for me!"

She put her hand on the significant bulge below his belt. "*Later*, my love," she breathed in his ear.

20

Scott drove the OFPD cruiser into Oneka Falls at a few minutes past two o'clock. He didn't care much for his role in the plan, but Benny had assured him it was necessary. And he'd said it was the most effective thing he could do for them.

He parked the car on the side of Union Street and got out. The old church was swarming with State Troopers, and none of them looked bored. He signed in with the trooper who had log duty and ducked under the tape.

"Scott!"

He turned and looked at Trooper McCarlson with a stony expression. "Don't give me any shit, Stan. I'm not leaving."

"No, of course not, Scott. You surprised me, is all."

"Can't sit in that fucking house alone for one more—" Scott snapped his mouth shut with an audible click.

"No, no. I can't imagine, Scott. If there's—"

"Want to run me through what you have so far?"

"Sure, Scott. Sure."

"But…just leave out the parts about…"

"Sure thing, Scott. Follow me. There's so much here…well, I've got to tell you that the forensics guys are going a bit nuts."

"This place hasn't been open long, from what I understood from OFPD's chief."

"No. A year and a half, maybe two. It flew under the radar until the anonymous tip came in. It was like a production line or something from the amount of DNA and other evidence."

"Any…any bodies?"

"No, Scott. Nothing yet."

Scott nodded. "Okay, run me through your working theory."

Carlson nodded and started talking. His cadence was fast, and his tone was all bubbles and candy-canes.

Scott put himself on autopilot and zoned out.

21

Toby drove the Odin Desperado back to the barn where he'd hidden it the first time. They'd gotten to town soon enough to see Scott turn down Union Street, and the trip out to the barn had been less than ten minutes. Toby had left the BMW for Shannon, so the garage area in the rear of the Desperado held Scott Lewis' Jeep Wrangler. The Jeep was a better car for their part of the plan anyway, and even if it wasn't, LaBouche had seen Toby driving the BMW. They might be on the lookout for a man in a red BMW.

He parked the big RV and turned off the engine.

"Go, go, gadget-RV," Benny said with a smile.

"I prefer to think of it as a Transformer," said Toby.

They piled into the Jeep and Toby backed out of the RV. "You should drive, Mike. I don't know Oneka Falls anymore."

"I thought your memory was back?"

"Well, yeah, but the last time I was here… Mill Lane threw me for a loop on my last trip. Ended up speeding through town, turning blindly."

"You could get a ticket for acting that way," said Benny.

"Yeah, and you've run out of friends on the police force." Mike said it with a smile but sobered right after he spoke. He and Toby swapped places.

"Still haven't been able to reach Jack?" asked Toby.

"No. Neither has his wife."

The three exchanged glances, and Benny shook his head. "Would it help her to know? Would it help you?"

"Of course, Benny," murmured Mike. "It would help."

"The town manager demon got him. You were on the phone with Jack right before…"

Mike squeezed his eyes shut. "I should have—"

"No, Mike," murmured Benny. "By the time Jack called you, his fate was sealed. There's nothing anyone could have done."

"Where is his body?"

Benny shook his head. "Not much left," he muttered

"*Dammit!*" yelled Mike.

"You know who is to blame for it," said Benny in matter-of-fact tones. "The best thing—"

"Don't you think I fucking understand that?" snapped Mike.

"I was just trying to—"

"I know. I know, Benny. Sorry." Mike put the Jeep in gear and drove east, away from town. They turned south on McMahon Road and skirted the edges of town. Once they were far enough south, they turned west until they reached 16, which brought them to the Thousand Acre Wood.

Mike turned onto an old ranger road—more of a pitted cart-track than a road—and crept into the forest itself. "Where do we park the Jeep? Will there be a nice sign to tell us? Park here to kill demons?"

Benny chuckled. "No, but I'll know where to stop. Plus, the dog-things will be in the area. Maybe."

"Oh God," breathed Toby.

Mike shook his head and kept driving.

22

Shannon had the sunroof open and the windows rolled down. It was chilly, but she wore a warm coat. Plus, she wanted everyone to see it was a woman driving.

She came into town from the west, pulling up to the one stoplight next to town hall. She didn't even glance at it. *I'm not Shannon Bertram. No. I'm a blonde. I'm cute, but not remarkable.* She still wasn't sure about what Benny had told her, but he seemed to be right about everything else. The worst thing that would happen to her is someone might think she'd gone crazy or stolen a BMW.

Chaz Welsh walked in front of the car and smiled at her. Her heart exploded. *Does he see me? What do I do? Do I run?*

Relax, Shannon. He doesn't perceive who you are. Your superpower is strong. Be calm.

Shannon didn't know how Benny always knew when she was freaking out. It was kind of cool, but then again, it was also kind of creepy.

After today, Shannon, I'll cut the cord if you want. It's up to you, I don't want to force anything on you.

She marveled at how different his mental voice was. Confident. Strong. *It will take some getting used to. We'll take it a day at a time.* He didn't answer her. *Does that mean he can't hear me all the time?*

The light changed, but Chaz Welsh was still standing in front of the car, smiling, chewing his gum. Shannon smiled and batted her eyelids. *Are you looking at little old me? Blonde little old me? I'm nothing special. I'm below your notice. You are not interested in me.*

Chaz's eyes drifted to the car behind her and his expression slackened. He looked around as if he were coming awake and with a shake of his head, crossed over to town hall. She didn't watch him go, she kept her eyes—and her thoughts—on the traffic light. As it turned yellow, she goosed the BMW, and it surged into the intersection. She turned right and then left on Mill Lane—Toby's street. Taking Mill to where Union dead-ended into it, she turned left onto Union and drove three blocks. She parked in front of a house two blocks past St. Genesius' Sanctuary of the Holy Mother.

Thinking about being blonde and unremarkable, Shannon slumped down in the seat and prepared to wait for her cue.

23

Owen roared into Oneka Falls, both sated and satisfied. The Barrett was in the trunk, and thinking about it made him want Brigitta again. She wasn't with him, though, which was upsetting, but she'd said she would meet him at the church.

God damn, I love this car. I love my rifle, and I love Brigitta! The thoughts made him warm and rosy. No woman had ever made him feel like that. Not even Stephanie. Not even on Stephanie's Death Day.

He fishtailed the car onto Mill Lane, delighted with the smoking tires and the expressions on the faces of the people out walking. Gunning the accelerator, Owen raced up to Union, where he slid around the corner again, laughing.

He parked in the rectory's driveway. The plan was perfect. No one in town would know where the fire originated—the perfect sniper's nest. The belfry of St. Genesius' was perfect. He'd be able to cover the entire town with the Barrett—it had more than enough range.

He got the big rifle out of the trunk and carried it by its handle. *It's my briefcase*, he thought with a grin. He carried the big box of ammunition under his other arm. He climbed up to the belfry, whistling an old disco jingle from the 70s. When he got to the top, he set down the rifle and the ammo, and he opened the shutters on all four sides. It was perfect. He had clear sight lines of every place Brigitta wanted him to cover.

No time like the present, he thought and laid down on his stomach behind the rifle. It would make one hell of a noise in the belfry, but that couldn't be helped. He scanned through the monstrous scope attached to the M82, looking for a likely target. He had the picture of LaBouche's "partner" in his pocket, but he didn't care if he shot that man or not. Part of him wanted to avoid it, despite what Brigitta wanted, just to spite the big yellow ape.

The hub of police activity was less than four blocks north. An old church, Brigitta had said. He did not understand why an abandoned church would interest a bunch of Statie motherfuckers, but, at the same time, he didn't give a rip about their interests—*he* was interested in seeing their blood splattered on the sidewalk.

Four blocks. No challenge. Not with an M82 in his hands. Brigitta was right though. St. Genesius' belfry was a perfect nest to shoot up that old church down the street. *Hell, maybe a few shots at short range would be good. Get me warmed up, acclimated to the weapon. I could go long after that with confidence.*

With a sigh, he pulled out the picture LaBouche had given him. *Might as well do this one as any other. Brigitta and her father would be pleased.*

24

"Here," said Benny. "Stop here."

Mike hit the brakes, bringing the Wrangler to a smooth stop. He killed the engine. "What now?"

"Now, we walk," said Toby. "But before we get out, you remember what we told you, Mike?"

"It hasn't been ten minutes since you last reminded me."

"Then you can repeat it back," said Benny. He lifted one shoulder and let it drop. "Simple, right?"

Mike's face tightened, and a hard smile spread across his lips. He forced a laugh. "You two are as bad as a couple of old hens." He flopped his hands in his lap. "But, whatever. Okay, there will be these things that seem like dogs, but they aren't dogs. They don't have eyes. They are part of Herlequin's menagerie. Their job—"

"We think."

"Their job, *you think*, is to herd the prey away from the edges of the forest, to keep them running. Herlequin is a goblin or gargoyle, but he's a demon so he can appear however he wants. He's a trickster; he may make us see things that aren't real. Okay? Good enough for you two?"

"Yeah," said Toby.

Mike snorted. "*Finally*. Let's go, boys." He sprang out of the Wrangler and walked around to the back, reaching inside and withdrawing a Remington 870 in tactical trim. He racked the slide.

Toby led the way, and as they walked deeper into the forest, an imposing darkness—a *gloominess*—descended. The trees loomed at them out of the murk.

"Yes," Benny breathed. "It was like this."

"Worse," said Toby.

Benny shrugged. "We were kids."

"*Scared* kids," said Mike. "Fear does strange things to perception."

They walked on, becoming ever more anxious the deeper they went into that artificial gloaming. The trees changed, becoming baleful and bleak, bald boughs bending toward them.

"Beautiful this time of year, isn't it?" asked Mike with forced jocularity.

Toby grunted. The forest seemed impervious to the season, to weather of any kind. *It's Herlequin's domain, and, like everything else, it bows to his wishes.* His mouth filled with the tang of some sort of metal: copper or brass. *Fear.* When the growling started, he had to fight to keep from running.

25

Scott left McCarlson inside shouting at one of the forensic techs, arguing about the chemical testing of the wooden tables. He stood on the narthex steps, hands on his hips. He hated waiting for the shoe to drop. Benny had emphasized that he had to hide his knowledge, his *awareness*, of Gray, that he had to play the part, but it was much harder than Scott thought it would be.

He glanced up Union toward Main Street, his gaze scanning along the rooftops. Benny knew about Owen and his perch, but he hadn't been able to exclude the possibility of another sniper. If Scott got hit in the same way he intended to deal with Gray…well, it wouldn't be good for anyone.

He turned his gaze toward the other, longer leg of Union, stretching his vision to see where the road again took a ninety-degree turn, ten blocks south. Again, he skimmed the roof tops, looking for signs of another sniper. He fought to keep his eyes from arrowing in on the steeple of the Catholic church down the way, but he could feel Gray's eyes on him, nonetheless.

26

Owen was scanning the old church through the long lens of the M82's tactical scope when the cop came out. He double-checked the picture and then grinned. It was him. LaBouche's partner.

He put the crosshairs of the scope on the man's right knee. *"Pow,"* he breathed. He moved the crosshairs to the man's left wrist. "*Pow.*" He scanned the cop's body, making the sound of radar pings under his breath. When the scope crossed the man's groin, he steadied it and put his finger on the trigger.

27

My turn, thought Shannon. She fixed a picture of the woman Gray had called "babe" in her mind. *Long blonde hair, narrow shoulders, chiseled features, pretty blue eyes, pale skin. I am "babe."* She opened the door of the BMW and got out. *I am* your *"babe," and I am naked.*

She walked up the block toward Play Time, moving fast. *I am your "babe," Owen. Look at me. See* me. *I am naked. I am waiting for you to notice me.* She glanced over her shoulder at St. Genesius' belfry. The slats of the blinds were open, and sunlight glinted off something in the gloom behind them.

See me, Owen. I'm right down here, my love. I'm naked, I want you to see my nakedness—I want you, *Owen. Look at me. Look at me. Look at me.*

28

The growling was getting louder and louder as if more dogs were adding to the chorus. *They sure as hell sound real*, Mike thought. He followed Benny, who walked without doubt, never second-guessing their route. He held the Remington at port arms, knuckles white, tendons creaking, trying to see in every direction at once.

"It's okay, Mike," Toby whispered from behind him. "Think of this as a welcoming committee."

"Yeah. It's one hell of a welcome."

"Remember, that shotgun might knock them down, but it's not likely to do much good otherwise. Conserve your ammunition. Only fire—"

"—if there is no other choice. I *got it*, man."

"Okay, Mike. No problem."

Ahead on the trail, a big black dog-thing stepped out in front of Benny. It turned and faced them, looking—if that term even applied to a thing with no eyes—right at Mike. Its lips curled, revealing long, sharp obsidian teeth. Its growl became a snarl.

"All part of the show," Benny murmured. He walked right up to the thing and held out his hand as if the thing was a neighborhood dog. "Hi, there. Remember me?" he said in crooning tones. "I've come back." The dog-thing turned toward Benny and cocked its head to the side, ears up like it was a normal dog. "I want to see Herlequin again. Will you take us?"

The dog-thing turned its head toward Mike, and he had the distinct impression of eyes boring into his. The snarl came back.

"Oh, he's okay. He's the Police Chief. Don't you recognize him?" The dog-thing whirled and trotted off a dozen steps before stopping and turning its head back toward them.

Mike didn't like this part of the plan at all. *Why bring all these demons or devils or whatever they were back to Herlequin? Why give him minions—help—in the fight to come?*

29

As Owen was tightening his finger, taking up the trigger's slack—in preparation for putting a .50 caliber round right through the cop's groin, a bit of yellow flashed in the bottom of his scope.

His heart swelled—it had to be her. *She said she'd come and now she's here, but why is she down there and not up here with me*? Owen took his eye away from the scope and looked over the barrel of the rifle, down at the street.

Brigitta stood on the sidewalk, half a block down from the old church—and she was naked. His pulse slammed in his veins and his mouth dried. "Babe?" he murmured.

Below, she waved up at him and smiled.

"Come up, come up," he called, but she shook her head and tossed her hair. He couldn't be sure, but he thought she was laughing. *A game, then.* He liked games.

At least with Brigitta.

30

Scott pounded up the stairs. The rifle was already in position, he'd set it up in the cold belfry before going into the church below him. He climbed the last set of stairs and then stood, hand on the belfry's ladder, slowing his breathing, calming his racing pulse.

When he was ready, he climbed into the belfry, careful not to move in a way that might attract attention. But Shannon was below, on the street, exposed. If Gray saw through her trick or became suspicious, she'd be dead in seconds.

Scott climbed into the belfry on his belly and snaked his way over to the rifle. He put the stock on his shoulder, worked the bolt and sighted through the scope at St. Genesius' steeple.

There was nothing left to do but wait.

31

Toby followed his friends—who followed the big, black dog-thing—into the sunny clearing ahead…the sunny clearing filled by the big tree…the tree with all the burls.

He had to admit that he was nervous. The tranquilizer gun was ready, magazines loaded, but still, he doubted the efficacy of the M99 against a creature as old as Herlequin must be. Bortha had been a nightmare—the M99 seemed unequal to the task, and yet Bortha was subservient to Herlequin. He shook his head. *Time will tell, I guess.*

Herlequin stepped from behind the tree, and when he did, a memory stole over Toby's mind. The burls were not burls. They were faces—faces of children that had gone to live in the tree.

Herlequin laughed. "Such a face, Toby Burton."

"Hello, Herlequin," said Benny. "Long time no see."

"Indeed, boyo, indeed. And you've brought a friend! How nice of you."

Mike shouldered the shotgun and aimed it at Herlequin's chest.

Again, Herlequin laughed, his leathery wings rubbing together and making the laugh sound like a thing out of a horror movie. "That pathetic toy is no use to you." He waved his hand, and in a blur of black fur, the big, black dog-thing launched itself at Mike.

Without thinking, Toby shouldered his tranquilizer gun and squeezed the trigger. The dart hit the dog-thing mid-leap, and the thing squealed in an undog-like way. It seemed to lay over on its side, but even so, the weight of its body slammed into Mike, staggering him, and he lost his grip on the shotgun.

"I'm disappointed, Toby," said Herlequin. "I thought I taught you better last time."

"Just do it, Toby," said Benny. "Do it, do it, do it."

With a feral grin, Toby stepped forward and began firing darts into Herlequin's chest.

32

Owen waved again, trying to get Brigitta to come up and join him. She just stood there, waving back. *Why won't she come up here? Is this like back at the hospital? Is this another betrayal?* He felt guilty for doubting her right away, but the thought remained.

Well, if she's not coming up, I might as well get busy. He resumed his firing position and put his eye to the scope. He could see the top of Brigitta's head at the bottom of the scope, but the cop had disappeared.

A madcap exasperation slammed into his veins along with a large dose of adrenaline. *Why, Brigitta? Why?*

33

Scott's finger ached with the tension of keeping the slack off the trigger. The rifle was on the cusp of firing, and if he twitched, or moved, even in the slightest, it would go off. He'd been holding the position for what felt like an hour, drawing slow, even breaths, pausing between each one so he'd be ready to fire.

When he saw the glint of reflected sunlight near the center of his crosshairs, he made a small adjustment to his aim, exhaled, and squeezed the trigger.

34

Mike ducked to the left, circling out of Toby's way. He still held the shotgun by the barrel, but only just. Reaching for the stock as he ran, he scanned the edge of the glade for more dog-things. The infernal things had shadowed their progress since the big dog joined the party, there must be more in the forest.

Toby's tranquilizer gun spat in rapid succession. The man they called Herlequin was staggering back with each impact of the darts. Mike only had the fight with Bortha to compare it too, but he didn't expect this fight to be this easy.

Benny was standing in front of the big, burled tree, staring at it with horror on his quivering face. He dropped to his knees and took off the backpack he carried and began rooting around inside it.

35

A rifle boomed above her, and Shannon ran into the yard beside her and around the side of the house. If Scott missed...she'd be Gray's target.

I'm invisible. I'm invisible. I'm invisible!

And Scott had missed. She knew it the minute Gray screamed with a furor that approached madness.

36

When sweat dripped into his eye, Owen ducked his head to wipe it away, and that was what saved him. The bullet hit inside edge of the big scope, shattering its optics, and deflected down into the breech of the M82. Owen pulled the gun over on its side and tried to work the bolt.

Owen screamed, but not in pain. "*Oh, you goddamn motherfucking pissant!* I never even got to *shoot* it!"

37

Toby circled to the right, pulling the trigger, sights centered on Herlequin's chest. Mike was somewhere to his left, but he would have to take care of himself for the moment. With each dart, Herlequin staggered, reeled, or grunted. *This is almost too easy*, he thought. When the gun ran dry, he ejected the magazine and slammed another home. He brought the gun up and faltered.

Herlequin was already down on his knees. His wings flapped twice, and, as Toby's mouth dropped open, dropped over on his face.

"That's it? He's down?" asked Mike.

Not taking his eyes off Herlequin, Toby circled around behind him. "I don't know, Mike," he said. "Remember, he's a trickster."

"Not one of those dog-things attacked," said Mike. "This was easy."

"Yeah," said Toby. *Too easy*. He prodded the big goblin with the toe of his boot, but Herlequin never moved. "Benny, let's drain his blood. I don't want him coming to ever again."

Benny was kneeling in front of the tree, looking worried. "Yeah. Yeah, let's do that."

"What is it, Benny?" Mike asked, but Benny just shook his head. His eyes darted toward the dark forest and scanned the trees. He pulled a rope out of his pack and looped it around Herlequin's feet. The other end, he threw over a branch of the ugly tree at the center of the glade. "Mike, help me." Together, Mike and Benny hauled Herlequin upside down, and Benny cut his throat.

"I expected more of a fight," said Mike.

"Yeah," said Benny, his attention back on the forest. "Me too."

38

Scott didn't know if he'd even hit the bastard, but Gray didn't return fire, and Scott took that as a good sign. Even so, he kept the scope centered on St. Genesius' belfry while troopers swarmed toward the building. *If a shadow so much as twitches,* he thought. *Fire free.*

39

This was too easy, Shannon thought. Gray had never even fired a shot. She ducked around the back of the house and peeked at the Catholic church across the street. Nothing moved.

The troopers from Play Time were pounding up the street toward the church. "He's up in the belfry," she yelled.

The troopers executed a tactical entry on the church's vestibule, and Shannon rolled her eyes. "The belfry," she muttered.

40

A thick stream of greenish-blue blood arced from Herlequin's neck and into the double-layered trash bag. Herlequin's muscles twitched as his life's blood drained, but other than that, nothing happened. It was almost boring.

"Why drain him here?" asked Mike. "That other guy was more of a threat."

"That's why," said Toby. He glanced at Benny, and it was a worried glance. "Are you sure, Benny?"

Benny swallowed hard. "I don't feel him anymore. The dog-things either." He shrugged, casting an uneasy glance at the woods. "It... He must be out."

Toby's gaze shifted to the tree at the center of the glade. "We should chop down that damn tree." Herlequin thrashed, but his silvery eyes remained vacant.

"Oh, he doesn't like that idea," laughed Mike. He bent over Benny's backpack and came up with a hand axe. "Let's see how he likes this." With a double-handed grip, he swung the axe toward the tree.

An unreasoning fear slammed through Benny's mind. "No, Mike! No!" he yelled, but it was too late. The bleeding form of Herlequin disappeared, and all hell broke loose.

41

She stayed hidden until the troopers led Gray out of the church, his hands cuffed behind him, his feet shackled. Breathing easy at last, she stood straight and walked to the street.

Gray's eyes tracked her, and in them, she read hope. *Yes. I'm "babe," and I'm coming to your rescue.*

A trooper stepped in her way, but she ignored him, looking over his shoulder, looking Owen Gray in the eye.

"Why, Brigitta? Why did you abandon me again?" His voice shook with emotion, and he sounded wretched, heartbroken.

"Because, *my love*, I'm not Brigitta!" *See me! I'm Shannon Bertram!*

His head jerked back as if she'd slapped him. "Who the fuck are you? How did you do that?"

"Do what?" asked a trooper.

"I'm Shannon Bertram," she said. "And I've got a crisp dollar bill for your troubles, you asshole!"

At first, Gray looked confused, but recognition spread over his face. "*You?* Chickenpox girl?"

"Damn right!" Shannon snapped. "Enjoy your time in prison!" She turned her back and walked away, bee-lining for Toby's little red BMW. *I love this car*, she thought as she slipped behind the wheel.

She started the engine, wanting to go pick up Scott and meet the boys at the park as they'd planned.

42

I knew it! I knew it was too easy! thought Toby as Herlequin's body disappeared like smoke. In the same instant, the air erupted with howls, snarls, and an eerie wailing.

Mike jerked the hand axe out of the ugly tree, and instead of sap, thick cadmium green blood poured from the wound. The tree writhed and thrashed, whipping its boughs around like savage clubs. A limb smashed into Mike and sent him flying.

Before he landed, dog-things began pouring into the glade, teeth bared, lips back. Toby started to move, jinking behind the tree, then back out, snapping dart after dart at the dog-things. Unlike the first one, the new-comers were resilient.

Mike rolled to the Remington shotgun and scooped it into his hands. He snapped the gun up to his shoulder, and it boomed, once, twice. A dog-thing keened and fell to its side, more cadmium green blood pouring into the grass.

Benny stood frozen, staring at the writhing tree. His mouth was moving, but no sound came out. "Benny!" Toby yelled. "Get out of there!" But Benny didn't move.

Boughs of the ugly tree were circling around behind Benny, as if the tree wanted to give him a hug. The bark of the tree shimmered, shining with a chartreuse light.

"The tree, Mike! The tree!"

Mike looked, and in one fluid movement retargeted the shotgun and fired, smashing slugs into the heart of the tree. He bent and fed shells into the shotgun's ammo tube.

Toby snapped his tranquilizer gun up and fired five quick shots at the tree. It was unclear whether the shotgun's rounds or the darts irritated the tree more, but it was clear that neither type of round did much more than that. "Benny! Move!"

Benny's eyes snapped away from the tree and locked on Toby's. Toby replaced the spent magazine and beckoned Benny with his chin. "Move!"

Benny looked around, saw the tree's limbs behind him and dove toward Toby, arms up to protect his face. He hit the ground and rolled to the right, avoiding two thick branches that slammed into the earth by a mere fraction of an inch.

The whole tree was shaking and writhing, but whether it was from pain or fury, Toby had no idea. He snapped the tranquilizer gun up at the same moment Mike shouldered the shotgun. They fired in unison, Toby's darts hitting the tree from the right, Mike's shotgun blasts slamming into the tree trunk from the left. A horrible keening wail split the air, and the whole tree shuddered.

"Look out!" yelled Mike.

Toby ducked and felt the wind of a passing tree limb. Still stooped he jigged right, then left, unslinging his pack as he went. "Have to reload, Mike!"

"Do it!" The shotgun boomed again and again, and the keening increased in volume. The dog-things stalked in circles, snarling and growling, unable, or unwilling to get close to the tree.

Toby knelt and began feeding darts into empty magazines. "Benny! What do we do? *What do we do?*" His attention on reloading, he didn't see Benny stand up and run at the tree.

43

She froze, her hand on the gear selector, her eyes locked on the rearview mirror.

Brigitta was sitting in the back seat, looking back at her with hatred in her eyes. "You *bitch*!" Brigitta hissed. "How dare you? How *dare* you!" Spittle flew from the blonde woman's lips and her eyes seemed to pulse with malevolence. "He is mine, do you hear? *Mine*!"

Shannon didn't know what to do. She stared at the apparition in the back seat, muscles locked in place, fear streaming in her blood.

44

Scott came down out of the belfry when the troopers entered the church. A grim smile played at the edges of his mouth, but he felt empty. Drained.

He left the hateful old church and walked out into the cool fall afternoon. He watched Shannon approach Gray and exchange words. She climbed into Toby's BMW and started the engine, but then she seemed to lock up like a robot running out of batteries.

Something stirred in the pit of his stomach. Something that both hurt him and scared him at the same time. He dropped the rifle and sprinted toward the car.

45

Benny understood. It was too late, but he finally understood. Herlequin wasn't a gargoyle or a demon or a goblin or an elf. He wasn't one of Toby's "traditional" or "undead" demons, though he played at being both. No, Herlequin was a "weird." Herlequin was the *tree*.

He sprinted toward the tree.

"Benny, no!" screamed Mike. He fired the shotgun in quick bursts at the trunk, spent shells peppering the dog-things.

Benny ducked his head, avoiding a sweeping blow from one of Herlequin's branches by a hair. Ten feet from the tree, he shifted his focus from the tree trunk to his abandoned pack lying in the grass. He dove, scooped up the pack, and rolled away. He dumped the contents of the pack out in front of him and pawed through it, looking for the metal canister Toby had given him to hold. "Your canisters!" he yelled.

Mike stood hunched over, shoving more shotgun shells into the loading tube when the thick branch slammed into his side. The force of the blow lifted him off his feet and sent him crashing into the trees.

"Mike!" Toby screamed. "Benny! Look out!"

46

"I…I…" she stuttered.

"You nothing," sneered Brigitta. "You *nothing*!" Her voice shook with near-uncontrollable rage, and spit flew from her lips with each syllable. "It's ruined! It's all ruined, and it's all *your* fault!"

Shannon's hands came back to life, and she scrabbled for the door handle, wanting nothing else than to be out of the car and away from Brigitta.

"No," said the woman in the back seat. "Look at me!" she snapped in a whip-crack voice.

Without thinking, Shannon looked at her. The visage of the blonde beauty fell away and what sat in the backseat of the car scared Shannon more than anything had ever scared her.

Brigitta was hideous. Her skin was black and riddled with weeping sores. Flesh hung loose from her bones, and her dry, brittle hair hung in purulent clumps. Her nails—claws—were long and age-yellowed. But it was her eyes that terrified Shannon. Her irises were crimson, and blood dripped from the corners of her eyes. They blazed with a pestilent, virulent hatred. "Now he's lost to us. Lost to *me*. You will pay for what you've done!"

47

The blow knocked Mike's breath away, and he almost dropped the shotgun when he crashed into the trees. His friends were trapped behind him, a score or more of dog-things between them. Worse, now that he wasn't within range of the twisting, slashing tree, the dog-things were coming.

Benny was screaming his name, yelling something he couldn't understand. Mike pushed his aching body up and finished reloading the shotgun. He had to get back to his friends, had to help them, had to *protect* them.

He ran toward the glade, the snarling four-legged nightmares speeding ever closer. One of them leapt at him from the darkness, and he fired the shotgun from the hip. The slug took the dog-thing in the neck and punched straight through it, misting the air with cadmium green blood. He fired again, and this time, the slug hit the dog-thing in the jaw, smashing through the back of its skull. The dog-thing's muscles slackened all at once, and it turned on its side in midair. Mike ducked, and it flopped through the air over his head.

Head down, Mike sprinted toward the glade, thumbing two more shells into the gun as he ran. The dog-things snarled and ran to intercept him.

48

Toby reloaded all three magazines, trying to watch Benny, Mike, the dog-things, and the whirling tree all at once. He slipped a magazine into his gun, shouldered it and fired five times as fast as he could squeeze the trigger. At this range, and given the width of the trunk, the chance of him missing was miniscule.

"Toby! Your canister!" Benny screamed.

Toby switched magazines and fired five darts in rapid succession. Who knew if the M99 was even effective against a tree?

"Your canister, Toby! I need it! *Now!*"

Toby glanced in his direction. Benny stooped low to the ground, arms outstretched, beckoning Toby. Like being struck by lightning, what Benny wanted to do dawned on him, and he stooped to fish through his pack for his own, fire-extinguisher sized canister. He pulled it out and threw it to Benny.

"I need Mike's, too! Get it!"

With a nod, Toby slung his pack, so it hung across his chest, changed magazines, and fired his five darts into the tree. The tree was shuddering, swaying to and fro as if in a strong wind. He slung his rifle, and sprinted across the glade, one hand holding an empty magazine and the other fishing in his pack for more darts.

Mike burst from the trees in front of Toby, eyes wild. "Dog-things behind me!" he yelled.

"Mike!" yelled Benny. "Give me your canister."

Toby grabbed Mike by the arm and tugged him inside the arc of thrashing tree limbs. "Get it," he said. "I'll keep the dog-things away."

Mike dug through his pack, found the metal canister, and threw it to Benny. "What else?"

"When I say, shoot the canister!" Benny rolled the three canisters to the foot the tree and turned to Mike. "Now!"

Mike fired at the middle canister, and flames exploded up the trunk of the tree.

49

Scott had sprinted halfway to the car when he saw something come over the backseat at Shannon. He raced to the car and jerked on the door handle, but it was locked. He rapped on the window, but Shannon was in a fight for her life, some banshee with rotting, black skin screaming and slashing at her.

He turned and yelled for help from the troopers standing around the church. Scott turned back to the car and drew his pistol.

50

Brigitta shrieked and scratched. She hit and bit, pulling Shannon's hair. It was as if a wildcat writhed in her lap. There was no way to get away, she couldn't even fight back because it seemed like Brigitta was everywhere at once.

Scott was hammering on the window with the butt of his pistol. Each blow making a muted *thud*, but not breaking the safety glass. He had no leverage.

She will kill me before he gets in, Shannon thought in a detached, almost clinical way. *Wait! That's it. I'm dead! No reason to keep hitting the dead girl. I'm dead, I'm dead!*

51

Scott hammered the window with the butt of his pistol again and again, but it wasn't working. It just bounced and skittered off the safety glass. The thing in Shannon's lap was tearing at her hair, gouging her face with her nails.

He could shoot out the window, but there was a significant chance of hitting Shannon. Even so, there was little choice. He set himself and aimed carefully.

Just when he was about to fire, Shannon died.

52

Fire cascaded in wide sheets across the tree, igniting the old wood. In the forest around them, the dog-things screamed—sounding very much as if they were the ones being killed. Toby hoped they were.

The fire spread through the tree as if by magic, racing up the trunk and down the branches. It popped and crackled as the flames hit Herlequin's blood and ignited that too.

The tree was shuddering and hissing, but there was nothing it could do but burn. Herlequin shrieked, and it was a deafening sound—like a thousand jet engines at full power. Mike stood next to him, shotgun hanging loose in his fists, staring at the burning tree as if hypnotized by it.

Toby tore his eyes from the tree, searching the glade for Benny. He was slumped on the ground next to his pack, clumps of burning blood and drops of liquid fire raining down around him from Herlequin's burning boughs. Toby sprinted over and pulled him out from under the branches. "Benny! Are you okay?"

Benny looked up at him, groggy and confused. "Is he dying?"

"Yes, Benny, I guess he is. Thanks to you."

"Good," said Benny and closed his eyes.

53

Dead! I'm a dead girl! shouted Shannon in her mind, lending all her mental reserves to her cries.

Brigitta stopped screaming, stopped attacking her.

Shannon glanced at her face and saw suspicion, disbelief. *No, I'm dead, you killed me. I'm dead. You ripped out my throat. You can believe it.*

Brigitta shifted to the passenger seat, never taking her eyes off Shannon's face. Her eyes narrowed, and she sat bolt-upright in the seat. "*No! No!*" she shrieked and disappeared.

Shannon slumped in the seat for a moment and opened the door. Scott was there in a flash.

"I thought she *killed* you!" he cried.

"Sorry about that."

"What happened? Where'd she go?"

"No idea," said Shannon, and a moment later, she collapsed in a dead faint.

54

The huge tree burned, and Toby smiled, thinking of the woman in his dream. He wasn't sure if it had been his mother in the dream, or if it had been Benny playing the role, but it didn't matter. Her face resided in his memory now, and he would never forget it. He remembered her name: Candace. She hadn't been the perfect mother, far from it, but in the end...in the end she'd tried to do right by him.

"Is it over?" asked Mike.

"I think it—"

Between Toby and the tree, the air popped, and a demon appeared. Her decaying skin sagged, and her brittle hair flew toward the tree on the currents of air feeding the fire. "*NO!*" she screamed.

Toby snapped the tranquilizer gun up and fired into her back. "Yes!" he snapped. He popped the magazine and fed the gun another. He fired that dry and repeated the process. Toby had hit her with fifteen doses of M99, and she reeled as she turned to face him.

"*You!*" she said, and it sounded every bit a curse.

Mike fired, the shotgun booming, drowning her out. The slug smashed into her and rocked her back a step. He fired again and again, backing her closer and closer to the tree. When her hair caught fire, she fixed them with a freezing glance while she beat at the flames with her hands. "You'll pay for your mischief!" she shrieked. The air popped again, and she was gone.

"What the hell was that?" Mike asked.

Toby shivered. "A teleporting demon," he said.

"They can do that?"

Toby shrugged. "News to me." They got Benny between them, supporting him in case the demon woman came back, and they had to run. "Is it finished?" Toby murmured.

Benny nodded. "Herlequin is dying—dead for all intents and purposes. The undead queen who just left us is another story.""

"What was in that stuff?" Mike asked, pointing at the torn remains of the chemical canisters.

"Chlorine trifluoride," Toby said. "Maybe the most flammable stuff in the universe."

"How long will it burn."

"Until he's gone."

"Until his blood and body break up?"

"Gone for good," said Toby.

"Good," said Benny.

"Hope Scott and Shannon are okay."

"They are," said Benny, sounding very satisfied with himself.

The fire continued to burn, and the darkness lost its hold on the forest around them. The horrible corpse of the tree burned to ash. As the sun burned the last of the murk out of the Thousand Acre Wood, the three men walked back to the Jeep.

55

When Mike pulled into the state park to the north of Thousand Acre Wood, Toby's red BMW already sat in the parking lot next to the woods. Scott and Shannon leaned against the side of the car, and while Scott looked unscathed, Shannon looked like she'd been to the roller derby.

"Shannon!" Benny yelled and hopped out of the back of the Jeep before Mike could stop. He ran to her side, but when he got to her, he stood there like an idiot, unsure of what to do.

"You're going to kill yourself, you fool," yelled Mike. *No, I'm not.*

Mike laughed and shook his head. "Do you believe that guy?" Together, he and Toby climbed out of the Jeep and walked around to the BMW. "You get into a fight with a wildcat, Shan."

Shannon nodded. "That's how it felt. It was 'Babe,' Gray's girlfriend. She's a zombie or something."

Benny shook his head. "She's one of Toby's undead demons. Her name's Brigitta and she dropped in on us, too, but Toby and Mike convinced her to leave by—"

"I can't believe the whole plan worked," said Toby with something like wonder in his voice.

"Of course it did," snapped Benny. "I said it would, didn't I?"

Scott cleared his throat and looked down at his feet. "Gray survived. The bullet hit his gun, and he wasn't even scratched."

Benny shrugged. "Doesn't matter. He'll never get out of prison. Not again."

"And you're sure about that?" asked Mike.

"Doesn't it stand to reason? Gray escaped from a maximum-security prison. They'll put him somewhere federal, I bet. Maybe that supermax in Colorado."

Scott's face twisted. "Are you saying that because you know—*saw* it somehow—or because you believe it?"

"It stands to reason," muttered Benny. He focused on Shannon and reached toward her, but then pulled his hand back.

"I won't break, Benny," said Shannon, leaning her head against his chest. Benny wrapped her in a hug and glanced around, eyes wide. The other three men laughed, but not unkindly.

Scott cleared his throat. "Did you... Was...was *he* with the boss, the king demon?"

Toby put his hand on Scott's shoulder. "No, Scott, he wasn't. I'm sorry."

"So LaBouche is still around."

"Oh, yes," said Benny. "He's still around somewhere. So is Brigitta. We need to be careful for a while."

"What do we do about Oneka Falls?"

"I've got an idea about that," said Benny. "Here's what we need to do..."

Dusk fell as they spoke, and high in a tree at the edge of the woods, a lone, yellow magpie looked down on them, watching.

I hope you've enjoyed this introduction to Oneka Falls and are dying to see what happens next. *The Hag* picks up where this novel leaves off and you can find it here: https://ehv4.us/4thehag.

To be among the first to know what I'm up to and when the newest book I write goes live, please join my Readers' Group by visiting https://ehv4.us/join. Or follow me on BookBub by visiting my profile page there: https://ehv4.us/bbub. Or, if you prefer to stick to Amazon, you may follow my author page: https://ehv4.us/amausa.

If you haven't already read my *A Rational Man* series, you can view all three books on Amazon (please note that if your local Amazon marketplace supports series pages for Kindle ebooks, all three links will point to it): Book 1: Wrath Child: https://ehv4.us/4wrathchild, Book 2: Black Bags: https://ehv4.us/4blackbags, and Book 3, Devils Dance: https://ehv4.us/4devilsdance. For my complete bibliography, please visit: https://ehv4.us/bib.

Books these days succeed or fail based on the strength of their reviews. I hope you will consider leaving a review—as an independent author, I could use your help. It's easy (I promise). You can leave your review by clicking on this link: https://ehv4.us/2revdk.

AUTHOR'S NOTE

I'll tell you this for free: I could get to like this writing thing. There's nothing quite like the feeling of finishing a book, and the dread that comes with knowing you will spend the next month (or six) editing and rewriting it, the anticipation of starting the next book as soon as you are finished with the drudgery of rewriting.

I write to entertain myself (and because I must), and, hopefully, to entertain you. I try not to follow current events because they make me sick. This isn't hyperbole, my illness takes stress and converts it into inflammation and pain. I discovered a couple of years ago that ignoring the news, the politics, all those things that we have no power to change or control, makes me feel better in a quantifiable way and has zero impact on my life. So there you go. But I can't help knowing some things that go on, and as I was writing Demon King, a certain gentleman who shall remain nameless (he deserves no publicity, no fame, not even infamy—he deserves to be forgotten) decided that shooting into a crowd of concert-goers would fix his problems. Owen Gray's exploits in this book are purely coincidental, and

I hope I've portrayed him as a weak-minded coward, which is what I believe these spree shooters are. Like Matt Greshin, I have no idea how to stop these individuals—if I did, I would be doing it. Now, I'm going to stop talking about this before my spleen (or left elbow) swells to the size of Connecticut.

Demon King was fun to write. I wrote it in two distinct chunks: the events of 1979 and the events of 2007. It was very interesting to see how the story changed with the passage of time (both in the story and in real life). While writing this novel, I wrote a blog post titled: *How long have you been planning this?!?*, that was about stories sneaking up on authors and doing something that isn't expected. I wrote it after the story killed both Craig Witherson and Jim Cartwright in a couple of days. I had plans for both characters, thank you very much, but Mr. Story didn't care. Not a bit.

If you are a Stephen King fan, you may have noticed an Easter egg or two. I hope you enjoyed them.

Here's another freebie: I wrote this book when I should have been writing the next book in the Blood of the Isir saga. In my defense, Toby had a hold on my forebrain, and he wouldn't let go. Everything I saw, everywhere we went, fit into Demon King as if they were meant for it. Sometimes you have to listen to that little voice, and sometimes you have no choice in the matter. I hope you will forgive me this brief detour from Hank Jensen's story.

The next thing I'm writing is titled Rooms of Ruin, and its book two of the Blood of the Isir. I've already started it, and it's as comfortable as putting on my favorite T-shirt. I have a feeling that the pages will fly by as the story unfolds before my eyes.

ABOUT THE AUTHOR

Erik Henry Vick is an author who happens to be disabled by an autoimmune disease (also known as his Personal Monster™). He writes to hang on to the few remaining shreds of his sanity. His current favorite genres to write are dark fantasy and horror.

He lives in Western New York with his wife, Supergirl; their son; a Rottweiler named after a god of thunder; and two extremely psychotic cats. He fights his Personal Monster™ daily with humor, pain medicine, and funny T-shirts.

Erik has a B.A. in Psychology, an M.S.C.S., and a Ph.D. in Artificial Intelligence. He has worked as a criminal investigator for a state agency, a college professor, a C.T.O. for an international software company, and a video game developer.

He'd love to hear from you on social media:

Blog: https://erikhenryvick.com
Twitter: https://twitter.com/BerserkErik
Facebook: https://fb.me/erikhenryvick
Amazon author pages:
    USA: https://ehv4.us/amausa
    UK: https://ehv4.us/amauk
Goodreads Author Page: https://ehv4.us/gr
BookBub Author Profile: http://ehv4.us/bbub